THE CANID CHRONOLOGY

BOOK ONE

A Journey's Beginning

ANGOLA HONE

Published in the United States of America
PO Box 657 10000 Bay Pines BLVD
Building 20 Bay Pines, Florida

Cataloging Data
Names: Hone, Angola, author.
Title: The Canid Chronology Book One: A Journey's Beginning
Identifiers: ISBN 979-8-9906180-1-5 (paperback) | ISBN 979-8-9906180-2-2 (hardcover) | ISBN 979-8-9906180-0-8 (ebook) | LCCN 2024909170 (print)

Cover, map, and clipart design by Tessa Sentell
tessakaycreative.com

Published August 31, 2024

Man, o, man, weren't thou first chosen?
Art shepherd of all to the Mistress beholden?
Thou ember diminishes, scattered apiece,
Inherited betwixt bipeds not of thine fleece.

–From Queen Illdari's archives

the
Canid Territory
of
Altharia
N
W E
S
TERRITORY'S BORDER
TOWARD CASDOOM DESERT
TOWARD ELTCINDALE
MOUNTAINCAT RIVER
OLD LEAKTOP
SANDBASK LAKE
MT. RECKER
WITFAST
PINKRUN
HUMANIA SEA
YARROWICK
OWTSKIRT
MIERBRAK
WHIMSIC FOREST
WHIM'S HAVEN
SHORTCUT ROUTE
ELVANUS RIVER
GUTREEK
AVIAN TERRITORY
TOWARD ELEPHANT TERRITORY
ENRISED

Contents

Prologue		1
I	Bartering Games	6
II	Of an Elf and Delsic Root	19
III	Nothing Shall Harm Me	33
IV	The Blacksmith	46
V	Furless Fiends & Foes of Fur	57
VI	The First Offense	75
VII	Straightening Affairs	82
VIII	Journey's Beginning	94
IX	A Last Day in Whimzic	106
X	Dilemmas at Owtskirt	118
XI	Alongside the Great Highway	130
XII	Interferers	142
XIII	A Soul's Humors	151
XIV	The Legion, the City, and the Vulpine Prince	164
XV	Rulers of Flintstone	176
XVI	Much Like My Old Friend	192
XVII	Guests and Ambassadors	207
XVIII	Royal Ball	221
XIX	The Second Offense	233
XX	A Bell Tolls	245
XXI	Looming in the Distance	252
Epilogue		266
Acknowledgements		269

-Prologue-

*M*orning mist dampened Sutter's tawny fur. Through its white veil, the sound of lulling waves perked his triangular ears. It was a gentle noise. Early summer provided no breath of wind to dispel the morning's fog or frenzy the waters upon the craggy shore. The sound and the strengthening scent of sea salt guided Sutter far better than his vision. Even as young as the animal child was, he could smell and hear better than most feathered or furless creatures.

A dark pile of coral rocks rose through the ocean mist before him. There was an even darker break between them. Sutter wedged himself through the narrow opening, shuffling sideways as he pushed his way through. His wiry tail scraped heedless against the tight, uneven walls where his own scent lingered from previous visits.

On the far side, the tiny pup came to a bank of fine, sable sand. Near this exit, in another crack in the jagged cliffside, Sutter removed a hidden reed pole with a fraying length of twine wrapped around it. With this fishing apparatus in paw, the pup strutted across the beach. He played a game with the breaking waves as he went, walking close when they receded, then backing off as they surged up the sand, teasing his hind feet out of their reach.

Sutter giggled. Of the dozens of coves which bordered the Humania Sea near his hometown of Gutreek, this one was a secret known to him alone. None of the bullies from town had found it. Fog now obscured the basalt cliff sides that semi-circled around the secluded bay. Come midmorning, however, the mist would lift to reveal the unique beauty of its black sands glittering in sunlight.

Born by the sea, Sutter had enough sand under his fur to never be rid of it. But he never lost his taste for crispy baked fish. Finding his favorite flat-topped boulder by the shallows, he scrambled atop it to begin his work.

Besides his own fur, Sutter wore nothing but ratty breeches and a strap which supported a knapsack. He removed a tin of worms from the pouch. The pup almost forgot a prayer of forgiveness to the Mistress for his poor bait, but dipped his head and flattened his ears a moment to do so. Bugs and the like were not considered Her creatures, and indeed, some avians even ate them, but Sutter's mother had warned him that one could never be too careful when it came to taking a dumb creature's life. Thus, Sutter prayed for his worm, just as he would pray for the fish soon to be lured to the hook by it.

Absolved then, the kit attempted to fix his thrashing nightcrawler to the barb. It proved a challenge. Fox and wolf toes might be opposable, but they were still fatter and clumsier than true fingers. "Itch you, lil' squirmer," Sutter muttered, almost pricking himself.

The pup's left ear perked. He dropped the defiant worm, alert, squinting out into the fog. The crunching footsteps he had heard did not resume, but he remained motionless.

Was the secret ruined? The heavy odor of fish and brine from the sea was usually enough to throw off other canids' noses, but perhaps Sutter had been followed through the jagged passageway?

There it was—the footsteps resumed. They sounded wet and heavy on the sand, and with them was another, quieter movement of fine, swishing fabric.

From the fog materialized a hooded figure, its face bleached white like long-dead coral. Tall, thin, and clad in dark, draping robes, the person's ghastly expression paralyzed Sutter upon his rock. Fear made every hair on his body stand on end, even to the very tip of his tail. The stranger's eyes were a cancerous shade of yellow. The pupils contracted as they beheld the small pup.

"Where are you from?"

The figure's voice was feminine, but oddly sonorous. It

carried unmistakable threat. Her grimacing teeth did not move when she spoke, and only then did Sutter realize the face was a mask that resembled a skinned skull. She held a staff fashioned of wood darker than the sands, and when the kit did not reply, she pointed its head at him.

"Local, what is the name of your town?"

"G-Gutreek," Sutter answered with a frail whimper. He saw the slender digits wrapped around the staff. They were true fingers, furless and adept. The child bowed his head just as he had during his prayer. This lady was an elf. A descendant of the Mistress Herself.

"How far is the Whimzic Forest from Gutreek?"

The tip of the staff, still pointed at the child, glowed with the low, golden light of wood being rubbed near cozy embers. Sutter blinked at it for a moment. He stopped trembling and relaxed before splitting into a wide smile. "I don't know," the kit now replied as though the imposing skull was a joking playmate. Indeed, he stifled a giggle. "Never been that far inland, missus. But m'pa has. He's a fox. Met ma on business in the Haven. She's a wolf."

The glow of the staff faltered from giddy gold into a feeble, blueish tinge. "You're a crossbreed," said the figure.

At once, gloom to match the staff's radiance crashed upon Sutter's expression. His big eyes welled with tears. "I-I'm not cursed!" he wailed.

The figure swept closer to his rock. Her staff's end remained honed upon the weeping child, her other fingers pinching the pommel of a hairline blade holstered beneath her cloak. Yet it was there the knife stayed. The slit eyes behind the mask searched the pup's face.

Up close now, she smelled faintly of flesh going fetid.

"No," the lady answered. "You're not. Tell no one of us, else you shall be."

The staff's arcane glimmer died. Sutter shook himself as though he had just emerged from the surf and at last found the sense to scamper off. The pup fled for his narrow crevice's refuge once more—away through the fog, and away from the number of voices growing on the beach.

The witch in the skull mask remained on the barnacled stone, staring after the canid pup. As she leaned on her stave, another hooded figure emerged from the mists behind her.

"Speaking with someone, witch?"

The man's voice was sneering and cruel.

"You'll refer to me by my title, deserter," the witch replied. "I spoke to no one."

"Then whose fishing gear sits upon the stone, *Lady* Dusklight?" He spoke the name with a mocking tone, then pointed to Sutter's rod abandoned at the witch's feet.

She said nothing.

"Cunning and pitiless. When I bartered for your skills, those were the qualities I was assured would serve us in our endeavors," the man said. "Yet you leave a witness to our arrival alive? Perhaps it was all a lie."

"A pup missing will draw more attention than one who spins tall tales," the witch replied. "Even should he talk, who will believe him?"

"Soft words," the man spat. "Perhaps I shall tell the Shadow your bloodlust lacks."

"You will find proof of it soon enough, and sooner than you'd like if you continue to speak so brazenly," the witch replied, holding up her staff. The end glowed again, this time a smoldering red, and off its knotted surface, a few embers danced. The man shied back a pace from the smiting yellow eyes. "Do not speak of my master," said the sorceress. "Have we not promised that pups aplenty will burn before we are through?"

"Before *I* am through," the man said, still wary of the staff. He lifted his chin, revealing a jagged scar, and breathed deeply. "*Home.*" He relished the word and the breath before turning to the beach at their backs. Dozens more figures were gathering. The raiders were hesitant. Furtive eyes beneath the many hoods watched the witch's skull face as though it were a fell omen.

"Why do you stand there indecisively?" the scarred man called to them, stepping to hide the mask from their view. "Behold! At last we stand upon the lands of our forefathers! Come now! Once more, we shall remind our foes who first unleashed fire!"

Behind him, deadly as wine to a dog, the witch listened to the men's cheers in silence, though her yellowish eyes did brighten for a moment. She gripped a knot in her ebony staff, for she was, after all, part fire just as they were—impending conquest sought to fan them ravenous and wild.

-Chapter I-
Bartering Games

*T*he claw grated against the whetstone. It reminded Ashiy that the hulking bear could shred a redtail fox like himself to bloody pieces if he spoke a wrong word. *But he wouldn't hurt me,* Ashiy thought, watching a spark glance off the bear's nail. *It's all part of the game. And it's time to play, Ashichuaba. Don't let your ears wince now.*

Ashiy crossed his forearms and stood straighter. He kept his bushy tail arched and still. Henyer's round ears almost brushed the ceiling beams, towering beast that the brown bear was. On the counter between them sat a motley assortment of damp, greenish scales—troll skin. "And how much did y'want for these?" the tanner asked, feigning disinterest as he examined his sharpened claw.

"Thirty faces," Ashiy replied.

"Gold?"

The fox gave a quick nod.

Henyer sighed, his fat stomach stretching the studded leather and silver acorn buttons of his vest. It was fine apparel of his own make, no doubt. Ashiy rubbed a hole in the shoulder of his own woolen smock. "Shouldn't y'be out back melting scrap?" Henyer's yellow fangs sneered.

"I've a few days off," Ashiy answered. An errant fly twitched his ear. The smell of the tanner's shop was insufferable. Sheets of drying troll leather hung like convicts from the roof beams. They wore him down with a stink of hair and gore. *How does he stand it?* The fox glared at his bartering opponent before replying, "What's it to you? I've got skins to sell, and that's all there is to it."

"You've certainly got some rubbish here," replied the bear,

sifting his razored nail through the wet folds on the chestnut countertop, "and certainly not worth thirty faces."

"Then I'll sell them elsewhere."

"Best luck t'you." Henyer's claw resumed its ugly scrape. Ashiy didn't move. This was the game's first stage. Both knew the other's bluff.

"I hear Wondo's looking to make troll leather a part of his inventory," Ashiy said. The grinding faltered for a moment, and he was satisfied to note a scowl slip across the bear's flat face. Wondo was a merchant. He also provided Henyer with his curing salt.

"Troll *leather*, not raw hide," Henyer parried. "You going to treat it for him?" Silence at this stage guaranteed lost coins, but Ashiy had nothing to retort. The tanner pressed his advantage. "Kid, if you're trying to sell something, you've gotta make sure it's something someone'll actually *want.*"

"What will you tan when all the trolls in Whimzic are extinct?" Ashiy gave a pointed stare to an empty rack on the shop's far side. "I'd want to take what I could before then."

"I'll unburden you of them for ten faces," Henyer said.

All that preamble for a paltry return offer. "That's not even two per!" Ashiy said. "I'd like to see you hunt one of those monsters yourself!"

This proved to be the wrong word spoken.

A single, honed claw slashed out to hover an inch shy of Ashiy's coal nose. It smelled of old blood. "I'd like to see the same of *you,* urchin," Henyer growled. "Insult my intelligence again and see if your sorry pelt don't join the rest." The claw jabbed toward the ceiling's décor, making Ashiy flinch. "You're thinking me dumb enough to believe a pup brought low an adult troll? *Ha!* What with? Those twigs and twine on your back?" Henyer's razor pointed at Ashiy's shoddy bow and chipped quiver of flimsy arrows, his words cutting deep.

"Can tell by the odor they're half-decayed. The creature was dead maybe—" two bursts of sniffing came from the tanner, "*three* days before you happened upon it. And these are only the thin bits from beneath the arm and knee pits, meaning whoever did kill the beast already removed the best surfaces. Did you carve yours off with *that?*"

Henyer eyed the dagger sheathed to Ashiy's belt. Its cracked pommel did not attest well to the hidden blade's condition. "You'd've had better luck using your own claws, even stubby as they are. Look as if they were trimmed with a bone saw," Henyer concluded, laying the scaley hides flat. "You're lucky to get ten faces for them. Ten faces and you get to eat for the night. You *and* your old crone."

"Twenty faces."

Ashiy's eyes narrowed, the defeat inflicted by Henyer's slow evisceration burned away by sudden anger. But the fox held the emotion subdued, still focused on the exchange.

Henyer's smirk became a half. "Ten, kid. Take it or take them away."

"Twenty faces."

Henyer, scratching his chin fur, evaluated Ashiy with a cold stare. Then, finally, he said, "Ah, what's a bit of charity?" The bear's laugh was ill-humored. "I'll fold, kid. But only cause I know that fool Buruk ain't paying you well 'nuff."

Henyer's wide arm swept the skins into a stack, pulling them away toward the shelves.

A sharp swat stopped him.

Henyer's paw retracted instinctively. It was a bold move—a diminutive canid smacking a hulking bear. They both ogled each other, surprised.

Ashiy recovered before a claw flew at his face again. "Gold first. And we'll shake on it."

Never breaking the glare, Henyer retrieved a clinking satchel from beneath the counter. One by one, the bear removed coin after coin from within and dropped each with a deliberate, resentful plink. The gold discs, each the circumference of a sliced banana, served as Altharia's prime currency. Queen Illdari's sweet, elven face slept on each side. How unfitting for such a countenance to shine in a foul shop where skins were husked from monsters.

At ten faces, Henyer's count hesitated. *"Twenty,"* Ashiy reaffirmed, tapping one hind foot, his tail flicking. Behind him, the tannery's door swung open to admit a wiry gray wolf with a chunk missing from his muzzle. A long sword bounced from his hip and in his forearms he carried a roll of hide the length of a carpet. With a more worthwhile vendor waiting, Henyer doled out Ashiy's remaining payment faster.

However, before he could sweep the fox away, Ashiy stuck an open paw over the counter. "Shake on it."

"Just take your faces!" Henyer slid the growl through ground teeth.

"A shake signs a deal," Ashiy said, unperturbed.

Fuming, Henyer wrapped one paw over Ashiy's with pressure enough to make the fox wince. "Our business is concluded, twerp." Henyer's scowl soured into a scathing grin. He leaned forward to whisper, adding the grip of his second paw and a sharp dig from his claw. "Just think…now you and the old crone can eat for *two* days."

Ashiy ripped himself from the bear's hold, snatched up the allotted coins, and brushed past the waiting wolf with a slam of the door.

He stood in the street outside. Fresh air flushed the tannery's noxious scents away. But Ashiy's soiled mood clung as he rubbed his sore paw, glaring at Henyer's closed door.

The bargain had, in essence, been successful. Twenty gold faces had been Ashiy's desired number from the beginning. But the image of Henyer's smug features sapped any mood of victory. Ashiy felt half-tempted to spit on the tannery's doorstep. *She's taught you better, Ashiy. Don't.* He wagged his head and retreated a pace in the direction he had come.

Then he marched straight back, puckered, and spit a fat gob on Henyer's door. Turning tail, he hastily resumed his stride down the central road of Whim's Haven.

Indeed, the hamlet Ashiy had called home for his seventeen cycles only had this one road paved with cobblestone. Wooden cottages with thatched roofs flanked its sides. All the other establishments in the Haven were tents connected by dirt pathways. One of the wooden buildings was shared by the tanner and blacksmith, one was an apothecary, and one was the Sheriff's headquarters. Directly across from these headquarters sat a tavern named Pelt's, which oversaw almost every illicit dealing in Whim's Haven. Settled at the heart of troll-infested Whimzic Forest where no true deputy wished to venture, the town had been founded as a refuge for bandits, plunderers, and scallywags.

Attempting to lift his mood, Ashiy whistled a hearty tune as he strode the streetway with his newly earned gold jangling in his purse and his ancient bow and arrows slung over one shoulder. A pair of drunken grizzlies were scraping by Pelt's Tavern.

Claws, curses, and fur clumps flew. Still whistling, Ashiy gave them a genial swish of his tail while dodging by. Then an outburst at the bar's door sent a beady-eyed raccoon all but swerving into the fox's arms.

The raccoon stank of drink and bellowed at Aggtree, the wolven tavernkeeper who had tossed him out, "NOT EV'N, FOR NO MINUTE—" a strong hiccup interrupted the curse, "DIDN'T EVEN DOWN A PINT, Y'SSTUPID—"

"Get off me, Harvick." Ashiy pushed the raccoon away.

Harvick teetered as he rotated, his mask splitting into a delirious grin. "A-sheee!" he drawled the fox's nickname. Altharians took to abbreviating their full names. Most were long, with many yipping and barking syllables. "A-shee, A-shee! Good to ssee'ya, friend!"

"Give it back." Ashiy extended his paw like an expectant mother.

Harvick tottered to the left, then, understanding his ruse had been thwarted, dropped all pretense of drunkenness with a frown. He held up Ashiy's coin purse. "Aw, I'da never taken from you, Ashiy. Just didn't know who I bumped inta is all." Raccoons had the best paws in Altharia, being so similar in dexterity to human hands. Harvick skilled his toward pick-pocketing. The thief squeezed Ashiy's pouch before returning it. "Feels a mite heavier than usual."

"I just did business with Henyer," Ashiy said, refastening the purse to his belt.

Harvick spit on the ground. "Itch that mutt. He cheat you?"

"No, I think I got the better of the deal." Ashiy began walking again. Harvick, hiding his devious paws in his cloak, fell into a casual stride with him.

"Fair on you, pleasure to hear it." Harvick nodded. "Henyer's gold is sweet to take."

"Did you *take* enough in there?" Ashiy nodded to the tavern. Few stayed for long in Whim's Haven. Brave enough north-bound travelers used it as a midpoint when short-cutting the main highway. It was something of a pastime for Harvick to slouch around the tavern, feign intoxication, and pry the odd coat and cloak of passing visitors for profit. Locals knew to keep the raccoon at two arms' distance.

"Agh! Nearly had a nice score, then the dog stood up! Thought I was jus' too friendly a drunk, so guess I avoided a beatin' at least." Harvick brushed his damp cloak. It was the only part of the raccoon which had consumed alcohol, providing him with a strong cologne. "When'll you let me give you a lesson, Ashiy? You've got small 'nuff mitts for pickin' a pouch."

"I'm not a thief." Ashiy inclined no judgment toward Harvick. To the fox, his statement was merely fact.

"If you only steal from other thieves, it's no crime." Harvick shrugged. Ashiy didn't reply, so he dropped the topic. The duo exhausted the cobblestone underfoot, coming to a winding vineyard of dirt roads. "You off to market?"

Ashiy nodded. "Then home."

Harvick's true smile lifted years off his ragged face on the rare occasions it surfaced. "Give your ol' lady a hullo for me, eh?"

As the raccoon turned and hustled his ringleted tail out of

sight, Ashiy almost asked him where he was going. *Better not to,* he decided. Harvick's mischief was none of his business, and no doubt it was sure to be quite illicit and doomed.

Out of habit, Ashiy gave his wallet a quick feel. It was still there.

A scrabble and a crash punctured the tent's silence. Ceramic shards and ink exploded over the floor, which, luckily, was dirt. "Sorry, very sorry!" Buruk, a bear closing fast on his fortieth cycle, clutched one paw to his sooty apron. He rubbed the fabric, sheepish.

An upturned palm remained presented before Buruk. Slender fingers curled, beckoning the bear's wrist to return. It was a delicate, furless hand the color of an umber olive and quite warm, yet Buruk trembled to let it hold his.

"It won't hurt."

"I know, I do—I'm givin' the matter t'much thought." Buruk stooped to gather what he could of the mess he had made. "Silly thing, innit? Can work around the furnace all day, but now, rememberin' when it happened…"

From her spot at the table, the lady allowed him to stall, tracing his movements with patient hazel eyes. They suggested a seniority of age not mirrored in the rest of her face. She was over eighty years old. Yet her striking features were narrow and sharp, lacking any wrinkle save those befitting a youth of twenty. Auburn hair, devoid of a single silver strand, was pulled behind two distinctive ears. Each of these ended in points.

Elves were a rarity in the Canid Territory. In a town as delinquent and remote as Whim's Haven, their presence was even more unfathomable.

Yet here Ceilia sat, her holy features wreathed by a dingy shawl. The modest tent she made home had not uprooted its stakes from Whim's Haven's outskirts in nigh seventeen cycles.

"Are you prepared to try again?" Ceilia asked. The bear hesitated, unsure of where to deposit the fragments of inkwell he had gathered. "Leave those. They'll be taken care of."

Cleaning efforts nullified, Buruk, feeling even more buffoonish, set the pile back on the floor, then retook his too-small stool opposite the elf. Their seats and table were the only proper furnishings inside the cramped shelter. Two bedrolls, a lantern, and a walking staff were secured with cords to the tarpaulin above their heads. Several patchy traveling trunks were stacked in one darkened corner, with an unlit candle, parchment, and glass vials strewn on the topmost trunk. These scant possessions were plenty to crowd the tent, especially given Buruk's included size.

The bear surrendered his paw once more, laying it atop Ceilia's palm. Under the lantern's light shone a most ghastly scar. Mauling fire had created a hideous channel of bald, mangled skin that ran up his forearm from where the T-shaped mark of a branded thief was displayed.

Buruk's expression contracted. Three decades had passed. His criminal habits had been broken, and the injury's pain had long receded, but the memory of agony was not fleeting.

"It won't hurt," Ceilia said again. "I promise you."

Buruk nodded. "On with it, Ceilia. I'll keep still."

The elf's other hand enshrouded Buruk's forearm, massaging it, and finding places where the skin appeared too warped for hair to regrow. Ceilia's eyelids closed. Buruk used her luminous face as an anchor to keep from jumping up again. How serene she looked! What an honor to be in her presence; a creature whose blood descended from the Mistress of all life itself…

Ceilia's index finger found the scar's origin. She needled it with her nail. Every muscle in Buruk's body went taut, but to his credit, he did not flinch again.

The lantern light, however, did for a brief gutter.

When its flame reformed, it found itself outshone by a second light. Buruk's tension fled at the same moment. His face, cast in sudden blue highlights, slacked. The bear's big eyes welled with uncharacteristic tears. "Ah…this-*this*-what's—?"

"Shh." Ceilia's hand continued to play over Buruk's arm.

The elf's face seemed even more divine when sky blue colors danced across it.

Buruk sobbed. Quietly.

"I've finished."

He blinked. Once more, the lantern's glow was their only illumination. Yet as she quickly retracted her hand, a few azure particles danced round Ceilia's fingertips before vanishing like lonesome snowflakes.

"I-I'm sorry, Ceilia, not an idea what come over me." Buruk's cheeks were soaked. "Cryin' like a cub."

"Not to worry." Ceilia's eyes were open now. For the wisp of a second, their hazel depths shone with a lingering sadness. Then she smiled. "Will you see the result?"

"Result?" Buruk was still distracted by his own outburst. "Yes-*oh!*" The bear inspected his arm, transfixed. The scarring had disappeared. Silky black fur fluttered upon the twisted areas it had formerly been unable to occupy, blending with the rest of Buruk's coat. Hesitant, Buruk parted the new hairs with his claw. Beneath, the thief's brand could still be discerned. Alas, to remove it entirely was to break the law. But now it was much easier to miss.

"I-It's wondrous, Ceilia, truly!" Buruk's tears were now joyous and better restrained. "Ah, y'have my gratitude, as always. And, not t'worry, I'll not disrespect the gift."

"You'd be the last person in Whimzic I'd expect to return to debauchery, Buruk," Ceilia said. "I only wish you'd allowed me to take care of it years ago."

"I wish it too." Buruk could not quit examining his limb. "I'd just heard—I knew it was magic healing…my, *I'm simply*—I'd never imagined a normal right arm attached t'me again!" The bear waved the appendage with a laugh. Then, finally, his mood steered in a businesslike manner. "What I owe you, Ceilia?"

"Not a face."

"I know real craftsmanship when I see it, Ceilia. And *this*—" he said, giving his arm another vigorous shake, "is masterful. I won't accept y'giving it freely."

"Not a face," Ceilia said again. "You've done enough for us already."

"Ah, not at all. Not anything worth this," Buruk replied. His stout ears flicked to the tent's entryway. A shaft of declining evening sunlight crossed their faces, giving both cause to shield their brows. The tent's flaps parted to admit its second resident.

This was Ashiy. His paws were full of parchment-wrapped packages.

"Mother, I've got a surprise—" Ashiy froze, noticing Buruk.

"Evenin', Ashiy!" The hearty bear did not lose a beat. His nose wiggled. "Got y'some tasty treats there?"

"Come in, dear." Ceilia beckoned to the fox before returning her attention to their guest. "Buruk, would you care to stay and sup with us?"

"Naw, Branny'd be jealous. I'd best be back afore dark." Buruk rose, pinching Ashiy's shoulder on his way out. "Can see the forge's work on you. Buildin' muscle, eh?"

"I suppose." Ashiy shrugged the bear's toes off.

"Reminds me. Meetin' Aggtree tomorrow about his expansion to the pub. Day afters, Branny'll need your paws at the bellows, right?"

"Well…I do have paws," Ashiy said.

"Right'n good. Report in then." Buruk smiled and wound his cloak around his wide neck. He nodded to the elf. "Ceilia, bless you 'gain."

"Take care, Buruk," Ceilia replied. With a wink, the bear bowed out, leaving the fox and elf to share silence. Ceilia found a broom tucked behind the trunks and set to clearing the dirt floor. She swept the ink splotch and a fair bit of dust outside.

Ashiy watched her return the broom.

"Don't give me that look," Ceilia said.

"I see enough of him as is, you know," Ashiy replied, finally unloading his packages onto the cleared table. A whiff of soot and metal lingered in the air. Buruk was the town blacksmith. Ashiy, on odd days, served as his most recent apprentice.

"Selfish thing to say," Ceilia remarked as she buttoned shut the tent's entry flaps. "He wasn't here for you. Healing that wretched mark was a long time coming. You know that the sheriff who did it didn't even shave the fur first?"

Ashiy massaged his own undamaged wrist. He had never known the punishment of flame, unlike the vast number of animals throughout the Haven. "No wonder it was that ugly."

Ceilia came closer to inspect Ashiy's items. "So," she said, "what have you brought?"

Ashiy loosened the strings from the brown parcels. Food provided a pleasant distraction, and the thrill of unveiling his spoils to Ceilia refloated his spirits. From the first untwined package came a sack of chickpeas and a small wheel of orange cheese. The second unveiled half a dozen chicken eggs and another satchel, this one brimming with grain. Then, with a flourish, Ashiy revealed the contents of the third package. This one was his favorite. Forest blackberries, a jar of spiced apple cider, and—

"Pastry rolls?" Ceilia's voice was incredulous. She did not have an animal's strong nose, but cinnamon was unmistakable. "Ashiy! Was Hogpipper out of bread?"

"Of course not! But these were *irresistible,* Mother!" Ashiy's whiskers twitched, pleased to see her delight. He had inherited his love for sweets from her.

"Oh, my, you tempter…and cider too?" Ceilia whistled. Then her eyes narrowed. "How much did this cost?"

There came the daily question. Already in the air, fall's nip was beginning to test summer's resolve. Eight months, forty days apiece in count, added to a complete Altharian cycle. Ceilia remained a scrupulous saver throughout each passing season, but she became especially miserly during the two summer months. In summer, Whimzic abounded with edible plant life. Berry bushes, fruiting trees, mushrooms, and wild crops provided both food and goods for the experienced forager to sell. Autumn and winter's long stays, however, made the woods barren. An allowance had to be stretched to purchase food during those months.

"Half of today's earnings!" Ashiy tossed Ceilia his change pouch. "On budget, and we still eat like royalty."

Ceilia parsed the ten faces out on the table. Her perplexity was not alleviated. "You earned twenty coins today?"

Ashiy twisted free the lid from the jar of cider, not to drink yet, just to savor the scent. "Yes," he said. Then, under his breath, "Maybe I don't need to become a smith after all."

Ceilia pretended not to hear the comment. The argument that could ensue over it was a tired one. "What? All from foraging?" She focused on him.

Ashiy avoided her stabbing stare. "Yes…"

"You've never foraged enough food to earn twenty coins before."

"No…"

"Ashiy. What did you do?"

"I sold off some things to Henyer." Ashiy shifted on his feet.

"Skins." Ceilia's eyes widened. *"Troll?"*

Ashiy grinned; a guilty smile braced for explosion.

"Are. You. *Mad?"* Not another person in Whimzic, fox or otherwise, could shatter Ceilia's even temper like Ashiy. She had her hands on both his shoulders at once, trembling, shaking him, latching on as though he could turn to mist in her grasp. Her words, always clear and composed with premeditated thought, tumbled out fragmented and aghast. "What possessed—? Why would you even—? *What were you doing in troll territory?"*

"It's the end of summer." Ashiy's face flushed beneath his fur. "The forest's picked clean everywhere close to town."

"So you decided to pick a bout with a troll?"

"No, it was dead when I found it. Long dead. Already skinned even. Wasn't like I was the first to find it. We'd be eating for months if I had." The excuse had no effect on Ceilia's stricken expression. Gingerly, Ashiy pried her hands loose from his arms and took them in his paws. *"Mother,* I'm safe. You don't have to worry."

Ceilia rolled her eyes. "The words to make me worry all the more." She inhaled. Ashiy felt her grip lessen. But her hazelnut eyes pierced straight into his cobalt ones. "You have the apprenticeship with Buruk now, Ashiy."

"Yes, but it doesn't pay!"

"We still manage." Ceilia gestured around at their modest tent. "Enough of the forest—it isn't a playpen. You must quit treating it like one. Do not stray that far again. Understand?"

"Yes," Ashiy said, containing his own exasperation. His stomach growled, imploring for the admonishment to end. "But really, Mother, look at all this. Wasn't it worth it?" Ashiy held up one of the cinnamon pastries, enticing her. "C'mon, you should pick the biggest one."

Ceilia shook her head. Then frowned. Then, inexplicably, chortled.

"What?" Ashiy's head tilted sideways, ears perked.

"Oh," Ceilia's face softened. A tinge of bittersweet joy in her voice struck Ashiy more than her scolding ever could. Her arms opened. Ashiy accepted the tight hug, nuzzling Ceilia's dark hair. "You're too good to your nagging mother, you know that?"

How very similar their heights were now. A single month might see him surpass her.

"I don't," Ashiy replied, embracing Ceilia all the closer. "I've been trying to treat her even better."

-Chapter II-
Of an Elf and Delsic Root

*T*here were many curious things concerning the relationship between Ashiy the fox and Ceilia the elf. Curious to the townsfolk of Whim's Haven. Curious to their immediate neighbors. And curious, most of all, to Ashiy himself.

Seventeen cycles prior, early morning light had fallen upon a new canvas tent pitched by the Haven's edge. It stood without fanfare; unassuming, patched, and weather-beaten. No thought was given to this newcomer. The tent's occupant went unseen and unheard, and they had not been recorded in the Sheriff's logbook, for the Sheriff of that day was even more of a criminal than the present one. Many travelers came and went without a whisper in Whim's Haven. The borough had hosted shadier rovers than whoever dwelt in that solitary, vagrant tent.

Months elapsed. The tent did not vanish from its site. Its resident might well have planted its stakes and then died within. If the newcomer had existed at all.

A full year passed before the rumor circulated of an elf sighted in Whim's Haven.

Some said she frequented the market at sundown when the bustle subsided and prying eyes were few. She disguised herself with a hood folded round her face like melting candle wax to hide her telltale ears. Such rumors became of keen interest to the locals who retold and muddied them at the pub. Elves were lawful. They were enigmatic. And often they were, a final rumor embellished, filthy rich.

What business could such a creature have in a place black as Whimzic Forest?

Explanations ran rampant, each vying to be more outlandish than the last. She was a spy from Eltcindale itself—an eye for the queen, sent to uncover conspiracy in the furthest reaches of Altharia. No, not a spy, but a princess, banished from the capitol, sworn to secrecy in this backwater hamlet out of fear of assassination. But then again, she could be a witch, renounced of her divine blood and bent on experimenting with unstable magic. *No, no,* better yet, she was—and so the talk went round and round.

Parties of young ruffians began ambushing the marketplace for glimpses of the hooded lady. Older crooks eyed cloaked strangers they passed in the streets with unease. For weeks, paranoid thieves and smugglers conducted their dealings as if Whim's Haven were a normal town—under cover of darkness or in secretive rendezvous rather than the accustomed broad daylight.

The elf's presence remained unconfirmed. Gossipers quieted. Rumor dissolved.

Then she appeared in the market one afternoon, unhooded, pointed ears bared, and uncaring of the shocked looks she garnered. The red fox kit she ferried puzzled the locals even more. He was well-fed and dapperly groomed. She set him atop stalls as she haggled with vendors. When he cried, she shushed and cooed him in her arms as if he was her own child. Upon retiring to the outskirt tent, she took the kit with her.

Reaction to the elf's sudden emergence was fickle. Much of the excitement surrounding her presence was owed to mystery, which did not persist with her anticlimactic reveal. There was not much to find interesting about the elf. She was a beauty, just as all her flora-borne kin were, but she had no scars, and practiced no dark sorcery. She offered a good-natured chat to any who approached her and only left her tent to purchase food or allow the fox kit to explore on wavering feet.

Still, certain bandits took unsavory interest in the little tent poised by the forest's edge. Many became convinced the elf was hoarding valuables and bided their time to raid her home after her next infrequent outing. A pair of wolves—quite unwise fellows who thought themselves sneaky—staked their own tent a few yards from hers, pretending to be neighbors. The day after hatching their ploy, they awoke to find the elf waiting outside. She invited them for tea, where, to their disappointment, they discovered her tent's interior was quite plain, with no treasure to pilfer. Her furniture and supplies were antiquated in a sense that appeared almost deliberate. Everything was second hand, any value beaten out of them long ago. The fox kit slept in nothing more than a ratty sling hammocked to the low ceiling. Her teacups' floral patterns were worn and the porcelain half cracked. After an overdrawn teatime, the wolves left dampened.

Word spread and criminal scrutiny dropped.

Whim's Haven, after all, was a historic den of oddballs, ranging from kleptomaniacal to murderous. A mother and adopted child offered little fascination by comparison. They were accepted as just another town peculiarity.

Years advanced. The fox kit matured. At five, he supplanted his caretaker in running marketplace errands—a surprising development that created a brief buzz. It was a rather dangerous business for someone so young to undertake in the Haven. But unlike most slum toddlers, the child spoke as if educated, and, to the dismay of many swindling vendors, he could read.

This talent was not lost on certain watchful animals. Most individuals in Whim's could not cipher for themselves and cornered the pup on several occasions to ask how he had learned. The child proved much more talkative than his reclusive caretaker, crediting her with teaching him, and introducing himself by the birth name Ashichuaba. Only when asked for his mother's name did the child hush, claiming, tight-lipped, that he was not supposed to share it unless the elf gave him permission first.

Indeed, the elf's name was safeguarded, but the secret began to disseminate. Whatever savings had sustained her through Ashiy's infant years had evidently run out. She began offering reading lessons to the Haven's illiterate populace at a very meek cost. For any who became her students, two conditions were enforced. First, they were forbidden to speak the elf's name to anyone who did not already know it. Second, their desire to read had to stem from an honest want to better themselves. They were not to apply the skill toward criminality. The scant few students who met this second requirement came to know the elf as Ceilia.

From these pupils, a steady, secretive community fostered. At first, only children learned, and parents who had settled and reformed their criminal ways but remained too poor to travel beyond the forest's borders. Word of mouth and curiosity admitted more, though Ceilia never accepted too many at a time.

Still, the number of illiterate locals gradually diminished. New, legitimate business fronts took form over the encompassing decade, Buruk's smithy among them. All owed their startup, in large part, to Ceilia's tutelage. With their success came a general respect levied toward the unseen elf from the average Whim's Haven resident. The Haven's most immoral folk continued to harbor meek derision, but the elf never interfered with their illicit prospects, and she preached no morality toward any animal who did not first seek it. Thus, no troubles were stirred, and she was left alone.

To the present day, Ceilia remained an enigma, though a familiar one, with friends aplenty who cared not for whatever buried past had brought her to Whim's Haven.

Ashiy cared, though. Quite deeply.

Most outsiders assumed he knew the elf's secrets. They were mistaken.

Ashiy had grappled against the mystery of Ceilia's past all his life. Half of his caretaker's identity remained hidden; a half he desperately wished Ceilia would open to him. For she had revealed to Ashiy only three snippets, and these only after a dreadful amount of prying over the course of many years: she had been a close friend of his true parents, they had both died in the months following his birth, and their names had been Dreer and Lavese.

Ceilia groaned, rifling through her trunk.

Ashiy's right ear twitched. Sprawled on his sleeping mat, his tail and a leg free of the blanket, he cracked open one eye. "What's the matter, Mother?"

"I've gone and used all my delsic." Ceilia began refolding the clothes she had displaced. "Greedy of me. I thought I still had one taproot left over."

Ashiy yawned. "Have the rest of the cider I didn't finish." He rolled onto his back. The spell of slumber was broken. Needlepoints of sunlight stabbed through the tent fabric at him. *Seventeen years waking under the same canvas...* Ashiy rubbed his eyes, then hefted himself upright.

Ceilia chewed her lip, stewing over the fruitless desire to check the now organized chest a second time. Ashiy nudged her shoulder, consoling her over the loss of her favorite tea ingredient. "Y'know, I'm beginning to think you have an addiction." Ashiy snatched an undershirt from the container to throw over his lean torso.

Ceilia chuckled. "You might have just pegged the nail to the notice." She sighed. "No delsic. Summer is truly over without it."

"Not yet, maybe." Ashiy struggled with his cloak's fastener. Ceilia had sewn it with a small button that his toes struggled to fit. "I'll look for more while I'm out in the forest."

Ceilia frowned. "Buruk and Branny don't need you?"

"Not until tomorrow. You heard him tell me."

Her displeasure was evident, but she did not contest the matter further. "You're not leaving without breakfast."

"I'll scavenge something," Ashiy replied.

"Out of the question." Two cinnamon pastries remained from the previous night. Ceilia chose one and presented it to Ashiy. Still fumbling with the button, he did not take it. "Here, open."

"Mother."

Ceilia persisted. "Open." Ashiy grudgingly revealed his

tongue. She stuck the roll between his teeth, then assisted him with the stubborn cloak.

"Thamkths," Ashiy said through a sticky mouthful.

"You stay out of troll territory." Ceilia clutched the cloak's collar. "And be back before sunset. Yes?"

"Back to eating poor." Ashiy licked his paws. Then he equipped his quiver and picked up his bow.

"When you become a graduated smith, we'll dine better," Ceilia said, kissing his cheek.

Ashiy made no comment on the matter, stealing through the entryway into the brisk air outside. He stretched in the morning sunlight, taking in the surrounding scenery. Scores of similar tents nestled amid the dewy grass, and thin strands of smoke leaked skyward from campfires. The scent of eggs, toast, and syrup drifted from them. He rounded away from his home's entrance to face the forest.

The woods were untamed in this direction. Whimzic, still shadowed with mist trapped beneath the close-knit canopy of its foreboding cedars, beckoned to Ashiy. His heart leaped to chase its call.

A few steps beyond the town's borders left all sounds of civilization muted. A few more, and the sight of Whim's Haven was swallowed by mossy trunks and waggling ferns. Ashiy strode amid a dark, green land. Pale summer asters winked where stray beams of sunlight fell. Bedding moths leaped up like dust from steps made through overgrowth. Speckled mushrooms peeped from the shades of bracken. Spindled tree roots warred with neighbors for space above ground. Ashiy climbed atop one that arched as high as his waist, surveying for a direction to embark.

Alive! This forest was alive with the promise of adventure! Ashiy had sensed it, tantalizing him since his initial foray at eight cycles of age. These choking roots did not encroach across the entirety of Altharia. Their reach encompassed a region some hundred miles in width. Beyond them lay mountains which prodded heaven's underbelly, rivers that whipped the earth like twisting lashes, cities whose noble masonry had witnessed centuries-worth of sieges, and, bards claimed, lands where islands were suspended in sky and cloud.

And I'll never see any of them.

The idea dampened Ashiy's usual surge of excitement. His ears wilted against his head as he remembered Ceilia's parting words. She was set on the idea of him becoming a blacksmith, having twisted Buruk's ear the previous month to take the fox on as an apprentice. Once Ceilia was set on a notion, the sea would be more apt to siphon its salt before she reconsidered. Smithing was a safe occupation, save you were careful not to light your fur. But it was a stationary practice. There would be no opportunity to venture out into the vast world. Out there seemed to be a place Ceilia was keen to forget.

What a bore it all seemed, to remain in one spot forever.

Ashiy gripped his bow tighter. Time to distract himself. If his expeditions through the forest were numbered, he refused to squander this one in gloom.

He gave his bowstring a strum. Its fiber was chafing again. Ashiy received it from Ceilia as an eighth birthday gift. Even under his careful treatment, its limbs were now chipped. Every week forced him to rebind the frayed leather grip straps, and the deteriorated rest was nearly too shallow to hold an arrow shaft.

Still, it accomplished its purpose.

Ashiy took a flying leap from the root. Midair, he produced an arrow from his quiver. Crouching low as his feet hit dirt, he yanked the string, and imagining the deadened tree several yards ahead was an oncoming foe, discharged an arrow.

Thiiiish!

"Argh," Ashiy growled. The projectile hurtled into a bush just shy of the stump. He had been moving too much. The fox straightened, nocked another, and focused upon the target with a single eye.

Thunk!

The arrow's butt quivered, its head buried in the decayed

bark.

Thunk! Thunk!

Two more followed in sporadic succession, creating a lopsided triangle. Satisfied, Ashiy shouldered his weapon and went to retrieve the stuck projectiles. He then sifted through the bush for the initial arrow. Pulling it out, he inspected its ratty feathers. They were peeling free of the glue. Ashiy sighed, placing the arrows back in his quiver.

He continued practicing. An hour a day was his habit and eight years had molded him into a fair archer, provided his targets were stationary. Lightning-shattered tree stumps and elephant ear fern leaves in his path were left pocketed with holes.

They were the only things he had skewered. Indeed, Ceilia had granted him the bow as a weapon for defense. "Keep out of trouble, but if you are *in* trouble, keep it at a distance," had been her words the day Ashiy received the weapon. "If I find you've used this to start a fight, I'll confiscate it at once."

The hour plunged Ashiy further into the forest, though the scenery could disguise the distance trekked from Whim's Haven. An elf or human might find themselves lost. But not Ashiy. The trees, identical as they might seem to others, had been landmarks known to him for many cycles. Besides, canids had their telltale noses. He could retrace his own scent back the way he came, as long as no rainfall washed it away.

Humidity rose with the day. The morning's trapped mist clung to the back of Ashiy's throat and he began to pant. Concluding his archery, he removed his suffocating cloak. Taking two of its corners in each paw, he tied them together as a makeshift sack. *Now time to fill it.*

Despite the abundance of foliage he had already passed, none of it held profit for a forager. The berry bushes were either pruned or past their prime. Non-poisonous fungi had been sniffed and dug out of their underground dens. Even edible sages and garnishing plants had been uprooted for miles encompassing the town. The summer season saw an abundance of foragers combing the woods.

In fact, Ashiy found it surprising he had encountered no fellow searchers yet this morning.

As if in defiance of this thought, a slight breeze carried to Ashiy a familiar scent. A minute later, the smell strengthened, and Harvick the raccoon emerged from the underbrush.

"What're you doing out here?"

Harvick jumped, a paw clamped across his breast. "Ashiy! Curse it all, you've given me a fright! What'd y'say, there?"

"I asked what you're doing out here," Ashiy said again, watching him closely. Harvick did not often drift far from town.

"What are *you?*" Harvick's response came with an uncharacteristic snap.

"I'm foraging."

"Well, ah, I'm…on a little meetup with a new business partner of mine," Harvick's voice dropped. There was not a lick of gold in Ashiy's wallet, so he allowed the raccoon to come nearer. "Can y'just give yer word you'll not tell anyone you've seen me out here? What y'say, Ashiy?"

"Sure, Harvick."

"Ah, atsa true friend." Harvick's consternation lessened. He gave Ashiy a lazy wink. "Stay safe out here, eh?"

"Same to you."

The raccoon scurried into the forest. Ashiy stared after him, not doubting for a moment the affable scoundrel's need for safe tidings outweighed his own. To meet with someone this far outside the Haven meant Harvick had really stepped into something sinful.

Ashiy did not even want a glimpse of what it could be.

Thus, he angled his path northward, opposite the direction where Harvick had gone. Scouring for another hour yielded a couple of tidbits. Ashiy sniffed out a hazelnut tree, but only harvested a handful from its boughs. They were an autumn yield, still with a month left to ripen.

Another small score came from a quaint family of rindchew bushes. They produced tough, brownish fruits with a rocky, bitter hide and even bonier core. Native to Altharia's mainland, the resilient fruits budded year-round and were essential for keeping canid or bear teeth sharp and healthy.

Ashiy made a rather unsatisfying lunch of them that afternoon, reclining in a tree branch as he gnawed the fruit's rough skin. Though he wished to press deeper into Whimzic, he would return home past nightfall if he did not begin doubling back within the next hour.

But I can't return with just these. Ashiy cast away a rindchew core, listening to it plunge through the foliage below his tree.

The veer north had not been made entirely to avoid Harvick's hijinks. It had been a temptation. There were more trolls in Whimzic's northern region.

Ashiy scratched a symbol in the tree bark with an arrowhead, teetering over the decision. By technicality, the whole forest was troll territory. A troll that stayed with its mother too long would be devoured, lest it grew large enough to cannibalize her itself. Thus, young trolls migrated through the forest in search of a den. Ashiy had spied a few of these rovers over the years. Though they had skin thick as chain mail, they were skittish if enough din was stirred. Decades of hunts and exterminations had deterred them from Whim's Haven proper, but the biggest and meanest of the brutes settled just shy of these instinctual boundaries.

Their muddy nests were a terrible danger to go near, but not without reward for the plucky forager. Trolls, vile meat-eaters that they were, ignored digestible plants.

I'll go to the same place I found that dead one yesterday. Ashiy shivered. It had been the first adult troll he had ever come across, dead or alive. With most of its skin rendered asunder, the creature had been a chilling sight—an eight-foot mountain of pure muscle and tendon sprawled on the forest floor, with wicked curved claws and incisors the size and thickness of Ashiy's forearm. *But it's dead. Too close to town. Alderly's deputies probably killed it. A troll nest without a troll—best take advantage of that before some other forager does.* Ashiy checked his cloak bag again. Three unripe hazelnuts and a shriveled rindchew mocked him from the bottom. *Can't go home with nothing.*

Ashiy shimmied down the tree and strode in the direction of the dead troll's den. *It isn't troll territory if a troll isn't around to occupy it anymore,* he reminded his hounding apprehension.

Still, the surroundings Ashiy soon discovered were grim reminders that there had indeed been a monster dwelling in them. The ground, formerly firm and grassy, became gluey mud under Ashiy's feet. Sap coagulated from white gouges in nearby trees where wretched claws had been sharpened. The odor of old excrement lingered in the air, choking out any other scent. Ashiy's heart thudded against his ribcage so loud he feared it would rouse the ghost of the goliath. He kept an arrow always primed on the bowstring, and any muskrat or insect that fidgeted in the thickets found it aimed their way.

Nothing to fear, Ashiy reminded himself. A scent of death had begun wafting downwind toward him. The rotting troll carcass proved his safety.

But the risk he'd taken did not produce its supposed rewards. Ashiy had failed to calculate just how much destruction trolls inflicted on their habitats. The torn-up earth had taken with it all greenery. Nothing much remained. *A waste,* he thought, shaking muck off his bare feet. *What a—*

Ashiy paused.

A delsic sapling winked at him from the base of one claw-raked cedar. Indigenous to Whimzic, delsics were saplings in name only. They grew only a few feet tall, the pallor of their stems almost translucent, and they developed dark, azure leaves. Belowground, however, they acted as parasites, latching to an existing tree's root system.

Ashiy knelt beside the delsic to excavate the dirt. The pale sapling was well-integrated. After a few minutes of scraping with his paws, he hit a network of afflicted cedar. Delsic infection turned their roots pearly white and very sweet in flavor.

Ashiy grinned. Just a few minutes and the day's fortunes were altered! Delsic root fetched a fair wage at market, perhaps even more so now that summer, its prime spreading season, was ending. And it was Ceilia's favorite tea flavoring. That alone was worth more than any gold. For the next hour, Ashiy spaded the soil with his claws and cut milky roots with his knife, humming as he worked.

Finally, the rucksack overflowed with roots.

Ashiy stood, clapping his filthy paws. He patted the cedar's trunk, smiling sadly at the large gash in it. First a troll's sharpener and then beset by a delsic—the poor tree had been through enough. "Here's hoping your misfortunes are over, friend."

Shadows were growing in the forest. *Goodness, that took a while,* Ashiy realized. Turning his gaze upward, he tried to gauge the sun's placement through the canopy. *Might not have time to sell today. Have to push it to tomorrow. But that'll be good. It'll give mother her choice picks.*

A scream echoed from the forest's depths.

Leaves rustled with a new breeze. A stench flowed on it that nearly made Ashiy gag. It was of fresh excrement, blood, and death.

The fur down Ashiy's spine raised on end. His ears swiveled. Something pummeled through the brush toward him, slashing through leaves, disturbing nearby lesser birds, hooves trumpeting—

Ashiy dove aside as an elk crashed into sight, barreling straight through the spot he had occupied. He saw antlers flash, the tendons of the dumb beast's fours pumping madly and crookedly, and the dull eyes roiling white with terror. Then it vanished into the forest.

In its wake, a trail of blood spattered over the earth.

Ashiy scrambled to his feet. In that instant, the forest floor began to pound, matching his elevated heartbeat. Footfalls, monstrous and thundering, closed in fast on the spot.

Ashiy had only a second to throw himself behind the beaten

cedar trunk before the troll entered his view. The fox scrunched close to the bark, flattening like paper, wishing he could meld with it.

But those claws could rend any flesh, be it tree or animal.

They dragged through the mud, talons black and razored. Deer blood gleamed on several of them. A mottled tongue stained itself ruby by licking them. Ashiy chanced a furtive peer around his hiding spot. The troll was gargantuan—ten feet tall, fully matured, and a male, judging from the prominent spines running down its hunched back. Gray skin rippled with muscle. A pair of tiny, slit eyes blinked in a scowl trained on the forest floor. The troll followed the blood trail left by its injured prey. Ashiy stopped looking.

Nothing to do but wait and pray. Fervent prayers. Prayers offered at the potential end of one's life. Ashiy closed his eyes, using the invocations to keep his breathing silent. *Mistress above, please let him pass! Don't let him find me!*

Deep sniffs came from behind the tree, guided by the troll's pig-like snout. Their eyes were all but useless. Ashiy shrunk, knees buckling in terror. He scanned the ground. His bow sat next to his delsic haul, and the crater dug next to it. All of it reeked of a fox's scent. Tasty fox. An ideal snack for such a monster.

Sniff. Sniff.

The snorts neared. Flight was hardly an option. No one could outrun the giant.

Ashiy tensed, quaking, still praying, understanding the only choice for survival.

Oh, protect me, please.

Drawing a sharp breath, Ashiy threw himself free of cover. Chest bared, he posed before the troll with wide flung forearms, and screamed as loud and deep as he could. The yell, delirious and droning with a confidence only the fear of death instilled, perturbed the troll. It took a single rumbling step backward, claws raised.

Ashiy's yell petered out. He inhaled, preparing to repeat it.

Hunching, with a cavernous, bloody mouth split wide, the troll produced its own roar. Ashiy's face was blown by the reek of rotted meat. His ears rang, the furious howl shattering them. All intent to scream froze like a spike in his throat.

This was no wandering troll. It was an adult, war-torn from long defense of the territory the two of them stood upon. And now it had another challenger.

Ashiy grabbed up his bow and fled.

Another bellow from the troll, followed by a colossal crack. The wounded cedar tree fell in a storm of shattered bark and whirling leaves. Somehow, Ashiy kept running, dodging thickets, vaulting fallen logs, cutting himself on briars.

In only a few careening strides, the troll cleared their distance. Wild swings tore at Ashiy's tail. He felt rushing wind as one missed, then he soared forward from a second glancing blow. Arrows scattered from his quiver. He rolled several yards before stopping, stomach-down on the earth.

Crushing fingers encircled Ashiy's legs as he tried to regain ejected breath. Weightless was the feeling of being hoisted into the air. He managed to shudder a gasp. The troll's face appeared even uglier upside-down; grinning, piggish, and only inches from his own.

Ashiy still held his bow. Weakly throwing a paw behind him, he found a single arrow stuck in his quiver.

He put it in the troll's forehead.

The creature's jaw careened back in an aggravated scream. Ashiy's vision ebbed. The hold on his pinned legs did not release, instead thrashing him around like a plaything. Growling, the troll plucked the arrow free of its cranium. Thick-skinned brutes. Their forehead hide was blubber, compensating for the tiny brain behind. If only he had hit one of the eyes…

Spent, Ashiy hung limp, unaware of the fanged jaws opening, throat gaping wide.

He imagined Ceilia's face, tear-stained and broken. A wreck of grief.

I'm so sorry, Mother.

-Chapter III-
Nothing Shall Harm Me

A flash of light. Radiant yellow. Like a final sunray dying in clouds. Ashiy felt weightless. He laughed, quite suddenly overwhelmed by deep mirth. This was cheer! Cheer that warmed like a holiday spent with beloved family. A golden land? Was this what awaited travelers on the far side of death? The happiness was as overpowering as a riptide.

Nothing shall break me, nothing will harm me, no harm will befall this poor fox. Nothing shall break me, nothing will harm me, no harm will befall this poor fox.

The thoughts danced around Ashiy's head in a chant not entirely his own. *Something's off.* He fought his logic through the incantation. *What's happening?*

Then came the pain all at once, as the uncaring ground abruptly ended Ashiy's freefall from the troll's grasp. His groan morphed into a hearty chuckle.

Ashiy opened his eyes.

Ethereal light surrounded him in a thin, yellow veil, as though he were enclosed in the upturned head of a canary tulip. Through its half-translucent petals, Ashiy saw a fight.

Shimmering in chainmail, a mighty gray elephant stood on hind feet, planted behind a door-sized shield. The troll's howling came to Ashiy's ears dampened and distant, even though its maker stood only scant feet away. Claws beat at the turtling elephant's shield, gouging hunks of wood, then cleaving the thick surface in two. Ashiy saw the elephant swerve backward around more slashes from the beast's talons, now defenseless, crying out something indistinguishable.

Another flash of smiting sunset emblazoned Ashiy's vision. He blinked, half-blinded, and saw the troll stagger with another curdling screech. It held a spot on its corded neck where smoke now billowed from its blistered hide. The creature's snout cast about, searching for the source of the new attack.

With the troll distracted, the elephant drew from his back a two-pawed greatsword. Moving with surprising speed, he slid under the troll's stumble to impart a shallow cut on the creature's thigh.

Glancing pain drove greater fury into the beast, making its next flurry of blows incontestable. The elephant could not dodge them all. His sword connected with one splayed finger. Ashiy heard a splintering crack and from the troll came an anguished scream. The sword went spinning from the elephant's grasp. Ashiy saw the black talon it had hit hanging by a hinge.

The elephant saw it too. Before the troll's roar ended, he seized the creature's limb and tore the talon the rest of the way free from the mottled finger. Somersaulting again beneath the wide legs, under a retaliating sideswipe, the warrior this time drove his opponent's own severed claw deep into the soft nook behind the right knee.

Clubbed by the force of the troll's wail, the light around Ashiy briefly shimmered like heat haze, then restrengthened. Ashiy elicited another bleat of laughter. His paw went to stifle his mouth, and he found his own movement sluggish, as though the surrounding light was a barely permeable liquid that both impeded and inebriated him. Yet the chant ringing around his head was no drunkard's croon. A feminine voice repeated all the stronger, *No harm will befall this poor fox. NO harm will befall this poor—*

This is magic, not death, Ashiy managed to break his own thought through.

He looked and saw a second fighter raise a knotted walking staff. Opposable fingers. A hairless face the color of yew bark. *Mother?* Ashiy clasped paws over his eyes. Even through them, the accompanying flare smarted. A noise like a thunderclap penetrated the shield. He lowered his paws to see the troll's own remaining claws scraping the skin raw around its ears.

Finally, blinded, deafened, and spurting black blood through its crippled leg, the monster relented its territory. Ashiy watched it hurl off into Whimzic, bawling as it went.

The yellow light around the fox faded. His unnatural glee sapped away with it, allowing Ashiy to perceive his thundering heart and racing head. He had nearly been swallowed whole! The fox's new grin was his own, and a shaky one, half-delirious. The trepidation of death fled, giving way to a rush that was only describable by a single thought, *What an adventure!*

But who were his saviors? Ashiy tested movement. The troll had dropped him a fair distance. His entire body hurt, a particular sear coming from his right forearm. He ran a paw over it and discovered warm blood from a mean gash. But nothing seemed to be fractured, so Ashiy stood, eager to meet his rescuers.

The elephant was retrieving his sword, cursing under his breath as he found a large chip where its edge had met the troll's razored nail. Then the warrior's beady eyes locked onto Ashiy. The fox nodded, about to offer his gratitude when the elephant stalked forward and slammed him backward against a nearby oak.

"What in Illdari's name are you doing out here?" The elephant's ivory horns quivered, his trunk arching a centimeter from Ashiy's nose. "You blasted idiot!"

Ashiy could not breathe. The hulking elephant had him pressed into the tree bark, igniting fresh aches. "I-I'm a forager."

"Eh?" The elephant's massive, papery ears flitted.

"A *forager!*" Ashiy spoke up.

"Don't you know troll territory when you smell it?"

"I—"

"Goodness, Evok! Let the poor fox be!"

The chiding voice was lit with concern, and equally confident in its authority. It belonged to the person Ashiy had heard while he had been in the light. Had she been speaking aloud, or had it all been in his mind? He glanced over the elephant's wide shoulders. Though linked by their pointed ears, youthful faces, and centenarian eyes, the elf was not Ceilia. Her hair was lighter, her tasseled clothing more ornate. The tip of her ringleted staff, held in gloved hands, still glowed like a dying ember incensed by the wind.

The elephant, Evok, kept hold of Ashiy's collar. "The fool's lucky to be alive."

"Yes, I believe he realizes that. Let him free."

Huffing, Evok did as instructed. Ashiy slumped against the bough, trembling. The elf traded spots with her companion, kneeling eye to eye with the fox. "Are you hurt?"

"I-I'm all right." Ashiy hid his cut arm, but winced, drawing the elf's gaze to it anyway. Her gloved fingers gently pried his paw aside. From a satchel, she produced a heavy roll of gauze and at once began mummifying the limb with it.

"Thank you."

"What a story you'll have to tell your friends now, huh?" she said. "A troll and an elf both met in five minutes?" She assessed Ashiy for further injuries. "Are you from Whim's Haven?"

"Yes, madame. Just a couple hours' hike from here."

"Oh, thank the Mistress! Did you hear, Evok?" The elf spoke over her shoulder. "We'll sleep properly tonight!" Evok made no reply, now sulking over the decimated fragments of his shield. She frowned but returned her focus to Ashiy, tying off the bandage in a tight knot. "What is your name?"

"By birth, Ashichuaba," Ashiy told her. "By shortening, Ashiy."

"Well met, Ashiy." The elf took his paw and brought him to his feet. "I'm Ithcianarus, of Eltcindale."

Ashiy returned her expectant stare, quite puzzled for a moment. Then, with sheepish realization, he made a deep bow. After a lifetime of living with Ceilia, he had lost the sense of reverence usually reserved for meeting those of her holy kin.

"You may call me Ithcia," Ithcia concluded with a lustrous smile. She directed her staff to the elephant. "And my protector here is called Evokkienn, if you'll forgive his behavior."

Evok snorted, indignant. His claymore snapped moodily

into his back scabbard. *"My* behavior? This brazen kit could've seen us killed!"

"I'm not a kit!" Ashiy bristled.

"And a mouth on him to add!" Evok's eyes were livid. "The number of adversaries I've felled in a month outweighs the number of your cycles, boy. Keep respect on your tongue's tip next time it flies at me!"

"Evok!" Ithcia stomped her staff a single beat against the ground. Evok fell silent, but his glower remained impervious to command. "Don't test him, Ashiy," Ithcia said. "His anger isn't without cause. Entering a troll's territory is reckless business."

"I know." Ashiy picked at his bandaged arm. "I'm grateful, truly, that you risked yourselves to save me. I just-I thought the troll in this area was dead."

"It's breeding season." Ithcia grimaced at the thought. "Two trolls tend to share land around this time of year."

Ashiy felt blood rising in his face. *Of course!* How could he have been so headstrong to forget such a vital detail? Yesterday's dead troll could have been the victim of a violent contest for a bride, and Ashiy had narrowly escaped the victor. He hung his head. "I don't know how to repay you both."

"You can lead us to Whim's Haven," Ithcia replied.

"I'm not sure that's enough."

"It'll suffice." The elf smiled.

"And I'll have a stern word with your caretakers," Evok's voice returned, lower but still simmering. "Poor parentage— that's where recklessness and disrespect stems."

Ashiy's head buzzed, hot anger rising at the remark. The retort left his mouth before he could stop it. "You can save your lecture! My parents are *dead.*"

Evok, skipping not a spare second, answered, "Then we saved the last in a line of boneheads."

"Evok! Enough now!" Ithcia looked aghast. She stepped between the duo, favoring to place a hand on Ashiy's shoulder. "Is there no one we can return you to, Ashiy?"

"No." The fox shook himself free, drowning the guilt of the

lie with anger. He began searching the ground, trying to find his dropped bow. "I'll take you to the Haven, then. We'd best get a move on before—" he spotted the weapon, "nightfall."

Ashiy's bow had been indented into the forest floor by a troll footprint, broken into three pieces. His heart stabbed for his treasured birthday gift. He left the unrepairable remnants behind, pointing homeward. "That way. C'mon. Follow me."

He set off without waiting for them to follow. Soon after, when a chilly bout of evening air shook the trees, he realized he had also stormed off before finding his cloak and the cache of delsic roots secured inside it.

However, a stroll worked wonders to quell foul moods and dangerous excitements. Within the hour, both had ebbed from Ashiy, replaced by curiosity.

There was another elf in Whimzic Forest, accompanied by an elephant no less! Each species was a rare sight, elves hailing from Eltcindale in the far north and elephants from the opposite south. To have both in the Canid Territory, in a remote place such as Whimzic, suggested something afoot. However, Ashiy dreaded to ask his companions their business lest it spur another lecture from Evok.

But as the lumbering elephant fell back a few strides behind Ithcia, the fox's inquisitiveness got the better of him. "Both of you are rangers?"

Ithcia nodded. Given the pair's aptitude for combat, Ashiy had suspected as much. Guild rangers formed organized fellowships across Altharia. They were trained warriors, the oldest parties founded by veterans of the feline centennial war, sworn to defend the queen's lands and uphold the laws therein. "If you're going to the Haven to apprehend a criminal, you'd best tread carefully," Ashiy said.

"That a threat, boy?" Evok prodded Ashiy's back. The elephant was striding closer than he had thought, almost trying to separate him from Ithcia with each stomp.

"It's a warning." Ashiy's whiskers twitched. "The Haven's locals are a tight-knit bunch. They don't give up their own to rangers."

"They?" Ithcia caught the word, brows creasing. "You're not a local?"

"I am," Ashiy replied. He paused, deliberating. "But not one of their own."

Evok's trumpeting scoff quivered Ashiy's ear with hot breath.

"We aren't here to arrest anyone," Ithcia said. "We're tasked with eradicating a horde of reanimated spotted in the region."

"Reanimated?" Ashiy shuddered. "In the Canid Region?"

Ithcia nodded grimly. "So they say. Though our own trail has gone cold since entering Whimzic's embrace."

Of sorcery, Ashiy knew little. It was an elvish art, though Ceilia refused to perform it often. And even when she did, she never elaborated on the practice. Ashiy did know necromancy to be a forbidden branch of the art, originated by a mad human insurgent decades ago. To reanimate the dead, bards rumored, birthed husks devoid the characteristics they had possessed in life.

Thoughts of magic reminded Ashiy of the peculiar happiness which had engulfed him during the troll encounter. Once again, his fascination came pouring out toward Ithcia. "I've never seen sorcery like that before. That's what it was, yes? That glow—"

"Yes, I'm sorry if you were disturbed," Ithcia interrupted Ashiy quite suddenly. "But there was little else I could do at the time."

"Disturbed?" Ashiy was taken aback by the reaction. "Why would—"

"Don't forget, it was *you* who necessitated it in the first place." Evok's trunk jabbed Ashiy's spine. "Ithcia's quick action is what saved you."

His nagging secured Ashiy's silence once again.

With the day went a slip in the temperature. Shadows lengthened under the cool evening breeze and Ashiy led his rescuers at a faster clip with mounting dread. They would be skimming close to nightfall by the time they reached Whim's

Haven. Ceilia was bound to rally a search party. As the sounds and smells of town drifted toward them, Ashiy's fears were realized. On Whim's outskirt paths, he collided with Buruk and his son, Branny.

"Hoy, there you are'n, Ashiy!" The smith's brown fur was still caked afresh with soot. He had been summoned straight from the forge, by the scent of fire on him.

"Your ol' lady's rounded some of us t'scour for you!" Branny said. The younger bear was a dwarfed but spitting image of his sire. He peered at Evok and Ithcia. "Who're these folks?"

"Travelers," Ashiy formed a quick excuse. "I'm late because I've been guiding them."

"Certainly not!" Evok said. "The rascal's *late* because he warred with a troll!"

"A troll!" Branny had a shrill voice for a bear, as well as a very loose tongue.

His face flaring to the tips of his ears, Ashiy realized his venture with the troll would likely be known throughout the Haven within a day.

Evok had caught another detail as well. "What'd you say?" he asked Branny. "The kid's *grandmother* has people hunting for him?"

"Well, she's his mother…I think?" Branny looked to his father for clarification.

Buruk shrugged. "She's right worried. Got a few close friends out is all."

"Go call them off!" Evok said. His iron grip took Ashiy's shoulder now. There would be no shaking it. "We'll return the kid."

"Right, g'night then." Buruk trundled off with a twiddling wave, Branny alongside him.

Ithcia turned to Ashiy, her expression keen. "You said you had no parents."

"I've got a godmother." Ashiy avoided her gaze.

"Well, that's a rather rude deception, isn't it?"

"Let's see her, eh?" Evok steered Ashiy, who, defeated, now

led their course toward his own tent.

Ithcia's hurt voice stung him. But the lie had not been entirely for his own sake. Ceilia was already secretive to the Haven at large. Outsiders made her even warier. Once, as a young kit, Ashiy had let slip her name to a roving robin in the market. Memory of the heated scolding and swats to the rump Ceilia had administered still made the fox cringe. On top of the whole troll mess, Ashiy knew a dire punishment would also be in effect for him bringing two absolute strangers to their threshold.

But, beneath his foreboding, Ashiy could not shake a pip of anticipation. Elves knew their kin well. What might be revealed when Ithcia and Ceilia were brought together? Could one of those glimpses into Ceilia's past, so precious in scarcity, be incited when the pair were faced?

"Oh, thank the Mistress! *Ashiy!*" Ceilia spied their procession from afar. She had been standing vigil at the mouth of their tent, a silhouette against the orange light inside, and sprang forth to embrace him.

For the moment, Ashiy's dread swept away. His eyes teared, buried against Ceilia's hair. Then she recoiled. Ashiy winced. The stench of the troll mud hung on his clothes, rancid enough for even the elf to distinguish. She pounded his chest with a balled fist. "You did it, didn't you? When the sun went down and you weren't-I thought you might have-oh, you wretched, foolish, *fool!*"

"I know, I-I'm sorry, Mother. But I'm safe."

"Thanks to us." Evok crossed his broad arms.

Ceilia noticed the rangers for the first time. Her gaze flitted to Ithcia, who was examining Ceilia with measured interest.

Ithcia used a pleasant tone to address her kindred. "You're Ashiy's…godmother?"

"I am." Ceilia's even-tempered reply was almost chilly.

"He was within an instant of becoming a troll's snack when we rescued him, madam," Evok said. His arms shifted with unease. He was clearly torn between the desire to reprimand

Ceilia and pay her the holy esteem he owed her kind. The latter won out as the elephant's tusks dipped in respect. "It honors me to return him safely to you."

"You have my gratitude, truly," Ceilia replied. "If you name a reward, I'll give it."

"None wanted." Ithcia curtsied.

"Then I thank you again and bid you a pleasant stay in the Haven." Ceilia did not return the gesture, instead turning Ashiy off toward their tent's inviting entrance.

"Except, if I may, sister," Ithcia's call beckoned a halt, though Ceilia did not rescind the back she had turned toward the rangers. "I'm quite curious to know your name."

"It's Havsenia, of Frost's Barrow," Ceilia lied. Without further conversation, she drove Ashiy into their tent and fastened its flaps as though warding off a plague.

"Sit," Ceilia bid Ashiy. He obeyed, bracing himself on one of the moth-eaten stools for a harsh rebuke. To his astonishment, however, Ceilia said nothing more for a long while. She hunched on their tent's threshold, using a small rip in the fabric as a peephole into the night. Her pointed ears strained for sound above the prattle of neighbors at their campfires and cicadas racketing in the forest.

"Mother?" Ashiy finally said, spooked.

No reply. Ceilia resealed the tent's tear with a licked finger. Then she hugged Ashiy's head to her bosom. He could hear her heart thundering beneath. He extracted himself from the embrace. "Mother, what's wrong?"

"You're hurt—let me see." Ceilia stooped, unraveling Ashiy's bandage with fragile care. Her fingers trembled enough to make the simple action a challenge. Her fear alarmed Ashiy. He wished she would berate him.

"Mother, please, what troubles you?"

"Everything." Ceilia's voice came quiet. She gave up at the bandage, throwing its tattered ends aside as she gripped Ashiy's shoulders, her face alight with a haunted fire. "Everything you do troubles me. The way you disobey me. The way you crave adventure. The way you brandish your life as if it were faces to cast away." Welling tears extinguished the blaze in her eyes. "You're so much like your parents. Your father especially. Seeing you grown these days is like watching him walk before me again."

Ashiy's own tears escaped, stinging. He leaned closer, enticed by his godmother's words, wanting more, so much more. All his life he had craved answers to the questions which came bleating out. "My father? I look like him?"

Ceilia nodded, her focus on Ashiy absent even as she tightened her hold on him. "You're too much like them—"

"Was his fur red like mine?"

"But not too much. How can it be otherwise? You're their son—"

"Was she pretty? Please, Ceilia, what was her voice like?"

"Their only son, their only legacy—"

"Tell me! *Please!* I want to know!"

"And today you nearly followed his fate! It's too similar, too similar, no, no—"

"His fate? What's too similar?"

"Dreer died in a forest, Ashiy! Without me to protect him as I promised your mother I would!"

Ceilia rose all at once, fearful memories guttering from her eyes like candlelight. Ashiy was left in the dark to blink after them in desperate shock. Her voice hardened. "I *will* protect you. Never again, Ashiy! You're never to enter Whimzic Forest again! You'll stay in the Haven where it's safe! You'll become a smith. You'll live out your days in peace, and settle down with a lovely vixen of your own, and be happy…"

Ceilia's words trailed off assured of their own prophecy. She peered into the night through the slit in the tent again.

Ashiy stood, glaring at her, possessed by a sudden wrath he had never known before. How could she dare to stand with her back turned, knowing it all, everything he had been and was meant to be, without an inkling to include him in any of it? His voice trembled to keep from resounding throughout the Haven.

"Why are you so afraid of those rangers?"

No answer. Ashiy burst with fresh tears. This punishment outweighed any other. It was too cruel. He had not deserved all this for sneaking into troll territory, had he?

"M-mother."

Ceilia looked at him, her expression regaining its composure. It softened as she saw Ashiy unconsciously fiddling with the unraveled ends of his bandage.

"My arm hurts."

She motioned for him to sit. "I'll fix it up."

This time Ceilia's fingers wound their expertise with nary a trace of trembling. She daubed cleansing sap over Ashiy's gash. A fresh bandage resealed it. Ceilia kissed the tender spot when finished. "There. Better?"

Ashiy's sniffles had died off. He gave a glum nod.

"Good. Why don't we eat something?"

The remainder of their evening played out in a pantomime of its usual course.

Once a sparking flint lit a campfire, their remaining foodstuffs were heated on a skillet for dinner. The elf and fox ate, ravenous after the day's lengthy course. They made a silent concession to split the final oozing cinnamon bun. Ashiy shed his rancid articles and bathed in a bucket of bone-chilling water. Ceilia settled herself at the cleared table with a quill and ink to perform her ritual of recording in her tattered journal. As she did, Ashiy, fresh and clean, but shivering from dampness, unfurled his sleeping bag to make himself toasty inside. He rolled away from the flickering lantern light to feign sleep at the tent's rustling wall. Half an hour later, Ceilia snuffed the glow and bedded down in her own bag.

There, in the dark and stillness, the day's magnitude weighed on Ashiy.

He did not shift in his nest, fearing Ceilia would hear him, so his thoughts churned instead. What to make of this conflict in his head? Forces of guilt clashed against fury like briny waves against simmering magma. Though many of the day's faults were his, Ashiy could not shake the idea that Ceilia harbored a greater offense against him.

She's not my mother, came his foremost thought, and it immediately made him sink his face deeper against his pillow in shame. He would never say such a heartless thing to Ceilia in daylight, face to face. *But she's not! And that isn't my fault! Maybe my real one wanted all the things Ceilia does for me now. But how can I know if she'll never tell me?*

Ashiy clung to a new revelation parsed from Ceilia's tirade. *He died in a forest. My father died in a forest. Was he an explorer? A ranger?* One of Ashiy's eyes shifted free of his pillow to behold his unbranded wrist. *No. Not a criminal, surely? But again, how am I to know?* A wry smile followed the eye's emergence. *Not a blacksmith though. No, blacksmiths don't up and die in forests.*

Ashiy's ears pricked. Ceilia's soft breathing announced she was asleep on the tent's far end. The rhythm began to lull Ashiy like a spell. As he listened, his thoughts began to ebb.

The final one murmured defiance.

We'll see if I stay a smith...we'll see...

-Chapter IV-
The Blacksmith

"*A*shiy, your eyewear."

Branny paused his hefted hammer, having snatched yellowish shrapnel from the furnace with steady tongs and set it upon the anvil.

"Oh, right." Ashiy pulled the leather-bound lenses from their resting place between his ears to shield his eyes from sparks.

The delay had cooled the lump into a throbbing orange glow. Dissatisfied, Branny thrust the shard back into the furnace. Ashiy grunted at the bellows, reviving the inferno within. Both animals watched it lick the metal strip, gauging the color.

The shard had once been the blade of a large rapier from Buruk's stash. His door and purse were open to any in Whim's Haven who wished to sell off broken equipment. Every few days a slew of shifty barterers visited, pawning off their rusted daggers, splintered tangs, and sanded blades. Buruk would remove the blades for smelting and repurpose them. Ashiy's initial creation at the anvil had been a refashioned pair of tent stakes. The set had been too cockeyed to sell, so Buruk had allowed him to take them home. Ceilia at once removed their previous stakes and, bustling with pride, tethered their tent with Ashiy's first undertakings.

Ashiy once suggested to Buruk that he might make a prettier penny repairing the weapons and turning his sellers into buyers. The genteel smith rejected the notion. "After missus Ceilia taught me t'read, I took a vow t'not do no fell deeds, y'see?" Buruk had shaken his head. "I'm a simple bear, but I know the types of critters who carry weapons 'round this haven. To know what I'd be sellin' might be used to harm another, it ain't right'n'good. The less blades, the better, I says. More nails. More tent stakes. More door hinges. More building tools. Things for liftin' fellow animals up. This'll be a right'n'proper Altharian town, soon 'nuff. You'll see, Ashiy. It don't happen overnight, but it started with your lady, and its growin'. We ain't just a smuggler's cove no more."

It was an admirable vow, but drained Ashiy's already limited interest in the blacksmith's craft.

CLANG! BANG! CLANG!

Branny's mallet and a cascade of sparks returned Ashiy from his reverie. He pawed at a warm glint that alighted on his forearm.

"Sorry. Y'all right?" Branny shuddered, his craft forgotten for a moment to ensure his partner was not aflame. Out of smithing habit, they kept a bucket of water nearby, soaking the fur on their paws and arms at regular intervals. Buruk's business, being a highly flammable one, had its furnace set apart from the structure that housed his ventures and that of the unsavory tanner Henyer. Ashiy and Branny toiled outdoors, in a spot dug out behind the building.

"Fickle fire," Branny said. "I'll be more careful." He whittled down the shard with a couple of lesser blows. A proper spike took shape.

It was to be one nail of a full order. Aggtree, the owner of Pelt's Tavern, had commissioned an expansion to his establishment and his builders needed something to hammer into their boards.

"Y'member the bard poem 'bout fire, Ashiy?"

Ashiy sighed. After a silent morning, he now sensed Branny's customary chattiness about to brim over. "I think I have."

Branny started to hum in an off-key swing, piecing forgotten stanzas. *"Furless fiends and foes o' fur…*foes o' fur…*rung from their flints flare none endure…those furless fiends and foes o' fur…*can you 'member any of it else, Ashiy?"

"It's been a long while since I heard a bard," Ashiy said.

"We ought'n go sometime we hear one's in market!" Branny twiddled his shard in the fire, almost dropping it from the tong's fingers. "Autumn's the time, betcha plenty'll pass through'n the next few weeks."

Ashiy was distracted from answering by a pair of foxes rounding the shophouse.

Fellows in species though they were, they at once struck Ashiy as miscreants. Both were larger than him, tan-pelted, and in their paws they carried a bundle of six broadswords wrapped in dark leather scabbards. One stopped behind Branny, sizing up the apprentices with a glittering, narrowed eye. "Buruk in?" The fox's voice was scratchy.

"Uh-huh." Branny directed them toward the door with his hammer, then resumed his chatter to Ashiy unperturbed. "Still'd like t'know the rest of that diddy, though. Y'think your mother'd have a scroll of it somewhere?"

The sandy foxes vanished through Buruk's door. Ashiy stared at its battered woodwork. "She might," he said, hefting their bucket of finished rivets. "I'll fetch more scrap."

Branny nodded him off. Dragging the heavy pail, Ashiy pushed through the entryway to discover Buruk at his table, mid-conversation with the newcomers in his storehouse. It was a tiny office crammed with boxes of nails, door hinges, and scavenged scrap metal. A menagerie of tools, ranging from scythes to hammers, hung from the low ceiling, making it a dangerous place to bang one's head.

"And I'm askin' how you'd come by such pristine steel?" The blacksmith had one sword unsheathed and spread over the chestnut wood. Its long blade was sleek and shining as it caught sunlight from the storeroom's singular, shuttered window.

"None your business now, is it?" One of the foxes said. He glanced at Ashiy and bared a fang. "What's the funny look about, scamp?"

Ashiy ignored him, holding the bucket up for Buruk. "Finished this lot, sir. Just looking for more scrap."

Buruk nodded, and he waved Ashiy on, still speaking with the customers. "Well'n, I'd say you'd best take 'em elsewhere. 'Fraid I can't afford to buy 'em."

"A price named'll judge that."

Ashiy began filling a new scuttle with ratty sword blades, taking deliberate time to remain indoors.

Buruk chewed his cheek. "All's I can offer'd be seventy-five faces."

Ashiy almost dropped one of the blades. *Seventy-five faces!* He turned the exuberant price over in his mind. *That's twice what he pays Henyer for rent in a month!*

"Barely twelve a sword, cheat!" The first fox was not as impressed by the figure. Ashiy stiffened at the accusation, but the other fox clamped a paw over his brother's muzzle.

"We'll accept," the second fox replied.

Paws shook. Buruk stood. "Right'n'good, then. Ashiy, stand aside would y'please?"

Ashiy stepped aside from the front of Buruk's locker, rattling his pail. Buruk withdrew a spindled key from his smock's front pouch. The padlock it fit was a device of the smith's own hammer and the vault which swung wide revealed several sacks of gold. Withdrawing one, Buruk allocated a few coins to the foxes.

Greedy gleams in their eyes, they departed. Buruk slunk the unsheathed broadsword back into its scabbard and began lining them all up in the locker's interior. Ashiy examined one of the weapons before the smith could hide it away, pulling it out a sliver from its fine casing.

"You should've checked all these before paying so many faces," Ashiy said.

"Why? That damaged?" Buruk asked.

"No." Ashiy relinquished the weapon to the smith's large paws. "But it's an easy trick."

"Wouldn't've mattered anyhow." Buruk looked grave. "You haven't 'prenticed long, Ashiy. I've been forgin' almost two decades and ain't never seen so many treasured blades in one place." The bear's locker door clanged shut. Ashiy looked at the reattached padlock hungrily.

"So they're worth seventy-five?"

"Each."

Ashiy's ears fidgeted. "Each?" he repeated. *"Each* sword is worth seventy-five faces? And that's what you paid for six!"

"Might be worth even more." Buruk shrugged. "That's tempered steel. Squirrel-make, each of 'em blades. Near unbreakable."

Ashiy whistled. "Must be stolen."

"I'd the same thought," Buruk said. "Why's I offered so little for 'em. Must be off someone close by, too, else they'd've tried gettin' a better price at market. Probably knew I melt swords down and thought it a fine way t'get rid their evidence."

Ashiy guessed it to be a rather foolproof theory. "What will you make them into?"

"Nothin'," Buruk said. He stopped a second inquiry by wagging a paw. "I could burn all of Whimzic in our oven an' it'd never burn hot 'nuff to melt such'n steel. Reckon we should try'n'find the proper owners."

Ashiy's ears deflated with his excitement. "You're just going to give them away?"

"If the owners can be found." Buruk angled Ashiy another serious look. "Now don't be makin' that face, Ashiy. How'd you feel if'n you lost somethin' so valuable?"

Ashiy cast a pensive glance at the scuffed floorboards.

He had been robbed once. Only once, which was somewhat a miracle considering his hometown. It had been during one of his first forays into the market in Ceilia's stead. A pair of wolves had pulled a knife on Ashiy, and with the same blade undid the coin purse on his belt. He had run home to Ceilia crying.

"I'm sorry it happened, Ashiy, but remember this feeling. It is a terrible thing to feel robbed, isn't it?" Ceilia's admonishments from that day came back to him with Buruk's reminder. *Forgot, I guess,* Ashiy thought.

After all, his pilfered coins had not left him for long. The same snarling wolves, both subdued and apologetic, had come to his tent the very next morning to return the whole stolen amount. Ashiy suspected Ceilia performed some magic on them, though she had denied it when pestered. Who else, though, could have ensured he was not crossed by ruffians from that day forth?

"That settles it, I suppose," Ashiy told the blacksmith. "Any ideas on finding the real owners?"

Buruk shook his head. "Not one. Hmm…" The bear scratched a round ear. "Maybe they belong to 'em rangers, y'think?"

"Evok and Ithcia?" Ashiy did not have to ponder hard to recall the troll encounter and his rescuers. "No. They didn't have black-clad weapons."

"An' there ain't six of 'em to be wieldin' six swords neither," Buruk said. He clapped his paws. "Well, keep'n ear peeled."

"Yessir." Ashiy turned to exit. Buruk, however, caught his apprentice on the shoulder.

"Oh'n best keep Branny in the dark about 'em swords, Ashiy. M'boy's, well, y'know—" The smith held up a paw and clacked his toes in a way which mimicked a jabbering mouth.

Ashiy smiled, arching his own paws like the round of a headstone. "Silent as Sepplecretem's tombs, Buruk."

Branny's voice indeed carried loudest, even over the surrounding din of Pelt's Tavern. Two days later, the order for Aggtree's nails, hinges, and window frames had been fulfilled and the smithing crew took up his offer of free drinks in addition to their payment. One mug chugged and the young brown bear's senses were daffier than a spider swinging from a web in a breeze. Branny swished an arm over the battered bar, almost pitching himself forward off his stool to intercept a refill slung down the countertop toward him. All the while, he talked at a volume suited to communication over a mile of gale-swept landscape.

"Cart-a-wheelin'! Issthe word I mean! Cart-a-wheelin', m'head's feelin' like cart-a-wheelin'!" Branny bust with laughter over the unplanned rhyme, giving Buruk cover to swipe his son's brimming mug and shove it toward Aggtree.

"This'n here isn't Ember Whiskey, is it?" the smith asked the barkeep.

Aggtree, a gray wolf with a leg given a permanent limp from breaking up a barfight too many, offered a disapproving head shake. "Barely a bite innit. Cub's a lightweight."

Buruk considered the cup before hazarding a sip. "Ah, takes from his mother, then. No more for 'im."

Aggtree gave a peddling glance toward Ashiy who was seated on the neighboring barstool. "What'll y'have?"

Ashiy glanced at the already soiled mug, further tainted by the spotted rag in Aggtree's mincing paws, and shook his head. "I'll keep my mouth dry."

"Dry mouths go in the gutter." The wolf's snarl deepened.

"Then make mine Buruk's second."

The smith rapped his tankard. "Hear, hear."

"Hear! Hear! Use'n ear!" Branny flicked one of his ears with a large grin.

Still glowering, Aggtree drifted off to wheedle other patrons. Ashiy treated the wolf's back with a wary eye but was soon distracted. The few occasions he had seen the pub's interior were cursory ones, when its doors had been pushed aside by the odd customer. He strained to organize every detail about him. Pelt's shuttered windows barricaded evening sunlight as though they'd been bribed by the scraggly chandeliers overhead to snuff out any rivalry. Thin candles in wire claws dimly illuminated the bar and centermost tables, allowing booths conjoined to the walls to conduct their liaisons in shadow. From these dark spaces came the occasional glitter and puff of smoke from a lit pipe.

"Y'sure you want nothin', Ashiy?" Buruk rubbed the fox's shoulder. "Not t'even take a bottle back to yer old lady?"

Ashiy smirked at the bear's jest and shook his head.

If Ceilia knew he was inside this lawless den of drinkery and debauchery now, she might be inclined to rescind his association with Buruk. Ashiy could not envision his godmother ingesting anything stronger than her tea.

"Bargh…" Branny suddenly doubled over, cradling his stomach.

"Need a step outside, y'do?" Buruk laughed. "C'mon, Agg keeps'n bucket out back. No, no, y'stay comfortable, Ashiy. Be back'n a moment."

The smith guided his charge off, leaving Ashiy feeling rather exposed at the barstool. He leaned back, wishing he had accepted Aggtree's offer, if only to appear more blended with the scenery. The wolf had evidently nursed Ashiy's refusal as a slight. He caught Aggtree's curled lip muttering to a rather intimidating eagle at the bar's far end. Both animals glared at Ashiy, so he left the counter, careful to maneuver around the bar's shifty patrons.

Serrated daggers laid flat on tabletops alongside gambling apparatus. Slash-mouthed wolves, foxes, and rats crouched over cards which still wore faint bloodstains from previous games that had ended badly. Ashiy avoided meeting any odd eye. He found a string supporting several petrified lumps of fur draped between two roofing beams. A misspelled sign above it gave him a shiver:

Steel'rs un beet'rs un deel'rs find beer.
Cheeters of cards lose thumselves un eer.

Ashiy slipped into one of the outlier booths, content to play the role of a shadow until Buruk and Branny reemerged. He reclined onto the seat's patchy leather, his nose wrinkling as he recognized it to be troll skin. Not long after, he detected distinct murmurs from the next stall over.

"And none sign of either. Warned you, didn't I? Never share 'rangements with unvetted outsiders. What were we thinking?"

Ashiy's ears fiddled. He tilted his head in a discreet effort to hear the lowered but urgent conversation. Harvick the raccoon spoke on the other side of the booth. The pickpocket sounded worried.

"We thought the same as they did—a few extra paws able to vanish once the work was over." Ashiy identified the second talker as Urus. He was a decent robin, not a local in the Haven, but the hatchling of a merchant who frequented the region.

"Vanish too well, they did." The third speaker Ashiy did not recognize. But the depth of tone and stark scent suggested a middle-aged sloth bear.

"Miserable kips." Harvick's teeth grated.

"Swearing'll do us little good now," Urus said. Then, after a pause, he continued. "My pap's leaving town tomorrow. I'm cutting with him before we're found out."

"What?" Harvick said, scandalized.

"Sensible." The bear agreed.

"You both can't leave! We need a plan!"

"Hunt my tent tomorrow—you'll catch naught but wind." Ashiy heard weight shift on leather as the sloth bear shimmied out of the booth.

Urus followed suit with a parting remark. "Smart coon, wriggle your own hide free."

An assault of hissed swearing at the bear and robins' tails failed to impede their retreat. With Harvick's affairs coming to a rather unexciting conclusion, Ashiy turned his interest to the rest of the bar. However, as the irate stream of profanities dried up, its final trickle let drip an interesting tidbit. "And curse their flea-ridden, itching mothers, all of them. Why, if ever I see one of them sandy-pelted pinheads, I'll make them the scabbards for their own stolen stash!"

Harvick silenced. Defeated. Or maybe catching his breath.

Ashiy, alert once more, calculated through the dropped information. *Sandy-pelted pinheads and a stolen stash, hmm?* The description was much too familiar to be a coincidence.

Before Harvick could collect himself and steal away, Ashiy slid from his booth and into the adjoining one. He adopted a pleasant smirk. "Hiya, Harvick."

"Feh, *what?* Oh." The raccoon had been distracted by a half-filled bottle. He seemed relieved to shift his attention toward the new company, but his crooked smile was taut. "If it ain't Whim's res'dent troll wrangler."

Ashiy cringed but pushed forward. "Having a nice evening?"

"Fair." But Harvick had lost his smile. "Say, I've not seen you in Aggtree's before."

"First time," Ashiy said.

"Well." Harvick toasted his bottle. "To many more."

Ashiy allowed him a long draught before proceeding. "Want to know where your stolen swords are?"

Harvick almost coughed up his drink. His eyes narrowed as he swallowed. "Lurking little eavesdropper! What, you've seen those two sand foxes?"

Ashiy nodded. "Even better—I know where the swords are. And I'll give them back for a hundred faces."

"You-y'little-*feh!*" Harvick threw up his paws, irked. "Foxes! All alike! Thought we were friends, Ashiy, and now y'want to swindle me?"

"Not swindling if you're swindling a swindler," Ashiy said.

"This ain't swindlin', Ashiy." Harvick leaned forward with fearful eyes. "I need them swords. We were s'posed to deliver them to someone else before them foxes decided they liked them for themselves. And I'm the fool who brought them aboard the scheme. I don't hand over the blades, and I'm liable to get skinned."

"Then sounds as if you're in dire need to pay me." Ashiy did not buy Harvick's sham terror for a lick. In a rare swell of confidence, he reached over the table and, winking, swigged from the raccoon's own bottle.

Fire lit Ashiy's throat. He spewed a mist of whiskey and dissolved into a fit of coughs. Sympathetic, Harvick scooted around to clap the young fox's back before reclaiming the bottle. "First, eh?"

"Y-yes," Ashiy croaked, eyes watering. How did anyone swallow such poison? "S-so we have a deal?"

A dry chuckle came from the raccoon. "I haven't the funds on my person, ya rascal."

"Bring them by Buruk's."

"Buruk?" Harvick's stare swiveled toward Aggtree's counter. The smith in question had resurfaced there with a much more repressed Branny. Both were casting about anxious stares for their fox companion, unsure of where he had vanished off to.

"Drop the payment by." Ashiy pushed himself away from the table to rejoin the duo before they spotted him in Harvick's company. "One hundred faces." He offered his paw and Harvick swept it into a vigorous shake without hesitation.

"Of course, of course." The pickpocket nodded fast, grinning. "Worth the price for a friend who's saved my skin."

Despite the lingering simmer in his throat, Ashiy felt elated over his bargain. Buruk sensed this uptick when he reappeared. "Ho, don't be tell'n me you've had too much as well, Ashiy."

"Too much?" The fox replied.

Branny, still looking a mite sick, nodded beside his father. "Ayup. You've a big grin on."

"It isn't from drink."

"What then?" Buruk smiled, infected by Ashiy's giddy expression.

"Oh, couldn't say." Ashiy smothered his cheer with effort. *Let it be a surprise.* No doubt the honest blacksmith would have returned the swords to Harvick at no charge were it revealed they had been stolen from him. *And what a terrible injustice that'd be. Buruk losing seventy-five pieces over someone else's misdeeds.* Ashiy dodged Aggtree's roving glance and tossed the idea of starting a tame card game between the smithing trio. *Just imagine the surprise on his face when the raccoon brings him a profit in a nice fat pouch!*

Indeed, Buruk's face would be surprised the following morning. Stumbling free of a lingering fog from the previous night's pints, the bear entered his storeroom to find his vault's door swung open upon its hinges. His very own pocketed key was left in the undone lock. And not one of the broadswords, nor compensation for them, was left inside.

-Chapter V-
Furless Fiends & Foes of Fur

$\mathcal{A}$ sheriff's duty was not supposed to be inherited. Whim's Haven's very first deputy had, like all town chiefs, been selected by the local populace. And the populace of the Haven in those days had required a figurehead to satiate the royal decree for public officers. They had elected someone willing to accept any bribe slid under his whiskers. The chain of this corruption now extended two generations to the current gray wolf, grizzled and half-deaf, who stood in Buruk's burglarized storeroom looking tired and annoyed by the summons of a legitimate crime.

Sheriff Alderly was not the only irritated animal present. Henyer stood with a dark countenance in the arch separating Buruk's diminutive chamber from his leather making workshop. Unlike the sheriff, the tanner's chagrin did not stem from apathy.

"A fool enough to bring something such as this near my own business!" The tanner's words demeaned. "You should be thankful they took nothing valuable of mine, else you and your obnoxious cub would be sleeping in the forest's clutches tonight, Buruk!"

Buruk turned over the key snug inside its opened padlock. He nodded to Alderly. "Any hope of findin' the intruder, y'think, Sheriff?"

"Ah?" Alderly shook his long whiskers with a lazy blink. After Buruk repeated his question louder so the deputy could hear it, the ancient wolf pointed to a fine, white powder scuffed on the floor. "Thief used salt to cover their scent."

"*My* tanning salt," Henyer said. "You'll reimburse me for it, Buruk."

"Yes'n I will, Henyer, *please.*" Buruk still sought vain hope from Alderly. "Salt didn't get all it, though. I can smell myself a raccoon, or maybe a rodent'a some sort."

"Half the Haven's coons and rodents." Alderly did not bother lending his own nose to the inspection of the pilfered safe. His uniform, robes of juxtaposing black and white, crinkled with a shrug. "What would you have me do?"

Outdoors, Branny sat upon the anvil with the forge leering cold and dark at him. The cub had his round face in his paws. Ashiy strode up for his shift to find his fellow apprentice drying big tears.

"What's the matter, Branny?"

Renewed sobs met the fox. Ashiy heard the muffled voices from indoors and decided to extract answers there. Upon intruding, the faces of the smith, tanner, and sheriff all snapped toward Ashiy as though expecting the culprit had returned to his handiwork.

"Ha, the troll-dung."

Ashiy ignored Henyer's affront. "What's happened here?" He looked between Alderly and the bereft vault. A precipitable lurch occurred in Ashiy's stomach before Buruk confirmed what was lost.

"Swords're stolen. Someone nicked in through the window last night."

Ashiy made himself impassive, staring at the ajar shutters.

"Not much to do, really," Sheriff Alderly reiterated, coughing. "Scent trail's masked and cold."

Buruk tried not to appear glum. "Ah'n I 'spose you're right, Alderly. Might be'n blessin' I lost 'em so. Whomever took 'em seems a professional thug. Took mine own key outta my pocket while'n I was sleepin."

"No blessings about this!" Henyer stamped a weighty foot. "Your rent's increasing, Buruk. Here I thought you'd said you ran an honest business, but you've got thieves crawling into my—" Henyer was interrupted by the heavy wallop of the storeroom door slamming shut.

Ashiy's rankled tail almost caught in the frame as he exited.

The fox stalked past Branny, offering him a reassuring shoulder pat in passing. *Don't cry, Branny. We'll see this thing resolved. Just wait,* he thought with rising heat. Ashiy encircled the smithy to set himself on the cobblestone street, ears seething flat against his skull, shoulders set rigid to cork his fury.

Harvick's ratty tent sat close to the market. Vendors at matchbox stalls were still organizing their wares as Ashiy dodged between them into the score of tepees penned close to the Haven's center. He had not visited Harvick in months, the prior occasion being to trade the raccoon for some odd scavenges. *Friends, ha! That's what he insinuated us to be last night?* Ashiy almost trod over a blackbird's campfire in his haste. Squawked curses assaulted his back as he continued through the close-knit shanty tents. *Blueberries for peanuts? Sure, Harvick would honor a small trade such as that. Should've known better than to trust him on a more valuable exchange.*

Harvick was missing from his tent, though when Ashiy thrust aside its tarpaulin and glanced inside, he found the raccoon's odor recent.

Ashiy crouched low, bracing his clever nose at the tent's threshold. He fixated on Harvick's lingering trace, allowing himself three sniffs to imprint the scent. It was a specific earth and alcoholic tang he could follow through the Haven's scent world of acrid campfire smoke, suffocating animal musk, and approaching autumn decay. Ashiy took off at once, eyes half lidded, maneuvering through senses potent to canids but unknowable to elves and birds. He bypassed people without notice, glancing at individuals as unimportant whiffs.

West. The raccoon had bisected the Haven westward. Then the unseeable track veered sharply away from town. *Where's he off to?* Ashiy thought, opening his eyes.

Harvick had entered Whimzic Forest.

Ashiy wavered before the brawny boughs. Ceilia's warning chimed at him from that dreadful night when she had mended his forearm; *"Never again, Ashiy! You're never to enter Whimzic*

Forest again!" The admonishment was a seal. For a suspended moment, Ashiy sensed that breaking it would usher some fell curse upon him. But he brushed the premonition aside with a bit of leaf which clung to one whisker.

I'm not going for my own pleasure. I'm fixing a wrong done.

Thus justified, Ashiy bound his nose to Harvick's trail and crossed the border from haven to woodland.

Whimzic greeted him in alluring robes. The forest's emerald summer trappings were beginning their molt to yellow and orange.

Ceilia's rule would have Ashiy miss such quintessential beauty.

He set aside his discontentment. *There's a more important task at paw.*

Harvick's smell strengthened, making it even easier to track. Other markers betrayed the raccoon's direction, too. Broken brush and twigs, leaden footprints, and shed fur provided Ashiy as clear a map to the thief as one drawn upon parchment. Ashiy was gaining on him. *But where's he off to?* Ashiy thought again. *This deep into the forest?*

The raccoon's path trended on a northern slant now. Ashiy had not traveled northwest often, even during his scavenging days. The forest ended sooner to the northwest than in any other direction begun from Whim's Haven. A two-day trek brought a traveler within sight of the endless Humania Sea.

Quite suddenly, Harvick's scent was overridden by one of putrid death.

Ashiy gagged, going only one step further before halting. Rotting flesh, dried blood, and rancid, wet decay engulfed his tracking nose. *What happened?* Ashiy cast about for the answer. Foliage and ground were beaten flat by many dragging footfalls. The prints left were too scuffed to identify the species of the walkers, but the terrible odor told him enough.

Reanimated.

Ashiy's blood coursed icily at the thought. What other group of monsters could jinx their path with such a deathly reek? And the crude knife on his hip was his only defense. Ashiy chanced another cautious sniff of the area.

It's an awful stench, but old. Maybe a day since being left. Harvick didn't run across these creatures...there! Ashiy picked out the raccoon's flavor again. Harvick had detoured after encountering the horde's taint. But a few minutes of chasing returned the trail on its arrowed streak northwest.

Then it veered sharply east. Only a moment later, it treaded back toward town, then redoubled back north once again. *He's lost,* Ashiy registered with grim satisfaction. That meant the raccoon was losing even more of his unknown head start.

Indeed, a few minutes later, Ashiy spied Harvick.

The raccoon stood doubled over, engaged in a breather, no doubt, from the load of the six contested broadswords he had been carrying. They now sat in the grass by his hind feet, pommels glittering in the sunlight. Harvick's waypoint was a small clearing with a mighty oak fallen across it. However, instead of succumbing to moss, the log's tall surface was etched with many equations. Numbers and crude symbols sliced in the soft trunk evidenced years of smuggling deals made and recorded at the site.

Ashiy slowed himself just shy of the clearing.

Crack!

"Who's there?"

Ashiy managed to crouch behind a maple as Harvick's stare sought the source of the snapped bramble. He inwardly chided his flat footedness.

"Who's there? I'm warnin' you to show yourself!" Another shard of metal glinted in the sunlight. Harvick had a dagger. The notion jarred Ashiy. He never knew the pickpocket to arm himself.

Harvick's nose wiggled high in the air. He cursed. *"Ashiy! That's you, isn't it?"*

Standing upwind had doomed him. Caught, Ashiy peeked from behind the tree. To his relief, Harvick pocketed his dagger, but Ashiy maintained a distance well beyond its reach should it reemerge.

"You *cannot* be here now." Harvick's voice was as unsettling as his weapon. Ashiy, for once, believed the mounting panic rising under his words.

"I'm not going to hurt you." Ashiy cautioned a stride forward. "But you should know why I'm here."

"I was tryin' to keep you out of it, y'headstrong fool!" Harvick's tone was low. Over it, from the depths of the forest, Ashiy deciphered the crackling of footfalls on dead leaves.

Multiple individuals approached the clearing. A strange scent preceded them. *Reanimated?* Ashiy's mind danced with visions of bloated flesh, lumbering strides, and the smothering stink of death as his nose worked toward the sounds his ears angled on.

Harvick quickly gathered the broadswords and thrust half of them into Ashiy's forearms. "If they question, you're my partner, understand? Don't say anything y'aren't asked!"

Ashiy gave an unconscious nod, still trying to pin down the unnatural scent as both he and Harvick faced the rustling forest.

From it came six figures, tall and hooded in pitch cloaks. Ashiy mistook them for elves at first, but beards on their exposed chins confused him. These were males. Elves were most dominantly female. Nor did an elf's features possess such squat roundness. *Humans,* Ashiy thought. His hind legs almost buckled, for what else could these strange creatures with their foreign scents be? Fire-starters. Enslavers. Foes which begat the first centennial war. Their presence terrified him more than a hundred reanimated ever would.

However, Harvick swept forward with a demeanor of business. "Ah, gentlemen," said the raccoon, presenting one of the blades. "For your inspection."

The leader accepted the graceful weapon. His dark eyes glinted like worn stones, and a streak of his stubbled chin was bald where a scar jagged across it. Ashiy suppressed a flinch as the man withdrew the sword from its sheath to twirl it, testing the balance. A human's fingers were double-jointed. Compared to an animal's stiffer toes, they were more naturally adept for swordplay.

Not withdrawing his cold eyes from the blade's flat, the man said, "We expected to meet four smugglers. Where's the other two?"

Harvick's throat clicked, dry. "They severed ties with our dealings."

"Severed ties?"

"Yes, for other arrangements. A pure business decision, y'understand." Harvick's chaffed nerves were audible. "Of course, they'll say nothing of these arrangements."

"Their tongues will stay silenced as though they were in cut throats."

"Y-yes." Harvick's polite grin faltered. "That's…a way to put it."

This time Ashiy did fidget back as the broadsword's point leveled at his chest. It seemed to amuse the man. "And you, redtail? Will you breathe a word of men amid their rightful lands once more?" Despite his fear, Ashiy hardened at the remark. Humans had no claim in Altharia. Theirs was to their island, quartered off by a raging sea. Nothing further.

"The blade is to your satisfaction?" Harvick directed the leader's attention aside.

"This one appears so. Give my men theirs."

Harvick relinquished his remaining swords, and when Ashiy dallied, swatted him smartly with his ringleted tail. Paws exchanged items with hands. Ashiy felt sickened and warped. Ceilia had safeguarded him from committing crimes all his life. Now he had just played a role in a deal odious enough to earn him a thief's brand, or worse.

The leader awaited his men's approval. Once each of them had strapped a blade to his hip, he gave another motion. A second man, bearing a large sack with odd protrusions over one shoulder, stepped forward and released it into Harvick's care.

"Our business is thus finished," said the leader.

Without a handshake, the six men withdrew into the forest leaving nary a murmur, like morning vapor dispelled by sun. Both Ashiy and Harvick stared after them in silence for a moment, the raccoon relieved, the fox stupefied.

"Mistress *above,* Harvick." Ashiy gave him an incredulous look. "What've you steeped yourself in?"

"A venture blacker than any I intend to profit on from this day forward." Harvick set down the mountainous gunnysack. "And you could've seen us both skinned! Why'd you hesitate to give them their swords?"

"Humans aren't allowed to carry weapons!" Ashiy said. "And as fine of weapons as those…how did you get them?"

"I'm just the deliverer. Those men had them smuggled from somewhere south."

"What do they plan to do with them?"

"Oh, come off it, you aren't my nan." Harvick scowled. "And this talk best not leave this clearing. Y'heard them—if they've an inkling we let slip they've been around—"

"What are they doing on the mainland?"

"Not my place t'ask and I've not a curiosity to find out neither."

"But—"

"Curse it all, Ashiy! Don't force me to threaten you!" Harvick shifted his cloak, revealing once more his dagger's hilt.

Ashiy quieted, watchful of the handle. He suspected the raccoon now capable of anything, and it pained him. "You're a true villain now, huh, friend?" Ashiy said, ears drooping. "Suckered me and wronged Buruk. Are you capable of murder now, too?"

It came with little satisfaction to see Harvick squirm under the question. He avoided Ashiy's stare, intent on rifling through the unseen contents of the sack. "I took them swords 'cause they were the price of my life," Harvick said. "My repayment to Buruk is keepin' him clean of the whole affair. As was the same for you, but y'chose to involve yourself further." The raccoon pulled a lengthy, dark object from the burlap and threw it toward Ashiy. Fumbling in his paws, he discovered a bow fashioned from ebony wood. "Here—for your involvement."

"An apology or bribe?" Ashiy demanded.

Harvick's lips snarled. *"Apology?* You think I owe you that? You attempted your little game, holding my own stolen possessions hostage! It was a dishonest thing." Harvick's livid expression fell. "I hadn't expected it of you, Ashiy."

"I-of-*me?*" Ashiy stammered, indignant.

"You." Harvick nodded. He tied off the neck of the rucksack, full of what Ashiy dimly realized to be more weapons. "You and your ol' lady always seem to manage without bein' dishonorable. So I thought, at least." Harvick hitched the bag over one shoulder. "Sorta admired it…but guess I was wrong." He made to depart but spoke once more over his free shoulder. "It ain't my threat, Ashiy. Do *not* tell anyone what happened here."

Like the humans, Harvick left.

Ashiy sputtered in the vanished raccoon's direction. He twiddled the new bow. Its string was fine and fresh. No doubt, being foreigners, the humans had no faces to pay with and had given Harvick lesser armaments to pawn.

How can he say that to me? Ashiy smoldered. *Dishonest? When he's out here striking bargains with humans? I shouldn't have given over those swords.* Again, he contended with a marred sense of failure against Ceilia's tutelage. But would it have only been the encounter with the humans which would cause her shame if she knew of it? *No.* Ashiy gripped the bow tighter. *So what if I knew those weapons were Harvick's before trying to sell them back? That's hardly worse than what he's been doing. Isn't it…?*

Three days passed, and there came no suggestion of human activity. Ashiy decided this would determine whether he would reveal what had transpired with Harvick in Whimzic

Forest. With no whisper of the men surfacing, his fear that they intended to use the weapons for some devious purpose finally subsided. Thus, he kept his silence.

The call of his new bow allayed Ashiy's fears further.

Ashiy had almost returned to the Haven bearing it that same day. But knowing Ceilia would pry a confession out of him about where it had appeared from, he instead secured it in a tree limb some distance from town.

The temptation to practice with it bound Ashiy like snaring bracken. The new weapon was a sleek mechanism, its cord woven of strong, unused fiber that he had to strain harder to bend. One of his former arrows loosed from it snapped in half. With a proper set of projectiles, Ashiy suspected it could puncture even a troll's thick skin. Every morning since the encounter, he had woken earlier, skipped breakfast with Ceilia with the excuse of mounting smith work, and stolen off into the forest for a few minutes of archery.

The robbery against Buruk formed the last of Ashiy's ebbing guilt, and it was by far the most pressing. To tell the smith where his swords had gone would mean outing Harvick, and Ashiy considered the idea. He had glimpsed the raccoon pawning off his odd weaponry at market, evidence that his trade yielded profit. But Ashiy doubted Harvick had made as much as the swords had been worth, and the potential exposure of the humble blacksmith to human wrath prevented Ashiy from turning the raccoon in. Beyond that too, many residents in the Haven would not take kindly if they heard he had done so.

I could sell off my new bow, Ashiy ruminated, whiling away at the anvil with his hammer. He hated the notion at once, searching for another solution which might recoup Buruk's losses.

Despite their misfortune, the smith and Branny seemed not to harbor an ill mood over the matter. Buruk conducted business with his usual jocularity, and as Branny bedded the furnace with fresh lumber, he hummed his disjointed tunes.

Presently, the younger bear interrupted Ashiy's conflicted

thoughts. "Say, Ashiy, you've been t'market as'a late?"

"Market?" It was the only word Ashiy caught as he fell out of his thoughts.

"Yeah! I was right'n what I said'n few days ago—there's a circus of bards blowin' through town. Goin' to put on a right'n'proper show this evenin', they says. Why don't y'tag long with pa and me?"

Branny looked so eager that Ashiy could not deny the invitation. When work concluded that evening, he rushed home to eat a quick morsel before the early sundown. As he speedily drank his bowl of lentil stew, cleared it from the table, and tidied his cloak upon his shoulders, Ceilia, seated opposite, offered him an appraising stare over her own soup.

"Off somewhere at this hour?"

"Bards are playing in the square tonight," Ashiy said. Then, under the duress of her raised eyebrows, he added, "I'm going along with Buruk and Branny. Buruk's granting us all a later start tomorrow morning."

"Mm, and you didn't think to extend me an invitation?"

"You'd…like to join?" Ashiy was taken aback.

"If it wouldn't embarrass you."

"No, not at all." Ashiy grinned, suddenly elated. He could not remember a single leisure event which had coaxed Ceilia from her tent. "You do remember how to interact with animals besides me, don't you?"

"Ha," Ceilia tutted. "Fetch my shawl, would you please, dear?"

She reversed Ashiy's jesting question on him ten minutes later. With one of her arms looped through his, they walked huddled close to combat the seasonal chill descending with the sun. Ceilia's other hand held her knotted walking staff. "It seems," she tapped Ashiy's chest lightly with its tip, "I don't even interact with you as often these days."

"I'm a working fox," Ashiy said. "Buruk's business is growing."

"Yes."

Ashiy evaded her stare. Sundown in the Haven saw ignited campfires at every cul-de-sac amid the hodgepodge of tents. Brisk bitterness in the air seemed to sharpen the blazes' smoky fragrances, enticing cozy warmth and companionship. Animals sharing log benches fanned paws and wings over drifting sparks. With Ceilia's shawl pulled low, the populace of Whim's Haven offered the duo no more than passing glances.

"I suppose it never occurred to me how busy you'd become," Ceilia's voice trailed.

Ashiy remained silent. There were many past occasions when he had let an unknown secret slip after suspecting Ceilia had already reckoned it. He must not reveal the morning excursions he was taking into Whimzic Forest.

"I'm proud, you know." Ceilia rubbed the arm holding her. "I've meant to say it to you so many times. Buruk says you're coming along well and working diligently. You're a great help to him, you understand?"

There it is, in her words, Ashiy thought. Each one seemed tuned to every facet of his guilty conscience. *But that's not intentional. She doesn't know.*

"I'm enjoying the apprenticeship more than I thought," he admitted.

Ceilia's hold on his forearm tightened with delight. She said nothing more on the subject as they neared the whooping and bustle from the marketplace. She suddenly became engrossed with masking her face in her shawl.

Festivities were in an upswing as they arrived.

Certain booths had been cleared away to allot space for three towering bonfires. Those that remained crawled with jabbering merchants seeking to take advantage of the gathering crowd. Aggtree had commandeered one stall. Rolling out fresh kegs from Pelt's, he was bent upon making the swelling throng just as cheery as they would be inside his establishment.

The bards were ravens. A band of black-feathered siblings and their elder father scattered around the dusty square, each hosting their own bonfire to distance their chants from one another and earn the most coin. Herds gathered around, attracted by warmth as much as by the music and fables.

To begin things right away, the youngest, a fellow with a streak of gold on his beak, drew those gathered in with a shrill whistle. "Hup! Hup! All you! Up! Up!" With this summons, he opened his maw wide and pointed it upward. The bird had no instrument or limbs dexterous enough to play one, but from his throat came the perfect mimicry of a fiddle's buoyant strings. He sang a jive fast enough to outrace a storm cloud's bolt. Hoots of approval rose from the listeners. The raven retreated, his chest contracting as his tongue played the role of a violin's bow, and dancers wove around his bonfire.

Ashiy and Ceilia skirted the group, hiking their steps to the jig while searching for Buruk and Branny. They met the pair of bears at the second bonfire, where the female raven twins were gearing up for their own act.

"Ho, there! Ashiy!" Buruk's voice boomed, even over the masses. As the fox and Ceilia joined him, he lowered his tone. "An' is that Ceilia'n there under th'hood?"

"It is."

"Honored t'see you." Buruk, with a clap to Branny's back indicating he should follow suit, bowed to her.

"No need of that," Ceilia said, casting furtive glances around to ensure their reverence had not revealed her to onlookers. She nodded to the corvid twins by the fire. One tuned an oblong, stringed device. The other wore a frilly dress which seemed to shimmer like water with every flinch. "What have we here?"

"Competition, looks like," Buruk replied with a smile.

They fixated on the twins to decipher what he meant. The sisters were flinging scornful looks at their young fiddle-imitating brother and the crowd of dancers he had mustered. Their own audience was being drawn into his. When he finished his first ditty and made somersaulting bows to uproarious applause, the sister in the shimmering dress gave her own whistle, louder and longer than his had been.

As soon as her note ended and heads turned, she took to the

air on nimble wings. Her sister began pulling notes on the tall harp with her wings. The flier twisted and vaulted, matching the music with airborne cavorts. In the dress, she appeared like water defying gravity, a torrent of rain threading its own path above the firelight. Their brother's audience splintered off, gasping and cheering. He started up another jig for those who remained, sending his sisters a scowl over his musical beak.

The harp silenced. Just as suddenly, the air dancer dove.

"Look out!" Ashiy and Branny ducked.

The music returned. They felt a breeze and the silken edge of the raven's dress kissed their ears before she soared high over them once more, lightly laughing. Ashiy and Branny joined in the subsequent applause.

"Miss'triss, above! Y'see that?" Branny said with a thunderstruck grin.

Having had quite enough of his sisters' distracting presence, the fiddler-imitator moved away from his own bonfire and toward theirs, hitching his throat tune higher so that it drowned out the softer harp. What ensued was a squabble, the sisters and the brother driving nearer and nearer, their music overlapping in an ugly clamor. The conjoined audience between them began guffawing, and many more were irked. "Ey, 'nuff with the trouble! How're we meant to enjoy your talents if yer troddin' on each other's notes?" came disgruntled grumbles. Ashiy, however, grinned.

In what seemed to be a discordant beat from their individual songs, the fiddle-singer and harpist hit an identical strum. Then another. Another. Their hostility melted, and suddenly their tunes combined in a merry chorus. The flying sister landed with a flourish of her oceanic gown, pulled Branny from the crowd, and mindless of his tripping and stuttering, began a lively waltz.

Cheers were immediate. Pairs of animals followed the bear and raven, scattering between the two bonfires. Becoming fluid shadows between them, they flickered under the harp and fiddle's united swing.

"Ah-ha! An act, it was!" Buruk roared as Branny was led by the raven sister. The young bear, twice her size, tried his dandiest not to trod on her clawed feet or break her fragile wings.

"Of course," Ashiy said, also chuckling. He turned to Ceilia. "Did you guess it too, Mother? How much coin will their little stunt rake them, you think?"

"They've certainly riled the party."

Ashiy's smile slipped. He could hear the stretch in Ceilia's cheer. Her fingers rubbed her temple. *Soothing a headache?* Ashiy wondered. It struck him how lonely she must have been feeling of late for her to tag along to such a rambunctious gathering. *She'd be readying for bed by this time, writing quietly in her journal.*

"Why don't we see the third fire, Mother?" Ashiy said, taking her arm once more. "Excuse us, Buruk." The blacksmith nodded, still engaged in the dancing, whistling to Branny as the raven directed his son about like a top.

The third and final bonfire occupied a much tamer area of the market, far enough away to find respite from the playful music and hollering crowds. Around the blaze were upturned logs arranged in a wide crescent. Ashiy settled Ceilia upon one and dragged a second up to sit beside her. An elder corvid served the centerpiece of the semicircle, storytelling in verse. The bonfire crackled behind his planked tail. He paused his current story to peck at his pipe and give his new listeners a welcoming blink with sunken, sickly eyes.

The delay gave a party of seated wolves the opportunity to heckle. "A'nuff with the child's tales, ol' bat. What're we to you? Cubs? Give us a tale fit fer ruffians. Don't you know the likes of the folk in Whim's Haven?"

"Bah!" A couple of feathers loosed from the bard's flippant wing. "I've seen harder crooks at elf-day feasts."

The hassling wolf stood, insulted. But a barking laugh from beneath Ceilia's hood distracted him. Ashiy gave his godmother a surprised glance, as did the elder bird.

"Ah. We've one who could vouch the claim." The bard clicked his beak on his pipe, dipping his head reverently to Ceilia. "What say you, elf cloven from the divine boughs? A request? My next yarn will be spun as a drape for your pointed ears alone."

Ashiy suppressed a smirk as the wolf, unsettled at being ignored, sat back down with a grumble and stared warily toward Ceilia. "Choose a good story, Mother."

Ceilia deliberated. "Tell them," she nodded to the wolves, "one about cats."

Ashiy found himself leaning forward along with the canines as the bard's lemon-hued eyes poured a dark stare toward the crackling fire. "Mm…cats…Foes of the second centennial are a fell subject indeed…but at an elf's request…" Another moment he haunted over the flames. Then, as though the grim verses came forged from their singeing depths, the wizened raven croaked:

"Alas, lowveld scores of shifting dunes,
Sea where liquid sands doth outnumber.
Sinking in thy midst bake crumbling ruins,
Under sun and hence rent asunder.

Cracking pyramids span myriad
Shambles wherein fierce residents graced.
Cats, foul rulers of their period,
A race for their savagery erased.

Oh, blood-drunk scourges, blasphemous beasts,
Sated their stomachs on flesh red hue,
Played murder a game for lavish feasts,
And new death raised their lives anew.

For saifs against the foes were tempered,
And found resurrection a trait feline.
Whet blades upon black hearts were rendered

Benign in use—cats' rebirths be nine."

Midway through his piece, the bard paused to take an obligatory draught on his smoker. His eyes shone bright, satisfied by the expressions of his younger listeners. They were impatient for him to continue.

Ceilia coughed and tapped Ashiy's shoulder. "Would you mind finding me some water, dear?" It was a ploy to get him away from a tale she regretted requesting. The history of the extinct feline race was a violent one. Loath though he was to miss it, Ashiy obliged his godmother's ask. He missed the bard's following stanzas while hunting for Aggtree's booth.

"Water? When'll ye take use of my true services?" The tavernkeeper was once again peeved by Ashiy. He waved an empty tankard at his muzzle. "Begone! You hold my line!"

"That isn't a way to treat your customers," said a rumbling, familiar voice. Ashiy, with stiffening muscles, turned to find Evok the elephant. The ranger blocked all firelight out with his bulk, yet his eternal scowl made his eyes appear to glow. "Though now I see this one, I understand the hostility. You're too young to be wasting alcohol on, kid."

"It isn't-I'm not drinking. I'm getting something for someone else."

"Surely."

"And it's water, anyway!" Ashiy said. How had he managed to fall into company with the two people in the Haven who disliked him?

Evok remained unconvinced. But Aggtree spat. "Feh! Water. Suck it through mud—I've none for ye here."

"That's what he asked for?" Evok asked the barkeep.

Another gob of spittle. Evok watched it glisten on the countertop. Then he slapped one of Illdari's faces beside it. "One tankard." He did not wait to be served from Aggtree's keg, but rather snagged the empty mug out of the wolf's paw. Uncapping his own hip flask, Evok stared the bartender down as he filled it to the brim with crystalline water. He passed it to Ashiy. "See that's the only substance you take tonight, kid."

The ranger lumbered off, leaving Ashiy surprised and Aggtree whispering curses. Evok rejoined Ithcia by the romping figures around the raven sisters' fire. Like Ceilia, Ithcia was also cloaked to mask her elven presence, though her gloved hands clapped loud and high in time to the music. *Wonder if they destroyed those undead they were hunting?* Ashiy felt a fleeting curiosity.

"Better return that mug," Aggtree murmured before Ashiy returned to the elder bard's bonfire.

Slipping back into the seat alongside Ceilia's, Ashiy offered her the cup. "You're too good to me, dear," she whispered. Ashiy nodded, straining to catch the bard's gravelly voice. His history on cats was winding down:

"Alas, lowveld scores of shifting dunes,
Desert where savages framed their blunder.
Sinking in thy midst wane unmarked tombs,
Under sun and hence rent asunder."

The ancient's voice trailed off, not this time silenced by a billow from his pipe, but by somber memory of dark ages past, evil captured fleetingly in a forlorn poem. His pale eyes, entrenched in meditation, stared unfocused in Ceilia's direction. The veil over them did not lift even as Ashiy led the begrudging wolves into a reward of applause.

It would never lift. Ashiy watched life in the eyes end.

A sword plunged through the old raven's back.

-Chapter VI-
The First Offense

*W*aking terror rippled through Ashiy. The blade point retracted, leaving a red hole in the bard's chest as he was pushed forward off its length like meat from a skewer. Above the dead bird loomed a figure outlined by the fire. It wore dark plate armor, its head covered by slotted iron over which the bloodstained blade rose, preparing to further butcher the bard's corpse.

Wrath struck Ashiy, though none of it his own.

It seared through him stronger than disbelief or fear. Blinding disgust almost made him pitch from his seat.

Murderer—your retribution!

A red beam of light, purer crimson than that cast by any flame, smarted Ashiy's eyes. It caught the killer in the chest, disintegrating the breast piece as though it were crumbling sand. The figure toppled backward onto the bonfire.

Ceilia had stood before anyone else, her eyes all rage, shawl in disarray, and slanted ear tips bared. Her staff's end, still aglow angry scarlet, remained angled on the spot where the attacker had stood.

Before the marauder had fallen upon his pyre, three more swarmed forth to take his place, war cries echoing under their helmets.

"Ashiy! Go!"

The wolves turned tail in abandonment. Ceilia surged forth, a lone tempest to intercept the fell knights. Her eyes and staff shone alike with red light. She moved fluidly, naught but her billowing cloak catching sword slices, fracturing the arms which thrust them, and throwing her opponents down dead with scorches from her staff. Ashiy, unable to remove his eyes from the hatred in her expression, was seized with a fearful realization: *She knows how to fight, my godmother. And formidably.*

With the new opponents vanquished, Ceilia turned and took Ashiy by the shoulder, driving him forward. "I said go! *GO!*"

Music had died, supplanted by screams. Chaos routed the square as more and more plated attackers cut indiscriminate, bloody swathes through the crowds of frolicking animals. Ashiy found himself churned in a sea of stampeding bodies, tethered to Ceilia by her hand, then smashed from its grip by a fleeing bear. Pain knocked through his face, and he stumbled for a moment, losing sight of Ceilia.

"Mother! Mother!"

A wolf grappling with a knight blocked the way. The animal managed a blow to unseat the helmet. A human's face was revealed, with murder in his eyes and teeth gritted as he kicked the wolf back and hacked with a glittering falchion.

Ashiy pivoted to the side and indirectly found himself before the dual bonfires.

Here, a true defense had formed. Thieves' knives wormed between weaknesses in the humans' armor. Noble bears, Buruk among them, leveraged their size, hurling assailants, heavy claddings and all, then returning their own dropped weapons against them. At the forefront battled Evok and Ithcia, true rangers on display. Evok crossed blades with three knights apiece, and over him a ward glowed protection when blades were suckered between his own defenses, shattering their flats like glass. Ithcia backed the elephant, occasionally dazzling with scarlet flashes from her own staff that fragmented mail and bone alike.

Then, between gaps in the fray, Ashiy first glimpsed her.

A figure in a shadowed shroud strolled as though the bloodshed formed for her a throne room carpet. Slit yellow eyes were sunken beneath a face bleached white. Indeed, a porcelain face it was, set in a deep hood, imitating a human's leering skull. In one pale hand she conducted an ebony staff.

Threads of flame bent to converge on its tip as she neared one of the roiling bonfires. Waving it, the witch siphoned the blaze and redirected it, pummeling into merchant stalls and isolated treetops. There it lapped and spread as if given life of its own, branding the battle with a ring of hissing light and the acrid scent of charring timber.

Fear set in rampant as the fire. Oldest and most primal animalistic panic imbued Ashiy as he lifted his arms against the heated glare. By the defended bonfire, warriors scattered in similar terror, leaving the rangers alone to combat.

Paralyzed by his thunderous heart, Ashiy watched the skull-masked inciter intercept a fleeing reveler. He identified Harvick by the ringed tail and crusted dagger. The witch moved like the dancers had before they'd fallen dead, playfully dodging between the coon's frenzied cuts. Then, in a final bid to escape the enclosing flames, Harvick threw himself forward with a death scream of the same pitch Ashiy had made when he'd challenged the troll. The raccoon's yell petered, and he went limp mid-lunge. He fell. In her second hand, the witch twiddled a hair-thin blade. A few drops of blood left its milk-white tip, stolen from the raccoon's heart.

The yellow eyes met Ashiy next, branding him with an eternal fright even from yards of distance. Then they were gone. The witch bore through the market's wreckage, flames shying aside in the wake of her flowing mantle.

Hampering his fear, Ashiy realized the battle was subsiding as quickly as it had erupted. Humans retreated off into the darkness beyond the flames. A few scuffles were still being sorted, but those that remained turned in the animals' favors.

With the bloodshed finished, hiders and fleers reemerged. Voices pealed out over the crackle and crash of ashen booths collapsing in on themselves. In his ebbing shock, each word seemed to float to Ashiy like slow wisps amid the smoke.

"Enchanted fire, steer clear!"

"Water! We must put the blaze out!"

"Help! Help!"

"Bring a healer!"

"Where's my brother? Has anyone seen my brother?"

This familial plea stirred Ashiy. *Ceilia!* Where had she gone?

Ashiy flung himself over the battleground, staying well away from where fires still hissed like adder nests, searching the frightened huddles of faces he passed. He saw Evok and Ithcia both mustering a group to draw well water for dousing anything alight. The fiddling raven sat dumbly by his bonfire, head bloodied, staring at his sister's harp shattered between his sprawled legs. Aggtree stumped past, drowning himself in great draughts from a tankard as his right arm seeped from an ugly gash. Henyer, who had bush leaves stuck in his fur from hiding, pilfered gold from dead animals' pockets. One of the wolves who had been listening to the old bard hunched, prodding the still form of his packmate. Other animals picked through the downed bodies littered throughout the market. Ashiy's heart thundered. He could not look among them for Ceilia. He *would* not.

He collided into fur that smelled of blood, but also familiar soot.

"Ashiy!" Buruk took the fox's shoulders. The smith had a wild glint in his eyes that Ashiy thought must be reflected in his own. "Branny! Y'seen him?"

"No! Have you seen—"

"BRANNY!" Buruk pushed Ashiy aside.

His son stumbled toward them, part of his shoulder blackened from a close encounter with fire. At the young bear's side was the raven who had been dancing with him. Her swirling dress was now ripped, but she seemed otherwise unhurt and remained close to Branny as she searched for her family. The apprentice may well have taken the wound on his shoulder in her defense.

"Father!" Branny threw himself into the smith's embrace, ignoring the aggravation to his injury. The safety of each other's arms brought about tears from both. Watching them deepened Ashiy's worry. He wanted to be in Ceilia's arms. He wanted to wake from this horrible, burning nightmare and find her ready to lull him into a more peaceful dream.

"B-Buruk." Ashiy approached the pair of them. "Have you seen my mother?"

Neither of the bears seemed to hear him. The corvid sister spied her brother by the bonfire and fluttered over. Another tearful reunion sealed in a hug.

"Buruk!" Ashiy tugged the blacksmith's paw.

At last, Buruk disentangled his pulled arm. The other remained clasped around his son. "I saw'n her fighting by the bonfires. I think—it's all'n blur—"

Ashiy wasted not another moment. With a place to search, he streaked away. The bonfire was not far, its earnest blaze dying in its circlet of stones, smothered by the first human collapsed upon it. All around lay still forms, shadowed by the flickering embers.

In his haste, Ashiy trod one and felt cold iron. Finally, his gaze drew downward. It was the corpse of another human attacker, his face darkened by a visored helmet. One motionless hand still held the pommel of a broadsword. *No.* Ashiy's fur raised straight down his spine. He kneeled and picked up the weapon. Its balance was familiar, as was the dark leather of the sheath attached to the dead man's hip. *No. No—*

"No!" Ashiy whispered, casting the sword away as though it could sting. It clanged off the human's shoulder greaves and the metal gave way, revealing a fatal wound. Something had burrowed through the man's armor as though it and the flesh beneath had been sodden paper. *Sorcery damage,* Ashiy registered. He stood again. Worrying over the sword would have to wait.

"Mother! Mother! Where are you?"

Ashiy's alert ears heard a shuffle. The bonfire's dying light revealed to him a fragile hand rising, bloodstained and shaking, from a pile of lifeless figures. Ashiy was on all fours at once, pushing the heavy carcasses aside.

There were many of them. Nearly a dozen had been smitten with magic from the twisted staff now fragmented in pieces.

Ceilia lay with one of the wooden shards clutched to her chest, her eyes still faintly raging against the foes scattered around her in the dust.

Her divine elven blood was mixed with theirs.

"A-Ashiy!" Ceilia had been reserving her strength to utter the name.

For just a moment, he scuttled back at the sound of her. Still in his mind remained the terror of fire, and he had seen it shine a brilliant scarlet in his godmother's eyes.

Then, ashamed, Ashiy knelt beside her, though a response lodged in his throat. Staring into Ceilia's face, he saw the fury vanish as she recognized him, her eyes returning to the comforting hazel he had always known. And the knowledge that he was there, that he was alive, seemed to signal some deeper, pivotal light in them to recede. She fought to keep it with each breath, but he could see it sinking.

"Ashiy!"

Say something! His mind wailed at his caught tongue.

"I-I'm here, Mother." Ashiy felt rigidity leave her body as he held her. The light receded further. Ashiy leaned his head closer to hers so that she might have something to fight for. "I-I'm here, I'm unhurt."

One of her hands found his face and twined a clump of fur.

"I meant to tell you so much…so much…forgive me…"

Could Ceilia even see him anymore? The light was so distant. Ashiy kissed her forehead, nuzzling his face against it so that she might feel his warmth and his tears.

"I love you, Mother. I don't care what you never told me. I love you."

A subtle movement in her throat. "My kit…my Ashiy…"

Ashiy heard her final heartbeat.

All which followed seemed to occur as though its thud had deafened him.

There was a silent period of darkness enveloped in her scent of old parchment and sweet root, which he separated from the blood and marked never to forget. Then followed a silent twilight of weightlessness, where he felt his limp embrace detached from her and himself buoyed by Buruk's strong arms. And finally, the silent descent into fitful slumber after being laid in his sleeping bag, where wakeful moments of tears interspersed throughout the night and well past a mournful dawn.

-Chapter VII-
Straightening Affairs

*T*he floorboard's creak clearly betrayed the hiding spot beneath. Evok pressured his foot against it a second time. His action did not go unnoticed by the wolf with mild mange and mincing paws who stood in the empty doorframe. The door itself had been bashed inward, lying splintered between the pair of them.

"Ah-ha, y-yes, I've not made an effort to clean yet."

The canine referred to the blood, dried in spatters against the cobbled wall, but still damp on the floorboard where it had pooled under a now removed corpse.

"The reason behind that?" Evok settled himself into a chair, ignoring its sagging protest to look over a mostly barren desk. The heftiest item upon it was a thick volume bound in troll-leather. Evok licked a toe and began to leaf through it. "Shouldn't have the Sheriff headquarters reeking of gore."

"I-It was my father's—" The wolf's voice trembled too much to warble further.

"When's the last time your father kept a proper log?" Evok tapped the book's open pages. "Far as I can tell, my partner and I were the only travelers recorded in years. And that's because we knew to come and check ourselves in."

"Couldn't say, sir. I'm unsure if he knew how to read."

Evok grunted, finally eyeing the disheveled wolf before him with full scrutiny. The fellow was now being thrust into duties meant for sprier bones. He looked to be nearing his late fifties, and the squint in his eyes suggested they were going blind. Still, he was younger than the Haven's previous late sheriff. "You're Alderly's son?"

"Firstborn."

"Of many?"

"Very many. But I was first."

"And I've heard in this town the office of sheriff is passed down through lineage?"

"No, sir."

Evok's glare sharpened. The wolf brushed his ears with a fidgeting paw.

"There'll be the normal vote. My father was well-loved, is all…the vote'll carry to me."

Evok slammed the logbook shut, making the wolf flinch at its flurry of dust. With more prolonged groaning from the chair, the elephant leaned back, his trunk curling upward for an exasperated moment, then he returned to a hunch. "Well-loved, eh? Where were all his lovers on the eve his blood painted this room, do you suppose?"

Evok's tiny eyes had a commanding effect. When they darted to the noisy floorboard again, the wolf looked there too. "I know you've already removed what gold used to collect under that," Evok said. "Of my advice, I'll grant you this—if you're a good animal, you'll give it and any of the rest your father stockpiled to a truly worthy successor. Let them better this town your family's allowed to go to ruin. If you're only a decent animal, at least parse it between your siblings."

"Y-you're not going to confiscate it from me?"

Evok grimaced. "Ill-gotten it may be, but it still belongs to your family."

"That it does, that it does." The canine nodded a quick assent, adopting a polite turn of mood shed of his former anxiety. "Well, ah, is there anything else I can do fer you, then?"

When Evok provided no answer, the wolf bowed and took no heed of the blood he tracked on his padded feet upon exiting. The ranger resumed inspecting the logbook. Important documentation, a town codex was. Altharian deputies were required to date the arrival and departure of travelers, and the birth and expiration of locals.

Evok removed a list written on a scrap of parchment from

his pocket. He fetched a ratty quill and nearly empty inkwell from the desk's drawers and titled a line: *Sixteen deceased. 5th day in the Month of Rodent. 1495.*

The elephant warrior was grave in his work. The names to record numbered only five, for the other animals killed in the attack had been loners without families to identify them. Thus, of these, Evok marked only their species.

The floorboard squeaked again. Evok did not allow the noise to disrupt his concentration, scratching the final name with his pen.

"What are you doing here?" a voice asked.

Evok expected the wolf had returned, but it was not so. This speaker's voice held a note of sorrow over a loss that truly dwelled within.

"I can ask you the same," Evok told Ashiy.

"I want to see Sheriff Alderly."

Evok watched the young fox, trying to gauge his grief. "Sheriff's dead." His tusks nodded at the tarnished wall.

"He…dead?" Ashiy took stock of the headquarters, only now seeming to notice the door bashed inward and lying fractured at his hind feet. "How? When?"

"Same as the rest—two nights ago, during the attack." Evok frowned. "Alderly was discovered here the following morn."

"They did it?"

Evok recognized the malice in Ashiy's voice. He shared it, but the ranger replied evenly, "More likely than not. What business did you have with the late deputy?"

"I—" Ashiy shook his head. "I'm turning myself in."

Evok set his quill down. "In? What for?"

"I helped them. I helped the humans." Tears of shame distorted his eyes, yet Ashiy confessed without averting his gaze from Evok's probing stare. He wished to be run through by the elephant's great sword.

"Explain."

"I was there for a weapons exchange with them. A few days before they attacked."

"You made a deal with these humans?"

Ashiy shook his head. "Not me, no." He relayed to Evok the encounter as it had occurred, beginning with the foxes trading blades to Buruk, and ending at the point when he had seen the humans depart with their gains. Evok listened intently.

"Where's this Harvick now?"

"Gone." Ashiy dipped his head.

"Fled?"

"No, I saw him during the attack. The witch killed him."

"Witch?" Evok said.

"You didn't see her?" Ashiy shivered at the remembrance. "She was darkly clad, and she wore a horrible mask."

"I did not cross my blade with her, no." Evok glanced at his logbook. He crossed the word *raccoon* from one of the deceased. "Was Harvick a birth name or a shortening?"

Ashiy shrugged. Years of seeing the pickpocket steal about, and the notion to ask had never even crossed his mind. Evok marked the name *Harvick* in the codex, then returned his attention to Ashiy. "Seeing as there's no sheriff to sentence you, I suppose the duty falls to a ranger such as myself." Ashiy hung his head as the elephant deliberated. "I give you none."

"None?" Ashiy bristled. "I helped—"

"You were entangled in something beyond your control, kid." Evok waved a foot. "More than those six humans took part in the attack, and with more equipment than those swords. Whatever their purpose for this butchery, it seems long premeditated." For a moment, Evok's usual gruffness lowered. "Now, what shall I write in the codex concerning your elf?"

An answer stung in Ashiy's throat for a moment before he gave it. For even unto the grave, he felt compelled to conceal Ceilia's name. "Havsenia. That was her birth name."

Perhaps Evok saw through the lie, for his quill's tip hesitated. "Are you certain?"

"Yes." Ashiy listened to the quill scribble, unable to watch it. "If you won't arrest me, let me do something to help."

"That was my intention," Evok replied, drying the fresh ink

with a gentle blow from his trunk. "As a witness to the humans and their attack, your testimony would be quite valuable. But on that matter, I've first got to consult with Ithcia."

Ashiy, though taken aback, took Evok's agreement in stride. "Good. I've something I need to talk to her about myself."

Darkness descended ever earlier upon autumn's passing chilly eves. Seated on the ground, Ashiy watched flames swell and sway under the thrall of terse breezes that were lengthening their breadth just like sundown's growing shadows. Other evening campfires were lit amid the surrounding shanty tents. But Whim's Haven had never been consumed by such odious silence. Brigands, bandits, and brawlers of the town had alike found the sudden violence to their community sobering.

Ashiy's tent stood dark. An open flap waved free, allowing wind to rustle the fabric within. *Two days ago, we left it together,* he thought, listening to the noise. How surreal the idea seemed.

The illicit bow sat across Ashiy's lap. Its retrieval from the forest had been his first excursion after that horrible night. Now as its sable limbs glimmered reflected firelight at him, Ashiy wondered how he could have ever counted the thing of any importance. He wished he still had his old bow. *Was the birthday she gave it to me my fifth or sixth?*

From the pathway, a cloaked figure came to rouse Ashiy from his thoughts. Ithcia positioned herself with the campfire between them. For a moment, they sat sharing the town's wearied silence.

"I'm sorry for your loss, Ashiy."

"Thank you." Ashiy accepted the condolence numbly. His tears were not finished, but there was more to do now than wallow. "I wanted to speak with you about it. She never told me…I never expected…i-is there anything special I need to do?"

Ithcia's reply was soft. "We elves can be buried, just as any animal. The preference of most is to have a favorite plant grown over our resting ground."

"A delsic shoot…" Ashiy said. "The trees are infested with them every summer. I suppose…I'll find one. Thank you."

Ithcia hesitated a moment before resuming. "Ashiy, I must report what happened to her. My kindred are recorded carefully in the annals of Eltcindale. And the manner in which she died…" She trailed off, choosing not to linger over the subject. "Is there anything you would have me say about her?"

Ashiy stared hard at the fire that its brightness might disguise the sheen coming across his eyes. "I don't have words strong enough yet…can I find them on the road with you and Evok?"

Now he looked at her. Ithcia shifted on her knees.

"Evok told me of your involvement, and how he wishes you to testify," the elf said. "A crier has been dispatched to Witfast, but eyewitness accounts of the attack will serve better. In two eves, once we've helped matters best we can here, we'll depart for the canid capital. However, after our business there, Evok and I must return north to our guild. We will not be able to escort you home again."

"That doesn't matter." Ashiy gave his bow an absent stroke.

Ithcia noted it. "Their crimes are black and they will be brought to justice. But make no mistake, Ashiy, we do not plan to hunt the remaining humans."

"I didn't ask if you were."

"And I will only allow you to join us if you swear not to seek vengeance against them." Ithcia's tone was a forewarning. "Vengeance of this nature could only ensure more violence. Violence is ugly—an act my kindred detest above all others. One your godmother would assuredly have stood against."

Would she have? Her final moments, and the score she had slain during them, troubled Ashiy with doubt. Ceilia had not been the mentor of peace then that he had always known her to be. "I don't want revenge, I swear it," he still said. Indeed, who was left to punish? Ceilia had dispatched her immediate killers, even if other men remained at large.

Ashiy shivered. "But I can't stay here."

Ithcia nodded and stood to take her leave. "Very well. Then we shall meet you in two mornings." She departed, drawing up her hood as she went. In the dimness of the evening, Ashiy allowed himself to imagine it was Ceilia's form retreating from his campfire—a fleeting fantasy gone with a single twist of the flames.

In the morning Ashiy would take his godmother from where she now slept, protected at Buruk's smithy. He tensed. Rage threatened to sweep him off into the forest, off on the diminishing scent trail left by that murderous pack of men who had cast his heart in turmoil and his home in such dreadful disquiet. A vision came to him from the fire in its ring of stones. He saw himself taking the black bow in his paws, and burrowing arrows through dark armor. He heard the men inside it die with overdrawn screams.

The vision faded. Ashiy found himself gazing upon dulled cinders.

You always taught me better, Mother, didn't you?

He fed the bow to them—fresh kindling for rejuvenating the fire.

Ceilia the elf was buried beneath a tall red cedar. Buruk toiled to provide her a deep rest. Branny inscribed a sigil of a scroll and quill into the bark.

And Ashiy left a pale strand of delsic root clasped between his godmother's folded hands. One day, after the cedar's roots wound their way through the earth to them, her favorite tealeaf would bask in sunlight.

The burial marked a day of tears, but of warm gratitude, too. Ashiy was surprised by just how many animals stopped by his tent with bouquets, incense, baubles, and inquiries as to where they could leave the elf their offerings. Most had been Ceilia's former students. A few were vendors from the market who had admired her grit for bartering. Aggtree, the barkeep, was the most surprising. "Always secretly hoped yer lady'd give my place a try," the wolf said. "Best proof of my bar's charm would've been to entice an elf, yeh?"

Ashiy found an unopened pint from the gnarled patron amid the rest of the gifts left on Ceilia's mound when he visited the evening before his departure. He had checked them every day, touched by the amount.

As Ashiy stood beneath the cedar's somber boughs, he breathed deeply. On autumn air he could smell tinges of woody bark, the damp of fallen leaves, and the crispness of approaching frost. Everywhere now the forest was hunkering itself down. Plants were sleeping, shriveling, and dying.

Yet come summer, this same spot would be alive again. The churned soil Ceilia lay beneath would produce verdant grass. Warm air would ring with lesser bird calls, and the scents would be lush, thriving, and fragrant.

Ashiy exhaled. Ceilia was gone, yet he remained. He knelt, and, finding room between the condoling gifts, kneaded a paw into the fresh-turned soil for a final time. He said nothing. All the words they'd needed had been expressed between them in their parting moments. Ashiy left his godmother to rest.

He soon approached the enclosures of Whim's Haven. By habit, Ashiy's feet brought him upon the cobbled road. Pelt's Tavern was beginning to emit lined rays from its shutters. Buruk and Henyer's shared shop was dark across from it. Ashiy ambled his way around to enter from the rear.

He hoped the smithing pair were not asleep and was relieved to find both enjoying a mug of warm cider in the cramped storeroom. Buruk ushered Ashiy inside as soon as the bear recognized his rap at their door and provided him with his own tankard. They shared silence until their drinks reduced to a thin sludge at the bottom of their cups.

"I wanted to thank you," Ashiy told the bears at last.

"Nothin' thanks needed," Buruk replied at once.

"For the cape clasp you placed on the mound too," Ashiy said. "You made that, Branny?"

"I did," the younger bear replied. His burned shoulder was

a bundle of white linens, parts of the fur shaved around it. The tender wound made him wince when he moved, but he raised his cup. "Hope she'd of liked it."

"To Ceilia, eh?" Buruk said, his mug lifting too.

Ashiy's mug rose heavy to meet theirs. The rims clinked. They guzzled what little remained. As the fox placed his mug down, he drummed the tabletop. "I also had something to tell you, master Buruk."

Ashiy informed them then of how their broadswords had been pilfered by Harvick. Then of how he had been roped into the dealing with the men. And, last of all, Ashiy gave them notice of his intent to go with the rangers to report as a witness to the human attack. "So, I suppose," he concluded, nervous, "this means a hold to my apprenticeship. If you'll allow it."

While his son's expression had waxed from horrified to dumbfounded, Buruk had remained stoic throughout Ashiy's confession. The smith leaned forward, grimacing. "Well'n…a hold doesn't count it, I say. Sounds more like'n resignation." Buruk batted a large paw as Ashiy began to protest. "Nah, say nothin' of it. Since you've started I seen yer heart ain't innit for smithin'. Done me good work, mind you, not to worry 'bout that. But I figured, even were Ceilia still here'n all, I'd be troubled to keep y'round fer good. Might be somethin' in yer blood callin' you away." The smith extended a paw. "So go on, Ashiy. Y'do what y'need doin'. May the Mistress above bless you."

Ashiy swallowed. He took the big paw and returned a small smile as it shook him. "I'd like to repay you for the blades sometime though," he told the smith.

Again, that dismissive wave. "Evil things," Buruk replied, his eyes darkening. "Nuff's paid a'ready. Poor Harvick with his life, by'n sound of it. I want nothin' for them. Just promise to go'n help some other animals."

"Done," Ashiy replied. "I'll start with the two of you." He motioned between the bears. "Ceilia's tent is too big to bring, so I was hoping you'd both move into it. Have a proper place to sleep apart from your business and Henyer."

Buruk stroked his chin, then glanced at his son, scrunched on his chair. "We'll look after it for you, friend," Branny said, sharing his father's unspoken agreement. "And anything inside you leave behind."

With these affairs in order, Ashiy stayed only a little longer with his dear blacksmithing friends. They wished him well on the road ahead. He wished them well with their own fortunes at their craft and hoped for a perfect healing of Branny's burnt arm. Then Ashiy left the smithy for a final night in his tent.

Without Ceilia's breathing to lull him, Ashiy avoided bedding down to sleep. Instead, he burned the oil in his lamp late that eve and rifled through the old trunks to disturb the hated silence. Branny's promise to care for his possessions reminded Ashiy to inspect what he and Ceilia had owned. There was little to inventory. Clothes, mostly; worn but well-fit.

Then there were his mother's books. Ceilia had insulated the trunk's corners with them; dusty, curled-paged manuscripts with hand-drawn renderings of flowers, landscapes, and animals. All of these Ashiy remembered well, for Ceilia had used them to teach him to read, then done likewise for her other pupils. Tucked inside one, Ashiy found the folded square of an old Altharian map. Joyous memories resurfaced, for he had spent hours poring over its charted cities and roadways as a pup, imagining what they must be like, sparking his desire to see the enticing world beyond Whimzic's shroud. Ceilia had confiscated the chart after he had asked if they could travel to Owtskirt, which sat on Whimzic's northern border.

Two final objects Ashiy lingered over. Both were more personally Ceilia's than they had ever been his: her chipped tea set, and her diary.

For a long hour Ashiy dreaded removing them from their spots where Ceilia's hands had last stowed them. The tea set he'd never had much use for as he had not acquired the elf's disposition toward hot drinks. Yet now, taking it with a kind of reverence, Ashiy made a late fire outside and poured a steaming mint broth from the kettle. This he determined to sip at the table with his godmother's journal placed before him.

Like the map, the diary had once been a joyous object. From it Ceilia had read him her poems and short stories. But he had never been allowed to peruse the pages himself. The scant times he attempted to hold the book, he had been thwarted by Ceilia shutting it with an uncharacteristic snap.

Even now, that forbiddance hung over him.

Did she write about her former life? Ashiy thought, far from the first time. *If I read its first pages, would I find tales about times when she wasn't a hermit? Would I find out how she knew my parents?*

He could have the answers now. There was no one to keep the diary closed anymore. Yet Ashiy felt none of the thrill he once might have over the idea.

His lantern burned low, the hour late. He had to find some sleep. Tomorrow would be a momentous day, after all. Yet Ashiy could still not bear the silence.

Just the poems, he thought, putting aside his teacup. *I just want to reread those. She wouldn't've minded that…*

So Ashiy opened the journal and skimmed it fast, trying to find stanzas which rhymed. By fate, he stopped open on a page that contained several:

Won't you take the willow'd road?
Abound in green with rolling sod?
Says I to me, while winnowing on.
My soul worries the road I've gone,
Has wrought us on a route unbound
From wreathes of gold we once were crown'd.
No, says I, to me, once more.
My love with me, I'll walk onward.

Seeing Ceilia's handwriting let Ashiy hear her voice. Syllable by syllable, sentence by sentence, he could detect every smile and sadness in her tone imparted upon paper.

It was the same for the next poem he read, then the following, and the others following after that. At last, with his godmother singing in his head, Ashiy snuffed his light and finally found sleep.

-Chapter VIII-
Journey's Beginning

*T*here was a young oak listing by the northwestern edge of Whim's Haven. Evok had ordered Ashiy to meet the rangers by it at dawn. The fox arrived much earlier, more galvanized to rise than the sun itself. He leaned against the juvenile tree, twiddling a sturdy staff he had scavenged and whittled the previous day, watching the nearby pathway in the morning's chilly, creeping light.

Anticipation building from the previous night caused Ashiy to pace. He shifted the knapsack on his shoulders. Then he shimmied up the oak and reclined in its half-barren branches. With his back against the bark, Ashiy's need for sleep suddenly overcame him.

His light nap was soon broken by Evok's customary trumpet from below. "The kid'll make me regret this, mark my words."

"I mark he'll be a welcome change of company," came Ithcia's reply, and with it the gleam of a smile. "Yours dries fast."

Ashiy dabbed the sleep from his eyes and shifted to peer over his bough. The pair of rangers, oblivious, had relieved their shoulders of their own packings. Both wore long sleeves to protect their hairless skin against the autumn nip, though their garments were still light and nimble enough for travel.

"Sunrise," Evok said, nodding to the glow on the treetops. "He's late."

"Oh, ease up on him, Evok," Ithcia replied, lounging on her stave. Her somber voice dropped lower. "He's lost much this past week. It wouldn't surprise me if he were making some difficult goodbyes."

Wump!

Evok leaped a surprising number of feet as Ashiy's rolled sleeping bag struck the ground behind him. His greatsword was half withdrawn when his snarl found the fox perched on the branch above. "Or maybe," Ashiy said, making a limber landing beside the bag, "he's already here, and you're the late ones."

A gloved palm hid Ithcia's amused grin. Evok's sword snapped securely in its shoulder holster once more. "You think that business is funny, pup?" he growled. "Startling an armed animal like that? Think I couldn't have cleaved you in two had you been standing behind me?"

"That's why I was still up the tree," Ashiy replied.

"Oh, real smart." Evok's huffed breath stuck in Ashiy's nose as an odd smell of camphor. The elephant shook his trunk in the fox's face. "Listen here. We're bound into the thick of Whimzic Forest, with trolls looking to hunt us, and murderous men on the loose. Childish playing around will wear very quickly. Am I understood?"

"Yes, sir."

"Good," Evok said. "To add to that, I have some other rules." He paused, but Ashiy made no protest. "My duty is to keep you and Ithcia safe. The best way to do that is to make sure you follow my orders. If I say drink mud, you do it. No questions asked. No hesitation. You must promise that."

Ashiy glanced at Ithcia. She had struck him as the leader of the pair. But the elf nodded in reply. "Evok is a far more experienced ranger than I, Ashiy," Ithcia said. "It's a stipulation you must follow if you're to join us. Though I doubt any occasion to ingest something foul will be called for."

Ashiy held out a paw to Evok. "Then I swear it."

"Wonderful." The ranger was put in a better temper as they shook on it. "Now. We've dallied enough here. Time to go."

Time to go, indeed. The moment had arrived. Ashiy had fantasized about such an event for years—an hour when he would meet the end of the Haven's dirt pathways, not to trod them again until a long adventure returned him wizened and changed. Yet as he departed now, looking back at the clusters of shanty tents, Ashiy knew the awaited moment had come late.

Too much sadness had occurred these past few dreadful days. Part of Ashiy would remain in the town he had railed so long to be free of. For in all his imaginings, even those most daring and ambitious, Ashiy had never considered that he would not be able to return to Ceilia one day.

Perhaps that was what gave him such an equal sense of foreboding and thrill when the Haven whisked behind Whimzic's trees. With the rangers leading the way, Ashiy treaded forth into an unimaginable adventure.

How favored the unknown was to one's future!

However, there were a few things Ashiy came to understand as constants. First was his pack's load. He had not taken much but was burdened more so than on any previous outing he had made into the forest. A knapsack of cured foods from the market, a sleeping bag, several spare items of clothing, a fire-starting flint, Ceilia's diary (with the map stowed inside), his old knife, and the purse containing the remnant of the elf's savings all proved to be quite a strain. Ashiy's shoulders bore it well, thanks to his toil at Buruk's, but by the end of the first day, his legs almost buckled beneath him the moment he freed the weight from his back.

Ithcia approved of his supplies, at least. "Could be lighter, but you've done well with the essentials."

"Bah, what the kid's missed is a proper weapon," Evok weighed in with a grunt. Another thing Ashiy soon came to understand as a constant was the elephant's unwavering pessimism. He was a stern beast, rough and regimented, with a proclivity to view anything as a potential threat. "Whimzic's not the only place in Altharia abound with dangers. Even the highway's scourged by occasional bandits. A proper armament makes them think twice."

"In your case, perhaps four times," Ithcia replied, eyeing Evok's greatsword. Her expression betrayed that she thought it overlarge. "You've the proper idea with your staff, Ashiy.

A solid length of wood can defend just as well as a sword." She paused, twirling her own in her gloved hands, then added, "Most often, they don't impart a killing blow, either."

"I suppose so," Ashiy said. But he had not forgotten the crimson magic Ceilia had issued forth from hers; scarlet anger which had burned through iron armor as though it were fire devouring parchment. He supposed that a staff's deadliness depended on the one wielding it.

A new realization Ashiy came to was the magnitude of Whimzic Forest. In the first passing hours, its autumn grandeur went by in whirls of oranges and yellows, snippy scents, and a dim familiarity. During his foraging days, Ashiy had always pushed further and further. Yet he had always been calculated in his ventures, keeping in mind the need to backtrack before nightfall.

Now, when evening drew late, bringing with it the smells of nocturnal insects and lengthened shadows, Ashiy understood how small his knowledge of the forest had been. In the night, the trees formed black figures casting even blacker shades. Every rustle of the underbrush brought forth the fear that a beast was lumbering at them through a forest just beginning to silence for wintertime's approach.

Night fell fast, and a crackling fire provided tremendous comfort against the trees' swallowing depths. The trio fanned their hands, paws, and toes near it to get cozy even as their backs huddled against the dark.

"Won't this attract company?" Ashiy asked, nodding to the flames.

"In a more open country," Evok replied, shaking his head. "Whimzic's trees are thickly-knit—we're far from the Haven, and these woods will grow more untamed still in the coming days." His toes tapped his greatsword's resting pommel. "No, if we are to be run across by any foes this eve, it will be by blackest fortune."

"Which we shall pray the good Mistress wards against," Ithcia replied, dividing a loaf of bread from her pack. Evok shared a block of cheese, and Ashiy a few honeyed apples on twigs.

"What about reanimated?" Ashiy asked, causing a disgusted pause in the meal.

"That's a frightful subject to discuss before we bed down," Ithcia replied.

She sounds like Ceilia, Ashiy thought. Were all elves inclined to act motherly? "But they aren't a tall tale, are they?" he continued. "I smelled a pack of them that day I met the humans. You two said you were sent to hunt some, didn't you?"

"We did," Evok answered, flicking crumbs from his lap. "Though we didn't get the chance to find them. Walking corpses is all they are. Puppets. Violent to come across, but otherwise unthinking. As I said, a score of them would have to meet us by luck, and they'd be foul enough that even Miss Ithcia would smell them coming."

"Puppets," Ashiy said, accidentally allowing a sticky gob of honey to slide from his apple stick into the fire. "Who're their conductors, then?"

"We wondered the same thing," Evok replied, glancing to Ithcia. "Until you mentioned that witch the other night."

By dawn's first crack, Evok roused his charges with a stomping that shook the ground by Ashiy's head. "Up and eat, and let's start marching now! C'mon kid!"

They ate oatmeal mash cold as they secured their supplies, then they were off through the brisk morning with the trees around them yet draped in gray colors.

Ashiy's legs were creaky and sore, but he made no complaint besides yawning as they marched on. Before sunlight warmed them, they happened across the scent of a troll. But it was a day old and headed opposite the northeastern trail they were on. Keeping their eyes and ears on a careful lookout, they encountered nothing but a small clearing where they halted for lunch in the afternoon.

"What do you make of it then?" Ithcia asked Ashiy. "A day and a half spent on the road?"

"It's not much different from the days I've spent foraging," he replied, looking around at the identical maples. He was glad of the conversation. The hours spent sapped of it while walking had given him too much time to fret impatiently over the journey ahead and dwell over the previous week. "Evok's a stern taskmaster though." Ashiy lowered his voice a bit. "Doesn't he realize his legs are longer than ours?"

"The faster we move, the sooner we'll be rid of this forest," Evok interjected. His large ears did not miss much. "You've got younger legs than we do. Toughen yourself."

"He's got a point, unfortunately," Ithcia replied, removing a boot to massage her foot's arch. "It took us three days to reach Whim's Haven from Owtskirt."

"Indeed," Evok said. He stood up and began to pace. "So fit that shoe back to your heel and let's continue."

They did their best to follow the elephant's gaping strides, forced to maintain a jog to match him.

Ashiy withdrew Ceilia's diary from his pack, and, careful to keep its contents hidden from Ithcia's curious glance, removed the map. "Owtskirt is three days, huh?" he said, unfolding the chart to gain a grasp of scale. "How long shall we stay there?"

"A fortnight at most," Ithcia replied. Enough time to replenish their foodstuffs and log their visit with the town sheriff. She ran a finger along the map's fringe. "That's a handsome rendition, Ashiy. Do you know who penned it?"

"I-no," Ashiy replied. There was no signature on it.

Ithcia unfurled a map of her own from the fold of her cloak. It was on paper fresher and whiter than Ashiy's, though its illustrations were simpler and had many blotched spots. "Rangers are practitioners of mapmaking, by nature of how often we travel," Ithcia said. "I drew this lousy one. And it's only of the Canid and Elf territories." She compared their maps side by side. "Whoever fashioned yours was quite the conqueror! That's all five territories, a bit of the Snowline

Mountains, Wyldwood, and even a corner of the Southern Swamplands."

"I didn't realize it was so…comprehensive," Ashiy said, holding his map closer as Ithcia put away hers. *Was it Mother? Did she draw this herself?* He would compare illustrations from her diary later. However, he did not recognize the messy handwriting which labeled the chart's towns and landscapes. Ceilia's spidery lettering was neater. *Who then? Where did she get it?*

The Elf and Elephant Territories were the furthest removed from one another. "What brought you two together, then?" Ashiy asked Ithcia, nodding to Evok's sword-clad back.

"Work," came a grunt from the elephant.

"But you were both born in your territories?" Ashiy continued to direct his questions at Ithcia.

"Being a ranger unifies animals from each," she replied. "I was a healer from Agoroth. Evok was a soldier stationed in Hermatt. I believe when his tenure expired, he didn't know what to do anymore, so he went traveling and eventually joined our guild when he got bored with it. Is that about right, Evok?"

"That's the story," Evok answered without turning around.

Ashiy looked between the two. He could not help but think they were making their explanation simpler than it must really be. He decided not to press the matter for now. Years of living with Ceilia had taught him when to leave well enough alone when prying into the past.

"I've always wanted to travel like this," Ashiy said. "Always heard stories from bards or ruffians in the Haven about famed guilds that explored new areas of Altharia or fought evils that arose in lands already known. Maybe I should become a ranger myself."

"It's not as famed as all that, kid," Evok replied. "Few find the same renown as an errant prince."

"Errant prince?" Ashiy asked.

"You haven't heard that one?" Ithcia asked him.

"Can't say I have."

"Are you certain?"

"Yes." Ashiy's whiskers twitched. What was the elf's overdrawn stare for?

"It's to his city we go." Ithcia tapped an upper edge of Ashiy's map. "Witfast, Fox Lord Eckner's capital. The old gray was a spry swashbuckler in his time. Headed his own guild comprising his closest compatriots. Their travels took them far from The Canid Territory's seat. There were many times when it was thought Prince Eckner would not return to his lordship, whether due to death or simple disownment."

"I never knew our lord was such a rascal," Ashiy said. In truth, he knew little of court and politics at all. Ceilia had never incorporated them heavily into his education.

"In truth, 'errant prince' has not been applicable to Lord Eckner for some decades," Ithcia replied. "He dwells now in Witfast as a proper servant to the queen."

"Will we meet him?" Ashiy asked with a surge of excitement.

"If our information about the attack is deemed worthwhile," Ithcia said. "Since we do not have a crier's wings, it will take us a couple of weeks to journey to Witfast. Any number of things could happen between now and then. Ideally, the remaining humans will be caught. If they are, justice requires them to be identified by those they wronged before punishment. That is why we've brought you along."

Ashiy recalled the callous face of the scar-chinned man who had threatened him that day when Harvick exchanged the woeful blades. "What kind of punishment will Lord Eckner give them?"

"Were it me, I'd see the lot hanged," Evok replied, the first thing he'd said that day that Ashiy liked.

"They should be dealt with…appropriately." Ithcia's answer was more careful. "Our relationship with the humans is strained these days."

"Has it ever *not* been?" Ashiy said. "They enslaved us foxes hundreds of years ago. Wolves, bears, and birds too, correct? That's what Cei—" he faltered, almost blurting his godmother's true name. "That's what everyone knows."

Ithcia's ear had not missed Ashiy's fumble.

Her stare became hard, but she did not divert the conversation's subject. "So it was," she replied. "Yet what everyone knows is often tarnished by what they also choose to forget. There are good men, just as there are bad animals. Were it not for our alliance with Humania, we might this day be walking a very different Altharia—one ruled by cats, not the queen."

Ithcia upended a small stone with her staff as she walked. "On the matter of these particular men, who they are and the motive for their attack must be determined. That will decide what Lord Eckner can do about them without harming our relations with the rest of their kin."

The way Ithcia spoke indicated the matter to be more complicated than Ashiy thought. The party lapsed into their usual silence as he pondered it. But all the deliberation in the world would not fill the place where Ceilia had fit in his heart. Fairness was a simple matter where the pain of her loss concerned him. Even were it not by Ashiy's own paw, he felt the humans who had attacked ought to be struck down.

No other kit should have to be orphaned.

The following night, they made camp by a stream. Its water was pleasantly cold against their throats, which were dry and hot from Evok's breakneck pace of travel. In its shallows, they caught some crayfish not yet driven underground by the brisk weather.

For Ashiy and Evok, these tiny crustaceans provided a welcome reprieve from stale bread, though the fox felt guilty roasting the critters over a spit while Ithcia watched on.

He knew better than to offer her any. Most Altharians maintained a diet that mixed that of the elven and elephantine races. Elves refused meat of any sort, believing it an evil to eat a warm-blooded creature simply because it had not been elevated to a greater intelligence and an upright, two-legged stature. Elephants ate plants naturally too, but as the sea bordered their territory's western edge, they did not refrain from eating any scaled or plated creature cast up by the blue.

"You're sure you don't mind, Ithcia?" Ashiy asked for a third time, hesitating over his first bite. She looked a mite paler than normal, but she waved his worry off.

"Traveling with Evok, I'm quite used to the smell of roasted sea-flesh," she replied.

"I'll swear away 'sea-flesh' the day I shake claws with a lobster," Evok said, already crunching a tail. "One that's my size, mind you."

Ashiy suppressed a laugh. That was an interesting sight to imagine.

The two animals ate their fill of the meat. Ashiy began to relax into a digestive torpor when something struck the side of his muzzle. He had barely a moment to yelp and catch the staff which had been thrown at him.

Evok charged him, greatsword raised above his shoulders.

Ashiy lunged, rolling off the log he had been sitting on. He heard a dull thud as the mighty blade fell upon the old bark, and Ithcia cried out, "Evok!"

Ashiy scrambled to his feet, brandishing the staff and trailing water. He had flopped into the bank's shallows. *What'd I do?* His mind churned. *Is he angry? I let him take that last crawfish—*

"Good move, kid," Evok said, hefting his sword over one shoulder.

Ashiy blinked, standing out of the elephant's reach, wary. Evok had removed the sword from his back, yet still had the blade clothed in its leather sheath. "What's happening?" Ashiy asked, glancing at Ithcia. She still sat next to the fire, though she rolled her eyes.

"You said you might become a ranger," Evok said to Ashiy. "To do that, you've got to know how to fight. You ever been in one? Almost becoming troll food doesn't count."

"Well…" Ashiy faltered.

As common as scraps had been in Pelt's Tavern and the Haven at large, they were something Ceilia had always warned Ashiy to steer well clear of.

"We didn't bring him to fight, Evok," Ithcia said.

"Defense is a proper thing for any Altharian traveling abroad to know," Evok told her. His attention refocused on Ashiy. "Your instincts are fair. Half-expected you to try to block my blow."

"And have you shatter my staff?" replied Ashiy. "And arms?"

"Sensible." Evok upturned his horns, pleased. "Evasion and deflection will be your foremost tactics should you run against an opponent such as myself." The elephant heaved his shoulders, making his big shadow from the firelight fall over Ashiy. "By that, I mean larger than you, which would fall under the category of anyone besides the average bird or an elf. Keep yourself out of reach and never endure a heavy hit if it can be helped, lest it tax your strength during the fight. Remember that, and you just might survive."

"Survive, right," Ashiy said, climbing out of the shallows. "Any other tips? Perhaps some that won't get me soaked?"

For the next hour, Evok instructed Ashiy on some minor basics of sparring. He seemed to be enlivened with the talk of swordplay, taking Ashiy's staff and training him step-by-step through several disarming maneuvers. Ashiy served as the puppet for these tutorials and grew quite weary of having his arms and paws twisted, yanked, and swatted by the elephant's deft toes. The surplus of valuable information soon made his head swim. When it was his turn to take the staff and try to disarm Evok's blade, his own movements were clumsy and skewed. He earned a few bruises from the ranger's dull scabbard and many reprimands besides, before Ithcia, who had been tending the dying campfire, called them off.

"Bah," Evok said, sending Ashiy's staff careening one last time. "There's a lesson in this too, kid. You know it?"

"That you're a real saphead?" Ashiy scowled, nursing a swelling knuckle.

"When you know yourself to be outmatched, be it by strength, armor, or weapon—run." Evok set aside his blade to stoop and eye Ashiy. "Run until the tides turn. Give yourself the chance to win another day. Bide your time. Find a way to usurp their advantage."

"Sounds cowardly," Ashiy said.

Evok spat between his feet.

"Don't think every fight's going to be honorable, boy. The age of the proud duelists, who faced each other eye to eye and never turned tail, went away with men overseas. When our ancestors overthrew the humans, it took attacks by night, and mud scratched in eyes. They used their teeth, their claws, their tusks, talons, sorcery, and any other tricks besides to overcome man's fire. No, the only cowards in a fight are those who don't defend their own family."

A twist became Evok's stern mouth, and Ashiy thought he saw a momentary pain in his beady eyes. But then the elephant turned and unfurled his sleeping bag for the eve. "So, if it's only your life to be lost during a fight, guard it, boy. The good Mistress above wouldn't want it spent."

-Chapter IX-
A Last Day in Whimzic

On the third day of travel, Evok awoke them to a dark Whimzic Forest when it should have been first light. A scent promised rain on the rattling breeze, bound to be freezing, and the party appareled themselves in long shirts and cloaks with the hoods drawn up.

Despite this odious turn of weather, Ashiy's spirits were lifted by the rest of the day's prospects. It was to be the final one spent in the company of his homeland's oaks, cedars, and overgrowth. Evok drove them at a clip which would bring them to Owtskirt come nightfall. *A new town,* Ashiy thought as they ate breakfast on the walk, losing breadcrumbs to the bellowing breeze. While Ithcia yearned for a proper cot, and Evok some fresh rations, Ashiy was fixated on the notion that he would at last see the Altharia beyond Whimzic's boughs.

The threat of rain acted as a favorable deterrent against trolls as well. Every one of the bare-skinned brutes detested such weather.

Unexpectedly, they came across another enemy scent that afternoon. Ashiy recognized it at once as human. A muddy path of heavy boot prints had been worn into the forest floor, festooned by saplings and brush trampled or hacked aside. They had traversed by recently, whoever they were.

"Headed toward the coast," Evok said, kneeling beside the trail. The trio stopped for a moment to investigate, holding their hoods against the wind.

"Escaping to sea?" Ashiy wondered aloud, unable to hide slight anger.

"We'll never know," Ithcia said. "They've gone away from Owtskirt."

"Shouldn't we follow and find out?" Ashiy replied, turning back and forth between the elf and the elephant. Evok still stooped, attempting to make a count of the men by pairs of feet. He gave up with a huff. Drizzle began to turn the tracks into frigid mud.

"These men created deep prints," Evok said, staring in the direction the broken path made. "Means they were as like as not wearing armor and weaponry."

"It's the men from the attack," Ashiy said. His heart began to thud more rapidly.

"We can't be certain of that," Ithcia replied. She tapped her feet, from impatience as well as cold.

"Not without seeing them, that is," Evok said.

Ithcia looked ready to smite the elephant with her staff. "You cannot be serious."

"The rain will come thicker soon, Ithcia. Any trace of them will be washed away with it." Evok hiked his sword higher on one shoulder. "I'm going to follow it. You and Ashiy wait here. If they don't turn up in half a mile, I'll reroute back."

"Have you lost every sense?" Ithcia's tone was shrill. "What happened to you defending Ashiy and myself?"

"That's why you're staying here," Evok replied. "What happened to your oaths to follow my instructions?"

"We shouldn't split." Ashiy stood between the pair of them. "If the rain thickens while you're away, you won't be able to find the scent back to us. Whimzic's a trickster. You can find your way in fair weather, but in this downpour, every tree will seem the same." Ithcia relaxed a moment as Evok considered this, though Ashiy continued. "If we go, we should go together, and vote on it. I'm willing, so let's follow the trail before the weather cloaks it."

"Only a half-mile," Evok repeated, breaking from their path. "Nothing shows by then, we bail. And both of you keep behind me. Always."

Ashiy obliged, staying almost near enough to Evok's haunches to be grazed by the elephant's needle-brush tail.

"You're-oh, you're both—" Ithcia bit her fuming tongue. She followed the animals as they sniffed their way along.

The men's trail grew stronger yard by yard. After traversing far less than half a mile, Ashiy lifted his nose. "Smell that?" he asked.

"Smoke," Ithcia replied. The campfire was near enough that even she could detect it.

Evok bid them all silence. He took his greatsword from its sheath and continued an onward creep toward the smell's source. With ample cover granted them by the forest's foliage, the trio skirted the edge of a small clearing.

In it, they spied their quarry.

A shallow stone embankment supported an A-framed shelter roofed by dense twigs and dead brush. This awning had been constructed long ago by a passing traveler, it seemed, for rain threatened to capsize the molding branches. Rivulets seeped upon the heads of five cloaked men huddled around a blackened steeple of twigs. Rampant smoke, though not much else, came from it. The men had a poor time keeping a fire lit with damp kindling.

Ashiy's hairs stood on end to see them. They were all draped in dark shrouds, but hidden armor glinted beneath their buckled knees and crossed elbows. Each man carried an armament. Two sported bows, and the others kept swords fitted awkwardly at their hips beneath their cloaks.

They muttered to themselves. The distance separating them from Ashiy and his companions ensured they could make out no words besides the occasional bark of a curse when a flint's newest spark refused to light. The rainfall became too constant to hear much else.

"What'd I say?" Ashiy said. "They're the same as the men who attacked the Haven."

"We should alert Owtskirt," Ithcia replied. "Though these five look lost."

"If they're cut off from the rest of their marauders, perhaps this would be an ideal time to question them," Evok said, rubbing the pommel of his sword. He glanced at his companions, and noting the unabashed anger on Ithcia's features, sighed. "Though you're right. I'll not risk a fight with the kid in tow." He tucked his blade away. "Let's be off."

Yet Ashiy remained honed on the men. A sudden, dangerous inspiration took him. One that would have made tricky Harvick proud. "Who says we have to fight them?" he asked as Evok and Ithcia turned to sneak off.

Before they could stop him, Ashiy stood and strode into the clearing.

Evok and Ithcia were too stupefied with shock to follow, and a similar look of surprise came across the men's faces as Ashiy called out, *"Hooh,* there! Might I catch some warmth by your fire?"

Without waiting for an answer, he pulled a smooth stone forward and joined the men's squashed ring around the smolder. For a moment Ashiy's heart dropped, and he thought his rashness would lead to certain doom when the men's hands flew to their sword hilts. His next chuckle held genuine nervousness. "Well, sorry to give y'fellas a fright."

"What's your business, vermin?" said the man who had been trying to light his flint and tinder. He was a lean individual, with a ginger beard and dark eyebrows. The flat of his blade was removed several inches from its scabbard.

"Jus' a traveler on his way home," Ashiy replied, memorizing his own details. Poor old Harvick had, on several occasions, forgotten a fib previously mentioned while feigning his drunken character. It would not do to be caught in one here. "To Whimzic Haven. Ever been?" A flurry of glances between the men gave Ashiy confirmation, but none of them spoke. The human seated nearest to him, a younger, freckled boy, made a nervous shift aside, betraying a wince where his right arm was swathed with bandages. "Cut, eh? A troll snag you?" Ashiy asked, causing the boy to start further.

"You're bold to approach us," the bearded leader said. "Don't you see we're humans?"

"I just saw a fire; didn't see who was makin' it," Ashiy answered, motioning at the dead ashes. "Maybe I'd've thought twice had I noticed, but what's the difference, really? In Whimzic I've seen all sorts in my time."

"You're young," another man pointed out.

"That's what-yes, I mean—" Ashiy thought quickly, "I *am* young, and I've still seen a lot of bandits, fiends, and the like blow through the Haven. Why should I be intimidated by some humans just as fierce, eh?"

"Where do you come from now?" asked another man, this one with an eye that did not align with the other but stared blankly at the shelter's sodden rafters.

"Owtskirt," replied Ashiy. "Visiting family."

"Which direction is it?" the young boy asked. Ashiy noticed a sharp glare given him by the bearded man.

"Hard to make in this rain, but abouts that'a way," Ashiy pointed at random toward the elements. "When it's stopped, I can show you fellas."

"Why would you do that?" the leader asked.

"Because," Ashiy shrugged. "It ain't far. And Whimzic's no place to be lost. We all need friends, no? Speaking of," he dropped his tone lower, improvising, "if you folks ain't been to Whim's Haven, I tell you, I've got friends who could help you smuggle some things. If you be needin' stuff from the mainland over to your island. I'll tell them all about you when I get back. Five humans lookin' for some smugglers."

The bearded man's sword tip almost sheared the end of Ashiy's nose as he leaped up to withdraw it. "You won't tell a soul about us," the man said. "Give us your pack."

Ashiy made his movements slow, undoing his backpack straps. "No need to threaten, now," he said with a loose smile. "If silence is what you want, so be it. But no need to steal—"

"Take care of the fox, Horely," the leader addressed the younger boy as though Ashiy had not spoken.

"Me?" Horely's voice cracked.

The lazy-eyed man ripped the pack from Ashiy's paws and

snagged one of the fox's arms in a painful clench before he could stand. "We can't have *it* giving away our whereabouts," the man growled. "Dusklight will have our guts if we ever manage to regroup with the others."

"It's just a filthy animal, Horely." The leader waved his sword before Ashiy's face. "Take out your knife—"

A great roar and shrill scream shredded Ashiy's ears. Wind blew rain beneath the shelter's awning, and the hand that had Ashiy's arm went limp as Evok's mighty greatsword cleaved his captor's shoulder. Behind the charging elephant, Ithcia's staff lit with crimson essence and her face whirled with uncharacteristic fury.

"Behind us, fool!" Evok swept Ashiy aside with his free arm as his other shook his bloodied weapon at the four remaining men. "You best have learned something useful!"

With an angry cry to match the ranger's, the bearded man and his lackeys swept forward, focused on Evok. Blades smote and slid off one another in the rain. Ithcia's staff twirled like a baton, upending feet and blinding eyes with shades of red that made Ashiy's teeth grit and foam in hatred.

The instant when combat came to its peak, so did the rain's volume. It dropped in sleeting buckets that crumpled Ashiy's shoulders and soaked his hood down flat against his eyes and muzzle. He staggered away from the sounds of continued battle, muffled through the downpour, and found respite beneath a tree.

One of the humans caught him there.

"Y-you-*murderers!*" It was Horely, the boy, brandishing a long dagger that he slashed through silver rain. Ashiy lunged aside, defenseless. He had abandoned his staff by the campsite.

Ashiy ran, and he felt the dagger nip the wet end of his tail. "Get back here! You-you-they're right—just filthy animals!"

I can lose him, Ashiy thought. He could see almost nothing. Rain lashed into his eyes. It would make the human boy just as blind once distance separated them.

Yet the same rain made the ground slippery. Ashiy's feet slid in a muddy patch, and when he faltered, a great weight crashed into his back.

The fox and the boy fell, the latter on top. By some miracle, the knife's first stab missed Ashiy's head and went flying from the kid's hand.

Ten slick fingers locked around Ashiy's windpipe. He kicked and scrabbled like mad against the boy, but found him far stronger. Half-blinded by mud and ebbing air, Ashiy saw dark eyes staring down at him. As they locked with his, they widened. The fingers on Ashiy's neck eased. With airflow came a clear idea. Ashiy drove mud from his paws into those shocked eyes.

"Aargh!"

The boy reared back, clutching his face. Ashiy, from instinct, found his opponent's knife where it had been discarded in the sludge and jabbed it upward.

Blood, much warmer than the rain, splattered Ashiy's face. The boy made a strange croak, now clutching the blade plunged into his collar. He fell facedown into the muck as Ashiy scrambled aside. There, he moved no more.

Ashiy stared at the body. Its dead limpness filled him with a strange panic. He could not bear to look longer and fled into the squalls of rain.

The precipitation lessened into a dull pittering and pattering upon forest leaves. With its abatement, Ashiy's thoughts became clearer. The first one which hammered him was, *How could I have been so stupid?*

Ashiy's flight through the forest brought him to another outcropping. This one had a small alcove shielded from the storm by a great oak whose roots twisted free of the earth to make a low canopy. There he lay until the frenzied buzz in his head receded into worry.

It was late evening now. The temperature fell. Ashiy's clothes and fur still clung to him like sap; cold, wet, and making him shiver. He had no spare garments. All had been lost when he'd fled from the human camp. *How could I have left my pack?* Ashiy kicked at a clump of grass. *With my food. And my staff. And Ceilia's—* Ashiy bit his lip to stave off tears. Her diary was inside, too. His godmother's last essence imparted on earth, maybe lost to him forever. *Stupid, stupid, Ashichuaba!*

Ashiy could not retrace his scent trail. The rain had expunged it. Clouds still courted the sky, making the sun impossible to find. They would also keep the stars from helping Ashiy navigate his course.

His stomach expressed loud displeasure. He had retched it empty earlier. Even afterwards, his nausea remained. For though the rain had long rinsed it away, Ashiy would never forget the blood spurting against his fur.

"Ugh." Ashiy doubled over, shivering now on his haunches. *Horely. That was his name. I killed him. An intelligent creature dead by my paw.* His clenched paw beat the ground. "Stop," Ashiy said aloud. He could sort these teeming emotions later. *When I'm safe. Out of the forest. Back with Evok and Ithcia. To mope here is stupid…stupid, stupid…*

What had he learned for all this folly besides? His ploy to wheedle information from the humans had yielded nothing but a title. *"Dusklight,"* the one man had named a superior. Ashiy knew the name not, but surely someone must?

He clung to this thought and made himself stand. To remain in this clearing would do him no good. Even if he must walk through the night, he reasoned circulation would keep him warmer than shelter. Making a guess at direction, Ashiy began off into the untamed wilderness.

He wished for a scent to find his way, yet all that came to him was fast-decaying humidity. The lingering scent of rain would have been a rejuvenating smell were it brought in a time of lesser peril. But this shower had been a curse. Ashiy felt he had entered its pall one way and come through it in quite another. As evening shadows deepened, silence fell, and Ashiy saw eyes form from crevices in tree bark and damp leaves.

They were the same eyes of the boy who had been lessening his fury, growing scared at the capability of his hands. *He was letting me go, wasn't he?*

The forest's silence was unbearable. *"Ithcia!"* Ashiy's first calls were no more than whispers. *"Evok!"* Then he repeated them thrice more, until he was braying to the fading light above, both for his lost companions and, when they brokered no answer, for Ceilia, Ceilia, *Ceilia!*

At last, wearied and hoarse, Ashiy collapsed into a rough thicket, fearing his mad yells would attract more devious night prowlers. Trolls were sure to be abundant, lounging outdoors now that the hated rain was finished.

Night almost arrived when a new scent came to Ashiy.

He sat up straighter in his bush, wiggling his nose toward its source. It did not belong to Evok or Ithcia, nor a human or troll. An earthy, peltish smell it was, of fur and a being of warm blood. Ashiy's ears detected the noise of pads upon slick grass and exposed roots.

A wolf emerged from the forest, fur and cloak both black as the oncoming night. In his paw bounced a stout blade, sharpened on only a single edge and barbed at the tip like a fishhook. He leveled it at Ashiy's bush. The wolf's own nose could sense the fox, too.

"If you can stand, face me." The stranger had a brittle voice, soon to morph from a youthful tone into a deep baritone.

Ashiy, too relieved to care how ridiculous and half-crazed he might appear, obeyed. He raised his empty arms. "I'm no enemy," he told the wolf. "Just lost."

"You do seem…shaken," the wolf said, tilting his head. He had mismatched eyes. The right iris was dark, but the left was a striking bleached blue, almost snowy, and shone in the failing light. "We heard you making 'nuff din to wake a cemetery."

"We?"

"Stand down, Frelik. He's got nothing to harm us."

The wolf sheathed his sword, and in the same instant, from somewhere behind him, Ashiy heard another, quieter slink of metal returning to its covering. When he turned, a brown-furred fox smaller than himself pocketed a knife. The second stranger had crept soundlessly, and as their scents were similar, Ashiy had confused his with the wolf's.

"Greetings!" the sepia fox said. "My name is Frelikatas! Although you are welcome to use my shortening, Frelik, just as Ziliacsonn here did. His goes by Ziliac."

"Um, hello," Ashiy replied, a bit spooked.

Frelik circled around Ashiy. He was quite a bit shorter, and less built than his companion, but seemed more cheerful. "Were you driven into the forest by the attack, friend?" Frelik asked.

"On Whim's Haven?" Ashiy asked. "In a way."

"Whim's Haven's been attacked too?" Ziliac replied, clenching his sword's pommel. "Human work?"

"Yes." Ashiy's mind reeled. "Where else have they struck? Owtskirt?"

"Just this morn'," Ziliac replied.

"There's scarcely anything left of it," Frelik added, shaking his head, "from what we can tell. We're just travelers passing by. When the humans attacked, they burned it quickly and sent most residents scattering. The sheriff sent out those who were left to look for everyone who went and hid."

"Who are you?" Ashiy faltered. Both canids seemed too young. "Rangers?"

"We will be," Ziliac said. He pivoted, giving an impatient flick with his broad tail. "You're looking too bedraggled to talk here. Let's return to town. It isn't far."

Ashiy followed his finders, blessing the Mistress above for his favorable turn in fortune. Frelik continued to be a steady questioner, and soon Ashiy informed the pair about his own recent encounter with the men and the assault on Whim's Haven. However, he left his account free of his ill-made weapons deal, as well as Ceilia's death, and when he told of his separation from Evok and Ithcia, he hesitated at its ending. "The rain got me lost. One of the humans chased me, and, well…"

"What?" Frelik listened closely, his mouth hanging open.

He looked like a pup enthralled by a tense bedtime tale.

"I got away," Ashiy replied, haunted again by the dying boy.

A growl came from Ziliac. "I hope your friends survived. By the sounds of it, they at least killed a number of those monsters."

"I hope the same." Ashiy's heart dipped. "We're bound for Witfast to report on the attack."

"A proper quest, huh, Ziliac?" Frelik exclaimed. "That's our destination too, but—" The brown fox ceased mid-sentence. His cause for silence was known at once by his peers, whose noses all crested the air as a rancid odor wafted toward them.

Ashiy knew its source at once. "A reanimated."

"Only one," Ziliac replied.

As if summoned by their summation, a figure lurched from the forest ahead. The creature must have once been human, though now it moved with none of the grace attributed to life. Dressed in rags, its reeking skin was pale gray, flayed in places, and the eyes in its head were aglow in the falling evening. Two sockets burning a faded yellow found the young travelers, and in the same instant alighted into spurts of red demon fire. The mottled mouth gave a shriek which raised Ashiy's fur on end.

Shnk!

Ziliac's blade flashed from its sheath, twice making precise cuts. The undead's two rotting arms were hacked, though it continued sauntering forward without bleeding. "What are you doing?" Ashiy cried. Ziliac spun, blade whistling to lob the monster's head from its shoulders. Finishing the maneuver, he kicked the armless, headless torso, sending it crashing to the ground.

"Mincemeat," Frelik said as Ziliac holstered his saber. "Can't help showing off, can you?"

"I don't know what you're talking about," Ziliac replied, though his smirk was a stretch pleased with itself. "C'mon."

Had Ashiy not already emptied his stomach earlier, he might have vomited as they left the corpse in the thicket. He still heard the teeth clicking in the decapitated head as he passed it.

"We've seen several while traveling through Whimzic," Frelik told Ashiy. "Strange that this one should be so near Owtskirt, though."

They came to the end of the forest at last. The trees thinned, as did the thickets and underbrush. Through them came a new overwhelming scent, that of idle brimstone and cooling flame. All at once, the forest fell away, and for the first time Ashiy saw field land, flat and unbroken, expanded before him. Wavy grass settled under a post-rain breeze, and upon it flickered orange lights which Ashiy first mistook to be rays of the setting sun.

A moment later, as the canids stood looking over the openness, he realized the lights were being cast by Owtskirt's remnants. The town, erected on the lip of the forest, stood some half-mile distant. Its damaged dwellings offered pillars of smoke to the night sky.

-Chapter X-
Dilemmas at Owtskirt

*H*ateful flames arose from the windows of fallen cabins and tinged the edges of blackened tent frames. Where they no longer burned, rain had turned former homesteads into mires of soot and tar. But that same precipitation might also have been sent as a savior to beset Owtskirt.

The town was smaller than Whim's Haven—no more than an outpost given a population surge by several decades of mingling roamers. Ashiy saw the pain in Sheriff Eandu's eyes when the corsac spoke. He knew the name of every animal killed during the previous day's attack. *Probably dined or dealt cards with each one as well,* Ashiy thought.

Ashiy spent the prior night drying off with Ziliac and Frelik, encamped some distance from the town's wreckage where they could not be smothered by its persistent smog. Several dozens of the town's survivors had joined them. That morning, they ventured back to find what remained of their homes.

"The fire's enchanted," Eandu warned. "Leaped from animal to animal it did, as if we was more flammable than wood or dry grass. Thank the Mistress for that downpour. If you find any places still burning, keep clear."

It was a caution well-given. As Ashiy walked down Owtskirt's main streetway, he heard hisses and saw sparks leap from the charred skeletons of neighboring cabins. "Just like humans," Frelik murmured beside him. The sepia-furred fox had a preoccupation with talking to himself. Before bedding down on a borrowed sleeping mat the previous night, Ashiy had heard the lad naming star signs, even though the sky had been too black with smoke to see them. "Just like humans," Frelik repeated, shying aside from another sharp fizzle. "Discoverers of fire. 'Course they'd know how to enchant it."

"It couldn't have been an elf's work?" Ziliac asked.

"No elf would do this," Ashiy said, sidestepping a scorched timber fallen on the dirt road.

"If you say so," the wolf shrugged. He turned to Frelik. "C'mon."

"What are you two going to do?" Ashiy asked.

"What rangers are sworn to—protect and help the people of Illdari's Domain," Ziliac replied, puffing his chest. "What about you?"

Ashiy surveyed the devastation around him once again. Animals picked through debris, cowering from embers, and called for loved ones missing. It all reminded Ashiy of the attack on his own home. "Sounds like a plan of action worth joining," he told Ziliac.

Over the following few hours, the trio made themselves indispensable to the recovery efforts. Ashiy helped a vagrant black bear unearth a few unspoiled sacks of flour from his dilapidated bakery, then assisted a mother kestrel in searching for one of her lost chicks. They did not end up finding him, though Ashiy encouraged her not to lose heart. "He's got wings, after all," he told her, drying her tears with a gentle paw. "We'll pray to the Mistress he'll fly home once the smoke clears."

Frelik helped the town's healer, a soft-pawed grizzly, tend to several wounded survivors. Though he seemed unfamiliar with salves and settings, he proved himself an ample and attentive learner. Soon several animals wandering about could thank their bandaged limbs and cooled burns to Frelik's care.

Of the three, Ziliac quickly became bored with simpler matters and proved himself a most fearless firefighter. The split-eyed wolf, first dousing himself with water, charged into several smoldering buildings with buckets to combat any fires still raging, be they enchanted or not. His efforts inspired a similar rousing in the townsfolk, who formed a small band that rallied behind his quest to banish flame. Their crusade came to an end, however, when Ziliac emerged from the remains of the town pub with a bright flicker on his cloak's hem.

"ZILIAC!" Frelik exclaimed, dropping a mortar of yarrow.

His friend whipped his cape free and flung it to the ground. The fire leaped up in sudden haste from there, igniting in a burst that looked, for the slimmest instant, like a human hand, fully formed, trying to catch Ziliac's fur. He jumped away, freeing his sword. A hit from its barbed blade drove the fabric into the earth, smothering the flame.

"Nothing to fear," Ziliac murmured. Yet when he lifted his blade, fire clung to it, running like liquid for Ziliac's paw on the handle.

Once more, he missed its touch, this time by throwing the sword aside. Nearby animals scattered, while Sheriff Eandu appeared alone with a pail of muddied water. The flames hissed out a final time as he emptied it.

Without being touched, the length of the sword remained aglow, dull red as if freshly pulled from a furnace's heart. "Watch it, boy!" Eandu exclaimed as Ziliac reclaimed the weapon. "Didn't I warn you that some fires were enchanted?"

The sheriff inspected the three young charges now gathered before him, scratching a stiff ear with one stubby claw. "Right then, travelers," Eandu said. "I thank y'for y'hard work for us. Fine rangers y'd make, I'd say. But best now we salvage m'quarters. See if'n the logbook survived that we can record your names and deeds inside."

Ashiy, Ziliac, and Frelik welcomed the respite. They went with Eandu to the sheriff's former office, which, like the rest, had not escaped partial destruction. Its thatched roof was now charred away, leaving only the sky for a ceiling. The windowpanes had melted like wax. When they entered through the forced-in doorway, ashy sediment leaked from the surrounding walls. The one on the far side had caved in from the combined damage of fire and heavy rain.

"Was fortunate to be out for cards with some fellows," Eandu remarked. "Large horde of the men went right for my quarters." The sheriff used two fragments of what once had been the legs of a desk chair to begin sifting through the rubble. "The logbook might not've survived."

Ashiy and his peers fanned out to uncover the lost volume. They were unable to locate it, but when Ashiy finished his sweep by the building's northwest corner, he found something else of greater importance. "There's—look here—it's a boot! I think the ceiling caved in on someone over here!"

Indeed, a leather boot, torn and silt-stained, peeked from beneath a pile of collapsed beams and stone. The others scurried to Ashiy at once but did not begin clearing debris. All of them were held in place by an apprehension which the fox had not voiced.

Most animals did not wear anything upon their arched or taloned feet unless they were very wealthy or members of a guild or battalion that commissioned heavy armor.

The shoe sticking free of the rubble belonged to a human.

"Don't know if they've made it," Eandu said, hunching slowly to get beneath one of the weightiest timbers. "But I suppose we ought to check."

Working with caution, they managed to heft aside the beams and scatter fallen thatch, confirming, bit by bit, an iron gauntlet with five creased fingers, and a furless, oddly splayed arm. At last, they dragged the motionless man free to behold his rounded ears. The bent arm seemed to be the rogue's main injury, though a dried bloodstain on his head told of another wound hidden in his wild mane of hair. A wheeze expelled a cloud of soot over his scraggly beard and made his rescuers all hackle in fright. It was the only sign of the man's survival.

"What do we do?" Frelik asked, deferring to Eandu.

"What else?" Ziliac's voice was venomous. He grasped his scorched sword's hilt.

The sheriff's own expression exhibited a similar rage. "I'd ask you to go outside, young'uns," Eandu replied. At his belt appeared a knife. "I'll handle this."

Frelik trembled and turned for the quarter's marred threshold. Ziliac nodded respectfully and followed suit.

Yet Ashiy's paw flew to catch the sheriff's wrist. "Stop."

"This innit business of yers, traveler." Eandu's fangs bared.

"I've lost as much as you have to men." Ashiy's voice remained steady. "I know your pain. But he's more useful alive if we can reawaken him. He could tell us about his cohorts. Where they come from. Where they plan to take their fires next."

Ashiy looked to Ziliac and Frelik for assistance. Timid, the brown fox shrunk behind the wolf. "It's a fair idea," Ziliac said, twiddling his whiskers, his darker eye glinting.

Eandu's arm trembled in Ashiy's grip for a moment, then the sheriff sighed and pocketed his weapon. "If that's your suggestion, take him 'way from here. With as much as these men've done to us, I won't be the only one to want justice in blood. Take the filth and be off before my folk see him."

The sheriff offered no further help. Stripping the man of his iron gauntlets and breastplate that he might be lighter between them, Ashiy and Ziliac took the injured man between an armpit apiece. With Frelik coming to their aid, they ferried the arsonist through a deteriorated space in one of the building's sodden walls.

A fair distance from Outskirt, yet close enough to see the scant campfires set by its surviving townsfolk, Ashiy, Ziliac, and Frelik found a suitable embankment by the edge of Whimzic Forest to make an isolated camp that eve.

Frelik set the unconscious man's arm and cleaned his head wound.

Afterward, Ashiy managed to filter some water past his cracked lips.

Ziliac tied the man to an oak using rope he had scavenged.

"You can't bind the arm with the sling!" Frelik exclaimed as Ziliac pulled the bindings taut. "And look at his head! I don't think it's best that you let it slump forward like that!"

"Oh, shut it, master healer," Ziliac replied. Despite his

testiness, he allowed the man's set appendage to hang awkwardly free of the coils. It could be put to little use, as maimed as it was.

Ashiy pulled his cloak tighter against him. He had begun to roast potato chunks over a spit, prepping to slice and melt cheese over them once cooked. The food had been gifts from those they'd given aid to that day.

Ziliac settled across the fire from Ashiy, cross-legged. He offered a glib cheers with his canteen. "Good thinking, by the way," he said. "Stopping Eandu like that. We might've missed out."

"Missed out?" Ashiy answered, pausing the turning of his spits.

"It's obvious what we do now, isn't it?" Ziliac said. "If he survives, we'll take that pink-skin with us to Witfast."

"We will?" Frelik piped up. He had been inspecting Ziliac's handiwork. Their captive slumped against the ropes, held upright to the tree bark like a sagging doll.

"Course we will," Ziliac replied. "Think of the reward we'll get for turning one of these rogues in. Ashiy's right—he's bound to have useful information."

"That wasn't—" Ashiy stopped under Ziliac's multicolored stare. How could he explain his reasonings? Why he didn't want the man to be killed? How he was still sickened by the remembrance of another's blood spattering his face? Ashiy didn't even understand himself. "Witfast is a long way to drag a human, even if he were conscious."

"Which is why it'd be great if you'd join us." Ziliac nicked one of the potatoes off the fire, cursing as he juggled it between two scalded paws. "Keeping him in line could go better with a third."

Ashiy gazed on, past their camp, to the trees of his old forest. The moon shined bright and unfettered by clouds as it began its trek over the nighttime vista. Its radiance revealed no figures emerging from the woodlands. Evok and Ithcia were still missing, a day later, and Ashiy had not forgotten them. *They'll show here,* Ashiy told himself, just as he had comforted the kestrel missing her offspring. *Both of them were too experienced...they've just wasted a day looking for me. They must realize I'd have found my way to Owtskirt.*

"I'll sleep on the idea," Ashiy responded to Ziliac's unbroken stare.

"We mean to make off tomorrow," the wolf replied. Under Frelik's questioning glance, he added, "Every eve spent here is one that the rest of those humans use. Who knows where they plan to strike next?"

In this foreboding mood they dined and then bedded. Ashiy had been granted a new padded bag from one of Owtskirt's decimated tents. He tried not to imagine that a prior owner, now likely dead, had cozied inside it just a few days ago.

As their campfire burned to cinders, Ashiy heard Frelik's small voice naming constellations once more. "Illdari's Pinnacle...The Traveler...Lemon Crest..." Ashiy shifted on his mat to face the younger fox.

Frelik lay on his back, eyes filled with starlight. "Sorry, I'll be asleep soon," he whispered. Several feet away, Ziliac was already snoring. "Counting constellations soothes me before bed."

"That's all right," Ashiy said. The day's events made sleeping a complicated chore for him as well. "What's that last one you named?" Ceilia had taught him several star clusters, but in a forest where trees often crowded out parts of the sky, Ashiy never became adept at remembering them.

"Lemon Crest." Frelik pointed. Under his direction, Ashiy spied a bumpy line of pinpricks twinkling as close neighbors in the night sky's northeast. "Or sometimes it's called Orchard Line. They received their name from, uh, believe it was the old astrologer Itri. She lived near an orchard of lemon trees and could always identify that set by the outline they made on the orchard's treetops..."

"What of that one?" Ashiy asked, pointing to another star at random. It was rather calming to free one's mind of the day's burdens and mingle with the gleaming expanse.

Frelik had the memory and tongue of a wizened bard, elaborating on each new constellation Ashiy inquired of. He began with Illdari's Pinnacle, which had once been named Iralda's Pinnacle, and would one day be renamed again for the succeeding elf queen. It glimmered the brightest, its pinkish-red radiance almost comparable to the oval moon and marked the northernmost point of the sky. Next Frelik told Ashiy of The Diamond, The Traveler, and Risen Pretender, the first constellation which men tried to name without the guidance of elves. It did not always point the way west like they thought, but only aligned for a few days in the present Month of Rodent. Of these and more, Frelik continued to expound until Ashiy's wide yawn signaled him to pause.

"You're learned, Frelik," Ashiy said to encourage his friend; he was not bored, merely exhausted. "You and Ziliac are from the south? Who taught you so much?"

"Oh, my parents, I suppose," Frelik replied. "But me as well. Not all alone, of course; they sent me to a tutor. But I've got a love for reading. Sepplecretem, our home, is a place where many animals are brought to be buried and their deeds recorded. I grew up in its archives, reading stories. All of them. Any I could find. Probably would've become a recordist for the Marrows, if not for…"

Ashiy noted Frelik's furtive look toward Ziliac's rising and falling back. "If not for what?"

"Well, I thought I'd learn just as much on the road as a ranger as I would being stowed away in a dumb, musty library," Frelik replied. Ashiy felt certain the brown fox was repeating persuasions made by Ziliac. "More than that, I'd be doing things instead of just reading about them. So I came with Ziliac, to become a ranger with him."

They both lapsed into silence.

Ashiy meditated on Frelik's sentiment. It was not so different from his own, after all. *I wanted to leave Whim's Haven for so long, he thought. See the world. Do new things. Well, now I am, aren't I?* Was it all he had dreamed of so far? There had been many hurdles—the worry about Evok and Ithcia the most imposing at present—but certain good things had come of his ventures too. Helping the townsfolk of Owtskirt, for one.

Ashiy turned his head to watch Frelik once more. The younger fox's breathing had steadied, his eyes fastened shut. *I hope you haven't left anything as important as I have behind,* Frelik. Sleep pulled down Ashiy's last thoughts. His final one mourned over Ceilia's diary, still lost somewhere in Whimzic's depths.

Near morning, a ragged cough and foul curse awoke the three animals.

The human surfaced from his coma in violent spirits, struggling against Ziliac's knots. "You blasted wretches!" The man's voice was hoarse, still tarnished with ash. "Where'm I? Release me! I'll see you choke on yer own severed tongues!"

"You're in no position to make threats," Ziliac said, evil-eyed at being so rudely woken.

The prisoner did not cease squirming.

"Stop! You're going to injure your arm further!" Frelik tried to still the man.

The captive batted the fox off with an ill-advised fidget of his bad elbow. "Get away!" He gritted his teeth, agonized by the motion. *"Filth!"* He spat toward them all, cursed until his voice was well and truly worn, and only then deflated against the tree.

"I'd guess after that you're pretty hungry," Ashiy said, licking a paw. He had begun another fire and cooked a meal during the tirade, this time of flat cakes given to him by the baker he had assisted the day before. Rising sunlight made the food's color and steam very appealing. Ashiy undid a small stopper of syrup to let the sweet smell also entice. "Maybe tell us where your friends all went, and we'll share."

The human answered nothing further, avoiding any look

cast his way. Though he hungrily licked his chapped lips. "We really must let him eat something," Frelik quietly told his peers when only a few morsels remained between them. "He won't recover any strength tied down and starved."

"Let him remain weakened," Ziliac replied.

"If we mean to bring him with us," Ashiy said, "he'll have to walk some of the way."

Ziliac rounded on him. "Then you've decided to join us?"

"I—" Ashiy realized he had spoken without thinking. Now under Frelik and Ziliac's expectant gazes, he came to a decision. What more could he do while waiting for Evok and Ithcia here? Were they alive, they would still be bound for the same destination. *And if they're...* Ashiy shook his head at the thought. He did not desire to linger in doubt. "I feel I should come," he told the pair. "If there's any hope of getting this human to Witfast before his kin do more harm."

"Swell," Ziliac said. He scarfed a final helping, then stood and drew his sword. The blade now sported a permanent black scar from being touched by living fire. Ashiy and Frelik hurried to their feet, alarmed as he strode toward their bound prisoner.

"Ziliac!" They both cried as the burnt blade fell, causing the human to gasp. It sliced through his ropes, wilting them away, leaving the man freed. Yet before he could comprehend his release, the wolf had him by his fractured arm, dragging him through the dirt.

"Ziliac!" Frelik exclaimed once more. "I'll need to set it again!"

"Then you'll set it again," Ziliac snapped. His attention was on the man, screeching and cursing under his torturous grip. "Shut up." He pinned the captive, now weeping, in the dirt. A pull on his hair forced him to stare over the embankment's rim, across the field lands to where Owtskirt sat, now as nothing more than flame-maimed foundations. "Look," Ziliac seethed. "You're suffering's less than those who remain there in that burned town. Your life ought be forfeit now, but we saved it. You hear me, fiend? We should've let those in Owtskirt have their way with you, but you've been spared so that you might atone for these treasons."

Ziliac's barbed blade slid beneath the man's neck, causing him to become motionless. Both Ashiy and Frelik froze their breaths. "If I think you're unable to do that, I'll enact Owtskirt's postponed justice. On my name as Ziliacsonn, on oath to the Mistress above, you'll not live another day should you run, or refuse to inform on your companions when we bring you to Witfast. Is that an understanding?"

"Mutt, itching animal, curse you—" Ziliac's pressing blade dispelled the man's curses. "I-I understand."

"Then you can prove yourself first by giving us a name," Ziliac replied. "Yours. Though it'd give me just the same pleasure to refer to you as furless or patch-head."

"M'name's Stromic," the man answered. "Stromic in full, unlike the names y'furred savages have—long as a bat's wingspan."

"Very well, Stromic," Ziliac said. He gave one last twinge to the man's arm, satisfied with one more outcry, then put away his saber. "We're bound for the Great Highway."

Ashiy allowed himself to breathe once more, though he smoothed the straightened hair on one arm as Ziliac passed him. The wolf began rolling up their sleeping mats. Frelik gave Ashiy a shrug and began creasing his own bag.

Stromic remained grounded, nursing his twisted arm. Ashiy brought him the pan of flat cakes, though he kept a wary distance while the man struggled to eat one-handed. Afterward, Stromic flung the skillet aside like a troll finished gnawing a bone and attempted to reapply his drooping arm to its sling.

"You'll let my friend Frelik tend to that," Ziliac told Stromic, his voice still carrying an edge. "And if you give him trouble, I'll do it myself. But the method of healing I see best would be a messy amputation."

Stromic made not one complaint as Frelik reset his fracture, though they could all hear the terrible way the man grit his teeth during the endeavor. Once it was done and Stromic proved he could walk on shaky feet, Ziliac called for a departure from camp.

"Time to move," said the wolf. He whipped his tail at Stromic's heels. "My sword's flat will sting greater than that."

-Chapter XI-
Alongside the Great Highway

For Ithcianarus the elf and Evokkien the elephant,

I left this message to let you know I'm unharmed and I hope that you are as well. Just as we planned, I'm continuing on to Witfast, though now with a new purpose. Sheriff Eandu can tell you more about it. I will pray we meet again, and that the Mistress guards you both.

-Ashiy

Thus read a brief letter Ashiy entrusted to Sheriff Eandu in Owtskirt. He took a detour into town, granted enough time to write his message and acquire a few more supplies by their prisoner's waning endurance. Though they had only walked a half-mile stretch through the grasslands, Stromic paled, sweated, and at last came to a heaving halt. His injuries incurred great weakness, and no amount of threatening from Ziliac could make him continue without respite.

By the time Ashiy got back to his new companions, the man's color returned somewhat, and they were able to march him onward. The grasslands sloped into a band of lolloping hillsides and valleys. Owtskirt and Whimzic Forest were at the travelers' backs, some distance to the southwest, and when Stromic's injuries necessitated another pause, they stood upon a gentle plateau from where they could glimpse Altharia's Great Highway.

Ashiy recalled it from his map, lamenting the chart's loss along with the rest of his items from home. The highway was a vast, rock-paved road worn smooth by centuries of travelers hailing from Eltcindale to Ramsburgh, divine north to smoggy south, and every branch in between. It had been laid in the age when mankind's industry dominated Altharia. Before their rule, the Mistress's elevated animals knew no more of highways than they did constructions made with mortar and shingle. In that early era, many species were still scattered across the wildlands in nomadic tribes. Men had subjugated them with fire, with the lash, and with their armies that moved swiftly along the Great Highway to reach every territory.

If his first view of the road his ancestors had built heartened Stromic, he did not display it. "Will y'starve me longer?" he growled. "You'll get no information from a corpse thinner than a summer undergarment."

They indulged in a hasty lunch of dry biscuits, honey, and bunches of clover gathered during the day's walk. Before giving Stromic his share, however, Ziliac bent down to eye the feverish man seated on the ground. "On the matter of information," the wolf said, "you'll get a fuller stomach now by sharing some."

"You're the dog." Stromic scowled. "Don't think y'can train me." Ziliac took a thoughtful munch on his hardtack. He blew several sticky crumbs across Stromic's face. "Mutt," the man murmured. Ziliac was unmoved. "Mongrel. Cursed *split-eye*—"

"DON'T!"

Ziliac's kick to his sternum halfway rolled Stromic down the hill. The wolf's face contorted into a terrible rage, his dark eye blazing bright as his snow-blue one as he tore after the man with a paw on his sword hilt. "I *dare* you call me that last name again!"

"Enough!" Ashiy leaped between them, paws planted against Ziliac's chest. The wolf blinked, still abuzz. Ashiy held him firm, despite being a head shorter. "What does it matter if he tells us anything? We're taking him to Witfast for others to interrogate! Calm yourself, Ziliac."

Ziliac pointed at Stromic over Ashiy's shoulder. "Breathe that insult again, and you'll breathe no more, patch-hair!" Then he turned and scooped up the remainder of his dropped meal.

Ashiy looked to Frelik. He gazed off at the distant highway

as if nothing else existed. Sighing, Ashiy attempted to bring Stromic to his feet, but the man pushed away his paw with a growl. He accepted his food with a similar smoldering wrath, though the renewed pain in his arm kept him silenced.

Ashiy thought of a new reason it had been wise for him to join the company. *Stromic might not live another day were he to travel alone with Ziliac. Mistress above, that wolf still might kill him, even with Frelik and me here.*

"It'll be strange business to travel the highway with a human," Frelik said, still monitoring the roadway. "It might not be a good idea."

"Why not?" Ashiy asked.

"Rangers patrol it," Frelik replied. "Suppose, with all the destruction men have caused in the area, they run across us? What if we're arrested? What do we say?"

"The truth," Ashiy answered. "He's a prisoner from Owtskirt. If rangers find us, I'll be happy to have them give us assistance."

"Steal our man and all the glory for his capture from us is more like it," Ziliac said. His temper had cooled. "We *do* want the glory for bringing him in, don't we? Guilds will be impressed to hear of it. You're on to something, Frelik. I say we ought to follow the road at about the distance we are now. Keep it in sight but stay far enough away that we don't invite eyes from other travelers."

"Not take the highway?" One of Ashiy's ears quivered in annoyance. "If we go alongside it instead, those who do see or smell us will think us more suspicious!"

"We won't be seen or smelled by anyone," Ziliac replied.

Ashiy made several other counterarguments, such as inclement weather obscuring their sight of the highway and worry that rough terrain would slow them and tire Stromic faster. But since the wolf convinced Frelik, that settled the matter. Rather than continue forward to the highway, the party took to their immediate left so that they could follow it at a distance going north. Ashiy now brought up the rear, unable to shake the idea that Ziliac had bound them on an illogical course of travel. *Why, more than suspicious, we'll look like outright morons!* Ashiy thought, trudging one moody step after another. *Fighting our way through bracken or tripping over brush when there's a perfectly paved road just a half-mile off!*

Hills and countryside they advanced over in this manner, often giving pause for Stromic's health. Long before sunset, however, they knew they could not push the human further and discovered a small brook by which they could encamp for the eve. This time, Stromic did not beg for sustenance, but settled himself with his damaged arm awkwardly upon his unraveled bag and was asleep before sundown.

"Think we ought to secure him?" Frelik asked as they waded into the stream for dinnertime minnows. "I won't sleep well otherwise."

"He's more exhausted than we are," Ashiy replied. "Wouldn't be able to make it far if he fled in the night. We'd be able to smell him out immediately."

Indeed, for the next several nights, Stromic made no attempt to escape. Their slow travel became even further taxed as the land fought them with denser brush, groves, and pockmarked areas of rocky gulches. From time to time, Ashiy cast a longing gaze toward the Great Highway, a flat, inviting stripe in the distance. He glimpsed the specks of travelers or oxen-pulled wagons that were making better time upon it. "We're already decided on our path," Ziliac responded when Ashiy reiterated the idea of merging. "Don't ask again!"

The wolf grew more irritable by the day. He sometimes seemed as tired as Stromic, with his blue eye beginning to tinge red. On several occasions, when they were delayed by pebbly embankments or impassable briars, he forced the party straight up or through them rather than veering aside for an easier path. Hunger would soon become an issue when their supplies ran out, and it was a sore topic, particularly between Stromic and the animals.

"Can't stand this grassfood," the rogue bemoaned one

lunchtime. Much of what they had to eat were leaves, shoots, and greenery scavenged along the journey; fall shriveled most berries and sent flowers into their shrouds. "Witless animals. I'll never understand how y'can live on a mainland teeming with meat yet eat none of it!"

"Because we're not monsters," Ziliac replied.

"Monsters, feh!" Stromic said. "Wish to the Great Flame on high that cats had taken these lands—then at least I might now be dining on venison or rabbit instead of uprooted dirt!"

"Next village or homestead we find we'll get some stew ingredients," Frelik said. "We're all hungry, after all."

"You mongrels don't know what it is to be hungry." Stromic clenched his good fist. "All this food running about and y'hunt none of it. In Humania, we've barely enough of anything to go 'round. Were we not on an island with fish on all sides, we'd have all starved long ago."

It was the most he had spoken over the past several days, and none of the canids were too keen to have him blabbering more. The notion that Stromic's accomplices were likely killing lesser beasts and devouring them during their marauding only strengthened their hatred for the men. They were pleased to have Stromic quieted by travel when they started up again, and that evening he flung himself down as usual, his traveling cot barely laid flat before he slept.

Clouds overtook the night. Their darkness proved fortunate, for it revealed the flickering lights of a distant town not visible by daylight. "Maybe Yarrowick?" Ashiy suggested, trying to summon his lost map to mind. "Never been. But the highway runs right beside it."

"Looks as if the town hasn't been touched by the humans, either," Frelik said, relieved. "We should buy some stew items. Perhaps see if there's been any rumors about the attacks."

"You both go," Ziliac said. "I'll stay here—we can't bring *furless* into town."

With this plan set for the following day, they bedded down.

Ashiy had scarcely gone to sleep when a commotion brought

him out of a nightmare. A specter of the boy from the forest, spitting blood, raced away as Ashiy sprang to his feet. The vision's yell became Stromic's. He grappled one-armed with Ziliac. Both flung curses at each other.

"Mangy canid! Let blight take you—"

"Dare you to touch him again, patch-head! I'll slice you open!"

Once more, Ashiy made himself the barrier to keep the foes apart. Ziliac's blade caught on his shirt and made a small tear, but this time the hound's fury retained its adamance. "He tried to kill us, Ashiy! Tried to nick Frelik's knife! But I've been staying awake! I *knew* he'd been feigning how weak he really is!"

Frelik stood to the side with all hold of slumber gone. "H-he was standing right over me," the brown fox said when Ashiy looked at him. Frelik clutched his dagger to his chest. It had formerly been secured at his hip. "I heard him and woke right up. He had it halfway drawn from my holder!"

It took a lengthy stretch of the night for calm to settle over their camp again, and it was only secured after Ziliac bound Stromic to another tree. With his venture foiled, however, the man's threats became more vocal, his curses screams intended to keep them from sleep. "We'll take you all, mongrels! Each of y'will lose your tails, your ears, and your tongues before I finally slice your throats! It will be like the old days of Humania restored! You'll be detestable slaves! Itchers! Filth! Man shall rule beast once more, just as the Great Flame intend-*mph!*"

A gag of rough rope gave the animals a reprieve from the threats, though through it the man still foamed more.

After the night's commotion, they arose the next day close to noontime. They held a brief discussion over what supplies were needed from Yarrowick and pooled what little gold they all carried for purchasing them. However, Ashiy volunteered to remain at camp with the captive instead of Ziliac.

"I don't know," Ziliac replied. His deep glower was returned with equal venom by Stromic, still tied and muzzled.

"You've bound him well," Ashiy said. "And you're a scarier figure, Ziliac. You'll get a better bargain off any haggling merchants."

"Scarier?" Ziliac's coldness impressed at once upon the red fox. "In what way?"

"Well—" Ashiy faltered. Ziliac's intensity simmered in his pupils, their color mismatched but united with firm, unblinking focus. Ashiy remembered well how infuriated the wolf became at the mention of them before and rustled a different excuse to keep him away from Stromic. "Tougher, I mean. Look at me and Frelik. Both of us are at least a head shorter and a tent stake skinnier."

"He's got a point, Ziliac," Frelik said. "And you've got the sword."

"Mm." Ziliac looked unconvinced but decided to be pliable. "Fine. Leave Ashiy your dagger, leastways, Frelik."

Frelik undid his sheath from his belt and gave it to Ashiy with a wink. After a meager brunch of wild carrots and bush beans, Ziliac and Frelik made off in the direction they had seen Yarrowick's gleams during the eve. Ashiy watched them swash a trail over the grassland, still keeping out of sight from the highway.

He felt Stromic's gaze on the back of his head. The man had no other target for his ire now. Sighing, Ashiy scraped clean the wooden plates from their meal and arranged everyone's traveling packs.

At last, Ashiy met Stromic's holding stare.

"If I remove the gag, will I just hear more curses?" he asked.

One of the man's eyelids twitched. Ashiy untied the rope from his lips. "Water," wheezed the man at once. "Stupid rope sponged my mouth."

Ashiy let him lap from his canteen, keeping a constant stream tipped for him. "Hungry?"

"Keep your grassfood," Stromic spat. He shifted against his

constraints, wincing. "You mean to keep me tied? My back's in agony and I've had nothing to brace me against the night's cold."

"If you'd kept to your sleeping bag, you would've stayed warm," Ashiy replied, though he draped his own around the shivering man.

"I'll slit your throat, redtail," Stromic reminded him for the dozenth time.

"Talk like that'll earn you the gag again."

A sullen silence fell once more, save for an occasional swear under Stromic's breath as he adjusted his stiff position. Ashiy watched the sky, the sway of the grove's trees, and a bug scuttling through the grass. It had been days since he'd had spare moments for germinating thoughts. *Since the morning before I lost Evok and Ithcia,* Ashiy estimated. That had been seven days prior. Three more would make it a full Altharian week.

The hour dragged on. Ashiy watched the scattered progression of travelers on the far-off highway. A brisk breeze carried to him scents of manure, cut timber, and grains from unseen Yarrowick. *They're taking their time,* Ashiy thought about his companions, consulting the sun's position. He yawned, but aware of how keen Stromic's stare became toward him afterward, he stood up to pace. Bound though the man might be, Ashiy would never dare to sleep alone under his crafty watch.

"Who's Dusklight?"

The question sprung from Ashiy's thoughts on the whim of a resurfaced memory. Stromic straightened against his tree's trunk, suddenly and militarily attentive. A tremor of terror rippled across his face. "How d'you know her name?" the man asked.

"Her?" Ashiy replied. His eyes widened. "That was her I saw? The witch with the skull-fashioned mask?"

"If you saw the witch, you'd not be alive to stand before me. You'd have been a meal for our flames."

"I did see her," Ashiy repeated, struck by a daunting realization. "And she *was* the one contorting the fires in Whim's Haven! She was with you in Owtskirt too, then? Is that it? Dusklight's your leader? A witch from Humania?"

"An elf," Stromic said. "From your own mainland."

The man's grin widened at Ashiy's shock, though the fox was swift to extinguish it. "You're a liar," he told the captive. He must be. "An elf would never cause such violence."

"What do you know of elves, redtail?" Stromic replied, delighting in the way he had rattled his keeper. "There are many sympathetic to our cause! We're not so very different! Only in ears!"

"And heart," Ashiy replied. Yet a fissure in this resolve formed with another memory—that final one of Ceilia; the malevolent way her eyes and staff had crackled when she fought the rogues. *She only did that to defend me,* Ashiy combatted the remembrance, hating it.

"Only because they're all women, feh!" Stromic grunted. "You'll see, redtail. Just you see. Who else but an elf could march on their own capital city? Who else could hope to take Eltcindale?"

Ashiy whirled to his feet. "That's what your band is planning?"

"We *will* take it, mongrel." Stromic spit a gob at Ashiy with glee. "What will you do then? Will y'be so smug when the heart of Altharia is razed to cinders? When we've slaughtered all its people just as we did in your Whim's Haven and Owtskirt?"

A hot flame of new anger arose in Ashiy's heart. He strode away from the now-laughing Stromic, wiping off the filmy spittle the man had lodged onto his whiskers. "If your Lady Dusklight is as violent as you claim," Ashiy's long breath ended with the hint of a smile, "what'll she do if she learns you've blabbered all this to me?"

Stromic's chortling died. Ashiy was pleased to see his face whiten.

When Ziliac and Frelik at last reappeared on the horizon, Ashiy felt ready to burst. He had to keep himself from running ahead to intercept them and share the schemes Stromic spilled. He finally told them the moment they were relieved of their scores from Yarrowick—fresh vegetables, cured fishes, and a canteen of brown stock.

They were similarly astounded by the humans' scornful ambitions.

"Well done, Ashiy!" Frelik exclaimed. "We ought've let you question the fool sooner!"

"Indeed," Ziliac said, and for the first time Ashiy saw him offer a true smile. It was a hungry thing, full of jagged fangs. "But evil news! We can't halt to make stew tonight, Frelik. C'mon! We've got to move swifter!"

Glad he allotted time earlier to situate their packs, Ashiy made no complaints about being off the highway for once as they departed. Nor did he groan about the redoubled pace which Ziliac demanded, even from Stromic, for now the wolf was convinced the man possessed more endurance than he had let on before. Yet oversleeping and making the trip into Yarrowick had delayed their journey. The town was still a glowing speck at their backs when nightfall forced them to a halt for fear of twisting their ankles in hidden rabbit dens.

"We shouldn't've tarried in town," Ziliac cursed. "All for rumors we already knew."

"Yarrowick's residents have heard of humans about?" Ashiy asked.

"Yes, and they've been on guard," replied Ziliac. "Men haven't shown their faces there, or else the scent of this one," he gestured to Stromic, "might've been recognized on us."

They'd been forced to camp in an area of choking grass. A fire could not be started for fear of catching it ablaze, thus they ate some of Frelik's stewing ingredients raw. Rather than bed in their bags, they beat makeshift dens in the reeds by bowing them aside and stacking deadened thrush atop them as an insulating roof (a tactic Frelik had read of). Once completed, the thick, grassy dens were very cozy and could be accessed the same way as a napping bag—by worming one's way inside feetfirst. Stromic was the last matter to contend with before they could sleep. With no proper post to tie him against and his broken arm making it a cruelty to cuff his wrists, they distrusted bedding. They established a watch on the man. Frelik took the first vigil after drawing the shortest inch of a broken reed, cloaking himself against a night threatening to bluster with chill.

Ashiy would replace Frelik after a few hours, and he wasted no time funneling into his den to catch as much shuteye as possible. It still seemed a feeble amount. No sooner than he had drifted away, soothed by the darkness and the insulating heat of his den, Frelik ruffled his head to switch watches.

Mistress watching, what torture! Ashiy thought as he crawled out and accepted Frelik's knife. The wind's cold latched onto him with fangs, and he longed for the toastiness of his den as Frelik clambered inside. He took stock of the other two reed burrows. Ziliac and Stromic were wrapped snugly within each. Intermittent gales jostled the tips of the human's dark mane. *How do men survive without fur? No chance he'll attempt something on a night frigid as this.*

Ashiy rubbed his eyes as the air stung them, still determined to stay awake. The wind was a boon in a dreadful way. Its harsh bellow, hissing through the grassland's dry reeds, cut Ashiy every few moments, providing him a focus for wakeful thoughts. *How do men stand winter without fur?* he thought again, drawing his cloak's hood over frosted ear tips. *Elves, too. To think mother's kin live in the north...*

The thought of Ceilia blotted Ashiy's thoughts with anger and doubt. Thinking of men and elves in the same line reminded him of Stromic's claim about Dusklight. The laughing wind offered no comfort against such treacherous ideas as an elf siding with mankind. Again, Ashiy recalled the night when his godmother had given her life. Had she not adeptly slain a score of rogues before her own fall? Her eyes had been afire with the violence she always taught Ashiy to avoid. *I felt her rage, somehow,* he recalled. *Through her magic. It seared.*

Ashiy wished for fire now; the wind numbed his toes. *Fire, fire, fire...*

A fire crackled before Ashiy. Turning a drowsy eye to the sky, Ashiy saw it tinged a morning red. He had fallen asleep, and once more, it seemed to last but the snap of an instant.

"I'm sorry, Ziliac, I was about to rouse you for watch—"

Ashiy's fumbled words trailed away. His blood ran colder than it had been throughout the night. Ziliac did not man the fire across from him.

A massive black bear hunched over the flames, one eye slashed blind and scarred over the lid. Upon his bent knees, reflecting the firelight, he fiddled a curved scimitar. "Quite ahright, redtail." The bear grumbled. "Yeh've done well."

-Chapter XII-
Interferers

$\mathcal{A}$ pair of shaggy wolves, gray-pelted and glowering, hunkered behind the bear's broad shoulders like furled wings. They tapped their claws upon the flats of swords with chipped blades. At once Ashiy knew the trio to be bandits, even before spying the thief brand welted onto the bear's wrist. It was in the way their eyes assessed the corners and folds of his clothing, appraising him for valuables and defenses. In Whim's Haven, Ashiy grew accustomed to such furtive, filching stares.

"We won't trouble you, if you do the same for us," Ashiy told the thieves. He mirrored the bear's nonchalant mannerisms, splaying his empty paws before the fire the newcomers had begun. "As rangers, we're bound on an errand. We aren't looking for bandits today. I thank you for the fire and can offer you some breakfast in exchange."

His thanks was not wholly genuine. The bandits dug their pit for the blaze far too shallow. A stray gust would find no trouble lighting the dry grasslands which penned them in on all horizons.

"Rangers?" One of the wolf twins exchanged a glance with his flanking brother. Their coyness had been rattled by Ashiy's calm.

The bear, however, tutted, unconvinced. "Y'ain't rangers," he said, his smile stupid but his reasoning, unfortunately, a mite wittier. "Too yung."

"We're bound on a rangers' mission," Ashiy replied, nudging the fire's kindling closer together with a twig. "As animals of Altharia, you would do well—"

The wolf twins rose to brandish their swords as Ziliac wormed free of his den and charged with his own blemished blade extended. "What's gone on here?" he snarled.

"We've got guests for breakfast, Ziliac," Ashiy said, keeping eye contact with the bear. The wolves' large leader had tensed, gripping his own pommel, but the red fox's measured calm kept him seated. "Breakfast and conversation would be best here," Ashiy told the bear. "Look at us closer. You've chosen poor marks. We've nothing of value which you could pawn."

"I like his sword," said one of the dogs squared with Ziliac, licking a crevice between snaggled teeth.

"See if you like it sunk in your belly," Ziliac replied.

"It's scrap!" Ashiy said as he stood, allowing the threateners' sword tips to angle on him, still with his own paws displayed peacefully. "I'll count to three, and we'll put all of them away. *All of us.*" Ashiy showed Ziliac a fearsome glare. "Now, one… two—"

"They might have nothing of value, but *I* do!"

Stromic fumbled free of his grass den, a terrible distraction that caused the wolves to back away, spooked. "A man!" The bear stood to his own feet, curving his scimitar toward Stromic with the shock of encountering a haunting spirit. "Stay off, man! Whut's this about?" The bear directed this accusation at Ashiy, but before he could form an explanation, Stromic cut in once more.

"Gold! Much gold as y'can carry apiece if y'three take me to the coast! What do y'say to an easy bargain?"

"Frelik! Shut him up!" Ziliac howled with a murderous look, but he was unable to turn his back on the bandits and their weaponry to strike Stromic. Ashiy, too, was pinned between the escalating groups. He felt a growing heat by his foot. But rather than glance down, he looked for Frelik. Where was the brown fox?

"Why ought'n we trust a man?" the bear asked. For all his greed, he kept wary of any hairless being. "What guld can y'promise?"

"Don't—" Ashiy saw cogs slowly shifting between the bear's tawny ears.

"He's deceiving you, fools!" Ziliac yelled.

"*Quiet,* curse-eye," one gray wolf cried. "Wur hearin' an offer—"

The canine had no chance to finish his words before Ziliac went berserk. He threw a wild onslaught of blows at his foes that they could only dodge back and away from.

Ashiy's thread of peace severed. He finally looked down and saw that a trail of fire had broken free of the pit. A second later, the kindling exploded in a torrent of sparks as Stromic hurled a hidden stone into it.

Fire needed no enchantment to devour the dry reed and grass beds. Even as Ashiy stomped several orange butts into the earth, flames strengthened by the wind formed several fortresses amid the brush. Their forces burned fast, spreading like too much ink dropped upon the center of a page. The breaking dawn was outshone by a brilliant firestorm upon the plain.

Ashiy coiled his tail around himself to keep it safe. He saw Ziliac, still a frenzied blur, driving the bandits further back with crazed swings, and they, daunted by his rage and the fire, turned to flee. Yet Ziliac caught one of the twins, raking a claw across his back, and with a yell of equal fury, his brother pivoted to defend. Both wolves, interlocked by paws, went crashing into the blackening grasses, biting and yowling death threats. Ashiy staggered forward to intercept them but found himself cordoned off by a sudden leap of orange conflagration.

Somehow, over its roar, he detected a fainter noise—that of a pained grunt and a dull thud. As Ashiy turned from the fearsome heat before him, he saw Frelik balled on the ground, just fallen. Behind him, fires flowed like two curtains closing, and Stromic could be glimpsed for a moment before their flourishes covered his escape.

"Frelik!" Ashiy rushed to the younger fox, fearing him dead. Frelik unfurled, still gasping, nursing a blow to the stomach. His den, reeds thick as a haystack and a score drier, became a sudden inferno. "C'mon! Run!" Ashiy pulled Frelik upright.

But where to flee? Fire blistered in all directions, the very ground under their feet cracking and scalding their toes. A moment more would leave them scorched pillars of ash!

Ashiy threw himself in a random direction, keeping a pincer grip on Frelik's paw as they ran through smoke that choked and burned their lungs. By luck, he had gone where the blaze spread thinly, and in another moment they were through!

Though they gulped clean air, they could not quit their race. The blare of crackling twig and chaff still filled their ears. Even when it was far behind them, they continued to hurtle on in primal fear of man's creation. They were animals panicked by the threat of fire and an acrid, agonizing death.

Water jolted the pair to their senses. They crashed into a stream by the edge of the grasslands, Frelik plowing into it on all fours as Ashiy stopped dragging him. For a moment they soothed their palpitating heartbeats, thanking the Mistress for their miraculous escape. On the horizon they saw, yet again in so many days, an arsonist's vapor rising against the sun.

"W-what happened?" Frelik asked.

"Bandits," Ashiy replied. He suppressed a white-seared bolt of anger, though it was not against those he had just named.

"Ziliac?" Frelik asked, pulling his whiskers. "Where'd he go? Did he get away?"

"We've got to go back," Ashiy said, his dripping steps taking him onto the stream's slender bank. "Just a little way, to see if we can find him."

They made a tenuous trek back into the reedlands, eyeing the dark cloud caused by their former campsite. After a few moments, they spotted a figure that swayed and faltered like the grass he stumbled through. Then the person halted for a moment, also locating the two foxes, and began a straight break toward them.

"Ziliac!" Frelik's voice flooded with relief as his friend drew nearer. "Thank the Mistress!"

"YOU FELL ASLEEP!"

Ashiy saw the outrage in Ziliac's eyes from several yards

away, tremulous as the ember trails falling from the singed edges of the wolf's ears and whiskers. Though Ashiy sidestepped to avoid his shove, Ziliac routed, seeking to fling him onto the ground. "Fell asleep! You imbecile! You-you-!"

Ashiy did not care about the wolf's limp, be it from burn or sword cut. His own anger flung out, and instead Ziliac found himself sprawled on his back. He blinked disbelief at the sky.

"Have you lost your senses?" Ashiy cried. Ziliac made a grab for his dropped blade, but Ashiy stepped on its flat. "Going to fight me now, too? That's your unfailing solution, isn't it? Attack anyone who crosses you?"

"Those were bandits, you dolt!" Ziliac seethed up at him. "You were going to let them rob us?"

"Rob us for what? *You're* the dolt!" Ashiy responded. "If you'd given me another moment and not had your sword waving at them the whole time, they'd have left us alone! They were already spooked by Stromic—"

"Yes! The man!" Ziliac's head spun, making Frelik cringe. "Escaped?"

"H-he kicked me," Frelik replied in a small voice, his ears wilting. "I-I was crawling out of my den—"

"How d'you lose a fight with someone who had only *one* good arm?" Ziliac shouted.

"Did you win your fight?" Ashiy asked, slipping his foot off the wolf's sword to check the blade for bloodstains. "What became of those other wolves?"

"Both of them and the bear made off, thanks to you!" Ziliac snapped. "Had to fight them alone! Were you both not such useless—"

"We didn't have to fight them at all, I told you!" Ashiy roared.

They continued a groundless argument that persisted until both Ashiy and Ziliac throttled their throats hoarse. Frelik, with his alone undamaged, suggested they drink from the brook and soak what parts of Ziliac were still liable to catch fire.

Ashiy deliberated a moment before following them both

again. Ziliac's behavior disgusted him, and he was beginning to formulate a grudge against Frelik's cowardice to weigh in on either side. Ashiy crossed the stream to remove himself from the duo and swigged angrily from his canteen, mirroring Ziliac's refusal to offer him even an accidental glance.

A while later, Ashiy detected Frelik's approach by the petty splashes his wading made. "Breakfast," said the younger fox, meekly extending a clay pot of cold broth swimming with raw vegetables. Despite the ordeal, Frelik had managed to retain his backpack. Though his stew, it seemed, would never be brought to a full, warm fruition.

Ashiy accepted the meal without thanks, stubbornly avoiding looking at him just in case Ziliac could be seen downstream over his shoulder. "We think the fire's burned out," Frelik said. Ashiy hazarded a peek toward the fieldlands. Indeed, the smoke had become bare wraiths now dallying in the sky. Still, he made no observation of his own. "We're going back," Frelik continued. "See if we can catch Stromic's scent trail."

Only because the younger fox sounded near tears did Ashiy shrug and reply, "Fine."

They made the trek through the grasslands in terse silence until they came to the place where the fire had smoldered down to ash. Here and there amid the char, cinders still winked. But the night's persistent wind had settled, offering the isolated coals no vehicle to fresh kindling. It was hard to identify the site of their camp, but eventually the trio discovered a place more flattened and blackened than the rest. They confirmed it by uncovering some of their old cooking pans and flintstones from the soot. All their other supplies had been consumed.

Ziliac kicked a skeleton heap of branchlets. They collapsed in a weak cloud of ash. "Can't smell anything but smoke," he muttered.

That much was true. The fire had incinerated scents just as adeptly as it had the landscape. By unspoken consent, the canids fanned out, noses ducked toward the acrid ground for any trace of their quarry.

Doubting Stromic would chance being sighted near the Great Highway, Ashiy forged his own search southward in the direction they had come. By noon, he arrived at another low, rocky hill which had broken the fire's advance. He remembered surmounting it the previous day. Here Ashiy gave his hacking throat and watery nose time to recuperate. Across the field, Frelik saw him set his rump to a large rock, and, still sniffing, worked his way over to sit beside him.

Ashiy looked to the sky. How clear it was today; a rare autumn delight when the sun could shine warm upon one's fur for the noontime spell. The morning's smoke made little lasting gain on the periwinkle stretch. Yet Ashiy wished for gray clouds that could reflect his terrible mood.

"Thank you, by the way," Frelik said.

"What?"

"You saved me." Frelik rubbed his wrists. "I'd have been a lit tinder had you not pulled me out of there. I wanted to thank you. I'm in your debt."

"It's nothing," Ashiy said. What trouble it was to keep a grudge against gratitude! "I wouldn't leave anyone behind."

Frelik watched the distance. Ziliac had become a dark speck, dipping in and out of the tides of dead grass while investigating scents. "You've got to forgive him," Frelik told Ashiy. "He didn't mean all of it."

"He can apologize himself," Ashiy replied.

"Of course, I'm not, *ah,* I'm not doing it on his behalf." Frelik paused. "He's not all wrong for being angry, either. You *did* fall asleep on your watch."

Ashiy stood up, caught. He had been attempting to stifle that nag of guilt all afternoon. "Let's keep hunting."

Frelik nodded. They both scurried up the hill. From its flat, they marked a small wood to the west. "If Stromic came this way, I'd reckon that'd be his mark," Frelik said, nodding to the trees. "Hidden from the highway."

They jaunted toward the shroud, on occasion taking moments to snort at stray stems that had been snapped, or indentations in the dirt which could be vaguely interpreted as footprints. Yet the ash left clinging to their fur and clothes infected their nostrils so badly that the foxes couldn't determine possible trails belonging to Stromic.

"I'm going to fetch Ziliac," Frelik said once they came under the wood's shade. "Maybe he's had better luck. Should we meet by the hill soon?"

Ashiy checked the sun's position. "Perhaps," he said. "We can't waste the entire day. With most of our things burned, it might be best we go back to Yarrowick."

They parted ways.

Ashiy, facing the forest, cursed. They had information from Stromic which could still be brought to Witfast, true enough, but how aggravating it was to lose the despicable rogue himself! Ashiy trooped into the wood, cutting briars aside with Frelik's knife to alleviate his frustrations. *And backtracking to Yarrowick will waste more time!* he thought, whacking a thorny vine which clung to his tail. *Who knows where else the humans have struck by now? How close to Eltcindale have they marched? This is stupid. I should go back now and—*

Ashiy's heels braked. He swiveled his face the way one does when passing a doorway too fast to catch sight of something odd in a room. There it was! Hanging off a crunched nettle bush—Stromic's telltale rank of sweat and fetid mackerel! The fox leaped onto the trail, now allowing saplings and greenery to clip him unpunished as he went. It was a fresh scent, though after a few minutes it swerved from a straightforward flight. Ashiy zagged to follow, vexed to find it intermingled with another odor.

He didn't get to the wood's cover quick enough. Ashiy inhaled dirt, so furiously he was working his nose to the earth. *Was it someone from the highway? One of the bandits from our camp? Whose trail is this?*

The theory of the bear and wolves' return did not worry Ashiy for long. An unmistakable crackle of bulk tromping foliage came to him from ahead, as did the waft of Stromic and whatever animal had chased the man. Ashiy held firm his dagger, prepared for a confrontation.

Yet at the final moment, he realized he knew the stranger's scent. It was confirmed a second later. Stromic stumbled into view, tainted by the smell of smoke. His bad arm was still pouched in a sling, but a new cloth gagged his lips. A gray foot righted the scowling man by the scruff.

Stromic's new keeper halted as they encountered Ashiy, all three of them blinking with frank disbelief.

"I think you lost this, kid," Evok the elephant said at last, making the man wince under a firm pinch.

-Chapter XIII-
A Soul's Humors

Since his first encounter with Evok, Ashiy never imagined he would be seized by a joy strong enough to want to embrace the stern, trunked warrior. Yet this happiness surged over him now, seeing the elephant with Stromic as a prize to reunify them. Were it not for the ranger's pronounced grimace, he would have succumbed to the temptation.

"You've recaptured him!" Ashiy replied, casing his knife. "And it's even better to see—"

"Ashiy!"

His spirits surmounted new heights at Ithcia's gasp. This time, he had no restraint. The elf ducked around Evok and flew at Ashiy with open arms. How close to tears he came, to feel comforting hands, so much like Ceilia's, wrap around him and squeeze his breath away. He returned Ithcia's embrace and was all questions when she pulled away. "What happened with the humans you fought? When did you get out of Whimzic?"

"Don't neglect your respect, boy," Evok growled. He took his grumpiness out on the back of Stromic's neck, throttling the man's head downward.

"Oh!" Ashiy looked to Ithcia, then began to bow.

"For goodness' sake, there's no need of that, Evok!" Ithcia replied, dusting Ashiy's sooty shoulder to summon him upright. "What on earth happened to you? Looks as if—"

"You're going to dote on him now?" Evok interrupted his companion. "After all your fits at me? As if I were the one who told him to go and antagonize those men? Where're his reprimands?"

Ashiy could have accepted all the scoldings in the world from both rangers, so he laughed, and so did Ithcia, and before they finished, even the corners of Evok's mouth lifted from an outright frown to a neutral crease. "You're a fool," Evok told Ashiy. "But no fool I'd wish to see dead. Next time, run your plan across Ithcia and me first, eh? I'll box your ears."

"Can you—" Stromic's gag slipped, "ease up? Going to tear my skin off!" He attempted to wriggle out of Evok's grasp.

"Quiet," the ranger said, readjusting the man's mouth tie. "Let's be off."

During the brief hike from the woods, Ithcia informed Ashiy of what she and Evok had been doing during their days apart.

Defeating the encamped humans unscathed, the rangers bent their efforts at once to locating Ashiy, not even waiting out the downpour which had separated them. "Had a head cold ever since," Evok added with a wet sneeze.

They assumed he survived upon finding Horely where Ashiy had stuck him. With the rain washing away scents, however, Evok had been unable to track his whereabouts or the path to Owtskirt. The rangers repositioned themselves the following day when the skies cleared. Ithcia insisted they scour the forest in fear that their young friend had managed to lose himself deeper inside it. Failing to find him, they prayed that fortune had led Ashiy to Owtskirt, where they finally headed on the third day after their separation. Only then did they discover that men had ravaged it, and Sheriff Eandu gave them Ashiy's note.

"Couldn't have included more details for us, eh?" Evok spoke up again. "Sheriff said you made off with some other 'yung-uns', but was all huffy and refused to say what for. Wasn't till I smelled your trail that I realized you'd taken a human hostage."

By now they had come to the wood's end. Evok sneezed again. It was a thunderous bellow, making both Ashiy and Ithcia jump. "Curse these grasslands!" Evok wiped his trunk on Stromic's cloak hood. "Allergies to worsen my cold!" He scowled at Ashiy. "Would you also explain why you've been making a tear through this rotten countryside instead of the road beside it? Been unable to puzzle that one!"

"Ah!" Ithcia fanned a palm over her eyes before Ashiy answered. "These must be your new packmates."

Ashiy followed her gaze. Frelik and Ziliac crested the hill where they had loosely planned to rendezvous. All of his previous ire with the duo returned. For a moment, he almost wished they had continued to search the burned field on the hill's obscured side. Then he could have departed alone with Evok and Ithcia.

Yet the pair drew near, and their shock was evident. Taking his blackened blade, Ziliac folded both paws upon its hilt to kneel. Frelik followed his companion's example, both quivering for a moment facedown before Ithcia addressed them. "What are your names, good wolf and fox?"

"Ziliacsonn of Sepplecretem," Ziliac replied, lifting his gaze. When Frelik proved too dazzled by the elf to speak, he added, "And this is Frelikitas, of the same origin." Ziliac's gaze strayed over Ashiy to fall with hatred upon Stromic. "We thank you, fair lady, for bearing this wretch back to us."

"You're most welcome," Ithcia replied. She smiled at Ashiy. "Your new friends are very polite."

Yes, impressed now, aren't you? Ashiy wanted to jeer at Ziliac's stunned expression. The wolf had never quite believed his story about journeying with an elven ranger. "I wouldn't've been able to take that cretin so far without them," Ashiy replied instead.

"And we're happy to remove him from you now," Ziliac said, turning to Evok. The ranger raised an appraising brow at him.

Then he sneezed.

"Rat it all!" Evok murmured. To Ziliac he said, "I think it better we keep him. By the highway, five mornings will see him jailed under Flintstone Fortress."

"The highway?" Ziliac said.

"Yeah! Was just asking Ashiy about that!" Evok said. "What's the idea of all this off-road hiking?"

"Well, we were afraid of disturbing travelers." Frelik almost certainly at once regretted speaking as Evok's intimidating stare settled upon him. "O-or being arrested by other rangers… for being with a human, and all."

"What?" Evok looked as though he had been told his breeches had fallen down around his ankles. "You all daft? There's not a ranger faithful enough in all Altharia to patrol the highway this far from Witfast! And anyone brave enough to ask your business you tell to mind their own! Mistress above, *that's* what's gotten you all traipsing in these hinterlands? You're lucky not to have run across bandits!"

The glare Ziliac offered Ashiy dared him to reveal that morning's antics. He gave the wolf a grin to antagonize him further. "Well, forgive our inexperience," Ziliac returned to Evok. "But this is still our quest. If you steal the man, I still expect Frelik and I to be credited with his capture."

"Steal him? Is he a fine brooch?" Evok answered, becoming very peeved. "Furthermore, he was alone when Ithcia and I chased him into these woods an hour ago. Let go of your pride, pup! This man is an enemy of Altharia. What matters is he's delivered to Witfast with all speed, not who gets the glory for it! Indeed, I will steal him from you. Might be the only way he's ensured a jail cell."

Both animals bristled, Ziliac's mismatched eyes mounting a blazing fury and Evok tensing with cold discipline, to the point where Ashiy thought the two might draw weapons on each other. He was a twinge disappointed when, after a moment of silent standoff, the defiance in Ziliac's expression extinguished and he dipped his head.

"Yessir." Ziliac responded as a soldier recognizing a superior. "I apologize. The man's charge is yours. If you would still have me, I'll do what you say to help bring him to Witfast."

Evok nodded. Then he shook all those present with another hollering sneeze. *"Ugh!"* He shook his trunk, despising every species of grass. "We get onto the road, first off!"

No more threat of ankles left twisted by hidden prairie dog burrows. No more added soreness from the raw dives and climbs of sheer inclines. No more burrs left between toes or fur and loose articles of clothing caught upon wildland fauna. As Ashiy felt the first few smoothened cobbles of Altharia's Great Highway beneath his feet, he wondered with fresh exasperation why they had avoided it for so many days. *No wonder Evok asked if we were mad,* he thought. *I may not be a crier, but on this trodden path, I'll fly!*

True to Evok's words, their enlarged group made excellent time with solid paving stones beneath them. The road stretched wide enough that the six of them—two foxes, one wolf, one elephant, one elf, and one man pulled unwillingly along—could walk side by side with ample space for oxen-driven carts to pass alongside. Purveyors of such wagons were merchants bound between towns. Near evening, Ithcia bid one of them to halt so they could purchase cured foods.

In addition to vendors in carts, the fine weather ensured the intermittent passage of other travelers making their way on hind foot and claw. All of them passed by from the north, coming from the direction Ashiy's party was destined. None overtook them from the south, a fact that satisfied Evok. He would have taken it as a sign his companions were slacking. They halted only a few times to ask passing travelers if they knew how far the way to Witfast remained. These individuals always gave short replies then returned to the road at a freshened pace, each one unnerved by either Stromic, Evok's mighty greatsword, or both. Several confirmed the canid capital was five days out.

Along the way Ashiy told his own story of events that had occurred since he had seen Evok and Ithcia last, sometimes letting Frelik fill the gaps in his memory. Certain parts he glossed over; his killing of Horely was one matter he wished in vain to forget, as well as the fiery encounter with bandits that morning.

What concerned him most was sharing the information Stromic had let slip.

Evok reacted to the news of Eltcindale's impending attack with a dismissive flicked ear and rolled eyes. "Ridiculous," he snorted. "The man's taken you in."

When Ashiy and Frelik protested, Ithcia added her own skepticism. "Eltcindale's built upon holy lands where my peoples' magic flows strongest. The queen's capital has never been taken, Ashiy, not even by felines during the year of their red ravage. This human band sounds more as if they're trying to copy Keld's failed insurrection. Just like those men, they appear to be raising corpses for their ranks. They are terrorizing the countryside at large since their numbers are too small to mount an attack anywhere greater, and they, too, will see their aims fail—not even worthy of being marked a centennial war."

"But these men have—" Ashiy paused. "Stromic claims their witch to be an elf."

"Then you need no further proof of his deceit," Evok growled. "What nonsense."

"Is it?" Ashiy asked Ithcia.

She deliberated. "My people would not align with such violence," she said at last. "My own suspicion is that this witch you mentioned is a human trying to pose as one of my kin. Keld's enchantresses were known to do the same to sway more fur-traitor animals to their side. They even wore skull-fashioned masks like the one you've described."

"But all of them were only humans in disguise?" Frelik chimed in, interested by the historic turn of the discussion. "None were elves?"

"None," Ithcia said, and for the first time Ashiy recognized an edge in her tone. "Keld's sorceresses practiced arts of fire conducted from their hands, just as all men do. Just the same as this witch who has burned every town she's come across. We elves are beings cloven from Eltcindale's trees. Fire's destruction is abhorrent to us. The essence our staffs emit is much purer."

A memory of Ashiy's rung untrue with Ithcia's words. "But Dusklight used a staff to direct the fires she made."

The elf stared at him. "That cannot be possible. Wooden staffs do not conduct flame."

"That's what I saw." Ashiy shrugged, unnerved by her sudden intensity. "Though I'm below a novice when it comes to understanding sorcery."

"Men do not practice sorcery. Their arts are of pure pyromancy." Ithcia shook her head at Ashiy's confusion. "Take my word for it, Ashiy. Fire cannot be wrought from flora. Likely, if this witch used a staff, it was one made of stone," Ithcia said. She quickly resumed speaking to divert the subject. "Furthermore, I've never heard of an elf called Dusklight. It's a name that does not strike me as elvish. More human. Some of them do take after the feline way of using words instead of sounds for naming."

"Maybe she's using a fake name," Ashiy said. "Elves sometimes do that."

Only once the reasoning had left his mouth did he realize the basis he had drawn it from. He avoided Ithcia's narrowed look.

"Of course this witch is a human!" Evok wanted an end to the debate once and for all. He clicked a nail off Stromic's head. "A prisoner will make up any number of lies to save his own skin, isn't that right, furless? Why do you think I've been keeping his babbling mouth covered? We'll find the truth when he's brought to Witfast. Lord Eckner will have wiser interrogators for him than our lot here. Ones who can debunk his smokescreens and decipher the truth."

"But suppose there *is* an elf with them?" Ashiy was too stubborn to allow the matter to rest. "Suppose, just this one time, they really do know a way to take Eltcindale? Shouldn't we at least send a crier to alert the queen?"

Ithcia took Ashiy aside with one hand around his shoulder. "Even if we could find a crier of high enough rank, the message would be met with the same response we're giving you now, Ashiy. You've spent your life in a secluded forest—you just don't understand how ludicrous the idea of Eltcindale being captured is." Ithcia lowered her voice, allowing Evok and Stromic to go on ahead so that her next words might be heard only by Ashiy, Frelik, and Ziliac. "You're underestimating that man's intelligence. Murderous though he may be, he's no fool. I think he pretended to let his plan slip."

Ashiy stewed a while longer during the walk. He hated the notion that Stromic might have pulled wool across his eyes so easily. "What do you both think?" He posed the doubt to Ziliac and Frelik.

"I'd trust an elf's assessment," Ziliac replied. It was the first thing he had said to Ashiy since their scuffle, and he remained short.

"I think they're right," Frelik said after more careful thought. "Stromic's smarter than we've owed him. He did bide his time, pretending to be weakened, trying to get at my knife. And he managed to escape us this morning."

"Then if not to attack Eltcindale," Ashiy growled, "what's their plan?"

Wrestling with nagging suspicions left Ashiy tired by evening. Nightfall did not part them far from the highway. Indeed, they found a mound of chopped firewood left at a bend where the cobbles came alongside a stream. A note upon it claimed the bundle a gift for any fellow travelers who could make use of it, for the gatherer had assembled too much and could not bear its weight for their continued trip.

The campers set about varying tasks. Frelik and Ithcia kindled the fire and began the long-awaited stew for their starved companions. Ziliac gathered sages and other requested herbs while Ashiy and Evok cleared enough ground for everyone's sleeping bags and cushioned it with fallen leaves.

When Evok dug into his massive pack, he trumpeted his snout. "Ah! How could I've forgotten?" He withdrew a second, smaller knapsack still damp from rain. Ashiy recognized the item at once, elated.

"My pack from Whimzic!" He snatched it.

"Ithcia made me lug it all this way for you," the elephant grunted. "Said it'd be a good reminder that I'd let you get lost."

"Yeah, of course." Ashiy only half-listened. Familiar spare robes, his crummy rusted knife, and a fire-starting flint were flung out in ribboning arcs. For a moment his heart skipped a painful knock, thinking he had reached the bottom without discovering the jewel of his desperate search. Then his toes curled around a hard corner of dog-eared leather.

Ashiy drew out Ceilia's diary and hugged it. To have it again was to have a tiny piece of her restored to him. He did not relinquish the precious manuscript all throughout dinner, dutifully keeping drips from Frelik and Ithcia's scrumptious veggie stew from hitting the binding.

"What's that there?' Frelik asked Ashiy, always curious about literature.

"My…mother's writings," he answered, aware that the others gathered about the fire were also taking notice. He had never told Frelik and Ziliac about Ceilia. "She was an elf. Like Ithcia."

"How does that—*what?*" Frelik's eyes widened.

"Does he look like a wretched crossbreed to you, Frelik?" Ziliac asked, licking his bowl.

"Not my mother by blood," Ashiy clarified to Frelik, flushing under his fur as he scowled at Ziliac for the jab. "My godmother, I should've said."

To Ashiy's relief, Ithcia distracted them all with a call to wash their dishes in the brook, then, as they lingered by the firelight before sleep, regaled them with a song.

"Divine heights, divine heights, eyeing sapphire sea to golden steppes, to the Leaktop of the west.

Dost thou see, dost thou see, our Mistress clad in amber cloud among the brightest stars lifted?

As she walked, as she walked, when the world, first bloomed, flowed with life under her first steps?

Newly bloomed, newly bloomed, breathing breeze, lacing

trees over formless fields which swept.

Then alone, then alone, grew her daughters, chose her bipeds, and with them dwelt a time content.

Dost she weep, dost she weep, o'heights where frosts wail and travelers' hearts scream 'turn back!'?

Come again, come again, down your slopes at the end when the age of centennials has went.

Our Mistress, dear Mistress, dwell again with your chosen, a time where all tears are spent."

Ithcia's sweet voice, coupled with crackling flames, proved a potent tonic. Yet as his companions' heads nodded low, her mournful verses stirred Ashiy's heart. With the reemergence of Ceilia's diary, so too came the forebodings which had kept him from first investigating it cover to cover. *What will I discover of her between these pages?* Ashiy massaged the volume's surface. *Who were you, Mother?* Though it hurt, he remembered the regret he'd heard in Ceilia's final words to him. *What things did you never tell me? I promised you they didn't matter, didn't I?*

Whatever secrets the book might hold, they could wait another day.

Ashiy slept in his bag that night still embracing the diary, the faint smell of his godmother's written ink pressed to his heart. It became an ingredient in his dreams, wherein he saw his lost godmother, first happy and smiling, then alight with a horrible rage. Men in dark armor swarmed her like ants to a carcass, each sent flying back with bursts of wrath. Yet they were only replaced by a dozen more until Ashiy was hacking through their midst with a kindred hatred. His godmother's eyes were consumed by it, losing their gentle serenity. Then they changed, becoming the brown, frightened eyes of Horely, and Ashiy drank blood spouting from the boy's mortal wound.

"Ah!" Ashiy thrashed himself awake with tears dampening his face.

Dawn was near. A careful glance around told Ashiy he had

not woken his compatriots. Even Stromic, who before bed had put up a ruckus against the new knots Evok had taught Ziliac to secure him with, was fast asleep.

Fearing they would be roused by the frenzied hammering in his chest, Ashiy freed himself from his clinging bag, at last leaving Ceilia's diary inside it, and sought clarity by going off to the stream. Cold water against his face calmed him, yet cleansing away the nightmare proved more difficult. Ashiy found a sloped, moss-covered stone in the shallows to sit upon. He watched faint moonlight ripple in the current that enveloped it.

"Ashiy?"

Ithcia's coo from the bank made him start—he feared it was a piece of his dream. The elf looked ethereal; a fading, moonlit phantom to be dispelled by the pink blush of dawn on the clouds. "Trouble sleeping?"

Ashiy nodded, hoping the darkness would hide his tears.

Ithcia joined him on the roomy stone.

For a while she, too, watched the stream. She did not pry.

"I dreamed about the boy," Ashiy said. "The one I…killed."

"Yes," said Ithcia. "I thought it might be that."

"How did you know?"

Despite the morning's cold, Ithcia pulled off her right glove. "You said earlier you know little about magic, Ashiy?"

"Magic?" The question threw him. "Yes, not much…she didn't use it often."

"None of my people can claim to understand it fully. Elves can use it with a staff, or, like humans with their fire, we can bring it about through our hands." Ithcia twirled her fingers, and there on her palm flickered a light. A gentle light. It resembled flame which sputtered but did not frenzy. But it could not be a flame, for fire was not sky blue in color. Ashiy felt his sorrow deepen when lost in its hue. He wept when its purple afterimage was all that remained aglow on his lids.

"W-what's happening to me?" Ashiy asked, swiping his running nose. "I shouldn't feel this way! Shouldn't I hate them?

Men? But I-I couldn't even let Eandu kill Stromic!"

"My kin believe our magic to be an essence of the Mistress herself," Ithcia continued, "an essence capable of healing and creation, or of the most rampant destruction, imparted when our soul's humors meld with hers." She shook her head at Ashiy's bewildered expression. "*Emotions*, Ashiy. They dictate what deeds sorcery can accomplish, its power, and even the color its manifestations take."

"Is that why I felt so sad just now?" Ashiy asked, still blinking aside the brief light's imprint. *And that's how I knew my mother's rage,* he thought, *the night she died?*

"When elves use magic, I feel their emotions? Just now, I felt *your* sadness?"

"My sadness, the Mistress's sadness—they're both the same." Ithcia laid her hand on his shoulder. "I'm very sorry for you, Ashiy. I'm sorry you know the guilt of taking a life. But you have to know, what you're feeling is a good thing."

"Why's that?" Ashiy made a feeble chuckle.

"Because in ages past, elves and animals alike have too often forgotten the toll that comes with extinguishing many lives." Ithcia watched a few leaves winnow by in the current. "The Mistress's essence has waned from Altharia most in times of bloodshed. Long ago, every animal, even a fox like yourself, could tap into its store. Now only elves can be conduits. Yet in warfare, even our strongest casters were unable to temper their emotions to the Mistress's own. They were severed from her completely when numbed by sorrow and grief. The Mistress hates violence, Ashiy. We ought to hate it too."

"Even against humans?"

"Indeed," Ithcia said. "They're one of the Mistress's creations too, after all, even if they forget it themselves. They used to be able to wield the Mistress's magic before they became obsessed with fire." She touched one of her keen ear tips. "They're not even so different in appearance from my people."

She picked a droplet from the end of Ashiy's whiskers. "So don't lose these tears in times to come, Ashiy. Mourn those slain by your paw. Never seek to increase their count, though occasions may come when you must again defend."

Her words were not wholly a comfort, but they strengthened Ashiy enough, and though his worries about Ceilia remained, he held confidence now that Ithcia's philosophies must have been similar to those that guided his godmother.

This world, Ashiy thought as he and Ithcia endured the cold wade back to camp. *Is it any wonder she tried to keep me from it?*

-Chapter XIV-
The Legion, the City, and the Vulpine Prince

*O*ne species of traveler missing from the road was birds. Foxes, wolves, and bears, all sauntering with walking staves, were predominant, with the occasional rarer sight of a mouse or rat. Yet the only signs of birds were the shadows cast when they passed the sun, and by the time Ashiy looked upward, distance or cloud already hid them.

On the final leg of the party's journey to Witfast, the Great Highway began to clutter with animals. So many now contended for space that the autumn air clung with an odor of mange, heat, and labor. Such a sudden influx of travelers, merchants, and envoys told Ashiy that Witfast was near, even before Evok's questioning of a tall, bat-eared fox confirmed the city would reveal itself before dusk.

On the horizon, quite suddenly, arose a gray shape, fathomless in size. Ashiy thought it to be some trick of light or cloud, yet it darkened and solidified, fingering higher into the blue heaven. *A mountain!* Ashiy thought, awed by its immensity, even at so many miles distant. He brought out his map—another treasure he was glad to have returned. *Recker's Rise? It must be. Mistress watching, if it's that big, how much taller could its cousins in the Snowline Range be?*

Soon after the mountain's appearance, a flock of robins soared over the road's bustle. So close was the current of air left by their wake, travelers on the road ducked. With their attention drawn, the redbreasts began piping their crier's message. "Hear ye, hear all now! Take heed commands from Orin, General of Flintstone, enforcing edicts from Lord Eckner!"

One of the robins, dressed in thin, yellow-striped leather, alighted near Ashiy's group, parting the throng of now attentive onlookers. His head sported a small cap, the rim adorned by one of his own plucked feathers. It had been soaked in pollen, dyed a sunny yellow like his fleet clothing. The robin righted his hat before launching into a practiced speech.

"General Orin issues forth with several battalions from Flintstone! From this noon hour, the Great Highway is to be cleared until they pass, that the soldiers might make all haste upon it!" From a small pouch by his hip, the robin withdrew a scrap of paper. Its white sheen displayed golden wax embossed by the crest of a haystack embedded with many armaments. "By decree of Lord Eckner, his seal brandished here, clear the way!"

Collective groans of confusion and vexation arose from the crowd. "Why's the army been sent about?" complained one tawny bear with an ill-shaped sack bowing his shoulders. "I've places to be!"

"Must be out to slay the humans," murmured another traveler, unseen in the crowd. His theory was debated between a chorus of other grumbling voices.

"Humans? No humans been in Altharia in a hundred years!"

"Yes 'er is, y'daft! Haven't y'heard, thu've been settin' fires in th'territory!"

"Fact, lookit that! There's one right there!"

Though his fellows had already taken wing to carry the order further down the highway, the robin who made the decree pivoted to find the source of the gasps which went up among those gathered. Already half taken-off when he wheeled, he almost crashed when he saw Stromic restrained at Evok's side. "You there!" The robin called to the elephant, readjusting his cap once more. "What's your business with that man?"

"He's a prisoner bound for Witfast," Evok responded. "A member of the marauders who burned Owtskirt, still at large."

"Not so at large anymore," the robin said, sweeping the ranger aside so that they could confer without as much eavesdropping from every ear now turned their way. Ziliac, Frelik, and Ashiy stood shoulder to shoulder to shield them and Stromic from sight. "General Orin goes now to confront several camps sighted on the territory's eastern side, by Elvanus's banks," the robin told Evok. "Reports say men have been hunkered there close to a week. If this one you have is indeed part of their number, his information would be most welcome to the Lord of Flintstone."

"That's why we're bringing him," Ithcia said, dismissing the quick bow given by the bird. "Would you send word to General Orin's detachment?"

"I'll do you one better," the robin replied. "I'll beat my wings hard and return to Witfast within the hour. Lord Eckner will prepare one of his captains to greet you. In the meantime, take my paper, seal, and scent." The bird, first rubbing one wing over it to infuse it with his smell, gave the wax-stamped parchment to Ithcia. "Continue by the highway. When you do come across Orin's forces, show it to them that you are not punished for remaining on the road."

"Many thanks," Evok said. "Your name would be good to have as well."

"It is Wexendell," replied the robin. "The general shall know me by Wex."

With that, Wex left them coughing in the dust stirred up by his wings and squinting after his form as he torpedoed northbound above the clearing highway. Ashiy and his friends abandoned curious and irked looks from the sidelined travelers as they walked on the now open path. At one junction, half an hour later, a white-eared bear hailed them. Alongside several other fellows, he stood guard over a curtained palanquin forced to stall by the roadside. "Ho there!" The bear's booming shout rang. "Didn't you hear? The highway's to be cleared!"

Evok glared. Ithcia waved the emblem Wex gave them without a pause. As they left the litter behind, Ashiy heard a snooty voice wail from beneath its canopy, "What could make them more special than I? I'm a princess! Tell them again I'm a personal guest to Lord Eckner's ball!"

Once they'd gotten past the unseen whiner, Ziliac stood

straighter as he strode beside Frelik. "This is something, isn't it? To have the road cleared for us, by royal decree?"

"Not for us," Ashiy reminded him, sidling alongside the pair. "For Witfast's soldiers."

"You're fit to spoil everything, aren't you?" Ziliac said, though not angrily. Indeed, days stretched without an apology had left Ashiy and the wolf more weary than infuriated with each other. "What do you think, Frelik? We must look like proper rangers now."

"Well, it is nice, I suppose," Frelik said. "More excitement than we've seen in a few days, for certain."

Ashiy could not disagree there. The highway's novelty had worn by the second day spent following it. He had yearned to take every dirt path they passed which branched toward hamlets and temporary camps. The unending fields, brooks, and occasional woodlands of the Canid Territory's countryside had become a monotonous landscape graying with winter's approach.

Frelik made a pink yawn. "Think we'll have a proper bed in Witfast?" he asked.

"I should hope," Ziliac said. "Then maybe you'd quit wasting yourself getting firewood we won't use." He referred to a habit Frelik had adopted since they discovered the gifted bundle of fuel. Frelik, inspired by the gesture, now rose earlier than the others each dawn so that he could collect and leave kindling for other travelers.

"Not a waste," Frelik said.

"Anyway, what'd be even better is food," Ziliac said. "Proper food. Not this grazing and leftovers from odd merchants."

"Hear, hear," Ashiy replied. "I say the only reward I'll accept from Lord Eckner is an edible one!"

Each of their stomachs then rumbled, though not for want of a meal. A thrum that shook the highway's looser stones grew in strength each passing moment. Ahead, the quake's source soon presented itself in a billow of upturned dust.

Warriors of Witfast marched in regimented lines. Poles

draped with scarlet banners rose into the air, straight as picket fence posts. All bore the fox lord's sigil—the same crest imprinted on Ithcia's paper—of the haystack serving as a sheath for many swords. These were no passing rangers, equipped with the barest essentials for battle, but foxes, wolves, bears, and the irregular elephant armored in polished plate. Ashiy marveled at the craftsmanship of the armor, all of which suited its wearers' varying sizes, dependent on species. Embossed on the breastplates, tucked on the shoulder cuffs, and burnished on the helmets, glimmered the haystack crest. At every soldier's hip bounced a straight sword, and on each of their backs, like a tortoise's hexagonal shell, was a buckler of firm wood and brass.

So determined were their looks, and the synchronized march of their steps, that Ashiy and his friends at last veered aside lest they be trampled. Their eyes smarted as sunlight gleamed off the armored warriors. Ashiy's heart swelled. Altharia will be saved. *The humans will stand no chance against these noble animals.* He felt certain of it. Yet the pang of another thought darkened his mood. *Where were these soldiers when Whimzic was burning?*

Their unlawful presence on the road had not gone unnoticed. A trio detached from the countless battalions to intercept them. These were knights of renown, their armor tinged with gold. Between the holes in their helmets where their ears poked free, a large plume curled and saluted any onlooker. The maroon fox in the center of this approaching trio touted the longest plume of all, and his aging whiskers were stiff when he barked toward them, "You'd best be those rangers Wex informed me of, else I'll have you all quartered in stocks for obstructing my soldiers!"

Ashiy noticed both Evok and Ziliac struck firmer postures. Yet Ithcia, moving with the grace of a leaf floating on an autumn wind, held forth their scented seal. "General Orin?" she asked.

"Indeed, lady of the Zenith," Orin replied, dipping his tall plume in respect. "My task, and that of my troops, lies upon our lord's east border, but I may spare some to escort you back to Witfast. Do you require us?"

Ithcia looked to Evok, who had taken to tethering Stromic to his own waist by a taut leash. "That won't be necessary, sir," Evok replied. "Go in victory. Dispatch this fiend's comrades."

"We mean to," Orin said, a hint of relish in his old smirk. "Soaravic, captain of the Flintstone Guard, is highest in command at Witfast in my stead. I have no doubt our lord will send him to meet you at the gates."

Their salutations concluded, Orin and his captains melded back into their fray of soldiers. After a few more minutes spent waiting, Ashiy and his friends watched the rear-guard pass, leaving them on an empty road in a settling smog of dust.

Witfast, the first human city freed from their harsh rule, was one of the most enduring in Altharia. Men designed it, in their age naming it Blackstone, but it had been built by generations of enslaved animals. From the mountainside's unyielding obsidian, a fortress had been chiseled around an ancient, abandoned bell tower of elven make. It had great walls, greater turrets, and a lesser throne where second sons of the old human kings lounged in regal envy. In those days, the mountain had another name than its current one of Recker's Rise. The Parted Peak, men of those faraway ages had dubbed it; a solitary outlier standing many miles apart from its even stouter Snowline backers. The rest of the men's apartments, terraces, and homesteads were set upon its gradual summit by divisions of class.

Fort Flintstone and the city at large were saved from thirst by the Mountaincut River, a mostly subterranean waterway flowing beneath its bowels. It emerged just beyond the city's mighty outer ramparts, forming a larger and more natural moat below Witfast's wide gates than any that could be dug with tools. The Great Highway fed onto an arched bridge with wooden bracers that could be collapsed against invaders in times of siege.

Ashiy trod along this overpass now, stunned in the deep shadow of the imposing city gates. The miles of houses with their fuming chimneys rose like books in a stepped stack. Fort Flintstone's parapets rested high above their thatched roofs, and the peak of Recker's Rise pillared even taller than the fortresses' looming belfry. The mountain had no equal crafted by hand or paw. Its height bisected the late eve's purplish clouds.

"Your mouth's frozen open, Ashiy," Ithcia said, amused.

"Men built this?" he asked. All he had ever known were cramped canvas tents, nailed crossbeams, and cobblestones held together with mud. He could never have imagined civilization existing on such an immense scale.

"Their imagination built this," Ithcia replied. "All but the bell tower, which was a construction of my people before men's prominence."

Ashiy gazed at the imposing spire. Even at a distance, its architecture stood apart. Where the rest of the fort had walls hewn to form sharp edges and unyielding walls, the single tower was a rounded, elegant thing, with a belfry pocketed by graceful, arched windows. Its stone, too, appeared less sable and more faded than the rest of the fort.

"If the rest is their work…how much bigger are places such as Agoroth?" Ashiy paused. "Or Eltcindale, for that matter?"

"Now you understand how foolish is the idea that such a small band of men might be able to take our capital," Ithcia replied.

"How did we ever take *this* from them?" Ashiy asked as they came off the bridge to the narrowed place which segregated the white gates.

"Oh! I've read of it!" Frelik piped up. "And of why the city is called Witfast now, and why the fox lord's sigil is a haystack—"

A great blare drowned out Frelik's excitement and forced all of them to fasten their paws over their ears. The ponderous bugle had been sounded by a vulpine knight, similar in appearance to those of Orin's forces, though his armor was far lighter. A score of other soldiers came to stop Evok, still tethered to Stromic.

At their head strode a stocky brown bear with the telltale feather between his scar-chipped ears to signify authority. As he approached, Ashiy saw an even stranger sight upon one of the bear's shoulders. A silver fox pup rode it, comfy as though the chain mail was a posh cushion for his tiny rump. His fur shimmered and shone, still young and downy, as he swayed with the bear's measured marches. He used the captain's ear as a ballast whenever he pitched. Indeed, the kit nearly toppled several times, seeming to make a game of startling his carrier, who each time splayed his paws to try to catch him.

The sight reminded Ashiy of himself with Ceilia at such a fledgling age. *That's a troublemaker there,* he thought of the pup.

"Captain Soaravic?" Evok addressed the bear, though the tilting kit distracted him as much as everyone else.

"Indeed," the beleaguered captain replied, saluting. "You're the rangers Wex told of—"

"There *it* is!" The fox pup sat upright on Soaravic's shoulder, shrieking. He jabbed a toe at Stromic, who winced and looked as though he would find no greater pleasure than to strangle the pup's boisterous throat. "Man! A man! Be lucky my father's the lord 'stead of me, man! I'd have the captain slice off those fancy fingers—"

"Silceo!" Ashiy could hear Soaravic's teeth grate. "You promised you would behave—"

"Is this?" It was rare to see Ithcia stunned. "This is one of Lord Eckner's sons?"

"This is Lord Eckner's *one* son!" the kit replied, making an astute bow and once again almost forcing Soaravic to intercept his tip toward the ground. "Prince Silceo, that's me! I've given you a bow, now you all should give me one!"

"Silceo!" Soaravic barked again.

"Oh," the prince rolled his eyes, then winked. "Give me a

bow, *please*. Especially now that I've used the right manners."

"On behalf of our lord," Soaravic told the travelers, "I've come to take the human to Fort Flintstone's cells and extend Lord Eckner's invitations. As thanks for your service, he wishes you to stay as guests and dine in the castle, until such time as your business in Witfast has concluded."

"Guests in the castle?" Frelik exclaimed.

Ashiy shared his unabashed excitement. That they might be ushered into the castle and permitted to socialize in its tapestried halls was something more extravagant than the most adventurous fantasies he had imagined while growing up.

"We're honored." Evok said. "Though I, for one, would prefer to see the man locked away in person."

"As would I," Ziliac said.

"Then you may take the man with my guards here," Soaravic replied, motioning forth a few of his knights. "They will escort him by backstreets to a more discreet entry of the fortress. We do not wish to cause a stir among the people."

With dusk approaching, they delayed no longer by the gates. Before Evok and Ziliac parted from the others with Stromic, they all heard the bellow of horns and a jarring rumble as the stone doors were barred shut for the eve. "Meet you later," Evok told Ithcia. "Should you encounter Lord Eckner, give him my regards."

It would prove to be a fair hike before Ashiy, Frelik, and Ithcia reached Fort Flintstone's courtyard gates, even going directly through Witfast's center roadway. Though fatigued from traveling tirelessly upon the highway, Ashiy found his sense of wonder was an ample distraction from it. He had never seen a place with so many animals packed in together. Even at this late hour, Witfast's pavements and alleyways were crammed. Craft makers, revelers, shopkeepers, bards, vagrants, and a menagerie of residents all moved aside only for the warble of Soaravic's trumpeter. Once the captain strode by, with the silver prince still perched on his shoulder, the crowd closed in again like cornstalks in a dense field. Silceo attracted many whoops and whispers from these onlookers. He assumed a noble air, the little pomp, blowing an occasional kiss with his eyes closed. He kept his chin lifted in a manner that would have looked regal had he been older and had his head not been overly large for his torso. With the attention he drew, Ashiy thought it no wonder that Soaravic had Stromic escorted away in secret. A human, no doubt, would have incited much horror and agitation.

"A bit overwhelming, isn't it?" Frelik said, noting the way Ashiy stuck close to him. "I think the smallest home we've passed here is twice as large as my family's back in Sepplecretem. What do people use all of that space for?"

"It must be to breathe easier off these streets," Ashiy replied, wrinkling his nose as he almost stepped in a sludge-stained gutter. *"Whew!* The smell of so many animals in one place! How do they ever get used to it?"

The stench of refuse did not linger when at last they were brought into Flintstone's first outer courtyard. As fox sentinels clanged its iron rod gates shut, the bustle of the city dampened behind the fort's barriers. In the plaza's center, surrounded by hedges, a marble statue of a tall fox stood upon a pedestal from which a thin veil of water cascaded. Standing before the fountain, Ashiy admired its workmanship—soft fur and an expression of warm valor had been hewn from cold rock.

Soaravic's bugler blew a final staccato note.

"Hooome!" Silceo droned louder. At last, with a pronounced step into thin air, he made Soaravic catch and then place him on the courtyard's well-weeded tiles.

In answer to both calls, the locks on two high wooden doors on the far side of the fountain fiddled. Each door was etched with the haystack sigil, yet only the left opened when its knob turned. Three vixens, two young and amber-coated, one older and a mixed muddy-cherry color, spilled out to intercept Silceo as he toddled forward. They were all dressed alike in simple handmaiden frocks. "To bed now, to bed, my prince," one of the amber maids said, sweeping the pup into her arms.

"I'm not tired!"

"Don't fight your mother," the cherry vixen responded to Silceo's whining. "Kurino will fix you cookies if you're not fussy."

"Fussy!" Silceo protested. "Never!"

"He certainly was at the gate," Soaravic said to the lead maid. "Did not behave as promised."

"Snitch!" Silceo shrieked at the captain. His maid tapped his snout softly. A nod from the cherry vixen sent her and the prince vanishing through the door.

Ithcia led Ashiy and Frelik to approach. The lead maid turned to them. "Our lord's guests?" the vixen asked Soaravic.

"Indeed," the captain replied. Then, with a start, as though he had long been in the practice of making only short talk with the headmistress, he turned to the weary travelers and introduced her with a slightly embarrassed flourish. "Welcomed guests, may I present to you the Lady of Flintstone, Syleah."

Ashiy and Frelik almost shattered their kneecaps, falling to kneel on the cobblestone. Ithcia was again perplexed, eyeing the vixen's patchwork garments before inclining her pointed ears to the castle's lady.

Syleah curtsied her dress's frayed hem in reply. "Please, lady of the Zenith," she said. "Your rank likely eclipses mine. And you two, rise now." The matron turned to the humbled foxes beside Ithcia. "My love, Lord Eckner, is at the moment occupied, but wishes me to welcome you. I'll show you to your quarters and have meals prepared while you freshen up. You all must be famished."

Ashiy had never felt filthier as he followed Lady Syleah through the castle's oaken doors. His pelt, lengthening now for the approaching winter, was matted with knots, dirt, and dust. There had been few opportunities to bathe while traveling, and those had been only brief dips into wild streams, or tongue grooming without soap or any other deodorant. The castle's entry hall had a long carpet embroidered with emblems of swords, fire, and smoke. Ashiy treaded lightly lest he leave dusty paw prints upon their intricate designs. Each corridor they entered was better kept than the last, arranged with tapestries, display stands, and banners that screamed at Ashiy for his invading uncleanliness.

Yet Lady Syleah spoke nothing about it to her guests, leading them forward with her maids in tow, and with Soaravic and his soldiers to provide protection. *She must smell us,* Ashiy thought, keeping a cautious eye on the swish of Syleah's tail ahead. *We reek of refuse, and heat, and campfire smog from the road. Though why's she dressed like a simple servant?* Ashiy could find no answer and would not humiliate himself further by blurting out the question. *She seems like a patient vixen, at the very least,* was his only conclusion. He suppressed a snicker. *Of course, being Prince Silceo's mother, she must have to be.*

-Chapter XV-
Rulers of Flintstone

*A*shiy sank into the porcelain basin, fitting its gentle curve as warm water soaked his fur through to the skin. A conifer scent filled his nostrils as he leaned his head back against the rim of the pool, closing his eyes for a few blissful moments. It was, far and away, the most luxurious bath he had ever indulged in.

Across the pool, Frelik undid his haphazard shirt buttons as he dipped a foot into the soapy foam. "Can't believe Ziliac's gone to visit some cold dungeon instead," he said, ripping off the rest of his clothes and sinking into the water. "What a *castle!*"

Ashiy agreed with Frelik's assessment of their housing. The bathroom was a spacious hall, joined with three separate bedrooms given to the young canids by Lady Syleah. The bathroom must have been carved from the mountainside. Its sanded rock walls on all sides were windowless, making their voices echo and giving the pool's humid fog no way to escape. "Where do you suppose all the water wells up from?" Frelik asked, creating a soapy, bubble beard under his chin.

"The Mountaincut, I'd guess," Ashiy replied. "Though I don't know how it would be so warm."

"Enchantments?" Frelik asked. "Though those bowls in the stalls are a human invention. Plumbing. It uses pipes and devices and stuff like that. I read somewhere that Flintstone is one of the few places to have it."

"If we see him again, we should tell Stromic his ancestors were masters at making devices to move dung." Ashiy elicited a chirruping laugh from his fellow fox.

They lounged in the sauna, almost losing track of time, before toweling off and retiring to their designated bedchambers. Ashiy's quarters were twice the size of his tent in Whim's Haven. On the walls hung portraits of Canid Territory countrysides, their faded paints emboldened by the simmering glow of a fire lit in the chamber's hearth. Ashiy ran a paw over the four-poster bed's silken coverlets, springing the cushion beneath. *Softer than cloud!* he marveled. *How will I not fall right through when I lay on it?*

A humble knock on the apartment's door set Ashiy re-wrapping his towel about his waist. Before twisting its knob, he caught an unfamiliar whiff through the frame's crack. It was of fur, faintly scented with chamomile, grease, and a smokiness similar to the crackling hearth. Opening the door, Ashiy found himself looking downward into a puffy face with a velvet nose. The mouse bowed, folding her pink, ovular ears. "Pardins, yun mister," she said. "Din't mind Giku. She brings him new nightclothes, by Lady Sylih's orders."

Ashiy accepted the folded items from the servant's tidy claws. Though rats had been commonplace enough in his hometown, he had never met a mouse or heard their strange, squeaking accent.

"Thank you," Ashiy told her, turning over the wine-red clothing which smelled of lemongrass. It was soft as his bedding and had a lovely sheen. "Giku, was it?"

"Yi, sir." Giku nodded. "Live inny old girments in the baths. Giku'll wash thim. Ind once drissed, Giku'll shiw the misters the dinner hall."

With a second thanks, Ashiy closed his door and slipped into the nightshirt and trousers. In one pant leg, he discovered thin stockings. He had never worn a pair before. Trying them on, he found them too tight against his digitigrade feet and almost tripped trying to walk a circle around the room. *Hope it won't be rude not to wear them,* Ashiy thought, leaving both draped neatly on his bedspread. *If Lady Syleah's going around in servant's clothing, I'd hope I'd be pardoned for leaving them off.*

Ashiy heard voices in the outside hall and opened his door

again, pleased to see all his traveling companions. Another mouse guided Evok and Ziliac down the hall as Frelik came out of his own quarters next door.

"What're you wearing?" Ziliac asked, coming to a halt.

"They're comfy!" Frelik said, lifting a leg to display his cotton stockings. He did, however, slip and slide a bit more with each step on the granite flooring.

"You look ridiculous," Ziliac replied, brushing his own stolid traveling cloak.

"They look properly regal!" Ithcia appeared from her own private bedroom down the passageway. She flowed gracefully as ever in her own cerulean nightgown, though she had put on her old gloves once again as she spun her drying hair over one shoulder. "A pair of foxes that clean up well!" She nodded to Evok and Ziliac. "You two ought to do the same. Least you both have the chance to make yourselves presentable before meeting the lady of the castle!"

"You met Lady Syleah?" Evok asked. He motioned to the mouse who was waiting dutifully as a silent watcher to their conversation. "Gillin here said the lady's overseeing our stay. Need to give her my thanks."

"And you saw Stromic to the dungeons?" Ashiy asked the ranger.

"Back to his foulest curses when we had him chained," Evok replied. "Though we'll not have to suffer hearing them any longer. He's secure in Flintstone's bowels, awaiting questioning." With another grunt, one of his paws came to rest on Ashiy's shoulder and he spoke low, for his ear alone. "Speaking of, we saw Soaravic again, and I informed him you might have information of your own to share concerning the humans you met in Whimzic. Tomorrow, or perhaps the following day, he'll receive your testimony."

"Let's be off now, boys," Ithcia interrupted with clapped hands. She motioned to the rodent pair, Giku and Gillin. "We're keeping our guides waiting."

With Evok and Ziliac promising to join once they had

washed and changed, Ashiy, Frelik, and Ithcia were led along new halls and upper landings by the squeaking servants. The higher they climbed through the spiraling stairways, the blacker the corridors' brick walls became. An abundance of lit lanterns with cross-barred panes and clawed chandeliers were required to combat a feeling of spelunking. Though the hour was late, they found the castle well-guarded. Paired fox knights stood tall with their polished helms, creating a striking contrast against the archways. More patrolled every other passage; their senses of smell sharpened for any intruder's scent amid the castle's aged must.

Soaravic too, it seemed, was not yet ready to rest, for when the mice brought the guests to the doors of a dining room, they found the captain awaiting them. "Ho!" the bear growled at the servants. "No Squeakspeak! If you've something to declare to our guests, make it known by the natural tongue."

"Ipologies, mister!" Giku said, yet still giggling to Gillin. Ashiy had not even realized their many pips and chitters were a language. The mice closed the mahogany doors behind them as Soaravic brought the guests to their seats.

Their dining room was pleasant, a simple space bisected by a long cedar table. Its waxen surface resembled a dark pond reflecting the glass chandelier glittering above. A half dozen timber pillars supported the chamber's vaulted ceiling. Carvings of tribeland animals eating, dancing, and celebrating adorned each one.

From a side door, Lady Syleah entered. Still donned in a handmaid's garb, she led a line of well-groomed mice and rats who brought domed platters to the guests as they settled into seats with padded armrests. Ashiy could smell the warmth of fresh pastries, veggie stews, baked fish, and buttered potatoes even before the gleaming lids were lifted. It took all of his restraint not to dig in at once before Lady Syleah assumed her seat at the table's head and Soaravic took vigil in the shadow of her high-backed chair.

"Once again, I'm here to offer my lord's gratitude in his

stead," the lady of Flintstone said. She extended her paws as boughs of welcome. "Dine, honored guests."

They needed no further permission. With exuberant thanks, they attacked the meals laid before them, heaping more helpings than they had eaten in an entire week on their plates.

Ashiy attempted, at first, to mirror Ithcia's polite mannerisms with her silverware. He had not grown up using such cutlery; Ceilia herself had preferred the simplicity of using her hands to dine the way most common animals used their paws. After making a few embarrassing mistakes scattering his food, Ashiy figured how to better handle his fork and spoon. It did not help that Lady Syleah's gaze seemed drawn to him each time he looked up. He tried to focus his attention on his plate, taking care to chew slower than before.

A while later, the wide doors admitted Evok and Ziliac, both looking rejuvenated in their gifted clothing. The elephant especially appeared several years younger with his gray, wrinkled skin unclogged and cleansed of dust. Though he made a mistake as Soaravic seated him. "We've an elf in our midst, captain," Evok rumbled to the bear. "Why've you given a servant the head seat?"

Frelik, seated opposite Ithcia, yelped into his goblet when her kick missed her partner under the table. "Evok!" she hissed.

"I apologize, sir elephant." Lady Syleah's eyes swiveled toward the warrior, crinkled with faint amusement. "I told Soaravic we ought to give a lady of the Zenith better respect, but he insisted the territory's vixen preside over her own castle."

It took Evok another moment to understand his folly. When he did, his waist almost tipped the table in his haste to bow and beg pardon. "Many apologies over and over, Lady Syleah," Evok said, holding his tusks for shame. "Forgive me. I'm deeply sorry. I didn't realize—"

"You're forgiven, good sir," Syleah answered. She smoothed one of the countless creases in her skirt. "It's an easy error to make. Though I do not wear these commoner's clothes as a trick, I promise. I'm much more comfortable in them, you see, and the castle's servants are more comfortable around me as well. I was one of them once, a simple cooking maid of the castle, before—" Lady Syleah paused. Ashiy caught the flush in her face through the tips of her diamond-shaped ears. "Our Lord Eckner is very kind," she finished. "If you meet him in the coming days, you may make amends by not telling him I wore these old things around guests. It would hurt him so. Please, do sit and enjoy, sir elephant."

Still abashed, Evok seated himself and ate frugal portions quietly under Ithcia's disapproving glare. For all the ruckus that the ranger had caused, however, Ashiy discovered the humble governess's eyes were still narrowed upon himself. *I'm imagining things,* he thought, picking at his scraps.

"I do hope we aren't keeping you up, Lady Syleah," Ithcia said, reposing from her own empty dish. "We would just as happily have eaten in the rooms you've given us."

Syleah shrugged. "I'm a later sleeper than my mate," she replied. "Differences of age, I suppose. Lord Eckner meant to join, but I found him asleep in his study, inkwell spilled on his whiskers. These attacks by the humans concern him deeply— he's greatly pleased to have such noble rangers capture one of their number alive."

There it was again! Ashiy looked up from his dish to find Lady Syleah's pointed stare fixed upon him. "And *you've* met some of their leaders personally?" she asked him.

Was that it? The reason for her unreadable gaze? Suspicion because he had pulled himself into a smuggling scheme with the rogues? "I met a few of them, yes," Ashiy said, daubing crumbs off his chin. "Though briefly. I survived their attack on Whim's Haven as well, my lady."

"I see," Syleah responded. "What is your name, sir fox?"

"Ashiy," he answered, feeling sick. "By shortening, that is. Full name is Ashichuaba, of Whim's Haven."

"A pirate's town, isn't that?" Soaravic spoke from Syleah's side. The lady leaned forward in further tension for an answer.

"Less so nowadays," Ashiy replied, wishing he had never

mentioned it. "There's still plenty of criminals about it, but there's a lot of decent folk making it a better place." Was he casting himself into a deeper mire? Lady Syleah's stare remained impassive as he lapsed into a disgruntled silence.

It relieved Ashiy when the servants returned to clear well-licked platters and Ithcia led them in another chorus of thanks toward Lady Syleah. "Good night to you all," the cherry vixen bid them in return.

As the cheeping Giku and Gillin led their yawning guests back through the castle to their bedrooms, Ashiy still could not shake his embarrassment over the whole meal. "Least you didn't liken the lady to a mere castle's servant," Evok told him. "For both our dignities, why don't we forget the whole event, eh?"

Ashiy slept through the following morning for the first time in as long as he could remember. The soft sheets and mattress were better than any enchantment to keep him drowsing well into the afternoon. A pounding on his door woke him. Before he unraveled himself from his covers, Ziliac and Frelik invaded his chamber.

"What fine beds, huh?" Frelik asked.

"Very comfortable, but boring to look at," Ziliac added. "Frelik and I thought you might want to join us on an exploration."

By the wolf's grim tone, Ashiy figured it had been more Frelik's inkling to extend the invitation. Both of them were dressed once more in their casual traveling tunics and breeches, now spotless. Ashiy found his own garments hung and pampered in his wardrobe, just as Giku had promised. "We're allowed to roam?" he asked as he changed.

"Your ranger friends aren't in their rooms," Ziliac said. "And when I asked that servant mouse, she told us we weren't confined, far as she knew."

"What better chance could we have to see the inside of a

royal castle?" Frelik asked, aglow with excitement. He tripped on the stockings he still wore as he paced while waiting for Ashiy to fasten his belt. "C'mon, c'mon!"

Frelik's eagerness was infectious. From Ashiy's room they set out along the passage, and from each intersecting hall chose a new direction or stairwell by the toss of a golden face from Ziliac's pocket. Daylight afforded the castle better lighting than the previous night's gloom. It filtered through several halls in a rainbow played upon the walls and floors. Looking up, the canids enjoyed many luxurious windows with colored panes arranged in the likenesses of foxes, knights, and the ever-present Witfast sigil of the stabbed haystack. They soon became lost in the maze of corridors, looping through several rooms twice over so that even their own scent trails became crossed and confused. When they came across knights who refused them entry to places such as the belfry, higher towers, and throne room, they doubled back again and again, until at last, an hour or two later, they came to a sheltered hall lined with massive tapestries that spanned from floor to ceiling.

As they turned to enter the passage, they almost trampled Prince Silceo careening in the opposite direction.

"What's the matter with you?" the tiny prince exclaimed, leaping aside so Ziliac did not trample his silvery tail.

"Didn't see you!" Ziliac replied in a tone which did not quite convey royal respect. "What's the matter with *you,* running indoors?"

"None of your beestax!" Silceo replied.

"I think you mean bees*wax,*" Frelik said.

"No, a prince means what he means, and I mean beestax!" Silceo's tiny nose lifted. "How else would queen bees pay for their hive?" Stumped for an adequate answer, none of them could stop the princeling's following tangent. "Now, I'm ordering you all, don't tell my sissy you've seen me!"

"I didn't even know Flintstone had a princess," Ashiy said.

"Well, it does! And I don't want to learn reading, or history, or counting, or none of it anymore today!" Silceo replied. "So

Silcea can shut her muzzle! I don't need to learn anything else! I know everything. Look!" The prince beckoned at the hall's intricate portraits. "I can name every one of my great grandsires here!"

"That's who these depict?" Frelik asked, rubbing his lower lip, fascinated. Indeed, every portrait displayed a fox, each one silver-furred and linked by a similar stern disposition. Frelik pointed to the nearest, a vulpine lord whose eyes, even in oils, arrested with a shocking, ice blue stare. "Can you name me him?"

"Obviously!" Silceo moaned. "That's only Lord Recker, the first fox lord. My great, great, great, grandfox. Maybe one or two more greats—I don't need to know the exact one! The whole mountain was renamed after him when he overthrew the humans living here!"

"Of course," Frelik replied, nodding. He motioned to the neighboring portrait. "And that fox, there?"

Silceo named them all, moving down the line, displaying a fantastic trove of trivia related to each former lord and lady of the castle. All of the males' names played on the strong, royalty-reserved sounds of "N," "R," and "Eck." It struck Ashiy as odd that Silceo's own name contained none of these consonantal noises, although, he supposed he had yet to hear the young prince's full-bequeathed birth name.

"He's cheating," Ziliac murmured as they neared the end of the gallery. "All of these frames are labeled."

"Shut your muzzle!" Silceo said, making an abrupt halt and pivoting as he flourished before the final painting. "And this here's father, of course."

They gave this rendition a longer observation. Lord Eckner struck a handsome figure, like his predecessors, with dark fur gilded silver, ears thick with scruffy tufts, and a thin, narrow face. Yet the painting's artist had preserved the current lord of Flintstone's features with a hint of levity, Ashiy noticed. His long whiskers were poised at a mischievous angle across dark, crafty eyes. *Perhaps Silceo inherited more of his personality from him than Lady Syleah.*

"Ta-da! The end! I know everything!" Silceo made a theatrical bow. He turned to Ashiy. "You're from a robber's town, aren't you? I know that too! I heard mother telling father!"

"What?" Ashiy's heart made a frozen dive from his chest to his innards. "When was—"

"Shh! *Shh!*" Silceo's ears perked up. The rest of the canids strained to hear soft footsteps approaching from the adjacent corridor. Then the prince scampered away, hissing over his tail, "Have to go! Remember! Shut up about me!"

Silceo's tail corkscrewed from sight the instant a new young vixen sauntered into the hall. Her delicate steps fell short of the gaping trio, paws fawning over a paisley yellow bow tied around the waist of her pearl-colored dress. The finery complemented Princess Silcea's fur. Though her rambunctious brother had inherited his paternal line's platinum luster, her coat was a mix between that of her mother, Syleah, and her father depicted in the portrait. It shone a brilliant, fiery orange.

"Oh," the vixen's voice was breathy. Her sepia eyes darted between the three strangers. All of them seemed near her age. "Who are you all?"

Frelik's mouth was open, and he produced a dry rasp not unlike the Squeakspeak spoken by the mice. Ashiy was still struck dumb by Silceo's casual confirmation that his presence displeased the castle's lady. Ziliac, after giving them both an irritated glower, dipped his ears to reassure the nervous princess. "Guests in the castle, my lady. Ziliacsonn, Frelikitas, and Ashiy." The wolf adopted a fanged smile, which, paired with his split eyes, made Silcea shyly scuttle backward. "We brought a human prisoner here yesterday, and we've become a bit lost."

"Have you seen my brother?" the princess asked. "I thought I heard his voice."

Ziliac pointed down the hall. The three stepped aside for the princess as though she were a passing explosion of flame.

"You, er, you're very graceful." Frelik suddenly found his voice, but at a higher pitch than normal. He looked fit to melt under Silcea's astonished expression. "On your stockings, I mean! N-never worn any before this, myself. Been slipping around like the floors've been iced over."

The princess twinged a smile but hid it away almost at once. "If you're all lost, just do this." Silcea's lips pursed and a sonorous whistle rose louder from her throat than any word she had yet whispered. "A servant will find you. Bye now."

With that, the princess followed after her scampering brother's scent.

"You and your ridiculous stockings." Ziliac slugged Frelik's shoulder, though his friend was too bedazzled to notice. "You're some charmer."

"I did make her smile, didn't I?" Frelik asked. "What a *princess!*"

Ashiy would have found humor in his friend's smitten grin, were he not still reeling from Silceo's revelation. He gazed up at Lord Eckner's portrait, no longer finding mischief under its gaze, but austerity and power. *Lady Syleah discussed me with him?* he thought. *Why did I ever mention Whim's Haven? I'll be lucky not to get ironed with Stromic!*

"Misters lost?"

Giku's whimpery voice made the wanderers jump. The mouse, summoned by the princess's prolonged whistle, had appeared at their tails as if delivered from the black stone's mortar joints. "Yes," Ziliac replied. "Take us to the dining hall. We've yet to eat today."

Without a word, the mouse showed them her bald tail and wove them through the corridors. She guided them to where they had dined the previous night in a fifth of the time it had taken them to become lost throughout the afternoon. Inside the dining hall, already seated and half-stuffed, Evok and Ithcia traded scones and jams.

"There you are, shut-ins," Ithcia said, holding a teacup between her fingerless mittens. "Enjoy a late sleep for a change?"

"Where've you both been?" Ashiy asked, attempting to distract his anxious thoughts.

"In the city," Evok replied. "Logging our business with the constabulary. We told them yours as well—you can thank us. And we've been securing supplies for the road. With our task completed, tomorrow we'll be heading northeast to report back to our guild."

"You're not staying just a little while longer?" Ashiy's already dampened spirits were sodden through.

Ithcia offered him a sad smile. "Rangers have no den but the road, Ashiy. Remember, we did say that once we brought you to Witfast, we'd be unable to take you back to Whim's Haven."

"I know, I know," Ashiy replied, unable to soothe his glumness with the taste of a pastry. Blueberry tart only exacerbated his sickened stomach.

"On the matter of your testimony, we spoke with Soaravic," Evok said. "Seems you'll be staying in the castle a few days longer. The captain said Lord Eckner wanted to question you personally on what you've seen."

Ashiy's claws made a rigid scrape on his table mat. It was all he could do to keep from barfing, especially when he detected an envious glance from Ziliac. *"Personally?* I know almost nothing!"

"Well, don't say *that* when you meet the territory's sovereign, kid!" Evok scratched an ear. "Tell the truth. It's bound to suffice."

"In any case, you won't meet him alone for your first time." Ithcia had a better read of Ashiy's apprehension. "That crier, Wex, was just in to inform us Lord Eckner will dine with us all tonight as a recompense for missing the previous dinner."

"I come from Whim's Haven, my lord," Ashiy told his reflection, forcing it to harden his nerves. "I believe it was— no, no, *be certain,"* the reflection scolded Ashiy. He sighed deeply and repeated himself. "On the third day of Rodent, I came across three humans in the forest—Whimzic Forest—by accident. I had a feud with this crook named Harvick."

Evok had the correct idea, Ashiy reasoned. It would not do to appear useless and fumbling when Lord Eckner requested his information. Therefore, for several hours Ashiy sat on his bed covers, rehearsing accounts to a brass-framed hand mirror he had chanced upon inside his bedtable's drawer.

But it felt wrong to label his old neighbor as no more than a criminal. Poor, feigning, and ferreting Harvick. The raccoon had given his life trying to fight on the same evening as Ceilia, had he not? "A feud with this old friend of mine," Ashiy reiterated. "Harvick was a raccoon. Not a bad one. Marked a thief, yes, but that's how most of my friends were back home…"

Ashiy rubbed an ache between his eyes, growling. It all sounded so awful. How would a lord of the territory see anything in him but a detestable lawbreaker when he spoke of other deviants with such fondness? "All right, I'll leave that part out. An—an *acquaintance* of mine, a raccoon named Harvick, stole something from me and I was trailing him that day. When I caught him, it turned out he had been going to meet with these men …"

By evening, Ashiy settled on a monologue which placed him in what he hoped to be a favorable light. It was succinct and glossed over many finer details. If questioned too closely, no doubt the entire account would fall apart. *You're going to end up in the dungeons,* Ashiy's mirror regaled him. His well-oiled words had not convinced his reflection in the slightest.

Giku's knock and scent beckoned from the closed bedroom door. Ashiy snarled an upper lip at the reflection, shined one of his incisors, and accepted his doom by answering. In a ploy to appear less scruffy and criminal, before his speeches he had spent another hour in the baths, scrubbing, cleaning, and plucking stray whiskers and hairs. Even the infernal stockings had been considered, but for a deeper sense of dignity he kept his hind feet free of them. The servants had graced him with a green robe to wear for the meal, and it far outmatched any outfit he owned. It kept him from looking like a petty street urchin, at least.

His four friends wore similar attire of greens and blues when he met them with Giku in the outside passage. Frelik had his vest buttoned improperly, and Ziliac's brighter eye clashed with his muted ensemble, but despite these flaws, Ashiy put his fear aside for a moment to admire them all. *We could pass for proper royalty in these silks,* he thought. *Only Ithcia could before. Goodness, she's a vision of the Mistress in that lilac!*

Indeed, the olive-skinned elf imitated a purple flower turned on its head in her borrowed corset, the stems of her arms wearing a new pair of slender, snowy gloves. "Ready, Ashiy?" she said, smiling. Then she nodded to Giku who ferried them off.

Their extended jaunt through the darkening castle made Ashiy realize they were not being led to the same dining room where they had eaten twice before.

"Where are we going?" Ziliac asked their rodent guide.

"Ballrim, misters," was her reply. They came to a magnificent double doorway, garrisoned on each side by foxes under the same banner as Soaravic. So immense were these bulwarks of ebony woodwork, it required a pair of these knights to move their hinges.

The hall within made the visitors gasp.

The span and splendor of the space far eclipsed that of their former dining room. Tall windows on each wall, and a roof of twinkling glass, framed the descending sun and the encroaching arc of cold, autumn constellations across a clear night sky. Where the wing did not resemble a greenhouse, its sable pillars, molding, studs, and wainscots were adorned with lines of painted gold that caught and dizzied the eye of any who strode past them. What a sight those glittering embellishments must have been when seen through the whorls of a dance! The flooring revealed the hall's purpose as a ballroom. Its smooth, hexagonal tile was whiter than any other material found throughout the dark, obsidian castle. Hammered into diamond shapes were varied inset gemstones that designated where dancers should frolic and onlookers applaud.

But on this eve, a large table with gilded edges had been moved to the center of the dance floor. One of its heavy legs had left a faint scar on the tile. A servant no doubt received a tanning for letting it drag. There were ten seats, all high-backed and gleaming from wax polish. Giku directed Ashiy and his friends to fill those on the table's left side.

"This, fir you, mister," the rodent said, sliding the first seat out with deliberate care that Ziliac should take it. Down the number she went, seating Frelik next, then Evok, then Ithcia.

"I think you've made a mistake," Ashiy told Giku. He realized, with great trembling, that his seat resided next to where Lord Eckner himself would recline. "I'm supposed to be where Evok is, wouldn't you say? Between him and Frelik?"

"Mistriss Sileah gave Giku sitting orders!" Giku replied, dusting one of the chair's manchettes impatiently.

Evok, ever an advocate for the respect owed to Ithcia, was about to butt into the argument when a muffled clarion call drew their attention toward the closed doors. They shuddered open with great effort once more. Soaravic, dressed in formal robes, emerged first through the widening crack. His soldiers broke past their captain like water rushing over a ship's prow, armored and stoic. They marched in step to the same beat. Against the ballroom's supports, their ranks formed a guard that was dozens strong.

Once each animal stood in their proper place, Soaravic's thick voice bellowed louder than the trumpet's. "The esteemed family! Radiant Princess Silcea! Revered Prince Silceo! Their illustrious mother, the lady of the Canid Territories, Syleah!"

Under their captain's rhetoric, each member of the Flintstone rulership came forth.

Princess Silcea, now in a wondrous dress of silver-striped silks, moved like foam buoyed upon gentle waves. She slipped into her chair, the third one down on the right side, causing

Frelik almost to swoon directly across from her.

Silceo moved stiffly in a well-tailored waistcoat that constrained him only because of his hatred for wearing it. He took his spot next to his sister, his usual boisterousness kept in check, no doubt, thanks to their mother's presence.

Lady Syleah had at last shed her commoner's garb for a dress shining with ruby filaments. Its beauty, however, seemed to only accentuate how simple her features were. She was not unattractive but did not convey the vision of beauty her dear daughter was already blossoming into. Ashiy guiltily thought that Lady Syleah's maid rags did indeed befit her better. She even tripped on her ornate gown's hem before reaching her chair. Ashiy turned his gaze from the lady.

His heartbeat quickened as Soaravic paused for the breath of his final herald.

"And, in his power and might, the ruler of Flintstone, Witfast, and, by heritage and noble blood right, the whole of the Canid Territory, all bow to Lord Eckner!"

-Chapter XVI-
Much Like My Old friend

*A*shiy observed the table's well-sanded grain, his heart pounding profusely as he bowed his head low toward the ballroom's splayed doors. He heard firm footsteps on tile. With them came an offbeat thud from what Ashiy assumed to be a cane.

Then there was a laugh—loud, and rapturous, and full of pleasant humor. It reminded Ashiy of a reveler back in Pelt's Tavern who had downed one ale too many. When its bouts finished echoing, a rich voice said, "My, my, Soaravic, good bear, will that be how you introduce me in a few days? Or shall my titles extend thrice as long for a gathering many times larger than those invited here?"

Across the table, Ashiy heard Silceo snicker and a whap as his mother cuffed his ear.

"I thought it good practice, my lord," Soaravic answered. "It will be the same as next week, for the sake of custom. And honor. Both mine and yours."

"Mm." A twiddle of toes drummed along a hilt. "Well, my guests, I'm no elf queen, so you may sever your fascination with the plate settings and resume your seats for an old codger."

There was a cautious shuffle around the table, but none of them sat yet.

Lord Eckner stood with sly ease about his pose. He was older in person than he'd appeared in the portrait Ashiy viewed that afternoon. The darker fur underscoring his silver tint had been grayed by time, giving his pelt, head to foot, an ashen quality. Yet age did not seem to have affected his vitality. The paw playing atop his cane moved spryly, and as the fox lord carried the cane around the table, Ashiy saw it was not a walking implement at all, but an elegant sheath. Twisted like an auger shell, its helical structure resembled a single dark vine or sapling, coiled around the long rapier it housed. In some places, the remarkable, razor-sharp blade shone through. Indeed, it could have been a living sapling freshly plucked from the soil. A few verdant leaves nestled near the pommel, and the tip was pale white like the shoots of a belowground root.

"My love." Eckner paused to peck Lady Syleah's cheek. She accepted the kiss without relaxing her posture, though her whiskers did fidget with a smile. Her lord took his seat, leaning the exquisite sheath against one armrest. He gazed up at his still-standing guests with an expression of frustrated resignation.

"Sit, my friends. Look, my own rump is comfortable."

Chairs made shallow scrapes. Ashiy could scarcely understand how his had ended up next to the fox lord. He flinched as Eckner's voice boomed out, "I mean you as well, Soaravic! Don't even think about escaping back into the hall! Your physique will withstand an indulgent meal for once."

Indeed, Soaravic had begun to retreat toward the shutting double doors, yet he huffed and turned about, taking the tenth seat at his lord's request. It was the one furthest down, but still on the side occupied by the rest of Eckner's family.

"We thank you for the honor of your presence, Lord Eckner." Ithcia leaned over so that she could speak across Ashiy. "As well as for the sanctuary and meals you have provided us this past day."

Eckner waved a dismissive paw. "Save thanks for this meal until we ensure the cooks haven't singed it. This is an experiment, of sorts. I'm having them attempt a few new recipes."

The lord clapped his paws a single time. From shadowed corners of the ballroom, passageway entries hidden in the stone walls slid open and rodents scurried out with new platters. "It's my own thanks I'm giving," the lord said as the table filled with steaming courses. "Many times over! General Orin and I were about to issue rewards to anyone who could capture humans from this rotten band alive, and here you've come and turned one over without incentive!" Eckner's ears flattened in respect toward the elf. "You are rangers, true and loyal to Altharia. As a former ranger myself, I never find it a trouble to see such citizens well-repaid."

"Well," Ithcia said, a rare flush of color infusing her cheeks, "in truth, it was Ashiy, Frelik, and Ziliac here who initially captured the man. Evok and I were escorts after the fact."

"Ashiy, eh?"

Though Ashiy had been sitting by him all this time, it was only now that Lord Eckner's gaze turned his way. The lord's dark eyes pierced, but their jolly wink melted a few worries from Ashiy's thoughts. "Well, good work, Ashiy. May the food be worth all the trouble it caused you."

The palace chefs had endeavored with every skill to make dinner a delight. Once Eckner's family chose their first picks from the mountains of platters arranged along the table, Ashiy and his companions towered their own plates. Each new dish proved more pleasing to the tongue than the last. Some of the fare Ashiy had never experienced before. He took a snaking scoop of a dish Eckner called noodles and found them particularly filling.

"An old human ingenuity," Lord Eckner explained, twirling a mouthful around his own fork so Ashiy could learn from example. "The art of noodle-making was lost in Altharia until recently, when our tinkerer found the crank machines used to ribbon the dough in an old storeroom. She mistook them at first for some sort of ancient torture device, *ha!*"

"Not an unreasonable notion, where humans are concerned," Evok snorted. The elephant had been captivated by another curling dish, this one with suckers. But it smelled too much like meat for Ashiy to chance a taste of it. "Now, my lord, if I may ask, how did you acquire this squid? It's as fresh as though it came from the shores of Hermatt!"

"Shipped up the Elvanus and then ferried back down the

Mountaincut," Eckner said. "We've got a moor running beneath Flintstone's very foundations. The freshness is owed to ice and salting, I believe. My dear wife would know better. You can thank her and our criers for the extravagant ingredients. She sought them out by sending birds out to shop in every corner of Altharia."

"A simple thing." Syleah shrugged. "When the lord of a territory commands it."

"You're too modest, dearest," Eckner said. His eyes widened. "Ah, *no!*"

Ashiy almost fell backward in his chair as the fox lord stood with a sudden change to his relaxed tone. Yet he had not barked at the stuffed zucchini Ashiy had dropped from his fork's spears, but rather at Silceo. The devious little prince eyed a fist-sized platter that had been set down near Ithcia. It was the only one still sporting its lid and Silceo half-crawled over the table to sneak a paw beneath it. He had almost popped the odd, brown square he'd retrieved into his mouth when both his father's voice and mother's paw arrested him.

"Aw, what?" Silceo asked as Syleah confiscated the morsel. He banged a tiny fist, rattling his goblet. "I ate all my vegetables! I want a sweet!"

"Not that sweet, you don't." Eckner eased back in his seat once more, now chuckling. "That one is reserved for our elven guest alone."

Her curiosity now drawn to the rounded lid, Ithcia lifted it. "What a thing to find this far from Eltcindale!" she said in amazement, holding one umber square between two fingers. "Lord Eckner, this is cocoa!"

"Chocolate?" Frelik asked, his gawking eyes for once tearing themselves off Princess Silcea. "Isn't that a poison?"

"For most animals," Lady Syleah said, glaring at her mate.

Eckner shrugged, still chuckling, a hair nervously now. "We'll inform the servers only to offer it to those who can eat it. With an elf as our guest, I couldn't resist a taste test."

"I—" Ithcia tempered her eagerness. She set the chocolate

back on its pile. "I appreciate the gesture, Lord Eckner, but your lady's concerns are true. Though we elves can indulge in such delicacies, the amount of chocolate you have here would be enough to kill half the animals at this table were they to ingest it. I wouldn't feel comfortable with that in mind."

A change came over the table, with everyone shifting as far as the boundaries of their seats allowed to be removed from the dangerous dish. Ashiy memorized the cocoa scent. Indeed, he would have found it enticing to try, given its sublime bitter-sweetness, were he not privy to the consequences.

"Well." Eckner waved a paw, the only person still with a smile. "If it's in bad taste, I apologize, Lady Ithcia. I'm glad you've caught my folly. We'll strike it from the provisions before the ball."

Ithcia replaced the silver lid, though the smell of the chocolates continued to drape uncomfortably in the air. "Ball?" she asked, trying to brighten the fallen mood. "That's the reason for all these exotic dishes?"

"Indeed, a grand celebration!" Lord Eckner said. "It isn't every season a daughter and father reach a paramount age together, now is it, Silcea?"

Silcea, whose own furtive looks up from her dainty plate had only been aimed toward Frelik, shrunk shyly against her armrest. "Sixty years lived is more impressive than fifteen, Father."

"True enough," Eckner said. "But it's rare that a father and daughter's birthdays share the same date! It's to be a magnificent ball, right here in this very chamber! I've invited families from every territory, and a great host of them have confirmed their attendance!"

"Early wishes to you both, then," Evok said, raising his ale in a toast.

"You'll be welcome to attend as well, my good elephant," replied the fox lord. He gestured widely. "All of you, for that matter. As a continued extension of my thanks."

"Well, I cannot speak for our younger friends," Itchia said, "but, with your leave, my lord, Evok and I must report back to our guild."

"Ah, commendable of you both." Eckner fished one paw into his inner breast pocket, pulling out a folded piece of parchment which he waved like a conductor. "However, you might find yourselves allowed a reprieve from your duties. You belong to the *Pinions Fleet,* do you not? That school of warriors banded near Ruvio's Crossing?"

"Your agents serve you well, Lord Eckner," replied Evok, giving a respectful glance and nod to Soaravic.

"Your guildmaster is an old friend of mine." Eckner brandished the note again. "A very dear one. This letter from me, borne by Wex's wing, should convince him to permit you to stay in Witfast another week. I hope you'll consider it. A ranger's duty is the road, I well know, but sometimes the road affords stops better experienced than shunned."

Ashiy admired Eckner's maneuvering. His smiling request, smoothly put, absolved the rangers of any consequences from accepting it. Indeed, how much more guilty would they feel at spurning one of Altharia's most powerful figures? *But why go to all the trouble of keeping them here?* Ashiy thought with a new nag of unease. *Why invite all of us to an event so grand? Surely bringing Stromic here isn't worth all of this?* Could Lord Eckner simply have a kind heart, full to overflowing like a foaming tankard? He struck the easy image of a doting host, plainly ecstatic as Ithcia and Evok accepted his invitation.

The rest of the dinner proceeded as warmly as it had begun, with Eckner coaxing a few battle stories from Soaravic, who had served as a coast watching ranger for a while, scuffling with pirates and Humanian raiders. Ashiy was interested to learn that Evok had once been a soldier of the elephant capital's admiralty. Silceo and Ziliac squabbled over the final bites of cinnamon sticks, with Lady Syleah teaching them a game they could play by revealing a set number of toes hidden behind their backs to decide who ate how many. Frelik and Silcea were in a world all unto themselves, finally putting their timidness aside to discuss several poems they'd both read by the famed Jexoc of Chitterdale, a bard who roamed Altharia in centuries past.

Yet through the merriment, stories, and games, Ashiy could not reconcile his feelings about the fox lord. Eckner was an enigma. How could one who ruled such an immense pocket of Altharia hold himself so lax and carefree? *Especially when there are humans running loose, burning his land and people?* This thought ignited a spark of annoyance inside Ashiy.

At last, Eckner brought the banquet to a close. "The hour draws late. I think we've all digested—look at my kit!"

Silceo's big eyes drooped, his head sagging back in his chair. But he jerked awake at his father's words, licking cinnamon from his mouth's corners. "I'm *not* tired!"

"Undoubtedly." Eckner nodded. "But the rest of us are."

Chair legs shifted, and the diners all rose to their feet. However, Ashiy's conflicted thoughts became a solid lump of returned anxiety when Eckner directed his sword hilt toward him like a scepter. "You, though, my boy, I would like to have a private word with." Some of the lord's mirthful tone vanished. "I should like to hear about the humans you met."

Ashiy would have very much liked to pardon himself under the pretense of sleepiness, but he nodded instead. "Of course, my lord."

"Splendid," Eckner said. His spiraled sheath made a definitive clunk on the tiles. "Come away then—we'll use the servant passages." He walked toward a far corner of the room where the rodents had appeared from before, blowing a kiss to his wife. "My love. My guests. Have a good night."

When Soaravic began to follow them, Eckner paused. "Aren't you ever sluggish after a meal? Tonight, I've no need of a bodyguard. I trust our friend Ashiy here."

Though displeased, the captain could do no more than give Ashiy a warning stare. "I swear still," Eckner chuckled, "you'd better take your duties off and properly enjoy yourself at my ball, Soaravic!"

The wall Eckner brought Ashiy to appeared seamless. A light stroke, then a push from the lord's paw, revealed a massive seam which shifted open into a narrow passage. "A neat trick, no?" Eckner said, ushering Ashiy inside. "The humans designed an anthill's worth of tunnels in the walls so that they might keep their slaves from sight. As a pup, I memorized each one."

"Very impressive," Ashiy replied. Eckner's snickering reminded him of Ziliac attempting to show off, though the lord's camaraderie was better refined.

The tunnel branched aside from a room permeated with the scents of dirty dishwater, hearth smoke, and seasoning spices. Ashiy assumed it to be the kitchens. With another imprint upon another segment of masonry, Eckner brought them into a wider, dimly lit corridor.

"We'll speak in my study," Eckner said, setting a brisk pace. "A wondrous place to unwind after a fine meal."

Ashiy nodded his assent. His dinner threatened to regurgitate as his stomach bubbled. *I'm walking alone with the lord of the Canid Territory.* The idea, which would have seemed ludicrous just a few days prior, still seemed just that. *He and I in the dark halls of Flintstone. Best prepare that story you rehearsed, Ashichuaba.*

Eckner, however, would not permit him any silent practice. He lifted his sapling-shrouded blade. "I noticed you observing my sword's sheath." Eckner still bandied a tone that almost seemed to vie for Ashiy's admiration. "Elven-work, old as the castle belfry. An heirloom of my birth line. Queen Illdari granted a similar one to each of the territorial lords." Eckner's next chuckle rang exasperated. "The best thing I've inherited, I'd say, prisoner as I am in this fortress."

Ashiy was at a loss for a proper response. He wished he had Ithcia's penchant for eloquent words. "Fort Flintstone is very magnificent, Lord Eckner."

"Ah." For the first time, the lord's expression grew dark as he gazed into the shadowed recesses of the passages. "Halls and walls."

A dilution of patrolling guards told Ashiy that they had entered a wing of the castle private to Eckner's family, or perhaps just the lord himself. They ascended a spiral stairwell that did not open onto further landings for a long stretch, climbing the looped neck of one of Flinstone's high towers. After a while, Ashiy felt dizzied when he glanced over the curved banister. "Up and up, Ashiy. Almost there now." Eckner clapped one of his shoulders with a firm paw.

A compact step ladder and unlocked hatch at the stairwell's peak revealed a chamber that smelled of lingering must, paper, and bird quills. A piled trove of parchments and books peered from racks like hoarded whiskey bottles. These slanted bookshelves nestled between silvery curtains that glittered unevenly in the sparse light of a dying hearth. Eckner began searching the many drawers of a desk that was once imposing but was now brow-beaten and ink-stained from decades of use.

"Make yourself comfortable, Ashiy," the lord said, motioning to one of the armchairs lazing before the fireplace.

Ashiy moseyed to the seat yet did not use it. Finding spare wads of messages and drafts long crumpled, Eckner kneeled and used them to nurse the dying fire. Ashiy noticed, with some alarm, that the fox lord's paws trembled handling the papers. "Would you like me to—"

"No!" Eckner's grunt flicked away Ashiy's assistance. "Sit, I say. I'll have it roaring in a moment."

It felt like a breach of etiquette to settle onto the dusty wingback before the lord, but Ashiy obliged. Indeed, even after woodchips and logs had been fed to the rejuvenated flames, Eckner appeared in no mood to sit. A nervous, uncontained energy now seized him like sparks popping from the freshened fire. He paced around his own chair opposite Ashiy, brushing its padded back with a stiff tail, running his toes along the fringes, semi-circling—doing anything but occupying it.

"Should I tell you what I've seen now?" Ashiy asked.

"That would be best."

Following a deep breath, Ashiy relayed his encounter with

Harvick's constituents. It was not the fluid recounting which he rehearsed in his bedroom. Eckner's own confounding agitation scattered the details Ashiy had tucked away. Yet he managed the gist of the story without revealing, he hoped, too much involvement on his part. Indeed, giving up his well-rehearsed words brought Ashiy's story closer to the truth. He even included his own demand that Harvick pay him ransom for the bartered swords, which he knew must make him appear to be quite the villain.

Throughout it all, even when Ashiy stumbled over his words, Eckner asked for no explanation. When Ashiy reached the end at last, coming to the night when the rogues had attacked, Eckner still spoke not a word, like a monk vowed to silence.

"We confirmed from Stromic later that the witch's name was Dusklight," Ashiy finished. "Maybe that's a name you recognize? It could be a lie on his part. Evok and Ithcia didn't trust a word he spouted about her being an elf or planning to attack Eltcindale."

"Could be a lie, indeed," Eckner murmured. His incessant pacing at last ended. He faced the fire, where he meditated on the leaping flames a moment longer, then threw himself into his chair. The gaze he had averted from Ashiy during the telling of his tale now turned, bright and broiling with an intensity that petrified the red fox. "So, you lived in Whim's Haven. It was your home all of your life? Or were you nomadic?"

"I—" Ashiy floundered, not expecting the pry into his home life. "Whim's Haven was my home, long as I can remember. Though I was never branded a thief."

Eckner disregarded this last statement, his dark eyes unblinking. Ashiy felt as though he was about to become a cigar burn on the upholstery. "Did you live there alone? Surely someone raised you. Parents?"

Ashiy had kept from mentioning Ceilia throughout his story. Even now, before a lord, his loyalty to her did not waver. "Yes. My parents, Lord Eckner. They lived there too."

"Ah, now there you fib, my friend." Eckner's whiskers hiked

over his burning eyes, becoming, for an instant, the mischievous poser in his portrait. As though a bowstring released of tension, he folded back onto his chair and chuckled to the rafters. "Your father was of the slum, yes, but not of Whim's Haven. He lived here in Witfast."

A tensile shock took hold of Ashiy and bolstered him from his chair. He was now the frenzied one as Eckner lounged.

"What?"

"You look much like my old friend Dreer." Eckner's amusement and twinge of melancholy bespoke his sincerity. "When my dear Syleah saw you properly dressed and bathed, she thought so at once. And when she told me, I knew I must see you myself. Indeed, she did not err. It's as though I'm seeing Dreer anew, as we were when we were young rapscallions together. Ashichuaba, Ashiy…that was the shortening Innaceilia gave you?"

Ashiy felt faint. His feet grew unsteady, and he set one paw upon the chair's armrest to keep himself upright. "You—you knew *Ceilia?*"

"Sit down, dear boy. There was a reason I bade you to take the chair in the first place," Eckner said. "Exhale and inhale."

Ashiy swayed back into his seat, taking the advice for a moment.

"Yes, I knew her," continued Eckner. "Although not by that shortening. Inna was another friend. She and your mother, Lavese."

These were not lies. Eckner knew the three names Ashiy thought himself the only keeper of. His mother, his father, and his beloved godmother, who had never even revealed to him her full birth name. The thunderbolt of shock departed, and Ashiy's thoughts downpoured into a river of questions that began to muddle together. "You knew them all? How? When? Why would they—where could—but if—?"

"Breathe again, my boy." Eckner silenced him with another wave. "Inna-er, *Ceilia,* told you nothing?"

"No." Ashiy felt as though he stood on the precipice of a

great chasm. Could all his childhood frustrations and desires concerning his heritage now be at an end?

"Ah, I thought not, given that you said nothing to me first." A pain came over Eckner's face, and for a single flicker of the fireplace, his age seemed to muster behind it. "More's the pity. Nothing at all? Allow me to explain, then, so that things might be clearer for you. But where to begin?"

Eckner's eyes became distant in their meditation upon the hearth's mantlepiece. "Your father will do first, I suppose. I knew Dreer best, and he knew me best in return. As I said, he was an urchin from Witfast's low slums. A very ambitious little cretin. So ambitious that, as a kit no older than five, he snuck into Flintstone by way of the servant's passages. Not for riches, or valuables, mind you, for what child that age would find worth in those? Dreer was a constant pilferer of the kitchen. And it was I who eventually caught him."

Age began to recede from Eckner's features, now aglow with mischievous memories. Ashiy, as though listening to a cunning tale devised by a bard, drank them in, still almost rasping for breath. "Ten years his senior, yet I'd never seen a kit with such gumption! Ah, I liked Dreer from the onset, and saw no point in having my crusty father emblazon his wrist with the thief's brand. Thus, I enlisted Dreer as my personal retainer. For a time, he acted the role of my glorified sparring partner, bodyguard, and all-around errand-runner. Though he promptly maneuvered his way into being more than that. A *paid* retainer, not some measly servant. And beyond that, he became my ally, my confidant, and a most dear and worthwhile friend."

Eckner's unfocused gaze settled over Ashiy without seeing him. "And my mother?" the younger fox asked.

He had meant Ceilia, yet Eckner nodded and said, "Lavese, yes. She was a hazel-pelted fox. You have her tall ears and short whiskers—about the only features not from your father. She was born in this territory to a bridge family. They sent her to spend most of her growing years in the elven region, a plan of sorts by her well-to-do parents, or so she always insinuated.

They wanted her to learn the ways of healing, that she might care for them when they became old and sickly. I believe Dreer and I were harmful but welcome influences on her when she escaped to Witfast. Well-trained with weapons as any prince and retainer ought to be, we expanded her repertoire of skills. She outclassed us with the bow and arrow. More proficient at skewering a straw dummy from a dozen yards than sewing up a bloody gouge, by far."

Ashiy flushed with admiration. Such a tantalizing snippet regarding his mother; an unknown factor which must have, by parental trait, drawn him toward archery. *Was that why Ceilia gave me a bow to begin with?* he wondered.

"And Inna, or Ceilia, of course, was our true medic," Eckner went on. "More your mother's friend than mine at first. They had been students together, and Inna came along to ensure Lavese stayed free of trouble. One of the few things she failed at, in truth. Especially once Dreer and Lavese became infatuated with each other. Forced to tag along with us, I don't believe Inna ever did cease having conniptions about Dreer and myself, even after we became allies. Thank the Mistress we did, though. Her magic saved us countless times, healing and fighting."

"Fighting?" Ashiy asked, and through his mind raced the last vision of his godmother, bathed in wrath and crimson light. "What were you fighting?"

"Goblins. Undead. Bandits. Monsters. *Ha!* What didn't we clash with?" Eckner's tail thudded a joyful beat upon his seat cushion. "But Inna told you nothing, I must remember. Such a vital piece of my life, nothing but a mystery to you." The old lord sighed, scratching his chin. "We were rangers, Ashiy. A cunning band employed for adventure. Almost a decade spent on the road and in the wilds. Golden years. We made quite a name for ourselves, we seven. *The Missables* was our guild's name. A play on what the commoners used to call me—errant prince. I think it was Dreer who pegged it. He said were we to start a guild, 'The Errant Prince and his compatriots alongside would all go missing from Witfast.'"

"And you did?" Ashiy asked, unable to help but join Eckner's hearty laugh. "Even Ceilia?"

"Well, we had to have someone mature, now, didn't we? Between your parents, the twins, and myself, only she and Sevox, our crier, were stoics. So indeed, she became a *Missable*. Had some fun at times, I believe, even if she did hate our name. Oh, the tales I could tell you, Ashiy! Of our swath cut into Wyldwood, deeper made than any explorers have gone since into the goblin realm; or of the Elvanus boat race, or our Mt. Hallow surmount, raiding bandit camps, befriending the last phoenix—"

Ashiy wanted to drink them all in too. He hung on the edge of his seat, tipped forward and frothing over with questions about every story. Yet there was one that he had to know, even if it was the tragic sum of all the wondrous adventures that dazzled before. "How did they die?"

Weight like a millstone fell upon Eckner's face, his excitement smashed in an instant. "I-I, well, even that, Inna didn't tell you?" The lord's voice faded quieter than it had been all evening. "If she didn't feel it was her place to do so…where is she now, Ashiy? Still in Whimzic? She must worry for you."

Ashiy's own head bowed. He couldn't watch the lord's sorrow increase. "Still in Whimzic, yes," he said in his own mournful whisper. "Below a delsic shoot, to fret for me no more."

The hearth burned low, and the remaining cinders received no further fuel, aching hurtful orange like the two broken hearts which pondered for a drawn, silent moment. "She did always like that invasive root," Eckner murmured. "For tea. I'd forgotten…"

"Why did she never mention you?" Ashiy asked. "Or any of this? If you were all such close friends, what happened?"

Eckner's paws wore scratches onto his felt armrests. "Death removes our family from us, dear boy, and grief can wield that same power over those still living." His voice grew anguished.

"Complications arose during Lavese's pregnancy. They were enough to weaken her so that an odd fever caught shortly after your birth took her away. Dreer was inconsolable." Eckner hesitated, hiding his long face in his paws. "He sought to smother his grief, I suppose, by throwing himself back into work as a ranger…and was killed during an exploration into Wyldwood."

"Inna and I leveled blame at each other for them both. It caused us more hurt, in the end. And I'm sorry." Eckner fidgeted, then like an untamed beast threw himself from his chair and kneeled before Ashiy with a trembling paw on his knee. "Mistress *above,* I'm sorry for it all!"

The old fox's shoulders heaved a sob, but Eckner refused tears as he looked into Ashiy's eyes. "Inna took you, and some of the blame she shoveled on me must have weighed true, for I did not look for long after she disappeared. But I swear to you now, Ashiy, you'll always have a home here, should you need it. Had things ever been different, it would have been your home already."

The lord of the territory kneeling before me. Ashiy took in Eckner's desperate gaze. Yet he felt compelled to sweep forward, steeped in his own anguish and sorrow, and tightly embrace the old ashen fox. Eckner stiffened for a moment with surprise before returning the hug just as fiercely.

-Chapter XVII-
Guests and Ambassadors

*D*espite the night's revelations, Ashiy slept through it soundly. There would be still more to hear from Eckner, and plenty left to clarify. Yet the exhaustion which had settled between them in the study, filled with mourning over the lost years that they might have shared, prompted them to leave further details for later. *Funny, that,* Ashiy mused. *To finally be able to know it all, whenever I wish. To savor it like an unopened present. Months ago, I'd have torn such an opportunity apart all at once.*

Ziliac had not slept as well. His grumpiness was exacerbated every time Fedji, their raccoon seamstress, brought a measuring line near his midriff. "I swear, I might've eaten a few crumbs of that chocolate," he growled. "Indigestion pains all night."

"Better than pins!" Frelik said, his arms and legs splayed stiff as a pole-strapped scarecrow. The cuffs and shoulders of his new robe were pinioned to his wiry frame.

"I didn't stick you a'once!" Fedji snapped at him, several sharp tacks jiving between her teeth. She was a prim ringtail, swishing about the three canids in diamond-patterned trousers and a jacket with billowy trims. "This one, on the other— *hold'a still!*"

For once, Ziliac found someone who would not be menaced by his spitting snarl. "Don't prod my belly, I'm warning you!"

"I can stick you with one a'these," Fedji brandished a needle, then tapped Ziliac's sword pommel, "before you can unsheathe this a'noxious thing in the way of my measuring tape!"

Lord Eckner had commissioned the dressy robes, first for Ashiy so that he would be fashionable for Flintstone's ball. Lady Syleah directed Giku to give him an envelope of gold and a haystack seal to take to the Savvy Silks—Fedji's tailor shop.

She designed the best formal wear in Witfast. But even with the lord's familial promises to care for him, Ashiy felt strange accepting such lavish generosity alone and included Frelik and Ziliac in the reward. He had yet to reveal to either of them his connection with Lord Eckner, if indeed he ever would.

"Hard enough, all this work less than a week a'fore the whole affair," grumbled Fedji. "You three aren't the only ones to bust through my doors demanding fine robes. Seems half Eckner's guests forgot theirs a'home. Now I've to fight one I'm dressing!"

"Lucky enough that Flintstone still has some old human gowns for me to try," Ithcia said. She had remained unusually guarded while accompanying the boys' foray into the city, speaking only to Fedji about purchasing new gloves for her collection.

"Apologies again," the seamstress told her. "I've not many clienteles with long fingers."

"I suspected so, but it never hurts to inquire," Ithcia replied.

"Can't show up in your usual tatters, Ziliac," Ashiy said as the wolf snarled again. His own fittings were already complete. The parcel he held contained a resplendent, dark robe with a felt bow tie and crimson half-cape to be drawn across the left shoulder. By luck, it contoured his form perfectly, requiring no further adjustments.

"My usual tatters are comfortable." Ziliac winced as though Fedji's next pin mortally impaled him. "Not as if I'm trying to impress a vixen the way you are, Frelik."

Frelik blushed and fell silent.

From the front of the shop, a bell's peal announced the entrance of two large bears through the front door. Fedji tsked. Her storefront sat boxed between an alley and a mint in the center of Witfast. What little space not occupied by wall-length skeins of silk, mirrors, and several looms, was a stage for mannequins in confident poses. "Be with you in a moment!" she informed the cramped newcomers over Ziliac's fidgeting shoulder.

"We can wait outdoors." Ithcia's hand took Ashiy's shoulder. She squeezed Ashiy past the bears. Outside, they watched the crowds move through the streetway for a moment. Ashiy braced himself, feeling as he used to before being interrogated by Ceilia.

"How did your private evening with Lord Eckner go?" Ithcia asked.

"I told him what I knew," Ashiy replied.

"Everything about the humans?"

As he reflected on the night, Ashiy's original purpose to inform Eckner about the marauder's activities had paled beside the importance of discovering his past. "Yes," he said. "That and more."

"How much more?" Ithcia's directness left Ashiy with an uneasy suspicion.

"What do you want to know, Ithcia?"

"You seem distracted today," she answered. "If anything happened out of the ordinary, I would hope you'd consider us friends enough to tell me."

Ashiy upturned his gaze to watch the Savvy Silks signpost sway on creaky iron ringlets. It was emblemed with a pair of raccoon tails sewn together by thread and needles. "Eckner and I may have a connection that I never knew of before."

"Ah."

Ithcia's exhale was a confirmation. "You knew, didn't you?" Ashiy's gaze switched away from the sign. "Who my godmother was? Maybe even my parents?"

"I had very good suspicions and you let some things slip," Ithcia replied. "My kindred are well-documented, Ashiy. Innaceilia was known to be one of Lord Eckner's *Missables*. Queen Illdari herself even commissioned their services once. But I didn't feel it was my place to tell you, especially in case my suspicions were false." She toyed with a loose thread on one of her fingerless mittens. "I'm sorry if you felt the opposite way. I've no idea why your godmother hid everything from you, but as a fellow sister of the Zenith, I felt honored to keep her secret.”

“You’ve nothing to apologize for,” Ashiy breathed. Saying the words brought him a sense of relief. He smiled. “I’m just glad to have everything in the light. Finally.”

“Indeed, that must be a load lifted,” Ithcia said, but her troubled expression belied words left unfinished. “I just hope it was truly Lord Eckner’s place to reveal her secrets instead.”

Ziliac, with Frelik at his tail, came storming out of Fedji’s door just then, causing its bell to prattle like mad and Ashiy to reserve further discussion with Ithcia for another time. “Finally rid of this torture!” the wolf growled. “Let’s return to Flintstone!”

They left behind the pricking at Savvy Silks to climb toward Fort Flintstone. It was a slow journey. Fanfare had increased throughout the day, with great trumpet blasts echoing by the city gates almost every passing hour. These calls summoned onlookers to their windows, roofs, and roadway gutters to welcome knightly processions, veiled litters, and opulent animals from faraway territories with wild applause, hoots, and gawking.

Lord Eckner’s ballroom guests were beginning to arrive en masse.

Though he had seen neither hide nor tail of the fox lord during his first days in Flintstone, Ashiy and Eckner now became inseparable. The lord’s current business was preparing for the upcoming festivities, which worked him into early bedtimes and made him giddy with every jaunt he took upon his twisty sword hilt. Lady Syleah, by her husband’s decrees, set the servants washing all the windows, shining every blackened floor, and festooning every wall with ribbons of scarlet, gold, and gray. Most of these labors were accomplished by night, Ashiy assumed, for he never caught, by sight or sound, a single rodent scurrying about. Indeed, Giku and her fellow maidservants only appeared to attend to the whims of the guests now beginning to overcrowd Flintstone's halls and apartments.

Over the next several days, Eckner introduced Ashiy to every one of them.

There were dignitaries from the bridge holders, families of well-established canids who collected tolls on the territory's river causeways, as well as monitored wares hastened past them. Ashiy thought them all plump in the bellies where most foxes and wolves ought to be trim, and they smelled of copper, gold, and fresh water.

Ashiy also shook paws with neighbors from across these river-segmented territories. The eldest prince, "Higher-Scale" Vondaro, presided in one wing. The mothy-brown bear's rambunctious paw shake almost dislocated Ashiy's shoulder. He struggled to imagine how much more immense Vondaro's father, the bear lord Vahanaro, had to be if he were nicknamed "Lower Scale," referring to how a scale would tip if he and his son were compared upon one. Alas, the weighty bear lord could not attend. The lighter Prince Vondaro did so in his place, so Ashiy was unable to put his wonderings to rest.

A lesser delegation of elephants had come the long distance from Hermatt. Of their group, the highest royal was the youngest Prince Deliquinn. Though near Ashiy's own age, he carried himself with the same chiseled maturity and flintiness as Evok. No less rigid was his sister Darlene, eldest of the elephant lord Darnan's line, and the only princess in their ranks. She did not bother with dresses but clad herself in plate and mail like her brother. Distinguishing them from each other would have been difficult were it not for the way Princess Darlene's valiant tusks shone a rusted red in color.

Proper advisors, landowners, and animals of rank cresting just below royalty had been sent to represent the remaining Avian and Elf territories. Memorable among them was a single elf named Heidiona, who did not strike Ashiy as motherly, but had about her an unpleasant, blossom-past-prime aroma. Eckner introduced her as a member of Queen Illdari's Eltcindale court.

Another fascinating individual, though one not of any noble

rank, was Yerrwish, the guild master of a profitable band of rangers hailing from further northwest. Ashiy smelled grains of sand in his feathers, telling him that the finch had spent time in the Casdoom Desert, even before Yerrwish let it slip that his guild was plumbing old feline ruins for wealths of rumored gold.

All of these names, families, and ambassadors brought with them an entourage of exotic advisors, bodyguards, and servants. Ashiy met a pure snowy rat with red-tinged eyes bred from the Snowline Range, and an elephant bugler who used the hollowed, ancestral horn of his forefathers as a clarion. There was a wolf with mechanical ears who had served Altharia and lost his fleshly ones during Keld's insurrection, and a host of other animals who intrigued Ashiy with their smells and clothing from the land's distant corners. To brush with them all reignited the old wayfarer's spirit inside of Ashiy, and he found a new pity for Eckner through it all. *No wonder he's excited for this ball. To have all of these Altharians gathered in one place! What difference can there be between being confined in a castle rather than a forest? Walls, like trees, must all look the same once cooped up inside them long enough.*

Lord Eckner continually astounded Ashiy by including him in these meetings. Silceo or Silcea were often hilted to their father's side like a pair of fine dagger sheathes as he made rounds greeting acquaintances. Yet Ashiy was even more present than they were, especially after the young princeling was sent off for bursting out an erroneous comment, or the demure princess excused herself after receiving extravagant birthday wishes.

"If I were some of your guests," Ashiy said to Eckner after finishing a conversation with a pair of ravens, "I'd wonder if you'd adopted me for an added red splash in your heritage, my lord."

Eckner slapped Ashiy's shoulder with a booming laugh.

"Astute, Ashiy. Indeed, you are the son of my closest friend. I'd like to believe, were Dreer with us, he would have named me your godfox long ago. With that in mind, refrain from calling me by title. Do I really appear that stuffy to you, still? Mistress above, you'll sound like all of these guests." Eckner twirled his coiled scepter-sheath, snorting. "Although, in truth, I'm using you as a shield against some of them. Silcea and Silceo will thank you—it's a practice they tire of. You see, not all of these advisors and princes are here to toast my merry health. Once the ball is over, I'll have many inescapable issues of politics to discuss with them. *Ugh!* The thought drains me."

They almost wheeled a corner, but the lord splayed a forearm to check Ashiy behind its bend. Peeking round, they spied a trio of sable foxes wearing narrow caps and making idle chat in the passage ahead. "Tax collectors." Eckner sneered with distaste. He trotted off in the opposite direction. "No doubt looking to corner me about expenditures for the ball. Even you wouldn't be enough to save me from their ire. Come, let's sneak this way. I don't believe you've seen Cutter's Undermoor, have you?"

Cutter's Undermoor, as its name suggested, was a remote dock built deep beneath Fort Flinstone's very foundations. Access to the dim cavern could be gained by way of a rickety wooden platform operated by creaking ropework, levers, and pulleys. "An elevator, it's called," Eckner told Ashiy. He nodded to the guards stationed by the cranks to lower them on the unsteady plank. "For once, not a human invention, but designed by one of my great grandfox's tinkerers. The spiraling stairwell that men once used still exists, but many backs were broken carrying imports up them. The servants are very thankful for this device."

Though sickened a bit by the elevator's heart-stopping lurches, the view Ashiy had of the Undermoor was worth its ride. Expansive docks, lit by lanterns burning from arched poles, stretched along a dark, subterranean bank. The swirling, soot-muddied reservoirs beyond them receded into a massive cavern of malformed black shapes. Standing upon the Undermoor's musty planking, Ashiy heard the mighty torrent of the rushing, unseen Mountaincut. Entombed in the rock, the sound amplified a thousand times over. Ashiy remained apprehensive that the weight of the mountain, though upheld for centuries, would first rain its spear-like stalactites, then the whole of its bulk down upon them.

"Ah! Now here's a proper hideaway," Eckner said, breathing in the air. It was very fresh, hinting at openings somewhere far up and downstream of where the waters flowed beyond sight. "None to catch us but the servants."

Indeed, many rodents labored. A proper score of flatbed carriers lined the docks, with mice and rats toting barrels, chests, and other miscellaneous cargo off of them. Most gave the important interloping foxes surprised glances and curt bows. Others were too busy to give them any response at all. Ashiy recalled that Eckner had mentioned ingredients and other goods for the jamboree would be brought by way of the Undermoor. He supposed these were the necessities being unloaded now.

Yet as Ashiy and Lord Eckner watched the drudgery unfold, the shrill blow of a horn came from an invisible sentry upstream. The winking lights of a craft's signal lanterns appeared moments later, prowling from the dark river toward the well-illuminated docks. Stacking carefully whatever wares they had been hefting, the rodents scurried to make the port ready for the incoming vessel. Their bald tails seesawed and their whispery voices Squeakspeaked orders.

"Ah, a latecomer, I suppose." Eckner squinted as the ship's lights grew larger. "Syleah did say we never received our Wyldwood plantains."

An abundant rattling at their tails warned them the elevator was hard in use. A moment later, they turned to find Captain Soaravic lowered on the trellised platform, his expression intense. He was well-armed and dressed in iron raiments, just like the half dozen Flintstone warriors at his shoulders. "My lord!" Soaravic addressed Eckner. He and his knights stepped free of the elevator's cage, which groaned with relief. "Have Wex's wings flown him with greater speed than usual?"

"What's this, captain?" Eckner held his paw against his sword's pommel. "What news did you send Wex to deliver that you could not bring yourself?"

"News of that very ship's approach, my lord," Soaravic answered, nodding to the slim prow materializing from the murkiness. "Consider its banner."

Pale light graced the single sail masted from the caravel's swooping center. Upon it fluttered a patchwork heart turned on its head and plunged through by a spike. Entrails of gold and orange wept down from its stake. "What crest is that?" Ashiy asked, filled with an icy dread as though he'd been thrown into the raging river.

"The King of Humania," Eckner replied.

His calmness perplexed Ashiy. Eckner strode toward the human vessel as it swerved to a rest. Soaravic and his bannerets were swift on their lord's tail, though none yet drew their blades, awaiting either an order or violence. Ashiy felt quite useless, with no weapon to make him even appear threatening. He followed behind them all.

The rodents reeled the boat in with hooks and tethers.

Shaven, bare-skinned faces that could only be human peered over the ship's gunwales. When at last their boat came to a steady bob, a gangplank extended. Upon it, a pair of knee-high boots with tips sharp as an elf's ear made their way between the ship deck and the dock. The man wearing them had no pitch armor or manacled gauntlets, and no sword of any kind strapped to his hip. He came in a dark tunic and breeches with elaborate frills. His eyes were a startling blue, unsusceptible to the Undermoor's gloom. The billowing plume stuck atop the wide, floppy brim of his conquistador hat was phoenix orange.

The man halted upon the moor within a few feet of lord Eckner's firm stance. A mane of windswept tangles broke free as the man swept his hat from his head and surrendered a gallant bow. "Fox Lord Eckner." His almost musical voice spoke in a rich baritone—far unlike the ruffian mannerisms Ashiy had grown used to from men. It also betrayed his age, despite the mask of his oval goatee. He sounded as though he was in the decade of his thirtieth cycle. "An honor to have you greet us on arrival."

"I worried that my invitation to Humania had gone ignored." Eckner returned a curt nod. "Who does King Hearthunder send to the festivities?"

"A most humble ambassador of his court, your lordship," replied the man. "I am Ferdinand. Though when I was last in Altharia to ply trades from Lord Darnan, your people used…I believe it is referred to as a 'shortening?' I was pleased to be called Ferd."

"Ferd? Indeed, that's a shortening," Eckner replied. "You are the one who sent my dear Syleah a flatbed of squid and crustaceans for the occasion, are you not?"

"Indeed, that was I." Ferd beamed. "Though I lament the one lost en route and hope it does not leave some of your honored guests starved for Humania's finest."

"Many thanks." Eckner's gaze made rounds of the ship's side, where several faces remained in waiting. "Who sails with you, Ferd of the Humanian courts?"

"No more than members of my own household. Consul assistants, a few attendants, and my own dear wife, Kamila." Ferd tossed a strand of hair from his brow. "If I may be so forthright, Lord Eckner, may she come ashore? Sailing has sickened her ever so much, and she, like us all, will be heartened to enter the mighty fortress where our ancestors, the Ruvios, once dwelled."

The man made a cursory glance of his own, noting the way Soaravic and his knights gripped their sword hilts. He presented naked palms. "We've all come unarmed; even our knives for cutting lines and preparing meals were thrown into the river before we came under The Parted Peak's shadow. You may scour our caravel but will find no warring weapon of any kind."

"We'll scour it well," Soaravic replied.

"With your permission now granted, of course, emissary,"

Eckner said. "And I, in return, extend you mine, Ferd of Humania. It was my hope, after all, that I might peaceably invite men into Flintstone's hallowed halls once more." He presented the ambassador with the hilt of his wood-spiraled sheath.

Ferdinand's fingers alighted for a moment on the leafy pommel, then dusted his own forehead. The Altharian custom secured a cast of protection over himself from Flintstone's lord—a gesture of trust and peace.

Eckner turned to Soaravic. "Now then, captain. Servants can see to his vessel. I would have you escort Ferd and his companions to proper quarters. Syleah should have some already set aside. Inquire of Giku. I will be along momentarily."

Hesitant though he seemed to obey the order, Soaravic did not challenge it. A thin procession of men, all of them dressed in more simple attire than Ferd, filed from the gunwale and surrendered themselves to the bear's established guard. Kamila, the first female human Ashiy had ever seen, emerged last, her mate Ferdinand guiding her by the arm. Were it not for her rounded ears and faint reek of vomit, Ashiy might have mistaken her for a very plain elf. Though green from seasickness, she still offered Lord Eckner a respectful curtsy in passing.

Once the men and Flintstone's guard had all been whisked up the protesting elevator, and Eckner and Ashiy were alone with the rodents, Ashiy at last let loose the breath he'd been holding. "You invited *humans* to your ball?"

"I invited humans to my ball." Eckner nodded. "And the precise one I desired arrived. I would thank you not to use that tone around Ambassador Ferdinand, Ashiy. Though this is the first time I've met him, word has it he is a true peacemaker between Altharia and the exiled human royalty."

"How can you trust that?"

"You're speaking as a common Altharian does, Ashiy." Eckner sighed, rubbing his sword handle. "Marauders, enslavers, and old tyrants. That is the only perception far too many of us hold about mankind. But know this principle: how we perceive something is how it will eventually manifest itself to be. If there is ever to be any lasting peace between men and animals, as there was in times past, we must change how we view them, and they must change how they view us. That's why I have brought Ferdinand here, Ashiy. I would think you have the good judgment to see he is no murderous deviant."

Indeed, the ambassador seemed a decent fellow. Yet that was not a difficult feat, considering the other men Ashiy met had committed terrible atrocities. And he well remembered that the best hoodwinkers in Whim's Haven had been the ones who could disguise their motives under a mask with no cracks.

"How is our own murderous deviant in the dungeon?" Ashiy asked, thinking of Stromic for the first time since taking company with Eckner.

"Tight-lipped," replied the fox lord. "Our jailers have been properly frustrated."

"Are we—" Ashiy paused. "Do they use torture as a way of finding information?"

"We are not savages, Ashiy," Eckner replied, though he did not lock eyes with him as he polished a scuff on his sheath. "If it comes to it, we shall have an elf use sorcery to compel him to talk."

"Sorcery can be used for such a thing?" Ashiy was intrigued.

"To certain ends," answered Eckner. "It can be used to lull a person's feelings into a blissful state where they might reveal anything when questioned."

"Why didn't you try it immediately?" Ashiy asked. "Or, I wonder, why didn't Ithcia give it a chance, with all the time we spent with Stromic on the road?"

Eckner shook his head. "Many elves consider the manipulation of another's emotions to be even more invasive than a torturous device. They would prefer the consent of those being subjected to their arts."

Ashiy offered the lord a quizzical look and Eckner waved a paw. "For example, Flintstone's bell tower hosts an old elvish spell. When Witfast's soldiers are sworn to their duties, they are baptized in the waters of the Mountaincut, which well into the structure's base. From then on, they will feel a sincere and dire tug on their hearts to defend their home whenever the warning alarm is rung. However, those who do not wish to be subject to the magic may abstain from this baptism."

"Well, I can't think Stromic will ever willingly let an elf interrogate him," Ashiy said.

"No. However, if it comes to it…that is one reason I've invited your friend Ithcia to stay here." Eckner sighed. "But on these matters, for the comfort of our invited human guests, it would be best if they did not know of Stromic's imprisonment."

"Do you think this Ambassador Ferd knows these marauders are about?" Ashiy asked.

"I hope to find out what he knows," Eckner replied. "It could prove the measure of his trustworthiness and perhaps help reveal what our prisoner refuses to." The lord rubbed his temple. "There has been word from Orin, though. Wex reported the dear general and his troops are on the homeward march. Those encampments spotted by the Elvanus were empty when they sent fresher scouts."

"So, the humans crossed the river, you think?" Ashiy replied, worried. "Toward Eltcindale?"

Eckner waved a paw. He, too, had been dismissive of the idea that a storm was heading toward Altharia's highest capital. "We've sent criers to warn the Elf Territory, but they should prove to be false alarms. Most likely, the men used the Elvanus to carry them back to sea." Eckner gave a sad shake of the head. "You shouldn't trouble yourself, my boy. Let's be off now. There are still a few furred and feathered friends I'd like to introduce you to."

Ashiy was quiet as they awaited the elevator's return. Not to trouble himself with the humans seemed like folly. The notion of Eltcindale coming under attack lingered, and despite Eckner's assurances, Ambassador Ferd was not someone Ashiy would soon trust.

Men are still the reason Ceilia isn't with us now. Ashiy snuck a glance at Eckner. The fox lord's loose disguise of cheer and unconcern had reappeared. He whistled a buoyant tune which echoed off the cavern's rough walls. *How would he perceive his guests then, if I revealed that detail to him?*

-Chapter XVIII-
Royal Ball

"Ziliac. Hello? Get up, Ziliac."

The bared yellowed fang almost made Ashiy regret shimmying the sleeping wolf's shoulder. Then a paw lashed out, clenching his vest. "Easy there," Ashiy said.

Ziliac's quartz pupil did not recognize his rouser, lost in a terror quite unbecoming to him. *"Cannottakestair…"* he murmured. The lid over his darker eye flickered, then both eyes blinked and morphed irritated. "You?"

"Still dreaming?" Ashiy pried Ziliac's grip off his chest. "Or are you ruining Fedji's handiwork for spite?"

"What do y'want?"

"Didn't think you or Frelik should miss the ball. Only an hour away. Is this all you've been doing this week? Sleeping and eating?"

"What else is there to do in a stone pen?" Ziliac answered groggily, swinging his legs free from his four-poster bed. He rubbed smooth a tangle of whiskers and fur that had been plastered at odd angles from being mushed into his pillowcases. "With Frelik constantly reading, and you—you…what's with the interest Lord Eckner's taken in you, anyway?"

"The library again—that's where Frelik is now?" Ashiy dodged Ziliac's suspicious glower. "He wasn't in his room."

"Probably studying how to ask a certain princess to dance with him." There was rare humor in Ziliac's reply, even if no grin complemented it.

"No doubt," Ashiy said, supplying a smile. "I suppose I'll hunt him down while you bathe and dress."

"Never had so many baths while doing nothing to dirty myself in between." Ziliac pulled his head free of his undershirt.

"Dressing alone won't take me long."

"Putting these on might." Ashiy stroked the golden buttons, cufflinks, and clasps adorning his robes from Savvy Silks. "Had to whistle for a rodent to help me."

"No rat's dressing me."

"Well, have it your way, but I'm not watching you struggle." Ashiy grasped the bedroom doorknob. "You might want to leave your sword behind. For once. In case you want a female yourself to dance with."

Ziliac's responding snort could have passed for a chuckle. *Mother of miracles, perhaps our mutual disdain can still thaw,* Ashiy thought as he capered through the doorway.

Anticipation for the celebration culminated in an air of excitement that filled Flintstone's dreary halls. Faint music from stringed instruments, tambourines, and flutes had contributed to this lightened mood just as much as the cleaning and decorating with ribbons, crests, and wreaths. One could follow the sound of sonnets being recited behind the doors of the grand ballroom. But since Ashiy and his friends had last feasted inside the hall, its entrance had been barred and guarded. Lady Syleah permitted no one inside to see the orchestra rehearse, or the decorations mounted. All would be revealed soon enough, and if the lady's thoroughness concerning the rest of the castle's upkeep was any sign, the ballroom would be more splendid than it had been before.

An hour before its unveiling, the music first slowed, then increased to a chanting pace until, the moment before its first revelers were to enter, the song would become a wild dash to entice them as the doors finally opened.

Dressed in Fedji's shining doublet and crimson mantle, Ashiy skipped along with the lingering beat. His path through Flintstone soon distanced him from the music. He came to a silent chamber filled with vast casings of books, parchment, and armchairs tucked in remote corners. Flintstone's library, nearly empty at this momentous hour, was far larger and better organized than Eckner's private study.

Frelik had discovered a plush couch where he could imbibe literature. It was nestled in a far corner, beneath the stained-glass form of an elf asleep over her half-written scroll. Sunlight through the windows created a warm, relaxing place for Frelik to read. A mountainous collection of volumes and documents piled around him now, his snout stuck between yet another cover as Ashiy approached.

"You're a fierce book-devourer, Frelik," he said, his tail almost toppling one stack.

"Ah, uh-huh?" Frelik replied, his furrowed gaze still on a spidery line of text.

"Ready for the ball?"

"What?" Frelik's upturned expression told Ashiy that he was still comprehending his paragraph rather than the question. "Oh, *this?*" Frelik said, displaying the cover. "Was rereading anthologies from Jexoc of Chitterdale."

"That bard Silcea enjoys, eh?" Ashiy noted that the angle of Frelik's couch afforded him a narrow portal to glimpse a blackboard between several bookshelves. Frustrated equations and spellings were scrawled over it. Ashiy smiled, certain Frelik became distracted from his studies whenever the princess was present tutoring with her mischievous sibling.

"Yes." Frelik lifted his book to hide, but Ashiy lowered it again.

"Well, c'mon, it's time to stop spying on the princess and wish her a happy birthday."

"Oh, well, I-I've been thinking," Frelik said. "Ziliac'll want to leave to register with a guild after the ball, and what better chance do I have to peruse a fox lord's library than now? So, I thought I'd just stay—"

"No, you're not going to spend the evening in this musty place." Ashiy hefted Frelik up by the armpit. "What better chance are you going to have to attend a fox lord's *ball,* Frelik? Now that's something better experienced in the fur rather than through pages, don't you think?"

"I—I—" Frelik sighed. "I suppose. That's the same thing

Ziliac would say."

"Well, he's right for once," Ashiy replied, digging away some parchments from Frelik's feet. "Think of the tale of your own you can weave! How the dapper, lowborn fox from Sepplecretem won the heart of the Flintstone princess from her suitors!"

"N-no!" Frelik's abashed frown won Ashiy a triumphant grin.

The five sojourners of the road, Ashiy, Frelik, Ziliac, Evok, and Ithcia, convened in the hall just adjacent to Flintstone's ballroom. Arrayed in their new robes, they looked just as courtly and majestic as the rest of the procession shuffling through the opened doors.

Ziliac, however, had not relinquished his burned blade. The ratty belt which kept it holstered clashed with his otherwise sleek ensemble. His dark gray doublet almost blended with his fur, and a bright white cowl draped across his left shoulder matched his brighter eye. Frelik looked better in his evergreen vest, and all the practice walking about in his prized stockings had paid off, as he moved in them unfalteringly now. Evok and Ithcia, whether by plan or incidentally, matched one another in colors of burnished orange. Evok's tuxedo fit too tight, making him look like a tick about to burst, and Ithcia wore a lengthy bronze dress which she pinched and carried by the front hems to keep it from being trampled.

Yet even with their elegant trappings, Ashiy felt outclassed by the ballroom's splendor.

Every window, wall, and surface had been polished. Reflections of animals in them gave off the illusion that three times as many partygoers had arrived for the entertainment than were present. Hundreds of golden streamers interwove across the ceiling between the glittering diamond chandeliers, creating a canopy which resembled the underbelly of a great feathered oriole. More cascaded as if molten behind a raised platform bordering the far end of the ballroom. Here a high marble table stretched. Eckner and his darling Silcea occupied its middle on a pair of velvet thrones. Spanning at their sides were the rest of the Flintstone nobility and royals brought from other territories. At its furthest end, almost shadowed by an archway, Ashiy saw a single seat given to Ambassador Ferdinand.

Large as the ballroom was, all steered clear of its floor's gemstone center. Two other areas to its left and right had been allotted to the orchestra—a band of birds, rodents, and foxes. Their combined symphony permeated the space, no matter where one stood.

Entering into all of this majesty, a fleeting thought came to Ashiy. *My, Ceilia would have hated all this pomp!*

When the ballroom at last seemed full near to bursting, Lord Eckner rose from his seat. He held his twined scepter-sheath high, its wave commanding attention. Buzz and music throughout the ballroom silenced.

Ashiy lost Ithcia and Evok in the hubbub, but by fortune he, Frelik, and Ziliac had been prodded to the edge of the sacred ring kept around the ballroom floor. For a stray moment, Eckner's roving eye locked with Ashiy's, then the lord of Flintstone smiled. He lowered his leafy hilt. His voice rumbled throughout the chamber, "Fellow Altharians, nobles, animals, and elves of class, all of you, my friends! Today is my beloved daughter's fifteenth birthday!"

Roars went up from the crowd, a band of luxurious foxes near the head table lifting hollers highest of all. Princess Silcea, with her sunset fur groomed to a soft luster, and her periwinkle gown sparkling oceanic, looked like a creation formed from heaven. She shrank beneath the weight of praise.

Her proud father went on. "A feat which she has modestly told me is far eclipsed by the age I have reached this very same day. Yes, your lord of the Canid Territory now stands before you, creaking and decrepit, at sixty. Do not hold it against me should I forget your names in passing tonight. My mind is fit for naught but cobwebs anymore!"

There were laughs as Eckner exaggerated putting weight on his scepter and curled his lip on his gums. After a moment of this charade, the lord stood straight and crackled with excitement once more. "I'll suffer speeches and toasts made in my honor later!" Eckner declared, throwing down his sheath. "Our musicians have kept me in suspense these past days, and I can bear the anticipation no longer! Tonight, we've come to dance! Dance, sing, and be merry and wild as our ancestors once were upon Altharia's open plains and unfettered skies!"

"My *dear.*" Eckner wheeled to his immediate right where Lady Syleah sat wearing a thin crown and plain yellow corset. He offered her his paw. "Tradition states that the hosts lead the rollicking! If you would have me?"

Ashiy clapped with the crowd as Syleah smiled and accepted her mate's extended limb. Though he noted the applause for her seemed much more subdued than before.

If Eckner recognized a downshift in his entourages' good will, he did not comment on it. He nodded to Silcea. "Of course, I'm not the only honoree of this ball. My dear daughter shall lead off the dance as well. But, *hmm,* she has no partner! Are there any takers for the honor?"

If Silcea had not melded with the back of her chair before, she did now under the thunderous response from foxes, wolves, and even some bears who raised their paws, vying to be selected. Under her father's shining smile, however, she rose with regal dignity, a cloud alighting from a sterling mountaintop, and the volunteers shushed. The crowd of noble foxes puffed and slicked their whiskers in suspense as the young princess left the high table's sanctuary. She graced each with a wink and bow but passed them all by.

"Ah, so she'll favor no foxes today." Ashiy heard several whispers exchanged from the crowded company at his tail. "Very wise. No doubt she discussed the matter with her father previously. She's yet too young to marry. She'll chose a wolf or bear or some other species that will mean nothing to her future ladyship." Yet Princess Silcea, with a consoling smile, continued to float along the anxious line, dismissing lean wolves, muscular bears, and pining avians. With each rejection, Ashiy's own heart swelled in anticipation as the dreamy princess sidled nearer, feeling a leap of hope to be chosen.

Instead, she halted beside Ashiy and focused her gaze on the other fox tensed beside him. Frelik was petrified. The rest of the room, too, quieted, speechless.

Smacking his friend's shoulder, Ziliac said, "She wants your paw, lunkhead."

Frelik stuck forth a rigid arm. Curtsying, and with her ears growing pink, Silcea took it. A booming chuckle rose from Eckner, now waiting with Lady Syleah at the ballroom's center. "He looks a stout lad, doesn't he? Well chosen, my star!"

The lord's applause encouraged some from the guests, though many of the jilted foxes near the royal table knocked their paws together only once. Silcea led a dazed Frelik to stand beside her parents. "Who's that?" Ashiy heard the murmurs starting up once more. "A son of a bridge family? What house? I don't recognize him." Ashiy found himself sharing a dumbstruck grin with Ziliac. They jested about it, yes, but never truly expected such a scenario as the one that had just transpired.

"Look at his face!" Ziliac bellowed laughter that was thankfully dampened by the orchestra's sudden upbeat. Silcea and Frelik, paws entwined, began to sidestep, jig, and pirouette, the princess leading. "Like he's been told to go a bout with a ten-foot troll! Hoo-*oo,* didn't think his eyes could get that large!"

The lord and lady of the festivities were adept distractions from Frelik's bumbling motions. Eckner and Syleah demonstrated a liveliness, intricacy, and intimacy to their movements with the stately sweep of the orchestra, suggesting they had rehearsed together many times prior. Their eyes remained locked, parting for the briefest dashes during a spin or low swoop. When the song ended on a triumphant chord, Syleah spooned to Eckner's chest and they gave the applauding crowd a joint bow.

Frelik seemed ready to pull away, but Silcea held him fast. A new song began, played by bombastic fiddles worming a breakneck pace. With whoops and hollers, paired animals flooded the dance floor, obscuring the leaders from sight in a hopping, pinwheeling herd. Ashiy felt a nudge at his own shoulder.

"Care to lead, spiffy fox?" Ithcia smiled, her lace fingers inviting him.

"Will I!" Ashiy replied, taking them. The melody was reminiscent of banshee fiddling he had heard growing up in the Haven. With Ithcia on one arm, he entered the onslaught of fanning gowns and limbs and devoted every sense to the music's thrall. The world became a whorl of fellow puppets spellbound to rhythm, then the archways, then Ithcia's beaming features, then the other wall, then the shimmering streamers, and then back around again and again and again. A single song morphed into a second, then beyond that a third, and a fourth.

Then, as if sensing the need for a reprieve, the orchestra's chickadee conductor led a more downbeat song. Ashiy, breathless from exertion, allowed Ithcia to lead him from the center floor. "Thank you," she told him, not even panting. "You're not half bad."

"Same yourself," Ashiy said, vaguely remembering Ithcia's gown blooming like a petalled flower. "Hope Evok won't be jealous."

"That lug said earlier this morning, and I quote," Ithcia deepened her voice and spouted one finger over her nose's tip to mimic a trunk. *"'You won't catch me ripping this constricting serpent of a suit for a hundred animals to see!'"* She sighed. "The numb oaf. I suppose I ought to find him and still try to coax him onto the floor. He's currently giving respects to his brethren from Hermatt, no doubt."

With another thankful smile, Ithcia wove into the party. Ashiy, still struck for breath and now thirsty, looked around for a glimpse of his other companions. Frelik and Silcea were missing from the dance floor. Lady Syleah had reacquainted herself with her seat behind the high table. Lord Eckner lingered nearby, caught by a wide circle of officials in a conversation he looked in need of rescue from, but Ashiy decided he would leave that job to Silceo.

"Biviridge, sir?" A passing mouse in a bowtie toted a platter of precarious teardrop glasses.

"Thanks." The pulpy drink refreshed Ashiy, even if he did not recognize the fruit. Dozens more rodent servants bobbed through the crowd as he continued to scan it. They materialized from the walls' hidden gateways, exchanging plates. Upon these were samplers of the meals Eckner had boasted of the night Ashiy met him. Noodles were slurped. Squid was being requested over and over by the elephant prince and princess. Eckner had apparently been unable to resist his more daring temptations as well, for Ashiy saw one servant bequeath a tiny dish to Ambassador Ferd in his corner. He shuddered to see the man chow down several deadly chocolate parcels with relish.

Against his better judgment, Ashiy abandoned his search for his friends and made a cautious trek toward the human. That end of the room was far more breathable. The five-fingered emissary and his assistants were being given a wide berth.

"Ambassador Ferd?" Ashiy hoped he gave the proper address.

The man looked up from his cocoa and Ashiy smelled the sweet poison on his lips before Ferd's handkerchief daubed them. "Ah, good to see you, friend," said the emissary. "You were there at the Undermoor to greet us, were you not? I don't believe I learned your name."

"Ashiy. I'm a friend of Eckner's."

"Very good, very good. How might I be of service to you, Ashiy?"

Ferd replaced the lid of his chocolate platter and slid it aside. Had the ambassador noticed the unease with which the fox had viewed it?

Ashiy's tongue went powder dry. What had he been thinking to say to the man in the first place? A grievance about his people's rampage? An accusation about what motives had brought him to Witfast? *Your people killed my mother,* Ashiy thought. Yet he could not say that to the eager, inviting face flickering with a hint of uncertainty before him.

"Is it nice to see the inside of Fort Flintstone?"

Ferd's expression wavered, perhaps trying to discern Ashiy's own motive for posing the question. Ashiy had none, aside from his need to break the odd silence. "It's a *great* honor," Ferd replied, "to be able to walk the halls where my kin dwelled centuries ago. There's no other feeling I can liken it to."

The odd silence lingered, despite Ashiy's effort.

"I want to thank you, Ashiy," Ambassador Ferd said. "I see plainly that you are discomforted by my presence. Perhaps you've known only bards' yarns about my people's wickedness. Yet you, young lad, are the first to approach, aside from Lord Eckner and a few obligatory nobles. I hope, one day, courage like yours might mend the divide between animals and mankind."

Ferd extended a hand. Ashiy took it. They shook, human fingers and fox toes.

"Well, you might make a better impression if you took part in the festivities," Ashiy said, inclining to the dance floor. "Rather than skulking here."

"Perhaps." Ferd's mustache twitched into a smile. "Alas, my lady wife remains ill from travel, and I'm unsure that any animal present would be my partner."

"Ask Ithcia," Ashiy said, "if you see her. She's an elf, looking for people to dance with her."

"Very good, then! Thanks for the suggestion, Ashiy."

Happy to be excused by Ferd's nod, Ashiy drifted away from the high table. His resumed search for his friends brought him briefly past Lord Eckner. The fox lord was still engaged with other guests, but a catch between their eyes told Ashiy he had been observing the exchange with Ferd from afar. His imparting smile was very proud, indeed.

At last, Ashiy spied Ziliac braced against a far pillar and

hurried toward him. Frelik crouched beside him as though fighting a stomachache. Ziliac nodded at Ashiy's approach, sipping from a glass of his own.

"What's going on here?" Ashiy asked.

"I don't think she was supposed to do that." Frelik's legs shook. "The princess, I think she insulted all of those foxes. They've been scowling at me since we quit dancing."

Ashiy investigated the posse of vulpine gallantry with a glance. Indeed, they had become a distinguished battalion of animosity glowering in their direction from across the ballroom.

"Those prissy prats?" Ziliac fondled his sword hilt. With a fearsome smile, he lifted his glass in a toast toward the smoldering pack. "Looks as if the whole lot's never grasped a sword in their lives. Don't you worry, Frelik, I'll protect you."

"Are you saying you'd rather Silcea hadn't danced with you?" Ashiy asked.

"Or pecked you on the cheek when you finished?" Ziliac added.

"Yes!" Ashiy said, exuberant to hear this missed detail. "Is that what you're saying, Frelik?"

Frelik rubbed the phantom spot where Silcea's lips had touched below his right whiskers. "No," he finally responded, rising slowly into a proper posture. "No. It was worth it all."

The three of them dissolved into backslapping laughter.

Once they were through, Ziliac drained his beverage and looked about for a rodent to collect the emptied snifter. There were few to be seen now, even as the music's swell brought waves of dancers back to the center of the room.

Ashiy's left ear fidgeted.

Over the thudding of feet on the jeweled dance floor, and orchestra's jovial tones, he caught a sharper, metallic sound.

"We ought to find you someone to lollop with next," Frelik told Ziliac now.

The wolf snorted, still irked to find no bearer for his dirtied glass. "Not a chance. My dates are with more of these drinks. I'll make myself too stuffed to—to—what's that *clamor?*"

Ziliac's triangular ears righted and swiveled toward the far end of the hall, where the ballroom's mighty doors stood shut. More clanks and scrapes resounded from behind them, growing louder alongside shouts that were far from merry. A second before Ashiy identified the sounds of clashing blades and wounded combatants, the great doors shook. Dust fell from their colossal hinges just before both were pounded open.

Through their breach, a horde of men poured into the varnished ballroom.

-Chapter XIX-
The Second Offense

*O*verhead, the crystal chandeliers vibrated with the noise of a thousand shattered icicles, then were drowned out by the screams of dancers becoming refugees against the walls.

A familiar nightmare unfurled before Ashiy, of men clad in tar-pitch armor and wielding wicked broadswords. They forced their way into the immaculate ballroom, staining its floors with bloodied footprints, cursing, and brandishing soiled blades at the few who remained nearby.

Their reek confirmed the invaders as no hellish hallucination. A putrid smell made Ashiy gag. Indeed, it choked most of the room, expunging all former aromas of feast. For the men in the first wave were not dressed in plate nor clutching weapons. In tattered rags, with clawing stone-gray hands, they lumbered forward with unsteady strides, eyes possessed of a harsh red glow, flesh sagging from their skin. These reanimated corpses provided destructible shields for their handlers. Living men held three undead apiece by chains leashed around their roiling necks, giving the corpses loose restraint as they floundered at the terrified animals.

Then, from behind this line of unholy resurrections and reedy marauders, a man taller than his inferiors strode forth. He seemed to savor the silent dread of the ruined festivity. Ashiy recognized his cruel smile above the scarred chin. The man's sword, exchanged to him by Ashiy's own paw those weeks ago in Whimzic, dripped sanguine. He smeared more blood upon his stubble, cupping one gauntlet to shout, "Where was *our* invitation?"

Ashiy never heard so much mirthless laughter as that chorused by the officer's men. They rattled their monsters' chain leashes, making the reanimated growl and hiss along with them.

"Invitation," the leader continued, "into Blackstone—the sacred halls of our ancestors, where now filthy animals parade and shed and defile! We've made our own entry. We wish to entreat with the pretender lord! Where's Eckner? Is the host *missing* from his own festivities?"

There was a shuffle from the far back of the pressed crowd, close to the high table. Ashiy saw Eckner, head lifted high, cantering forth with his coiled sword yet sheathed. *What's he doing? They'll kill him!* Ashiy thought. He wanted to cry out, and indeed, many animals did. Some foxes nearby even jumped to bar their lord from coming to the forefront of the trapped guests. Yet he bandied them away, his dark, plotting eyes searching, searching, until they picked Ashiy from the crowd. Their gazes met, and with deliberate pointedness, Eckner nodded somewhere aside.

Ashiy followed the lord's stern arc, certain Eckner had imparted him a final message. He found the spot Eckner had indicated. It was the furthest corner of the wall, where the servant's entry remained an invisible escape. Ashiy looked back to the striding lord for confirmation. Eckner was now past, yet a subtle stroking motion made by his paw resembled the one used to open the brick doorway.

Ziliac gripped his sword, yet Ashiy stopped him from drawing it. "This way!" he hissed, taking him aside with Frelik following. Their distance from the ballroom doors hid their movements, as did Eckner's loud response to the waiting captain. "How can I invite a stranger?" The fox lord came to a stop just shy of the reanimated line, a frown offered to their grasping fingers. "Much less a murderer and plunderer?"

"I know this scoundrel!" A new voice arose from the animals' droves. Ambassador Ferdinand jostled through from his secluded corner. He came to the battle line drawn by Lord Eckner's stance, an accusing finger shaking rage at the tall and bloodstained knight. *"Monteague!* A former captain of my king's royal army! Turned a deserter and bandit rogue against his homeland!"

"Altharia is my homeland," Monteague rumbled. "And these fetid corpses are truer soldiers than any animal-loving fool who casts his lot with these mongrels!"

"They do appear feisty," Eckner replied, his nose wrinkling as a gob of spittle from one feral corpse latched onto his fur. "Poor souls. They doubtless have more wits than you, *former* captain. This offense against one of Illdari's capitals will see you all hanged."

"To speak of wits when you yourself have been so easily outwitted!" Monteague's laugh barked no humor. "Your city needs a new name, Lord Eckner, for it takes a slow keeper to allow one of the most impregnable fortresses in Altharia to be so easily taken."

"I admit, I'm curious to learn how you breached this far." Eckner's grip tightened on his sword pommel, a flash of anger allowing his resolve to slip. "Taken, though? An overestimation. Your forces here, even bolstered by your undead, seem hardly enough to hold Flintstone."

"We will hold it. Who will take it from us when we hold so many prominent nobles hostage?" Monteague downed his visor's slotted helm. "This exchange is tiresome, Lord Eckner. Put down your blade. Your life is forfeit, that's assured, but we'll murder only a few of the others if you surrender it willingly."

"Forfeit?" Eckner's features went feral with rage. He turned one shoulder, that it might ignite vulpine faces in the crowd at his tail. "Then count the life of every fox here likewise! Do you believe they'll surrender their lord? We are not cowardly turntails!"

Eckner's sword scraped free of its twining sheath, flashing toward the high ceiling in a display that the human rogues, for a mere instant, flinched to see. "Perhaps you believe that your many swords against my single blade shall win you the day? How easily you've forgotten, human, that we here are animals of Altharia! Our true weapons are not blades forged by your fires, for we are wielders of the claw, the talon, the tusk, and the razored fang!"

Defiant cheers, growls, and hisses erupted from the animals. Lord Eckner sneered with teeth as sharp as his blade's tip, and he pointed both at the deserter Monteague. "You ask, who shall take this castle from you? The same brave creatures who took it from your ancestors! Come see!"

The roar of the animals drowned out Monteague's snarled order. His men let their monsters loose. The reanimated leaped forth with chains trailing a prisoner's ruckus across the jeweled floor. They swarmed Eckner as he stood free of his roused peers.

By the time Lord Eckner had taken his ground before Monteague's decaying slaves and exchanged first words, Ashiy had stroked aside the brick portal into the servants' passages, flung himself through their stooping byways, and wound up in one of Flintstone's kitchens. The rodents were gone, though Ashiy could tell by scent that their evacuation had been very recent. Knives laid by vegetables half-diced. A ladle's handle completed one lazy turn in a stew yet boiling.

"Where're all the servants?" Ashiy wondered aloud as Ziliac and Frelik materialized out of the passageway behind him.

"Who cares! Why'd you lead us here?" Ziliac growled. "We should go back and fight!"

"No!" Ashiy hindered his turn. "Eckner motioned for me to escape. We might be the only ones who got out! We can—we can—get a crier out! Or—or—"

"Ring the bell tower's alarm," Frelik said. The younger fox flew to the kitchen's squat, half-arched door. He made a furtive glance both ways into the passage beyond, then, finding them unmanned, bolted out. Ashiy and Ziliac had no spare moment to question Frelik's rare certainty. They chased after him.

"Bell tower? What good's that?" Ziliac asked as they ran.

"It's older than the rest of Flintstone—elvish," Frelik replied. "There are studies made of it in the library."

"This helps us *how?*"

"It's said that soldiers sworn to the castle's defense are beckoned home when the bell rings distress." Frelik skidded around a sudden bend, almost making his compatriots crash into a Witfast coat of arms mounted to the wall.

Ashiy's own thoughts spun. "Eckner told me about that spell too!" he recalled. "It could tell General Orin and his forces to come at all speed."

"Ridiculous!" Ziliac said. "What—"

"Look!" Ashiy caught both his companions off guard, breaking their skelter with a sudden stop. They had almost rocketed past a balustrade which opened into the night. Glancing out, Ashiy expected to see the cursed orange glow of a city afire. But as the harried trio leaned over the railing, they saw a quiet Witfast stretched far below under sleepy moonlight. The fortress alone was imperiled. Distant torchlights meandering the streets told of a city oblivious to the battle taking place at their lord's estate. "Magic or not, the bell tower will alert the rest of Witfast at the very least," Ashiy said. "Constables and rangers from the city could reinforce the fortress."

"Agreed," Ziliac said. They fled from the balcony and down hallways once more. "Do you know where the belfry is, Frelik?"

"In this maze? No," Frelik replied. "I've been following the servants' scent trails from the kitchens. They'll know—"

Frelik quit speaking, gripped by a sudden terror which both Ashiy and Ziliac's noses also detected. Three reanimated, collared by two black-clad rogues, swept into the corridor ahead. The men spied the animals at once. With a snick, the corpses' fasteners were released. They bounded free, red eyes blazing.

Ashiy would have turned tail and bolted in the opposite direction were it not for Ziliac's onslaught. The wolf, howling, advanced to meet the undead in a spitting hail of slashes, leaving them dismembered in his wake. His true targets were their masters, his speed surprising them. They delayed a hair to draw their own swords, earning one of the men a fatal gash against his collarbone. His half-drawn weapon clattered against the stone as he fell.

Though deprived of several limbs, two of the reanimated survived Ziliac's wounds. One with a single arm, and the other with its neck hanging by a mere thread, came pawing at Frelik. He dodged aside, but the near-headless undead caught his robe's hem, tearing the fine fabric with an alarming rending sound that spurred Ashiy to action.

Freeing a decorative buckler from one wall, he placed his full weight behind the oaken circle and bashed it into the offending reanimated. In a hissing sprawl, it landed on the floor while its one-armed partner reoriented itself to attack.

Ashiy caught its swipes on the shield. Frenzied fingers moved against the wood like the scratch of a dozen cockroach legs. The reanimated's strength, even with only one arm, was formidable. Ashiy slammed against a passage column, pinned behind his shield.

"FRELIK!" Ziliac's roar cut over the din of his saber striking the remaining man's blade. He kicked his first victim's fallen sword toward Frelik.

But Ziliac's opponent used the distraction to take a swipe at his shoulder. More fabric tore, this time darkened with blood. Ziliac snarled.

Frelik did not squander his friend's sacrifice. He grabbed up the blade, and, unbalanced by its heaviness, made a lopsided slice at the monster attacking Ashiy. The fingernails against the buckler dropped, the undead now with two stumps at the knees. Yet it still came on, snapping at Ashiy's exposed hind feet.

Ashiy crashed his buckler's curved edge down upon the monster's head. Both it and the creature's cranium burst with a crack. Crimson light flickered from the reanimated's fractured eye sockets, leaping up his forearms like catching embers. For a moment, they blinded Ashiy with a ravenous craving. He saw

Frelik looking dumbstruck and almost pounced at the younger fox, yearning for a taste of warm flesh. Seizing his friend, the malice instantly flooded away and Ashiy took the blade in Frelik's paws instead.

He swung it at the last reanimated, which had risen to attack once more, and finished the progress Ziliac made on its decapitation.

Its thud to the ground coincided with a strangled cry from down the hall. Ziliac disarmed his opponent. The man's plea for mercy went unheard. His sword had not ceased skidding across the hallway before Ziliac disemboweled him.

"Both of you unhurt?" Ziliac asked, turning to his companions. He mopped his blade over his cowl, human blood joining his own on the expensive fabric.

"I think so," Ashiy replied, not taking his bruised shoulders into account.

"Y-your arm." Frelik tried to tend Ziliac's cut shoulder.

The wolf winced, drawing away from his touch with a scowl. "Shallow. C'mon. We have to find the belfry before we run across another patrol."

They left behind the bloodstained hallway. Ashiy tried not to look at the bodies discarded in their wake. To have escaped the patrol with no more than Ziliac's gash, and now with all of them armed with the vanquished men's swords, was a miracle.

Yet they had lost the servants' scent trails in the fight. At a loss for what else to do, they resorted to whistling, hoping to call a rodent for aid. Frelik tried first, though he used a soft note, scared to draw the attention of any more humans. "I don't think men hear as well as we do, Frelik," Ashiy reminded him. "We can chance being a little louder."

They whistled and whistled, yet their summons went unanswered. Hall after hall they continued through blindly, echoing each with the pleading signal, dreading another horde of rotted enemies at every corner. They discovered evidence of more on the loose, coming to passages where their hearts dropped frigidly at the sight of bodies. Several Altharian soldiers were lying, still warm, alongside unmoving reanimated long cold.

"Why does it seem there were so few guards posted this evening?" Frelik asked, stopping at one such junction to search in vain for pulses amid the dead. "How could all these men take the castle so easily?"

"Eckner." A ponderous realization seized Ashiy.

"What?" Ziliac said.

"He mentioned several times when showing me around that he was planning to give the night off to any soldiers who wanted to enjoy the festivities," Ashiy replied. "Even bragged about having enough ale to fill every belly in the barracks."

"Wonderful." Ziliac kicked an undead's limp arm in disgust and pulled Frelik away from the bodies. "Leave them! This is hopeless! Every animal in that ballroom will be dead by now! Oh, where are the servants?"

Ziliac threw his next long and shrill whistle down the length of the hall. After it died away, they were about to choose a new passage by chance and prayer, when a meek shuffle attracted their attention. Giku's face peeked around the corner of the hall, her pink nose twitching, tiny eyes furtive.

Ashiy had never been so elated to see a rodent. "Giku!" he said, approaching the cowering maid at a slow pace to not frighten her further. "It's us. Ashiy, Frelik, and Ziliac—Eckner's guests."

"Yis, ying misters." Giku nodded, though she did not extract herself from behind the wall's safety. Her gaze found the soldiers piled dead, and her nose wiggled at the metallic aroma of their blood. "Giku and her kin heard fighting. Her kin fled, but Giku is loyal. She hird whistle-call. Giku knows secret ways out. She can show ying misters."

"No, we have to get to the belfry, Giku," Ashiy said. "Flintstone is under attack! We have to alert the rest of the city!"

"Old elf tiwir?" Giku nodded. "Misters ilready close. Bit too dangerous. Misters should come with Giku. Escape."

"We can't do that, Giku." Ashiy came as near to the mouse as he could. By the tension in her claws, he feared moving any closer would cause her to flee. "Please. You must take us. Once we're there, you can go. But you must show us the way."

The mouse's sharp nails made a fretful chittering on the stone wall, but at last her felt ears folded in a capitulating nod. "Giku will take the ying misters. Fir Lady Sileah."

The servant scampered off without another word, followed by the three relieved canids. Giku moved much slower than they did, ducking behind suits of armor, and lingering at intersections—always working her nose furiously to catch unwelcome scents. She then found a tapestry of Mt. Recker, and, after fitting a narrow finger in its gilded frame, revealed a hidden passage behind.

Crouching, they followed the low tunnel at an even more minute pace. Ashiy's relief by now dissolved into an impatient vexation. Ziliac was right. They were taking too long. How many of his friends had already been slaughtered in the ballroom? *Lord Eckner. Evok. Ithcia. The Princess Silcea and her mother. Please, oh please, Giku, I hope you haven't tricked us. This isn't an escape passage, is it?*

Another few minutes elapsed, and Ashiy felt ashamed for having doubted the mouse. The byway came to a dead end. After flattening her ear to the plaster wall and hearing nothing, Giku pressed it. Torchlight flooded through a revolving door, and the mouse ushered her followers into the corridor beyond. They recognized it from their explorations just a few days prior. "To the billtiwir." Giku pointed left, though she did not exit the safety of her tunnel. "Always girded. Go in. Go ip. Nivir down. Nit illowed through the cross dir. Old rule." Her wiry paws began to pull the hidden door shut. "Giku goes now. Be sife."

Frelik caught the side of the door before it closed. "Thank you, Giku," he said. "You've been very brave."

The mouse replied with a timid nod and a small smile before her passageway sealed shut.

Though he made a hopeless stand against dozens of undead with gnarled nails and a reek of sure death, half a cackle left the lord of Flintstone's lips. It became a doggish growl as the drawn elven blade of prior lords, balanced in one sure paw, decimated the horde that crushed in. Reanimated were functionless without their heads, wherein the necromancer's magic dwelt. Thus, Lord Eckner's blade, its edge pristine as a rosebud's thorn, pruned them with artful arcs, cuts, and swipes.

Yet despite the bloodless score he incapacitated, there were too many for an aging lord. Eckner knew the twinge of spent years after a rotating twirl spread both shoulders wide. He winced. In that moment of hesitation, gnashing fangs sought the lord's nape.

Then the reanimated's weight lifted. Eckner saw, for a flash, the weaponless Ambassador Ferd wresting the monster and its mortal bite away with bare hands. It writhed in his hold, both men, living and dead, collapsing in a mad struggle.

A courageous wave of animals came to Eckner's aid next. Foxes led the wild charge, driven fearless and vengeful from seeing their lord take the brunt of the onslaught. What few of Soaravic's guards had been stationed inside the ballroom led the fray with glinting weapons. The majority held none at all, and they were the first to have their blood spilled upon the waxed floor. Reanimated gouged, bit, and killed.

Then their drivers withdrew hidden blades, and under Monteague's command, charged forth to slay the survivors. They found this no simple task. Though protected by their dark armor, and set against many creatures bearing no weapons, the men nevertheless found bird talons, fox and wolf fangs, and the raw strength of bears and elephants worthy challenges.

Seeking glory, one young rogue dodged an elephant's goring tusks and charged Lord Eckner as the silver fox worked the knot from between his shoulder blades. The boy slid on a puddle of blood, and, spotting him coming, Eckner batted aside a flailing stab. He drove his own blade through an opening in the armor just beneath his opponent's belly. Taking the dead boy's weapon as he fell, Eckner tossed it to Evok.

"Untrained and overeager!" the fox lord bellowed over the yowls of close battle. "We'll take them!"

Increment by bloody increment, with equal lives lost on both sides, the humans were driven back from the center of the ballroom, beaten toward the mighty doors. One by one, their reanimated fell. Eckner's assessment had been adequate. These were no true soldiers of Humania, but inept defectors. Were it not for their numbers, equipment, and undead, they would never have matched the gallant lords and honed rangers congregated for Eckner's ball. High scale Vondaro, his mighty bear mitts already dripping red from separating limbs, now wielded two straight swords. The elephant Princess Darlene crushed six men herself, her wounding tusks now shining brighter than their usual rusty hue. The finch ranger Yerrwish took flight, and with a pilfered dagger, sent one of the ballroom's glass chandeliers cascading down to pulverize three rogues. Ithcia, though missing her staff, administered her palms to the crests of the reanimateds' brows. Whispering the words of unheard incantations, she made their hungry eyes gutter out.

By force of will alone, the renegade Monteague held his men just shy of the doors. He remained the one human worth the scrutiny of better caution. Paired with an iron buckler, his own sword worked wickedly. He did not overextend when opponents drew close, killing far more than his underlings with stunning hits from the shield followed by swift hacks with the blade. Cruel cheers erupted from his men when he engaged the young elephant Prince Deliquinn and ended him with a thrust through the throat.

Dismayed cries arose from the animals to see one of their broadest combatants slain. Deliquinn's mighty sister flung foul curses at his murderer, yet she was too wounded herself to surge forth. Instead, Evok rose to stand over his fallen kin, the sword Eckner had given him facing his adversary.

"You die today, invader," Evok said to Monteague in a steady voice despite the thunderheads darkening behind his eyes. "You are unworthy to shed the blood of Lord Darnan's line!"

"Still, I have," retorted the fell knight, taking stock of the apprehensive berth now given him and the seething ranger. "No more need be taken! Surrender!"

"You'll not escape death, coward," Evok replied.

With this oath, he lunged forward to end his foe.

-Chapter XX-
A Bell Tolls

*E*ach brazier along the hall burned lower than the last. When Ashiy, Frelik, and Ziliac came to the doorway, they found a place snuffed of light. In the shadows lay two more Flintstone guards, steadfast foxes resolved to their posts unto death.

"Someone's been here already," Frelik said in a quiet voice.

Ziliac tested the air. "I don't smell any men."

Between the slain, the belfry's iron door was cracked ajar. A dim glow yielded across its face from the unseen room beyond. It evoked fear, that ancient doorway. The trio of canids stood rooted for a moment. At last, Ashiy plunged forward, his sword at the ready. Sure that his friends were close on his tail, he cast it open on groaning hinges.

Ashiy's first tentative step inside soaked into a damp floor. His fear dissolved away at once, transformed into steely resolve. *For all my friends,* he thought. *For Flintstone and Altharia!* He shouldered the door open wider and barreled inside.

Here, too, the torches had been doused. Bark and root latticework comprised the floor, which funneled at the center into a basin. A massive stone plugged it. Residue, lime, and moss caulked its edges. The surface, though eroded by water, still displayed a tangible crest. It resembled a faint cross with its four posts winged on the ends like scythes. Ashiy did not recognize the mark.

Their barging entry met no attack. Indeed, there was still no scent of men about the place, only a mustiness of ancient stone. Their footsteps slapped on puddles. Echoes receded into the beams and buttresses cross-hatching into the tower's heights.

"Elves built this?" Ashiy said softly. "What for?"

"Was once a pool, maybe." Frelik dipped one foot into the

basin.

"Strangest thing…"

"What's that, Ziliac?" Frelik asked.

Ziliac stomped up a spray from one puddle. "The water's aglow," he said.

It was. Whatever liquid had once pooled in the belfry's bowels shone a faint honeyed hue. Ziliac stomped again, this time with a rousing growl. "The bell's what matters, c'mon!"

They found two narrow flights of stairs at the chamber's far side. Both snaked along the bowed walls. One ascended nakedly up the belfry's hollow circumference. The other descended into the floor, where, just visible before its curve, the steps met another stone door. This one, too, bore the scythe-cross emblem shared by the basin's plug.

"What are we waiting around for?" Frelik exclaimed. Though the weight of his sword shook his arm, he raised it high in a charge up the single-file stairway. Ashiy followed after him in a similar candor. All his worries for his friends abated. They were ascending the bell tower! They would ring it for victory, and in the name of Illdari, blot every invading human from the castle! All of it now felt possible, a simple errand, even.

Yet Ziliac lingered behind his friends on the first risen stair, his expression pensive.

"What is it?" Ashiy asked.

Ziliac blinked. "A dream, but…" He shook his head. "It's nothing at all."

They took the steps by threes to fly after Frelik. The plucky younger fox raced up and up, now humming a victor's triumphant tune. Its melody waned the higher they climbed, the further, it so happened, that they distanced from the basin's pale tangerine glow. When it became no more than an ache below, and the trio found themselves taking the endless spiral now in the dark, Frelik stopped, allowing his companions to catch up with him. "That was—" His eyes grew wide enough to see the whites in the gloom. "Did you feel that too?"

"Magic." Ashiy had already guessed the source of their bold

attitudes. His own invincible feelings of vigor had depleted with the climb, though his heart still burned for his endangered friends. "We've taken no oaths, but I suppose we're enchanted like the soldiers of Witfast now that we've touched that water. Let's keep going. But cautiously."

Without end, the belfry continued to supply more steps. Ashiy felt a strange pop in his ears and remembered how staggering the tower's height appeared when seeing it from afar. His legs' joints became furiously sore. He leaned against the smooth stone with every hike. *Why couldn't they've put an elevator in here?* Ashiy envied the Undermoor's transport.

At last, Frelik brought them to a landing. Nippy air soothed their tired lungs through the arched, open frames of the steeple's peak. Through several of them, the shadowed bulk of Mt. Recker obscured part of the starlit sky. Peering through the others allotted a fine view of Flintstone's battlements and the distant city far below.

"We'll have to bring a telescope up here!" Frelik lingered by one portal. "What an incredible view!"

"Leave me out of that venture," Ziliac replied, rubbing his aching legs. "How do we ring this behemoth then?"

A mighty bronze bell loomed overhead with a waist wide enough to crush the three of them. From its gaping mouth hung a clapper of equal scale. Yet this knobbed striker was not fashioned of metal like the rest of the bell, but wooden and inscribed with runic shapes. A long, frayed cord drifted down. Ashiy reached forth to tug it.

He found slit yellow eyes perched above the bell's crown.

A wave of purplish light and a blazing hatred not his own swept Ashiy off his feet. His paw still outstretched, grasping for the clapper, when he hit the belfry wall and had the wind knocked out of him. He crumpled to the ground, his sword knocked from his other paw.

The skull-masked witch, lying in wait, alighted beneath the bell's wide lip. A thin dagger drawn in one hand severed the clapper's rope. The ebony staff in the other crackled with violet menace as she turned it toward Ziliac and blinded them with another flash.

The wolf rolled beneath the blast. He pounded against the witch with his burned blade, gouging chips in her staff as she deflected his furious blows.

Ashiy crawled onto all fours. He saw Frelik, terrified, maneuvering around the fringe of the duel, unable to make a cut of his own between Ziliac's wild strikes. "The—*bell*—" Ashiy only managed an unheard croak. They had to activate it, barring all else. But how, with its cord lying limp as a snakeskin on the belfry landing?

A horrendous yelp announced the witch had found an opening between Ziliac's attacks. He dropped, clutching a tendon in his thigh that had been raked by her blade. She almost sliced the howl from his throat, but Frelik's own wavering war cry intercepted her.

He came after her clumsily, his overbalanced sword swinging wide in his stiff toes. The witch chuckled. She danced around him, shimmering and shifting coyly.

Behind them both, Ashiy rose, standing in the grasp of split decision. Summoning what little air he had regained, he leaped for the bell's wooden clapper. He caught it between his paws, dangling in a swing, shoving it away toward the bronze rim as he lost hold.

Monteague's shield rose like the sunrise to fend off Evok's initial blow and found it a feint. Evok diverted his blade at the final moment, aiming instead for the deserter's thigh. Yet the man's fast reflexes foiled the maneuver. He pivoted aside. Their swords slid off one another without harm, reconnected, then, in a mean twist, the elephant found his flung away. Weaponless, Evok caught Monteague's shield. He wrenched it with both paws, pulling the man in close with his arm strapped to the underside.

But Monteague's other hand still balanced the sword. With

his opponent so near, he would not have missed another fatal stab.

It was then, however, that a great vibration passed over the hall, making shards from the shattered chandelier dance upon the floor. The strike of a great bell pealed out, loud and defiant.

The disruption hesitated Monteague's finishing thrust. His eyes, widening with uncertainty, flickered a moment to the chamber's vaulting windows where the high elven alarm tower could be seen as a shadow against the nighttime sky.

Evok seized the opportunity. He wound his trunk under the buckler and around Monteague's sword wrist. The blade fell free like a deadened twig as he throttled it.

The clapper only seemed to make a meek strike against the bell's lip. Yet the landing shook and those struggling there were deafened. The witch turned as the wooden striker's surface kindled with a golden glow.

Ashiy felt a pang of homecoming, of bravery, of will and wherewithal to fight to a bitter end. He glimpsed a similar fire take hold in Frelik's eyes, imbuing his next graceless slice with resolved valiance. It caught the witch. The very tip of Frelik's sword tore through the empty front of her hood and put a leering crack across her porcelain mask.

The witch recoiled. Both opponents stood for a disbelieving moment, each thinking that the blade had reached far enough to kill.

Then, with a hiss, the witch closed in and slid her dagger between Frelik's ribs. A faint gasp and the rest of the mettle in his eyes faded. Frelik fixed on some point under his beloved stars to observe, and there marked a close to his journey.

He fell.

The witch's fury could not be contained behind her now battered mask. Ashiy felt her wrath as she rounded upon him next, and though the world had grayed with Frelik's collapse, he knew something close to vengeful contempt when he realized the bell had fulfilled its purpose. "You've failed," he said to her, his weaponless paws outstretched. How hollow the false fuel of bravery felt beside his grief. Ashiy's eyes teared even as he laughed at his oncoming killer. "Failed, failed, failed, what was it all for then, Dusklight?"

The witch hesitated, caught by her name, perhaps wondering how her prey knew it. Then she screeched, an omen of death as her skull mask bore near, and her dagger raised to bring about another end.

Yet with an enraged howl and touch of hellfire sorcery, Ziliac propelled himself upright. Though his lame leg spurted dark blood, his saber, once baked by the vile enchantress's own flames, smote across her turned back. Its blow spun her sideways. Ashiy saw the witch's arched silhouette in the frame of one belfry opening. He threw himself headlong at her shadow.

She was surprisingly light. When Ashiy shoved her, it was like tossing aside a thin vapor. With another scream, the witch toppled over the steeple's side.

In a sharp whipping of cloak fabric, she plummeted out of sight.

Ashiy stood panting.

Ziliac's faithful blade clattered as his leg gave way beneath him—whatever resolve the bell's chime had given to him now expended. Still dragging his limb, Ziliac crawled to his fallen companion.

"We've done it, Frelik," he said. "Frelik?"

Ashiy closed his eyes, letting a mountain-born breeze swell over his fur through the frameless window. Ziliac had not seen. He had not witnessed the witch's fatal punishment.

Ziliac's shaking paw did not rouse Frelik, though the wolf still called his name. He called it over and over, until he was wailing it into the bell's chamber above.

And Ashiy, knowing nothing else to do and wishing to blot out the sound of Ziliac's weeping, took up his sword. He used it to reach and flick the bell's clapper again, several times, until its gonging vibrated his bones and drove the ache from his heart.

On their side of the ballroom, the remainder of the human forces quailed as though each peal from the tower loosed a volley of arrows. The animals would rush in from the city and outnumber them. General Orin's forces, too, would arrive home sooner than anticipated!

Monteague sought to detach from his grapple with Evok so that he might rally his wavering line. Yet the elephant, with his greater strength, still held the shield and the man's pinned arm. Before Monteague could retreat, Evok pulled him forward again, bucking. He grunted as his tusks dented Monteague's breastplate. Pain shot through one of them as he made another wild thrust, piercing the armor through, and hearing his opponent's mortal gasp.

The fighters parted, their breath spent. Yet Monteague spit blood. He held his pierced side as he melded into his stupefied line of rogues.

Monteague already knew himself to be fatally stricken. His nearest captains saw it on his face, and they turned and fled. It spurred a stampede of their forces, beaten, back past the ballroom's broken doors. Monteague's cruel eyes fixated on his slayer with a hatred soon to die, cursing Evok's bent tusk as he was buoyed along backward by his retreating men. "To the hall! The hall!" he gasped, attempting to regain control. Then, forgetting they had broken down the doors, he mustered an unheard order, "We'll lock them in, keep them contained!"

A thunderous cheer from the animals drowned Monteague's continued commands and curses. Flintstone was won! So too did their cry obscure the final tones made by the bell. In that moment, victory swept away all thoughts of what it might have cost to ring it.

-Chapter XXI-
Looming in the Distance

When Flintstone's mythic bell sang the night of Lord Eckner's ball, on the 35th day of Rodent, in the 1495th year, the whole of General Orin's forces felt a dire call kindled in their bosoms. It made them jolt awake in their sleeping bags. Still on the return journey from their fruitless raid, their final encampment was several dozen miles from Witfast. They suited themselves in armor and fled their tents, not bothering to pack nonessentials.

Even the grand General Orin himself had an orange glow about his eyes that made him bellow into the eve, "For home, for home at once! May we arrive by dawn! The city is imperiled! Our lord likewise! The Mistress grant us swift feet and stomachs to be sated by vengeance alone!"

In the city itself, the bell's clamor shook Witfast's populace awake in their beds. Not sworn to its deeper properties, at first they knew not the sound's source or meaning. Yet in droves they poked their heads from windows and doorframes, spilled into the streets, and gazed in stupefied wonder up to the castle and its clanging spire. The constables, at least, soon realized the alarm, and gathered in a force a hundred strong that marched to Flintstone's aid. They found its gates unbarred and guards lying wounded. The deputies stormed the castle.

Its human invaders had been scattered in terror. Monteague, the deserter, they abandoned in the hall just outside the ballroom. Evok's inflicted wound left his corpse bloodless before the city investigators found it. The final curse from his rigid lips went unheard by any creature.

Through their ancestors' halls the offending humans fled. With Eckner freed from the ballroom, he bent every able animal to scour the castle. The mens' haphazardly retreating forces were sniffed out, rank as they were with blood, sweat, and fear. A larger group of them made their escape through the Undermoor, buying themselves time by disabling the elevator behind them. But all the others were hunted down, ripped from hiding in distinguished trophy rooms, bedchambers, and hallways. They fought madly, especially when cornered, not allowing themselves to be taken prisoner. Three alone were disarmed and thrown into Flintsone's cold dungeons.

Amid it all, Lord Eckner first ensured his dear wife Syleah and their two children were unhurt. A brave band of party-going foxes and wolves had formed a wall around the fortress's lady and kits during the fight, battling tooth and claw to the death for their safety. Thanks to their sacrifice, Eckner did not find a single strand of their royal fur touched.

The lord then made a headlong rush for the castle's belfry. The bell tower had fallen quiet with the arrival of the deputies' reinforcements. Eckner rallied animals with loud cries to reach it before any vengeful men might get there first.

Indeed, few of his guards had ever seen the fox lord so agitated. When he found the tower's protectors dead, Eckner was almost beside himself. His age prevented him from the long climb into its heights, yet he paced just as many steps horizontally as he awaited news from the soldiers sent to retrieve the tollers.

A cry echoed from above at last made Lord Eckner stand still with unease, looking almost ready to faint as its anguish carried down. "Three young pups are up here, my lord! One dead, one maimed, and the last too stricken to speak!"

Ashiy had forgotten to return the small mirror to its place in the bedside dresser. He had been too excited before rushing off to fetch his friends, those few hours ago when the allure of Eckner's ball swooped his every heartbeat. A quick preen of his whiskers in the reflection, a straightening of his cape fastener, then he had left it discarded.

Now, pining into the oval, Ashiy saw his fur standing on every end, his eyes dark hollows. Half of the color now staining his robe from Savvy's came from blood.

Ziliac's blood, for the most part. Though strong bears had come to whisk them away from the ruinous bell tower, none had been able to pry Ziliac from Frelik's side. He spat and hacked and bit at anyone who neared his fallen friend, until at last the mismatched eyes recognized Ashiy kneeling close. *"He'll be all right, Ziliac. Come with me now, please?"* With a shuddering sob, the wolf had assented with a numb nod and allowed Ashiy to guide him, limping, down the endless stairs. He collapsed near the bottom, bleeding throughout the whole descent, and then the bears had at last taken Ziliac, speeding his mangled form away to the hospital ward.

Yet when Ashiy attempted to follow, he had been intercepted by Eckner's embracing arms. After grieving into them, in a whirl of aching steps and unheard words of comfort, he found himself back in his bedroom.

What am I doing here? Here's useless.

Ashiy thrust the mirror back into its drawer.

All over the castle, the humans were being expunged, no doubt. From the belfry, Ashiy had watched the city's mob of constables and rangers pool onto Witfast's streets. In a storm of bobbing torchlights and glinting weapons, they had entered the castle proper. Every now and then, he could hear a distant shout or clamor somewhere beyond his door. Somewhere beyond it lay Ziliac, perhaps dying. Evok and Ithcia's fates were also unknown to him. *Somewhere, somewhere, somewhere.* Ashiy threw himself back into the chasm of his cushioning bedsheets. *Somewhere Frelik's gone. Have they removed him from that awful tower yet?*

A firm rectangle prodded Ashiy's back. He dug it free. Ceilia's diary, his constant comfort to sleep with for so long, now only reminded him of another person lost.

Perhaps many hours later, the bedroom doorknob creaked.

The occasional outcries seemed to have long since abated. Ashiy must have slept, yet he felt too empty to have gathered much rest. He sat up.

Eckner was his visitor. Their gazes held each other for a long moment. Then the lord's eyes fell to Ashiy's lap and the mothy diary reposed on it like a coffin.

Eckner closed the door and made a furtive stab at the bedroom fireplace with his bare sword. Caked blood fizzled from its blade, making dark blots against the low embers. "Who was it, Ashiy?" Eckner asked, watching them glow.

"That witch, Dusklight," Ashiy replied. "She was waiting in the tower."

"I feared someone would be," Eckner said. "Why didn't you get out? Take your friends and escape?" The lord sighed before Ashiy could respond, the hint of a grin on his mouth. "Because you're Dreer's son. The same bravery blazes in your veins. You plucky pup, you."

"It was the same for Ziliac, too," Ashiy said. "He never would've fled. And neither did…" He could not speak Frelik's name.

Eckner nodded to the embers, an absent toe curling on his pommel. "And the witch? You made her pay?"

"She's dead."

"Good." The tension in Eckner's shoulders slacked. "I came to tell you that your other friends shall pull through. The elf. Your wolf companion was on the brink, but healers have brought him around. And Sir Evok, well, he might have saved us just as much as you did this eve."

Ashiy's relief was dull.

Eckner continued. "General Orin will speedily return, thanks to the alarm. The rogues have been purged from Flintstone. Most of them are dead. A scant few escaped by the Undermoor upon a commandeered barge. It appears that's how they made entry in the first place…"

The fox lord trailed off. Ashiy had quit listening.

After a long silence, Ashiy asked, "Why did this happen?"

"A question for any violence the Mistress allows to go unchecked." Eckner gave his cryptic answer to the hearth. It irked Ashiy that the lord continued to turn his back toward him.

"We knew that men were up to something in the territory," Ashiy said. "We brought you Stromic days ago! He didn't yield anything about tonight's plans?" Fresh anger blossomed in Ashiy's chest, and he frowned at his tainted, embroidered robes. Festivities, indulgence, and opulence! He had been so distracted by it all since learning of his relationship to Eckner. How miniscule its significance now seemed weighed against the life of a friend. "How can something like this happen? What have *you* been doing?"

Now Eckner turned, one lip snarled, though he hid the fang in an instant.

"You are not the only one who has lost friends tonight, Ashiy," Eckner's voice came evenly. "Do remember that. My soldiers. My people. Their blood spilled in my very halls tonight. That is something I will be burdened with forever." Ashiy heard the lord's incisors grind beneath his tight jaw, then release. "Why did this happen? Because the spirits of humans still call them home. The men who invaded tonight wanted to retake Altharia."

"You still think there's hope of bridging bonds with them?" Ashiy asked, not yet satisfied. "Even after tonight, you think we can have peace with humans?"

"My life was saved by a human tonight," Eckner replied, then shook his head, flattening his ears. "This is no discussion to have now, with the evil actions of a select few still rife in our hearts. Let it loom in the distance, Ashiy. There has been enough war and sorrow for one day. I did not come to engage you with the dreadful politics that will follow this event."

Ashiy wanted to remark that such a bloodthirsty night would not have its consequences staved off for long, but he allowed the matter to rest. "Then what do you want?"

Eckner's sword grated with a metallic whine as he leaned full upon it, sighing. "Your father," the lord replied. "On an eve as fell as this one, what I wouldn't give to have Dreer offer me comfort. Many similar times there were, in the aftermath of a battle…when I found my own father unbearable…Dreer made himself a constant confidant." Eckner noted the way Ashiy shifted beneath his penetrating stare. "But I'm not so lost in the past as many might think. However identical you might look, you are not Dreer. He's gone. I understand the pain of losing a friend, Ashiy. I wanted to make certain that you are all right."

Tears threatened Ashiy afresh. He clutched Ceilia's diary cradled on his lap. "I wish, of the three of us, it'd been me," he said. "I should've been faster, or more careful, or led the way first."

"But none of that happened." Eckner laid a paw on Ashiy's shoulder. "How many nights I wasted away in guilt, thinking of similar alternatives that I had taken instead for your parents. You must let it go, Ashiy. The guilt of your friend's death lies on that witch alone."

"Maybe," Ashiy replied. Several teardrops plunked onto the cover of Ceilia's diary. Looking up into Eckner's kind face, he found that the fox lord had marked their fall and became curious about the book. The same prick of anger rose from Ashiy's chest once more. "But how isn't it also yours?"

The grip on Ashiy's shoulder hooked. A return of the half-snarl from Eckner did not immediately vanish this time. "Come again?"

"All of the guards told to take off for the eve. Orin's forces sent out on a fool's errand. Do you think if you'd spent more time interrogating that rogue I brought, instead of focusing on menus and decorations, it might have changed what happened tonight?"

"You—you are in pain," Eckner said. "I understand that, Ashiy, but I warn you—"

"And you motioned for me to take the servant's passage to *escape,* you say." Ashiy began to think, ignoring the numbness in his shoulder caused by the fox lord's grip. "But why not tell Lady Syleah and your kids to get to safety? You were right beside them. You wouldn't have even had to signal. No, you wanted me to get out and get an alarm off instead. Just like something my father would have done. Did tonight remind you of old times again? You seem like you enjoyed it too much."

"Ashiy…" Eckner's face contained no trace of its usual mischief. It had become something dark and ugly with rage. Both of his paws trembled, one on Ashiy, the other on his sword. "You are speaking to the Lord of Flintstone."

Perhaps he should have cowed in respect, but Ashiy barked a single laugh. He shook the journal at Eckner. "Where was the Lord of Flintstone when Ceilia died? It was these same men who did it. You let them roam all over, pillaging, killing, all while you sat here fattening up for your birthday celebration!"

Eckner's claws dug, then catapulted his accuser back into the pillows. Ashiy heard a nimble buzz in the air like that of a furious hornet, then a dull thud, and a loud rattle. When he disentangled himself from the coverlets, he saw one mast of his four-poster bed had been hacked off, sent rolling over the floor by the lord's blade.

The bedroom door shook every dresser, wardrobe, and curtain in the room as Eckner slammed it.

Flintstone's hospital ward was a squat, cathedral space with a shallow tile pool inset in the floor. Morning light filtering through its windowpanes showed strands of blood drifting in the water, coagulating in its corners, the drains staunched by an overflow of bathed wounds. The chamber pounced upon Ashiy's nose with a reek of pus, injuries, and sharp medicinal herbs. Beds arranged around the pool were normally reserved for the royal families of the castle in times of sickness. Now, the dawn following the attack, many plain cots had been brought in to accommodate the unprecedented overflow of wounded.

Ashiy found Evok standing when he approached. Ithcia applied a pasty salve to his crooked right tusk, despite his winces and bemoaning. "I can endure a toothache," Evok said.

"Shouldn't be wasting space in this infirmary."

"A waste of space? How could anyone say that about the great router of men?" Ashiy said with a smile, causing both rangers to turn.

"Mm." Evok assessed him. "Router of men, *feh!* I licked *one,* and he was a turntail with a craven heart. What will they call you now, boy? General Orin's forces returned early this morning. Rumors abound about who summoned both them and the city's reinforcements with the alarm."

"Keep still," Ithcia said to Evok. It proved difficult to apply the cooling salve to his tusk while he spoke. She turned in sadness toward Ashiy. "There are other rumors too. I'm sorry about Frelik, Ashiy."

The dull ache Ashiy fought in his chest throughout the sleepless night roared at her kindness. He nodded but spoke no more of the loss. "I'm glad you and Evok are safe," he said. "Though you seem dark around the eyes, Ithcia. Have you been here with the injured all night?"

"It is my duty as an elf. Lady Heidiona has been just as present as I." Ithcia nodded down the lines of cots, where the stern elf from Eltcindale bandaged the remains of Captain Soaravic's right ear. It was far from the only injury the bear had suffered. He had been the last line of defense broken before the men's initial breach into the ballroom. Soiled bandages mummified his wide chest, yet Soaravic proved a durable creature, each breath coming with a lesser wince.

Ithcia continued, "I will rest when the afflicted find theirs."

"And after that? What will you both do?" Ashiy asked, gazing at the two, overcome by a notion that though he had only known them a short while, he had not treasured them enough in that time. *These two are fine rangers. Fine Altharians. Fine animals.*

"Report to our guild," Evok replied. "Serve Altharia in whatever way suits our talents."

"What of you, Ashiy?" Ithcia asked. "Is it back to Whim's Haven?"

Home. Ashiy had yearned for it throughout the eve, wondering if the first shoots of Delsic had sprouted from Ceilia's gravesite yet, and hoping dear Buruk and Branny had not found a better replacement since his absence from their bellows. Mistress above the heights, how could he have ever wished to flee from the Haven's battered pathways, shanty tents, and pleasant din?

"I'll have to see," Ashiy said to Ithcia.

After a few more pleasantries exchanged, Ashiy asked where Ziliac had been laid to recover. Ithcia pointed out the ward's furthest corner. Thanking them, Ashiy picked his way toward it, through the bustling nurses and over the blood-dampened floors.

In a bed with dirtied sheets kicked to its foot, he found Ziliac. Sunlight glowed faint blue over the wolf's quivering face, the effect of a nearby window where a waterfall was set in glass.

Ziliac slept, yet not at ease. His whiskers twitched, his mouth muttering a stream of sounds that Ashiy could not make out. He winced at Ziliac's torn right leg. The silken pants had been trimmed away for stitches to be sewn into his flesh from the length of his groin to the knee. *The bell's magic must have saved him.* Ashiy marveled that Ziliac had stood upon that very thigh to give the witch his final strike.

Although feverish sleep gripped Ziliac, Ashiy did not wish to let him endure it alone. He hunted for a stool and pulled it close to his bedside.

The meager scrape it made opened Ziliac's white eye. Only halfway seated, Ashiy was frozen in place by its frenzy. A last, delirious whisper rolled from the wolf's lips, *"Friendredhelpsyou…"* Then he came fully awake, both eyes opened.

"Morning, Ziliac," Ashiy said. He did not patronize him by labeling it a good one.

Ziliac's chest heaved. He looked away, into the flecks of blue glass suspended in the window's waterfall design. His paw clenched the bed sheet in a convergence of mad wrinkles.

A cracked voice breathed on the panes. "I've to return home."

"Back to Sepplecretem?" Ashiy asked.

Ziliac nodded.

"I know the feeling." Again, Ashiy's thoughts wandered to Whim's Haven. Was Aggtree finished with the expansion to his tavern? Were the wintertime dealers readying to peddle their illicit ember whiskey? "The healers will have you in shape to return. But it'll take a lot of rest."

"No!" Ziliac's sharp hiss threw spittle against the windowsill. "It can't wait. They need to know. I can't evade it."

"What?" Ashiy said, now concerned.

"Frelik." Ziliac's paws balled and corkscrewed against his eyes like burrowing mites. "It's my fault. All mine. I brought him along and now I've to return. His family has to know, has to hear it from me. He has to be buried. Mistress *above—*" Ziliac's mismatched eyes resurfaced, frightening Ashiy with the near-madness he saw in their despair. "How am I meant to tell them? I'll die too! What more can I deserve, though?"

Hopeless. That was the word to describe Ziliac in that moment.

"No." Ashiy gripped the wolf's paw. What did their petty squabbles from before matter? "No, Ziliac," he repeated, holding his friend's desperate gaze. "You'll come through it. For Frelik's sake, you'll find the strength. And if you need help, I'll go with you. Just say the word and I will. You won't be alone."

A bit of the grief tainting the discolored irises faded. With a sigh, Ziliac deflated against his cot, his paw slipping from Ashiy's hold, and fitful slumber overtook him once more. After drawing the distressed covers back over Ziliac, Ashiy went to summon a nurse. There had to be a sedative for the nightmares behind those closed lids.

On the way, a putrid odor of decaying flesh distracted him. It cut sharper over any other scent of blood in the filled ward. Ashiy was drawn to the source—a patient mostly hidden by a cubicle of drawn curtains. Through a slit between two,

Ashiy spied a limp appendage. Once a hand, its floor-dragging knuckles were bloated black and oozing pearly seepage.

"That's the man."

The supple voice startled Ashiy, and when he flinched away from the partition, Silcea also fluttered back a pace, clutching a worn book. Even in a downy sleeping gown, Flintstone's princess fit the image of an angel coming to guide the wounded into the Mistress's golden life forever. She sported no injuries, and no guard escorted her, suggesting to Ashiy that she had snuck out of her chambers to lighten the moods of those bedridden. Her eyes were bleary red. Had she spent the previous night as sleepless as he had?

"Man?" Ashiy soured at the word.

"He saved father from one of those undead monsters," Silcea replied. "I saw. But he's paid for it with several bites taken out of him, the poor ambassador."

"Ferd," Ashiy named the man. He felt little for his peril.

"Yes." The princess nodded. She hesitated a moment, hugging her book tighter. Ashiy saw the yearning and loss on her expression. She wanted to ask about Frelik but instead bowed her head. "Thank you for ringing the alarm. Father says were it not for you, we wouldn't have won the eve."

"He does, does he?" Ashiy replied.

"I never saw him so panicked," Silcea said, her stare shyly curious. "When the bell quit ringing, and he took animals with him to find you, Silceo complained he must care for you more than us."

The comment made Ashiy's tail fidget.

Silcea shook her head quickly. "My brother speaks out of turn, of course, as he always does. Father doesn't…well, what I mean is you mean a great deal to him. As if you were family." Ashiy could think of nothing to say to this. The harsh words he had exchanged with the lord the previous eve had not been reconciled. Silcea's whiskers twitched; she was as uncomfortable as he in that moment. "Of course, you will mean a lot to all of Witfast now, too, doing what you did."

"I wasn't the only one to climb that bell tower."

"N-no." Silcea's voice shook. She steadied it with a deep breath and said, *"'Oh, love the lost, whose names when time is asked is left at a loss.'"*

"Pardon?"

"Lament for the Forgotten Hero. Jexoc of Chitterdale." Silcea displayed the faded lettering on her volume. "The poem mourns that Altharia's greatest champions are those who give their lives in secret. It claims people prefer living victors with names that go on to be immortalized forever." The princess's tears returned, soaking her cheeks as she blinked at Ashiy. "You're the hero who lives on today."

"And the greater one is lost," Ashiy said.

His dejected tone made Silcea shake her head. "But you still give others hope."

What a rush it might have once given Ashiy to fantasize himself being named a hero by a radiant princess. Now, however, his tail drooped. "I can't say I feel much of it myself at the moment, Princess Silcea."

"I think that's normal when it comes to heroes," she replied with a small smile. "They can be another's hope, even in such dire circumstances when they can find none for themselves."

Ashiy surveyed the demure princess, admiring the strength hidden within her. *Even here, hurting, she's tending to the hurt,* he realized. *She's trying to lift others, too.*

"Thank you for your kind words," Ashiy told the princess, nodding. "May your heart be healed, Princess Silcea."

"Yours too, Sir Ashiy."

They parted ways. Silcea found an injured animal to kneel beside and read soft poetry to, while Ashiy continued to ponder her words. He flagged a nurse for Ziliac and returned to his troubled friend's bedside with the beginnings of a tired smile.

"'Oh, love the lost,'" Ashiy repeated the stanza aloud after the healer soothed the wolf's sleep with a sedative. *"'Whose name when time is asked is left at a loss.'* That won't be the fate of Frelik's name, Ziliac. We'll ensure he's remembered.

You'll see."

Ashiy reclined on the bedside stool, still aching at heart, though it was not all a hurtful ache now. If he took to the road with Ziliac in the coming weeks, it would not be one without challenge or further heartbreak at its end. It would not be an adventure to earn grand acclaim from a lord, nor to find the thrill in mapping uncharted territories.

To provide support for a friend would be a simple quest.

Yet Ashiy found himself content to undertake it.

-Epilogue-

*T*he moon and Flintstone's high bell tower converged to throw a long shadow across the fortress's eastern battlements. It stretched over lengths and lengths of slanted, shingled rooftops. Beneath them, the many barracks belonging to Sir Orin's garrisons had swarmed that day with activity as Witfast's soldiers returned home. Now all of them stood dark. In the aftermath of blood spilled and hard-won victories, grim silence held the brisk night.

A dark heap marred one rooftop. Shingles beneath the deformed body had cracked beneath its impact. The corpse was a spatter of twisted appendages and entrails, loosely wrapped together by the dark robes the figure wore.

Yet, under the thrall of the cold shadow, one crooked arm suddenly shot upward, as if in salute, and its dislocated elbow straightened with a ghastly crack. Like a puppet of tangled limbs, the other ligaments made similar snaps and creaks as though unseen strings pulled them back into proper form. Once they were all mended, the hooded figure stood tall. It stared toward the moon, with irises that changed in a blink from deadened yellow to moldy green.

A wet wheeze restarted the witch's lungs.

She collapsed on all fours, her newly fixed hand sweeping to lift the bottom of her mask as she coughed bloody bile against the rooftop. When she finished, the night resumed silence.

The witch readjusted her mask, her fingers nicking against the new crack on its surface. That was one fracture the vile sorcery had not fixed. Yet what a result was the rest of its power!

She splayed her digits before her, flexing them. Sunlight would reveal their skin grayer and spongier than it had been before the plummet, but for now the lesser moonlight made them appear to her as soft, newborn flesh. She wrapped the hand behind her back, feeling where the wolf's sword had torn the robes across her shoulder. An ugly gash in the flesh remained, deep enough for her to probe her fingers inside. Deep enough that it should have still been gushing blood. Yet it gushed none at all.

To cheat death would have sent most to their knees uttering joyful thanks, but the witch's gaze rose to scowl at the bell tower. Though its chime had long waned into silence, the fact that it had been rung at all assured failure. Failure to hold Witfast. Failure for Monteague's raid, fool and deserter though he was. Failure to secure the interest of Humania's indecisive court counselors across the seas.

Failure, most direly of all, for her master.

"Forgive me, love." She entreated the night's empty shadows as though they could listen. Her wretched whisper sounded guttural and congested. Had a lung been burst by the fall?

The dagger, milk-white in color, still clad the witch's hip. She tightened her soft hand around its wicked pommel. *Dusklight.* That fox had known her alias, burn him, which meant someone in Monteague's ragtag ranks had been talking. Any men who survived the failed assault might be coerced to speak further, even the deserter general himself if he now thought all of his hopes lost and his allegiance to the witch at an end.

"None shall talk," the ugly whisper pledged to the night. "No word shall spread."

Of that, she would ensure there was no failure.

Moreover, stretched before her was the castle asleep and unawares. Its libraries and lordly studies presented rife troves of information to glean from. Such spying could help her amend allowing the bell to peal out. The witch groaned. Amends had to be made, indeed, before she could hope to endure the disappointment she would face from her master.

But first to find her staff. Had it fallen with her? Perhaps landed on another rooftop?

Dusklight's nimble form vaulted, soundless, from beneath the dark cast of the belfry's shadow. Unseen, she flitted between the battlements as a creature bred of fire and flora, now too reborn of forgotten feline sorcery.

Acknowledgements

Coming to the end of the beginning now, I can still proudly say I'm the eleven-year-old kid who scribbled the first draft of Ashiy's story. That kid skipped a whole family Christmas party to sit on grandma's basement stairs, with his cousins wondering what he was doing, his mechanical pencil flying over a red notebook. Man, he was so giddy discovering writing for the first time.

I'm that way again now. Because that kid never thought the story on those wide-ruled sheets would become anything. And that kid would be a brat not to write down a list of thanks for those who helped him get here.

The first thanks, above all, goes to God and His Son, Jesus, for granting me the love for writing and a half-decent ability at it. The second goes to my parents, always steadfastly loving and supporting me as two pillars in my life. The third goes to my first few readers from high school, even those I haven't spoken to in years, who fostered the courage to share my stories. The fourth goes to my latest beta readers online, who I have never met in person, but their insights have been so actionable and valuable to craft the characters. The fifth goes to the stories, creators, and franchises that molded my love for telling tales, such as *Narnia, Redwall, The Underland Chronicles,* Ray Bradbury, Lemony Snicket, and *Pokémon*.

All the rest of the many thanks go to the professionals who have contributed to *The Canid Chronology* so far. Allison, my editor, who has been patient with all my first-time questions and worked diligently to refine the story. Tessa, whose artistic genius visualized the incredible book cover out of my scatterbrained imagination.

And finally, I thank you, my readers, especially if you stuck around through this rambling blurb! Without you, I serve no purpose as an author. I hope to continue entertaining with my tales, and that you will join me for the rest of the series.

I implore you all to keep working diligently for your dreams. Make eleven-year-old you proud. It's a fantastic feeling, I promise.

All the best,

~Angola Hone

This is an Indie Book!

Please consider leaving a review
to help it reach more readers like you!

The Canid Chronology can be rated online at most major book retailers.

Want More of Altharia?

Scan the QR Code to Receive:

"A Feline Elegy"

This *Canid Chronology* Short Story + Exclusive Digital Artwork is Free to Newsletter Subscribers!